HUMANS FROM EARTH!!

AN SF/HORROR ANTHOLOGY

EDITED BY
CHUCK MCKENZIE

First published by Daft Notions in 2026
Daft Notions - daftnotions.com
Melbourne, Victoria, Australia

National Library of Australia Cataloguing-in-Publication data.
Title: Humans From Earth!!
ISBN (Paperback): 9781923391093
ISBN (Ebook): 9781923391109

Cover Art by Greg Chapman – darkscrybe.com
Cover Design, Formatting & Proofreading by All In The Edit – allintheedit.com
Anthology Edited by Chuck McKenzie

Horror, Science Fiction, Short Stories

Note: spelling and grammar within individual stories may differ according to the conventions of the author and country of origin.

CONTENTS

FEAR OF THE (IN)HUMAN

A FOREWORD BY
CHUCK McKENZIE

I became aware of that most terrifying of concepts—of things that *look* human, but which absolutely are not—at a very young age.

Yes, I know this may seem a little off-topic for this anthology, but stay with me...

The first time I can actually recall feeling afraid of anything I was probably around three years old, watching a repeat of the 1970 *Doctor Who* story 'Spearhead From Space'. I'd been popped down in front of that TV show as a literal baby, and my first few years saw me exposed to a variety of monstrous aliens hell-bent upon wiping out humanity. Characters in any given story might be infected by extraterrestrial plagues, shot by death-rays, bludgeoned by reptilian claws, or even *eaten*. The stories themselves could be set anywhere or any*when*, what with the titular hero being able to travel in space and time, and many of the settings were appropriately fantastical and unsettling. None of this ever worried me much as a child, though, initially due to my lack of comprehension of what I was seeing, and then to my growing awareness that the creepy planets and evil aliens in *Doctor Who* weren't *real*.

'Spearhead From Space' utterly shattered that comforting reality for me. For starters, the story took place not on some weird planet in the future, but on present-day Earth. The locations were just like those that my mum and I might pass on any given day: a hospital, a factory, a high street shopping strip. All recognisably real places, all exceedingly mundane and ordinary. And into that world came the Autons.

The Autons were essentially just plastic shop mannequins, like those ones at my local shopping centre. Ordinary, everyday things that I might walk right past without a care. Except that the Autons, animated by an invading alien intelligence, could suddenly jerk to life and murder people. The scenes in which gangs of Autons smash through shop windows and slaughter early-morning commuters in the streets still live rent-free in my head over fifty years later.

Sure, the Autons didn't look *exactly* human, with their featureless plastic faces, but they were near enough to scare the pants off this three year-old. And, as time went by, *Doctor Who* introduced me to other beings that hid behind almost perfect masks of humanity, either as shapeshifters or by possessing the bodies and minds of unfortunate humans. By late childhood I'd become obsessed with such entities and, despite (or possibly due to) the fear they instilled in me, I began to seek similarly-themed fare elsewhere. By age nine, I'd discovered the malignant alien mimic of John W. Campbell's *Who Goes There?*, and a few years later was able to watch the amazing film adaptation by John Carpenter. By my teens I was staying up late to watch old movies such as *It Came From Outer Space*, *Invaders From Mars* and the *Quatermass* films on TV, and was going to the cinema to see *They Live!*, *Lifeforce*, *The Hidden* and *Species*. I was also reading classic novels like Robert A. Heinlein's *The Puppet Masters* and Jack Finney's *The Body Snatchers*. More recently, I have enjoyed Michel Faber's exceedingly creepy novel *Under the Skin*, and tracked down the criminally little-known films *There Are Monsters* and *Significant Other*.

Of course, not all *things* that pretend to be human are alien: Ira Levin's *The Stepford Wives*, Stephen King's *The Dark Half*, Stephen Graham Jones' *Night of the Mannequins*, Jordan Peele's *Us*, David Schmoeller's *Tourist Trap*, Christian Duguay's *Screamers*...all deal with replicas that are either supernatural or technological in nature, and all terrify me. And don't get me started on zombies. Zombies frighten me because they look not just human, but exactly like your neighbours, friends, and family—because that's what they *are*. Or *were*.

Someone once suggested that my fear was tied to The Uncanny Valley, which documented revulsion in some people of things that look human but which are either inhumanly perfect or slightly 'off' in some way. It was a fair supposition. Despite originally being posited to explain our reactions to viewing unrealistically flawless humanoid automatons, The Uncanny Valley demonstrably impacts anyone immersed in a book or film involving the inhuman pretending to be human, except that, in such cases, we respond to the creeping suspicion (or foreknowledge) that these entities aren't what they appear to be, and in anticipation of the big reveal and whatever might follow, rather than to visual stimuli alone.

That's not why *I* find such things terrifying, though. Not entirely, at least.

You see, there's another type of monstrous pretender, pretenders that don't trigger our alarms until it's far too late...because these pretenders are utterly human. The cannibals. The abusers. The tyrants. The predators. The serial killers. They dominate our media and books, in fiction and nonfiction alike. We are in equal parts fascinated, terrified, and appalled by them. There's a small comfort, no matter how frightening the journey, in being able to finish a book or a TV show or a film and go to bed that night knowing that you absolutely won't be replaced by a pod person as you sleep. But human monsters are real. We know this. We can all-too-easily imagine the very worst of them working alongside us. Living on our streets. Knocking on our doors.

I don't think I'm terrified of things that pretend to be human because their masks hide something alien. I think I'm terrified of things that pretend to be human because I've always known these fictional entities serve to remind us of a horrifying truth; a truth that aliens, should they ever encounter our race, will also discover:

That sometimes the monster beneath the mask is *just a human being*.

And those are the worst monsters of all.

Not all monsters look like monsters.
At first.

HOME CARE

Daniel Fox

The meteorite was only about the size of your fist, not even a speck when you compare it to the scale of the galaxy, but boy howdy did it do a number on the observation ship. One moment the ship was coasting around Earth's orbit, stealthed, gathering data, recording what those wacky Earthlings were up to, and the next it was plummeting, trailing vapour and sparks in its wake.

There were mountains and snow and great big trees and then the ship was merging with the ground in the roughest manner possible. Bangs and thuds and the squeal of a metal not found on this planet until the ship, about the size of a modest bungalow, came to a halt in a dense patch of coniferous trees. If one simply *must* crash land, there are uglier places to do it than the Rocky Mountains.

A hatch blew off and Impartial Observer 12 clambered out as best he could in the planet's heavy gravity. He had multiple scratches and cuts across his large head and slim body, all of them dripping watery blood that was more clear than it was red. He had managed to pull on his environmental suit, but hadn't done a good job sealing it, and his helmet wasn't clamped down at all, so that it wobbled back and forth as he staggered through the snow, pulling an emergency beacon behind him.

He entered a sixteen-digit code on the information pad attached to the wrist of the environmental suit. Behind him, the observation ship, which was a wonder of stealth and data-gathering technology, began to melt as multiple installed pods of acid ate at its metal.

Job one was to get away from the crash site so he wouldn't be detected. Job two was to hide out and set up the emergency beacon so his people could bop on down and whisk him away, before the locals knew they had a visitor in their midst.

Observer 12 accomplished neither of these tasks. The gravity and the foreign mix of air and his injuries all ganged up on him, and fifteen steps away from the dead ship his great eyes rolled up and he fell, face-planting in the snow amongst the sweet smell of fir and pine trees.

Softness.

Warmth.

It was still a bit of a struggle to breathe, so he was likely still in Earth's gravity. But he was out of the cold and lying on something soft, so things were looking up.

He opened his eyes.

He was lying in a bed. A human bed, which dwarfed his small form. The sheets were clean and crisp and tucked in around him. The bedroom featured log walls decorated with needle-points of biblical proverbs. A small number of what appeared to be medical monitors surrounded the bed, attached to him with small sticky pads.

He'd been found. By an Earthling.

Uh-oh.

He pictured vivisection. He pictured forced breeding with some of the awful-looking Earthling females. He pictured brutal interrogations about invasions by the notoriously paranoid Earthling leaders.

The bedroom door opened and in walked a middle-aged woman with a smile on her face.

"You're awake!" said the woman. She waved a plate covered in freshly-baked goods. "Do your people like cookies?"

Between his injuries, his exhaustion, and the effort it took to pump air in and out of his lungs in Earth's gravity, Observer 12 didn't do much talking over the next three days. Most of the time was spent sleeping, eating, and absorbing everything that the human female had to say.

Which, as it turned out, was quite a lot. She was, she happily proclaimed, "Quite the chatterbox." She proceeded to prove this true.

Her name was Olivia Gordon-Bextor. She spoke English (one of the seven major Earth languages Observer 12 had learned). She was a surgical nurse in the big hospital in the city to the south. She liked doing needlepoint and she was a big admirer of country and western music (the old stuff, none of this modern C&W where the men whined and the women barked). She had a sister in Boston and another in Winnipeg, which was a city way up there in Canada, don't ya know?

Three days in, Observer 12 took a deep breath and said, "My equipment. Did any of it survive? There was a machine. About this size." He held out his hands up at about the length of a loaf of bread. His long fingers shook from the effort. "It is a beacon. Very powerful. It opens like a…" he paused for a moment, searching for the word, "a briefcase. It will tell my people that I need to be withdrawn."

"Oh no, hon," said Nurse Olivia. "I'm afraid there wasn't much of anything left of your ship or your stuff except a big pile of melted goop. But don't you worry," she booped him on his small snub nose, "I'm going to take such good care of you."

And to her credit, she did.

She took careful notes, watching to see how Observer 12 reacted to mushroom soup and toast and her homemade chocolate chip cookies and Chamomile tea. She checked all of his wounds twice a day to make sure they didn't grow angry purple lines of infection.

Under her constant care, he grew stronger. Breathing became less of a chore.

"I'm so terribly sorry to take up so much of your time," said Observer 12 a few days later, sitting up against his pillows. "I am taking you away from your occupation."

"Oh doll, you don't have to worry about me," she said, sticking a thermometer in his ear. "Caring for people isn't just my job, it's my calling, you know? Ever since I was a little girl I thought, 'Olivia, you're going to do your best to bring some healing to this mean old world.' And by golly, that's just what I intend to do right down to my very last days."

"They do not miss you at the big hospital in the city?"

"I've got vacation days stacked up so high I can barely see over them. Now, you hush, we just need to concentrate on getting you back up on your little grey feet."

"It is a shame all of my equipment is destroyed. I had a medical scanner that could have taken care of much of the diagnostic work for you."

Nurse Olivia sat back, her head cocked like a bird's. "A medical scanner?"

"Yes. It worked by taking a baseline energy reading of a species, and then could perceive injuries and illnesses according to digressions in energy soundings."

"Well, I'll be! Do you think such a thing could work on us little old Earth people?"

"I am certain it does. I have scanned a number of you for my research on your species."

"Was it a great big thing?"

"Oh no." Observer 12 held out his hands to the size of a large cell phone. His long fingers no longer shook from the effort. "It was only this size. Quite heavy, but manageable. A shame it was lost."

"Mmm..." said Nurse Olivia, a finger across her thin lips. For the first time since Observer 12 had known her, the woman fell silent.

Two days later, Observer 12 managed to swing his feet out from under the blankets. He was too short to actually touch the floor while sitting on the bed, and he was a bit wary of making the drop while he was still not fully used to Earth's gravity, but he was pleased with his progress nonetheless.

There was a gasp at the doorway and Nurse Olivia came hustling in like he'd accidentally set himself on fire. "Oh no no, hon," she said, guiding his thin legs back under the covers. "You'll hurt yourself."

"I must leave you soon."

Nurse Olivia stopped fussing at the blankets. "What do you mean?"

"I must gather together the materials to create a new beacon."

"You know how to do that?"

"I know how to repair almost all of the equipment of my ship. I believe I will have to substitute in some materials because you have different elements than we do back home, but I am confident of my ability to make it work."

"Mmm..." said Nurse Olivia, shaking her head and heading out of the room. Observer 12 heard her filling the electric kettle. "I don't know if you've seen enough of our world for you to make your way around. I was an emergency room nurse once, and boy howdy, the things I've seen. The cruelty that we humans commit on each other would just about take your breath away. Gunshots. Stabbings. Poisoning. Strangling. Beatings. Throwing acid at each other. Setting each other on fire. And if they ever got sight of *you?* Oh my goodness, no no no. You're so much better here where you're not a strange creature, you're just another person in need of some good solid tender loving care."

The kettle whistled.

"But Nurse Olivia, I cannot stay here forever. I have a family back home. And if I am in such danger here, doesn't my being here place you in great danger too?"

She returned to the bedroom bearing a tray with a cup of tea and a plate of her cookies. She extended the tray's legs and settled it down over his lap.

"Your Olivia knows how to take care of herself, yes she does. So don't you spend a minute of your time worrying about me. Now listen to your nurse, and drink your tea."

Observer 12 drank.

Minutes later, he was asleep.

When he awoke, the medical scanner was on the bed-table beside him.

He had a difficult time focusing. He was a bit disappointed in himself. He thought he had been growing used to Earth's air and gravity. But apparently he wasn't acclimatizing nearly as fast as he had believed. Once his vision did finally clear, he picked up the device and put it in his lap.

Nurse Olivia came into the room. "Is that it? Is that the medical thingamajig?"

"Yes," said Observer 12. "I thought you said everything had been destroyed."

"Well, after our little talk I said to myself, 'Olivia, are you one hundred percent sure you looked *everywhere* around the crash? Huh? Did ya? That little old spaceship made quite a mess coming down, and who knows what might have been tossed into a tree or behind a rock?' So I bundled up and hustled my buns back up the mountain and what did I do? I scoured the ground, that's what. I kicked through the snow, I shook the bushes, and what did I find behind a big old maple tree? That! So, is it working?"

Observer 12 flipped up the cover and pressed the power button. Nothing happened. He opened the battery compartment. The battery, a series of living cells that looked like a small bit of lab-grown meat, pulsed with an arrhythmic and unhealthy beat. "It is not. I will need tools. Quite small."

"I can find you small tools. We use them for fixing eyeglasses and watches and all sorts of things." Nurse Olivia leaned forward. "It will really do everything you say? I'd be able to use it to diagnose anybody of just about anything?"

"Yes."

"Oh my heavens," said the nurse, under her breath. "Just think of how grateful they'll all be."

"Who?"

Nurse Olivia's head jerked with a quick, darting movement, like she had forgotten that she had an extraterrestrial in her guest bed. "Don't mind me. My mind just went for a walk without me for a moment. I'll fix you some tea."

Within half an hour, Observer 12 was asleep once again.

When he woke, there was a small case on the bedside table. It was plastic and grey, with a logo depicting a watch with its back laid open, exposing its internal gears and springs. When he opened it he found it was full of miniature screwdrivers and pliers and the like.

He got to work on the device. He enjoyed clear problems with definite solutions. The bio-electric battery had something like a hiccup. It had been stretched out of its nominal shape by the crash, and therefore needed to be coaxed back into its proper form. Hopefully then it would be able to resume its normal rhythmic pulsing, instead of the nonsensical jostling it was currently busy with in its compartment.

It took three tries before Nurse Olivia was able to get his attention. She was standing in the doorway to the kitchen, looking at the dismantled medical scanner, her hands clasped together in front of her. "So, how are we doing in here? Are we all fixed up? Is our wonderful little toy running along all tickety-boo?"

"No, Nurse Olivia, I am afraid not. These tools are not sufficient."

The Nurse's smile slid from her face. "Not sufficient?"

"They do not allow me to manipulate the biological portions of the device without damaging them."

These words flipped a switch in the woman. One moment, she was her usual good-natured self. The next, there was anger in her eyes and her lips were peeled back in a snarl. From A to B, in the blink of an eye.

"'Not sufficient,' he says! Well I am *so* sorry, your imperial highness. I guess me running all over the devil's half acre to find you those tools was just a waste of your precious time."

"I did not mean to insult—"

The nurse snatched away the pack of watchmaker tools. "Cost a bloody fortune." She shook them in his face, and for a quick moment, Observer 12 was sure she was about to beat him with the pack.

But she took a breath and stood back up. This other personality, this creature of anger, was rolled up tight and stuffed into the back of her mind. Her nurse persona resumed command.

"Well," she said, "these things happen. Don't they?" She tucked her greying hair back behind her ears. "Who said that life should be easy? Nobody *I* know, that's for sure. Dinner will be ready in a moment."

Observer 12 didn't know the term 'cracked.' But it's what he felt coming from this human female as she stood there, twisting her mouth up into a smile, a smile that somehow did not match her dancing eyes in the slightest.

Nurse Olivia returned with Observer 12's toolkit.

She put it in his lap. It was cold from being outdoors.

Observer 12 didn't ask if she went back to the shipwreck and looked around again and just happened to find the small box. He knew now that she wasn't just finding his things, she had hidden them away, and he knew that she knew that he knew, so it felt safer to just play along because he was pretty sure this human wasn't quite right in the head.

"So," she said, that strange, strained smile on her face, "now that you have your beloved little toolbox full of your beloved little tools, do you think you might be able to fix up that little old medical scanner once and for all?"

Somehow, that question didn't seem like a question at all. It seemed like a threat. Not so much a *Can you fix it?* as a *You had better fix it or else, buster.*

"Yes Nurse Olivia, I believe there is a good chance I can make the device operational once more."

"Good," said the nurse. "That's real good."

He got to work on the medical scanner, carefully coaxing the living battery back into its proper configuration. His mind slipped away from the worry of this strange woman, and he did not know how long he had been working before he looked up to stretch out a kink in his neck and realized the house was quiet. No humming. No cooking. No kettle whistling in the kitchen.

He put down the device. He slipped down the side of the bed, dangling before his bare feet found the wood floor.

He moved, quiet as he could, which was very quiet indeed, to the door and reached up. He turned the knob. Winced as it squeaked. He pulled open the door.

He halfway expected Nurse Olivia to be waiting on the far side of the door, crouched, ready to pounce on him with a plate of cookies and a cup of Chamomile tea.

There was the humming of the refrigeration unit. A drip from an old-fashioned faucet into the sink. Sunlight gleamed off the surface of the highly polished small table in the corner. Not a nurse in sight.

He searched.

Nurse Olivia had collected the medical scanner and his tools from the crash site. He didn't understand why she had lied about having them, but lie she did. Which meant she might have lied about the emergency beacon.

Was the beacon in the hallway closet? No. In the master bedroom, with its strong smell of potpourri? Not here either. There were no hiding spaces in the bathroom.

He returned to the kitchen. There was a door here, perhaps a closet, perhaps hiding stairs. Either way, it was locked. He thought he might be able to manipulate the lock with his tools, it seemed simple enough, really more of a suggestion that this door remain closed rather than a definitive locking mechanism.

But wait, his toolbox and the medical scanner had both been cold to the touch. Like they had been outside. Did she have his equipment in some secret stash in the outdoors?

He opened the rear door and pushed through a second screen door and then he was outside. Snow was falling, gentle and slow, quieting the world. The cold did not bother him. His home was on a world quite a bit further from its sun than Earth. And the snow gave him an advantage. It showed a path made by Nurse Olivia.

He stepped into the break in the snow. The nurse's path led directly back into the towering tree line. Without the path, he would have been pushing his way through snow that was up to his waist. As it was, stepping in the old footprints, he made good time.

The forest was a beautiful place. His own planet, so far from its sun, had land-flora that mainly consisted of lichen and moss and stubborn shrubs. Here, the trees were great towering things like sentries standing watch at a gate.

He hurried along, feeling proud that his body had adapted quite well to Earth's gravity and air. He heard a gasp.

There was a man there, dressed in a puffy blue jacket and a red woollen hat and he had two slim strips of wood strapped to the bottom of his feet and he was holding two skinny poles with pointy tips on the ends. The human male's eyes were wide enough for Observer 12 to see the whites all around the iris and his mouth was hanging low enough so you could drive a small truck in there and then the nurse was stepping out from behind a thick tree. Something metallic and bright flashed in her hand and then the bright metallic thing was in the man's back and the man was straining, his mouth even wider, and blood, thicker than Observer 12's own, was pattering down on the snow.

It took the man a few minutes to die. All the tension in his pained body released and he finally dropped down into the snow.

Nurse Olivia, her hand and coat sleeve coated in the man's blood, gave Observer 12 a grumpy look and said, "Now see what you've gone and done?"

It was around this point that Beatrice got involved in this whole affair.

Beatrice Astor was the Sheriff in those parts back when all this went down. I think some people underestimated her on account of she was a quiet-spoken woman, tall, a little on the heavy side. I think the fact that she gave off this feeling of comfort, like a vibe or an aura, is what made some figure she was a push-over. We once had a biker gang try to make inroads with a meth farm, and Beatrice went out to have a talk with them, all by her lonesome. Not only do we not have a meth farm in the area to this day, we don't even have the motorcycle gang. What she said to them remains a mystery, the kind of puzzle we all like to chew on when we get together at Charlie Buck's roadhouse for a couple of beers and a game of pool.

So it was getting towards the ass-end of October and Beatrice's day was filled with getting all the tires on the sheriff's office vehicles switched over to winter tires when she got a call about a couple of hikers that found a body up towards Thirtymile Lake, and it looked like some animals had been chewing on him for a while.

She wasn't so sure she was going to make it over the pass on account of the snow coming down pretty good, but the county boys had just plowed the highway so she actually made pretty decent time.

She got flagged down by a fella in red flannel who pointed her up the hiking path that went around the lake. "I'd go with you," the flannel guy said, "except, uh, to tell the truth I don't think I want to see that again. It was pretty bloody."

So Beatrice waved to the other hiker, a lady also in flannel who was sitting in the car, her head in her hands, and then she set out along the trail with her hands full of police tape, a flare gun, and a rifle just in case the animal in question, likely a mountain lion, came back looking for seconds.

The trail was getting covered in snow and the body was likewise a mound of the white stuff and despite all that she knew within five seconds of looking at the poor dead bastard that no animal had done him this violence.

Observer 12 woke up some place that was dark and dank and chill and smelled of earth and damp rock.

He could feel where his health monitors were attached to his skin. He could feel something underneath him, something not as a comfortable as the bed in Nurse Olivia's spare bedroom. A cot, perhaps. Restraints kept him pinned in place.

There was soreness across his chest. There were bandages wrapped around his upper torso.

There was a creak of a door and light swung down a set of plain open wooden steps. Nurse Olivia came down, snapping on a number of work-lights hanging from nails pounded into exposed wooden ceiling beams.

Observer 12 was in an unfinished cellar. The walls were plain cement showing dark spots of moisture. An old washer-dryer combo sat in one corner next to a wide utility sink. The rest of the room was taken up by medical gear—a large directional light, the health monitors, a cabinet full of bottles and bandages. He looked down the length of his body and saw that he was not in fact strapped to a cot. He was bound to a surgical table. The bandages circling his torso were stained with red.

He tried to ask Nurse Olivia what she had done, but although his mind was fully awake, his body hadn't quite caught up yet, and all he could do was mumble and moan.

There was no hint of cookies or tea this time. Just Nurse Olivia clucking her tongue as she snipped away the bandages to take a look at his chest. "You try and help," she said, more to herself than to her prisoner, "you really do. But some people, some very silly people, you can lead them to water but you just can't make them drink. And now look where we are. Look at what you've made me do. Do you think that gentleman deserved to die? Well, you want out into the world so badly, you simply can't go out looking like you do. So here I am, helping you again, even though you're determined to make the very worst decisions possible."

Observer 12 raised his head again.

Looked down his body.

There were two big sections of his chest and upper belly that were no longer grey. They were pink. *Human* pink. Neat stitches ran around the outside of the two pink diamond patches. It took him a moment to understand what he was looking at.

My skin. She's replacing my skin.

"Now Mister, I suggest you bear down and finally fix that medical scanner of yours, because I've got to tell you, I'm not sure that I've created a real good blood substitute for you. You might be sliding down a slippery slope toward hemorrhagic shock as we speak. And there's always the threat of infection and donor rejection, yes there is." She put the device and his pack of tools between his limp hands on his lap, and tilted up the head end of the surgical table.

"Your life may very well be in your hands, sir. I suggest you act like it."

A couple days later, Sheriff Beatrice was on the phone with the state police, seeing if they had any murders with the same MO as her cut-up hiker.

"Can you say that again, Bea?" said the Statie, a fella by the name of George Zimmer. He and Beatrice had known each other since before time was invented, and he was always really super good about helping Beatrice out when he could. But this time, he sounded stumped. "It sounded like you said 'patches' there."

"That's just what I said alright," said Beatrice, kicking back in her office, sipping hot chocolate with her feet up on her desk. "They cut big swatches out of the skin on the victims back."

"Now why on Earth would someone want to go and do a thing like that?"

"I've heard of biker gangs doing it. Reclaiming any unauthorized tattoos depicting the gang's vest patch. That or burning it out of the skin with an acetylene torch. But my dead hiker, he didn't look like biker material. Clean cut fella, no tattoos, drove an electric car. He worked in advertising."

"So if somebody wasn't collecting tattoos then they were just...collecting skin?"

"Maybe so, Georgie. Maybe so."

"Sometimes this job is just full of the yuckiest stuff, I swear to God. Anyway, let me just tickle the old keyboard here and see if we get any MO matches in the area."

Beatrice heard George entering the information at his end of the line. "So how are the photography classes coming along?"

"I'm getting to the point where my thumb is in front of the lens only half the time now, so they're paying off. Not quite ready for a showing of my greatest works... Okay, so the computer says no-go for skin patches state-wide. I tried for dead hikers, and we have two others in the past three months. One fell from a cliff, and the other got lost and died from dehydration. And there you have it. I guess it would be too much to hope any of the locals heard anything, huh?"

"There aren't too many people local to Thirtymile Lake. It's way the heck out there. Nearest thing was a lumber camp, a nurse, a retired couple, one of those corporate retreat places that's closed for the season. Nobody heard a thing."

"What's your medical examiner say? About the cut-out spots I mean. Were they all ragged, or were they done reasonably well?"

"They're cut out all precise-like. Maybe a doctor?"

"Or a hunter. Or someone that works in leather. I'd even go so far as a book-binder, creepy as that might be." There was a pause, then George said, "Did you say 'nurse'?"

"Well, are you or are you not the busiest little beaver?"

Observer 12 jerked his head up, pretending that he had not heard the nurse unlock the cellar door and come down the old wooden steps. He was pretending a lot of things now. Pretending that he wasn't disgusted by having another being's flesh replace his own. Pretending that he was weaker than he was. Observers were chosen for their logical minds. For their adherence to truth and facts. But 12, it wasn't just his skin that was changing under the nurse's tender care. *He* was changing. He was a pretender, now.

He pretended to keep working on the medical device, even though it was completely operational now, albeit a little dinged up from the crash. He pretended that he was grateful for the cup of tea. He pretended not to notice when there was a knock at the front door upstairs.

Nurse Olivia hurried up the stairs, closing the door behind her.

Observer 12 spit the tea back into the cup. He was, after all, an observer, and he had finally recognized a pattern of falling asleep after having some of the nurse's soothing teas. She had been drugging him to keep him complacent, and it hurt his professional pride that he hadn't spotted this sooner.

He had observed something else. The cellar was cool. Cold enough to bring down the temperature of anything sitting in it for some time. The medical device had been cool but not cold when the Nurse had given it to him. His pack of tools? The same thing.

Perhaps...

He slid down from the surgical table, the transplant on his chest burning like the absolute Dickens. It made him careful in his movements. Mincing. Slower than he would like.

He began to search.

"It's me again," said the Sheriff. "I'm just following up on that there murder we had."

"Is there any news?"

"As a matter of fact, I did find something out."

Nurse Olivia put a hand to her chest. "I hope there isn't some kind of maniac running willy-nilly all over the area. I'm so isolated here."

"That would be a worry, for sure. But actually, what I found out pertains to yourself. See, when I was here last, you told me that you were a nurse."

"Yes, I am."

"Welllll...that's not strictly true, is it, Miss Gordon-Bextor? You *were* a nurse. To get real specific here, you were a surgical nurse. I've been around hospitals a whole lot in my career. I know you nurses get to know the ins and outs of your division pretty darned-tootin' well, maybe even better than the doctors in some cases. Would you say that you got to know surgeries pretty good?"

"Oh, I suppose I did. I assisted in all sorts of surgeries. Heart, lungs, liver, hip—"

"Skin?"

"I'm sorry?"

"Skin grafts. Did you ever assist in anything like that?"

"That's a very specified field. It's not an easy thing to learn."

"But did you assist in any? I ask because the victim, his name was Michael, he had two big swatches of skin cut from his back by somebody who knows what they're doing."

"Perhaps one or two over the years."

"And let's go back to the fact that you're not actually a nurse anymore."

"That was a bunch of administrative baloney. Politicking. They wanted to cut down on the time patients were kept in our care. Cut them free early just to save a buck or two. I made my opinion on *that* subject known loud and clear, yes I did. And the bureaucrats did not care for what I had to say."

"Okay, yep, yep, I can understand your frustration. Now, when I talked to the administration fella on the phone, he said that you were rearranging patient charts so they had to stay in hospital care for longer than was necessary."

Nurse Olivia sighed and crossed her arms and looked out past the Sheriff at the cruiser sitting in her long driveway, the snow melting off of its warm engine hood. Sheriff Beatrice got the impression the lady was more annoyed at the interruption to her day than she was worried about accusations of a heinous murder.

Finally the nurse looked back at her and said, "I belonged to something. To a wonderful community dedicated to saving lives. And they kicked me out. *Me.* After all that I had given them... Do you want to know my philosophy? I mean about the big picture. About life. This great big journey we're all on together?"

"Sure."

"Do unto others. Oh, I know that's nothing original. But I truly believe it. Treat other people as you would like to be treated. Now me, if I had just gone through something as traumatic as a major surgery, I'd want to be kept in a hospital, within shouting distance of nurses and doctors, until I was one hundred percent sure I was okie-dokie. Or if I was lost and all by my lonesome in a strange land, I'd want someone to look out for me. To do their best to help me fit in. To protect me from dirty so-and-sos full of hate for anything different from themselves."

"Have to say, Miss, you've kind of lost me on that last part."

"Well, come on in if you're coming in. We're letting the heat out. And there's something I suppose you should see."

The beacon.

There it was, hidden in the clothes dryer, real and intact and the most beautiful thing Observer 12 had ever seen. He opened it, and the controls came to life at the recognition of his bio-metric identity reading. He entered the code, and…yes… there it went, sending his distress call to relays in orbit, and then further relays out in the space between the stars, tripping its merry way along quantum rivers of information. They might have already received his call of help in the time he was thinking about it.

Then the door to the cellar opened and Nurse Olivia came down the stairs followed by a larger human female in a brown uniform who stopped in her tracks when she saw him. Nurse Olivia spun and plunged a syringe full of a clear liquid into the other woman's leg. The other woman's eyes sagged as she reached for something on her belt, perhaps a communication device or a weapon, but it was too late, and she fell from the stairs down to the packed dirt floor of the cellar.

The Nurse came down the stairs, pulling a second, smaller syringe of the clear liquid from her pocket. She removed its cap as she looked at the beacon with all of its blinking lights. "You didn't go and do what I think you went and did, did you? Oh dear. Now I'll have to round up and protect all of your friends too. Honestly, you're going to wear me right out."

Observer 12 swung the beacon. He put his whole small body behind it and it hit the Nurse in her left knee with a pretty satisfying crunch. She yelled out and dropped, and Observer 12 made for the stairs. He'd get out of this house of horrors and hide out in the woods until his people tracked him down and then he would be off of this hell-scape crazy planet forever, someone else could take over observing these lunatics, he'd get a job back home with less prestige and fewer crazy people stapling strangers' skin to his body.

That was the plan.

But just as he made it to the bottom of the stairs the lady in the brown uniform grabbed his slim ankle and stared up at him in wonder.

She wouldn't let go.

She still held him even as Nurse Olivia was plunging the small syringe into his long neck and he lost track of the world.

When he woke up, his face was a stinging thing. The feel of nettles under his skin. The dart of needles around his oval eyes.

Weak. He was weak.

He sat up.

He swung his legs around.

Carefully, he made his brittle way down the side of the surgical table.

His feet slipped in blood. Human, his, he didn't know. Nurse Olivia was getting sloppy. Tsk tsk.

Up the stairs, out of the cellar. The door was not only unlocked, but standing open. More sloppiness.

Here now, the bathroom. He stood on the squared edge of the bathtub, his long toes curling over its edge, his hand pressed against the wall to balance himself.

In the mirror—a monster. Someone with his body, but his chest pink, and his face...gone. Gone and replaced by the stretched-out features of the woman with the brown uniform. Surgical staples and thread strained to keep the face attached to his head. The eye-holes were too small, hiding the shape of his true eyes underneath them. He opened his mouth to let out a shriek, and the sewn lips mocked the movement, twisting and bunching like ill-tailored cloth.

He stumbled out. Out from the bathroom. Out from that log house. Out into the snow and the grey skies. Out to see Nurse Olivia waving the beacon in the air up at a shadow in the bright white clouds, her pockets stuffed with syringes. Her greying hair was loose, flitting about her face as she screamed up, "Here! Here! Give *me* your tired! Your poor! Send your homeless, tempest-tots to me, yes! Here I am! I lift my lamp beside the golden door!"

Observer 12 raised his own arms to wave off the ship. *Go back! Go back! Not her! Not this planet!*

He did not know if they would recognize him as one of their own.

*A monster can simply be something
so far outside of your experience
that you cannot relate to it.*

DELICACY

Narrelle M Harris

Arrieuweet drew the curtain back with her fine fingers and peered at the nightmare approaching the house. Tall, in the way of their people, with pale fur on top of their pale-skinned head, coiled in an elaborate design. Nobody understood yet what the fur arrangements meant to these aliens. Social status? Gender? History? Rank? Two years and still no clue. They didn't seem to understand the questions. Communication was still difficult and inconsistent.

Some things rang louder than words though. Some actions were clarions.

Arrieuweet wished the Humans had never found her world. She wished her people had destroyed the visitors the very first time their exploration ships arrived. Only that had been tried, and the City of Song and Soil was now a blackened, burned plain.

The Humans had called it a misunderstanding. They'd reached out to make peace and build understanding.

Evil things. Colder than the night desert. Crueller than the desert sun. All the time showing what they called their *teeth* in what they swore was a gesture of friendship, but Arrieuweet and all her kind knew the truth of it. Humans showing their true natures. Even though Humans made songs too, those lovely melodies had to rise past those grim little bones growing from their faces.

Arrieuweet had lost track of the Human's approach, and when the rap came on the door she startled so hard her delicate body banged against the wall. She let the curtain drop and, shaking, went to open the door. She'd rather not let the beast in, but she was afraid of what would happen if she defied it.

Still, she glanced over her shoulder at the square of carpet on the floor which concealed the locked and sealed trapdoor. The precious things hidden in there should have been out in the desert, ripening under sun-heated sand, but she couldn't take the risk. Instead, the six spheres were bundled together in a blanket and stowed by heated rocks in the basement.

Let it be enough.

She opened the door and widened her yellow eyes to take in her unwanted visitor.

It showed its teeth. Pretend-friendly. Showing its intent.

"H-how can I serve you?" Arrieuweet asked, voice trembling. The song of it whistled slightly, a little sharp. Her neighbours would have known it meant terror. Did the Human not understand that? Humans generally said how much they loved the sing-song of her people's voices. Perhaps they enjoyed that note of fear.

"Hi!" boomed the Human, all teeth and noise and very little grace. "I'm sorry to bother you at home, Harriet—that's right, isn't it? Harriet? Someone at the depot said you might be able to help me."

"Yes?" A feeble whistle through mouth parts made of keratin.

"You know what I'm after, right?"

Yes, monster. I know.

"I want to find a truffle cluster. What's your word for them? Parreetia." The Human rolled the 'r' in a fair imitation of correct pronunciation. "I've come looking for parreetia. Jackson at the base says you speak our language pretty well, and that you might help."

Arrieuweet shuddered, her hard mouth clattering faintly. "I not know where to look."

"We know they grow out in the desert, and our surface scan suggests this is the perfect environment for them."

"Why?" Arrieuweet asked, her notes plaintive and distraught. "Why need? Why?"

More teeth were displayed in a wider mouth, soft, red and wet like the flesh of a berry.

"Man, they are so popular at home. Like truffles—that's a delicacy, a kind of fungus. People pay a bomb for them. Delicious."

"No," Arrieuweet couldn't play along. Whatever fate it meant to her, she couldn't be part of this.

"I'll pay you well, if that's the trouble."

"No. Please leave. No. No parreetia. Leave them alone. Not...not delicious. Not."

"Well, we know you guys don't eat 'em, but we humans, we like to experiment with food, all over the universe, and this stuff..." The Human kissed its fingertips. "Chef's kiss, eh? I can take one cluster back and make enough money to pay out my contract. Go home."

Sending this one home would be wonderful. Sending them all home, away from where they surveyed the planet and dug up the mineral wealth, according to the treaty, and where they sought rare plants and creatures and parreetia for their abominable tables according to no treaty at all. Like eating these things was normal and natural.

"No," Arrieuweet said again, the note hard and firm. "I will not help. Do not seek parreetia. Do not eat. Do not." She bundled the door shut, pushing hard, and although the Human with all its pink flesh and bony face and brutal height was stronger, it was so surprised that the door closed on them. On their terrifying display of mouthbones.

Arrieuweet pressed, shivering, against the door until the Human ceased its wheedling and its threats and skulked away. She waited longer, until she could no longer hear it. She peered behind the curtains again until she was certain that the awful thing was on the path back to the Human base camp.

Then she pushed the carpet aside, lifted the trapdoor and climbed down to the basement. She closed the door behind her, latched it.

In the basement she crept to the bundle and wrapped her arms around it. The tiny feathers all over her body ceased to bristle and grew soft, and her embrace became warmer and gentler, adding heat to the nest. She would have to add heat to the rocks, to keep the temperature high enough for the ripening. Not long, now.

She would try again to explain to the Humans. The town would try to explain again, and see if it made a difference to the invaders. She almost knew enough Human words now that she might at last succeed where there had been only failure before.

"No eat," she murmured to the spheres she cradled. "No delish. No delicatsy."

It had never occurred to her kind that Humans could make such an appalling mistake. With their keratin-hard mouths, the Singer-People would never have tried to eat the parreetia, even if they didn't know what they were. They would never have mistaken the spheres for the...the fungus Humans associated them with.

Arrieuweet warbled at the parreetia in her arms, and her beak-like mouth clicked a tippet-tip rhythm of reassurance.

You are safe, little ones, she sang. *My babies. My eggs. You are safe from the ravenous things with mouthbones. I will save you from delicious. My heartsongs. My children.*

*Nothing turns some men into monsters
faster than having
their masculinity threatened.*

TOXIC

Mia Dalia

The researcher and his colleague stand in a laboratory, surrounded by screens, each of them playing a horror show. It is unfathomable to them and their kind to watch such things recreationally, but they cannot look away, magnetized to the pixelated nightmares by a strange, gut-churning fascination.

Their job is to observe, study, and change. They have traveled a very long way to do it, and failure is not an option. Although disheartened, they are starting to question the possibility of success.

In theory, this, like many other great ideas that have failed, is supposed to be fairly straightforward, but nothing seems to go to plan.

The researcher and his colleague have studied the history of this world extensively. They know all about its grim record of devastating colonization, recurring globally for centuries. One nation obliterating another in favor of self-righteous, vainglorious pursuits. The history of this planet is written in blood.

It is no wonder they've never made it to distant planets; they are too busy tearing themselves apart.

The researcher and his colleague are well traveled. They have traversed the cosmos looking for the right place. It was a folly to think a single destination would meet all their criteria, but they are willing to work for it. To compromise, within reason.

They can do whatever it takes to adapt and blend in. They'll follow strange customs, wear uncomfortable skins, eat unpalatable food.

But they cannot knowingly put their own kind in danger. They cannot abide the rampant violence of this world.

It is only when the person in the corner moves—slowly, bone-wrenchingly, with a heavy groan—that I realize it isn't a corpse. I'm watching it—the careful stretch of gnarled limbs, then a curled-on-itself body that follows. Until it reaches the square of light in the center of the room. Our sun in here is a bare low-wattage light bulb. The illumination it provides is sparse, but I can make out enough.

It is a man. Age undetermined. Face near featureless. His eye appears to have been replaced with what looks like a giant purple grape. His nose has been broken one too many times and now is merely a squiggly line bisecting his ruined face. There is a flap of flesh hanging off one of his cheeks, raw and wet. His longish hair, matted down with dirt and blood, droops down to his shoulders like dirty mop strings. One of his ears has been boxed into his skull, looking like bruised cauliflower. The other one is missing an earlobe.

It's difficult to imagine this man ever matching his ID picture ever again, but it is still there, hanging on a rubber cord around his neck like a gruesome reminder. With broken fingers, he extends it to me. It reads 'Jay Sommers.' A nice open face, plain and friendly. The sort that makes me think Midwestern. Though we are not from anywhere anymore. It seems that we have always been here.

I crawl over to him, dragging a broken leg. Show him my own ID. Another no longer recognizable face.

Jay Sommers tries to say something, but all that makes it past his minced-meat lips are blood-tinged saliva bubbles. He does a twirling motion with one of his less damaged fingers. I understand just what he's after, so I turn my ID over, and there they are—my sins listed in laminate.

The man tries to show me his, but I wave him away. I don't care. Not anymore. It won't change a thing.

There's only one outcome here, only one way this thing is going to play out.

With something intended as a battle cry but coming out distinctly more wail-like, I push myself to my feet. My broken leg screams in protest. The rest of my bones echo it. I fold my hands into fists, which reopens the weeping wounds along my knuckles. And then I attack.

No matter what it takes, I tell myself, no matter what it takes. The man's form is blurring through the tears I don't realize I'm crying. Or maybe it's blood—head wounds are a bitch. His body is a punching bag, absorbing the violence too willingly, putting up barely any fight.

I don't stop to consider the fairness of it all. There is no *fair* in this place. Only your best to survive and your worst to get you killed. The purest distillation of life.

I will not stop until it's over. Because the only way out of this is over Jay Sommers' dead body. And he is only one of many. The names, the faces, do not matter. Only survival. It's them or me.

And I will always choose me.

Three days earlier.

"So, what attracted you to this project?"

I'm sitting in the blandly beige room in a bland leather-esque reception chair across from a wide plain desk and thinking: These are the eggheads that run this show? What a joke.

But Johnny swears they are the real deal, and, for all his faults, Johnny doesn't lie.

I do find the way they refer to this thing as a project amusing. Just another psych experiment, all in the name of science. Like it isn't meant to be the thrill of a lifetime.

But I get it, I do. I majored in marketing. They are doing a deliberate undersell, the way pretty girls in nineties rom-coms were put in dowdy clothes and glasses to amp up the final transformation. Sure, whatever, I'll play along.

"I just want to do what the poster says." Big grin. "Find my limits. Test my mettle. All that."

"Not the money?" One of the geeks quirks his eyebrow at me.

"The money is good too, of course," I answer honestly. I wonder how far-reaching the organization is. If they combed through my financial records, if they checked out my internet searches on declaring bankruptcy, non-extradition countries, etc., they would know just how much this is all about the money.

They make a production of looking over my preliminary scores. Can't say they weren't thorough, from psych eval to physical stats. I'm in tip-top shape, an organic-fed gym rat. Ready for this.

"So, it's three days," the other geek says, light refracting in his thick eyeglass lenses. "Do or die."

I nod, mock-solemnly. It can't actually be *die*; this isn't Ancient Rome, we're not gladiators. I figure this is going to be more of a *Fight Club* situation, a movie I've seen enough times to quote.

Johnny didn't tell me much, said he was sworn to secrecy. But the fucker made it. Paid off his debts. Said the limp wasn't permanent. And the few skin grafts were well worth it.

The thing he was able to tell me, the thing that stuck with me ever since, replaying itself like some mantra, is that he'd never felt more alive.

I can get with that. The rat race leaves me a dull boy. I've had my highs, but they left me low. All the usual thrills have long become familiar. It was fun at first, the partying and the party favors, but over time, repetition kills excitement.

Ask me when last I felt alive, and I'll stumble answering. Was it bungee jumping into Villarica, or crushing that merger with LaoCon? One's an active volcano; the other is a deal Wall Street rated as the most brutal of the year. Close enough. But it doesn't stay, that daredevil shiver up your spine. Everything fades. Leaves you wanting more.

If anything, it builds up your tolerance. The bungee jumping thing started with Skypark, a curated park-like experience, and revved up to throwing yourself into a tube of raging lava. There used to always be the next thing, waiting just around the corner. And now not so much.

The money situation doesn't help either. Another thing that started off so small, practically innocent, just a light skim. Now it's this...

I lock eye contact and tell the geeks that three days is nothing.

There's something like mild amusement playing in their eyes. Bet they've heard it all before. Bravado is a thing that sounds fake no matter how you serve it up. In my case, though, it's the real deal.

To quote a disco hit my mom used to blare to piss my dad off, *"I Will Survive."*

They shuffle papers some more, but it's all perfunctory now. The decision has been made, and everyone knows it.

The head geek pushes his glasses up his long pointy nose with his long pointy finger and attempts something like a smile. "Welcome to Project Y," he says.

I suppose they use the word project to give themselves a façade of legitimacy. No one really calls it that, though. It's just The Game. If a bunch of DNA-nerds wanna circle-jerk themselves by imagining this is about science, that's on them. If they get some profound insights into the Y chromosome in the process, more power to them.

Is this meant to be some sort of a study of the emasculation of modern man? Sure, yeah, why not? They are not wrong. Being a white, well-to-do man in this day and age has become fraught with dangers. Seems like you're no longer meant to succeed. And if you do, make sure to spend enough time apologizing for it.

Do I hate it? Oh yes, let me count the ways. But then again, it just isn't worth it. Bottom line is, I didn't make this world. I'm just doing my best living in it. Same as everyone. If someone doesn't like it, they can get the hell out of my way. So what does it make me? A monster? If so, a very modern one.

Day one is all about labels. The assignation of sins. Not the way I'd put it, but I'm not the one in charge. It's actually almost relaxing to surrender control so completely. In here, I'm just another fish in a pond trying to prove itself a piranha.

The woman in the room is an eerie doppelgänger of my ex, right down to the critical quirk of the mouth and a shrill voice. Someone did their research.

The more the morning progresses, the more I realize just how much research has been done here. What these people know about me is some Big Brother bullshit. Things no one is meant to know.

Yeah, I lied, I cheated. Who hasn't? Coveted? You bet. Didn't kill anyone, though. "Not yet," I joke. The woman across from me is not amused. My ex was a humorless drag, too.

I always thought my parents went to church out of spite. Whether they were spiting higher power or each other, I was too young to figure out. Probably the latter, they were experts at that. The unexpected pregnancy kept for reasons that had nothing to do with love, I was the glue that held their marriage together. A fact they never tired of reminding me about. Father watched football too loudly, Mother blasted disco. He drank; she smoked. Both cheated, clumsily, indiscreetly, with phone calls that went silent when picked up and lipstick smudges on shirt collars. It was likely a relief to both of them when an exhausted long-distance trucker crushed their old Chevy one February evening, swerving on black ice beneath the starless sky. It was certainly a relief to me.

With nothing for inheritance but bad memories, I was taken in by a dutiful, though indifferent aunt and immediately set off to excel. I had every intention of leaving the grey, hopeless life and grey nowhere town I was from behind. Studied my ass off. Played sports. Got a scholarship. Then another. Worked hard. Played hard. Kissed all the right asses, then rinsed my mouth out with the finest of vodkas. Got far. Got dangerously close to the top.

Don't pity me—this Icarus scorched his own wings—but I refuse to view it as anything other than a temporary setback. Hence The Game.

The woman across from me is taking notes, unimpressed. Her expression is an impassive flatline. Fuck her, I don't care. Just give me my sin card and let me move on.

Eventually, she does. I scored pretty high on all the mortal ones. As expected. Except on wrath. Interesting.

The sins are printed, then laminated to the back of my ID. The front of it has my picture and name. So much for anonymity.

My card goes on a cord over my neck, and I'm off to the gym. Some endurance exercises. Lots of them, actually. Only the ones who complete their sets get to eat tonight.

The trick is you only have so much time to do it and only so many machines. Some tussles ensue. Nothing major. I try to stay away, save my strength, but then I gotta hit the treadmill, and the machine is occupied. A fat fucker about my age is pushing himself to a heart attack. I wait, but he isn't getting off, and time is of the essence.

So, I do what I must. I grab him by the back of his shirt and yank with all my might. He face-plants onto the treadmill with a loud thump. It's slapstick comedy at its finest.

I kick him off and get on the rubber. Begin to run. The man gets to his feet slowly, swaying. He's mad but not enough to do something about it. Fat men seldom are, I find—too soft, too indulgent.

I finish just in time for food, but then we are in the cafeteria, and I wish I passed. Our food is *alive*. Mind you, I'm not vegetarian or, worse yet, a vegan. I've eaten steak so bloody it still mooed, but this shit isn't even properly dead.

I'm given a choice between crickets and an octopus. Instinctively, I choose the latter.

The summer I moved to my aunt's, I found out all about crickets. They weren't the cute vessels of conscience like their cartoon counterparts. Oh no. The bastards were creepy, loved getting into the house, and hopped on their disgusting stick limbs when you tried to kill them. I've hated them ever since. Octopus, on the other hand...well, I've had calamari.

This is *nothing* like calamari. These creatures are small but squirmy, wiggly. I have to use both hands to wrestle my meal into my mouth, and once it's in, I find myself rethinking crickets.

The damn thing is fighting to get out, and I don't blame it, but I can't help it either. The tentacles are prodding the insides of my mouth, looking for ways to get out.

Octopuses, I've read, are intelligent, able to flee the tightest of confinements like some multi-limbed Houdinis. I also read that their brains are evenly distributed throughout their body, every tentacle…

No, no, don't name the food, don't overthink the food. I close my eyes, take a deep breath through my nose, and clamp down. And then chew and chew and chew.

Tears are pouring down the sides of my face, but it isn't pity or mercy, it's shock. A perfectly natural reaction. Eventually, after what feels like an eternity, it is over. I drink glass after glass of water. It cleanses the palate but not the mind. I suppress my gag reflex and wait for what's next.

Sensory overstimulation, apparently. I am placed in a tiny box of a room where all walls, floor and ceiling are projection screens, and bombarded with imagery. The goggles fitted onto me ensure I cannot look away or blink.

The images vary from innocent, albeit creepy, cartoons to violent pornography. There's no rhyme or reason. The main theme seems to be all the things you'd never want to look at in real life.

I try to let my mind drift, but the pictures jar me time and again from any semblance of reverie. I'll just have to wait it out instead. That's my main strategy here. With most endurance-based things, really, from dating to work to life itself. *Sit by the river long enough, sooner or later your enemies will float by.* I'm not much of a philosophy guy, but that's one thing Confucius got right. Stuck with me ever since college. I haven't always had the patience, but I have always tried.

When I'm let out, the treadmill fattie finds me and sucker-punches me. I guess it's free-for-all evening melee time. I get up and return the favor. His fat absorbs my fist like a bowl of Jell-O.

Everyone is brawling all around us. Some desultory, some enthusiastically. It goes on until the sprinklers come on and douse all the fight out of us. Then we are ushered into cubicles that remind me of those tiny Japanese hotels, or the glass enclosures space travelers get suspended in for long interstellar flights in science fiction movies.

Good thing I'm not claustrophobic. Some people are, though. I fall asleep to their freaked-out murmurs.

Day two brings more mayhem.

There are no windows in most places, no clocks. Time is presumed.

Today there is no food. Just tepid water. And the trick of the day is to tear someone apart. Not physically, it hasn't come to that yet, but with words. Sticks and stones, bitches. Bring it, I say.

We are shown a montage-style video about the life of one of my fellow participants. It's as tedious as most people's lives are. But I am paying attention, I am looking for things that would get under his skin. And when I find them, I fling them at him like daggers.

Every weakness, every indecision, every shitty choice. At first, he plays at stoicism, but after a while, I notice he's flinching. Later he is crying, messily and ugly, but that's the point of the game, isn't it?

The time he didn't insist his girlfriend get an abortion and got stuck with alimony for eighteen years, the time he slapped his ungrateful brat and got slapped with a restraining order in return. The job he lost for being too honest. The one he got downsized from for systematically lying. Sheesh, this guy did nothing right, it seems. The abuse everyone's dishing out is harsh, but hey, people like this dude are practically asking for it.

When it's my turn, I sit up straight in the chair, relax my expression, uncross my arms. I'm ready for this. I don't care what anyone thinks of me. Never have much, really.

We watch the montage of my life. Where did they get all this? Home movies I hadn't seen in ages? I wonder if my aunt held on to them, then sold them to these people. The woman never turned down an easy buck or met a principle she couldn't skirt.

Here are my parents and I, our first Christmas together. The tree is crooked and thin, sparsely decorated. The presents are wrapped haphazardly. I'm wailing; my parents are fighting.

It continues in a similar vein. A procession of failed family occasions, celebrations, vacations. I watch myself go from a knobby-kneed, too-serious kid to a sharp-eyed angsty teen. No, that's not angst, that's real anger, simmering just barely beneath the surface, threatening to break through.

Here's Niles, a ludicrously named kid we used as a punching bag in school. A helpless freckled nerd who never seemed to cry no matter what we did to him. Back then, it only served to egg us on. We entombed him in lockers, held his head in toilets, threw him into trash bins. He never cried. He did kill himself, though. With a straight razor, which I secretly always thought must have taken balls.

Here's me and my friends at his funeral. Everyone was made to go; it was a huge thing. Here's us starting a brawl right then and there. Poor fucker couldn't even get a peaceful sendoff.

Here's me at my parents' funeral. Not a tear to be found. I shot up nearly half a foot that year, and my suit fits terribly. I'm practically scowling like some dejected punk rocker. Look at me, free at last.

Here's a girl I didn't rape in college despite what she said. I can't vouch for my frat brothers, but I know for a fact I was too drunk to do anything but sleep. I can never get hard while wasted, then or now.

Here's a girl who broke my heart. Or so I thought at the time. Now I realize we just used each other for a while, and that's fine. I believe the nature of all relationships is transactional. The rest are misfiring hormones and misguided brain chemicals.

Here's my next girlfriend. We broke up after she got an abortion; an abortion I paid for.

Here's me at my college graduation. My aunt didn't come.

Here's a job I got fired from for stealing. With what they paid, they should have expected it. Here's a job where I perfected skimming the register. And here's the one where I lied about a coworker so he got fired and I was promoted to his position.

It goes on and on, with narration. That same shrill voice as the woman from day one. Fuck her.

Slowly but inexorably, the clips are leading us to now. To my almost-pinnacled life that took a slide back.

The screen goes black for a moment. and a single image is burning in my mind, imprinted by the montage. The frame of me fucking some girl whose name I can't even remember. No idea how they got this...did she make a video at the time? But the face I'm wearing just then is one of maddening focus and something like frustrated rage. Not a good sex face. Not a good face at all. It's like she's not even there, like it's just me pushing and pushing myself toward some goal only I can see, something I believe I am owed. Like I'm fucking the world itself.

The lights come on, all too bright. And then the critique pours in. I let it roll right off me. Mr. Teflon, me. Shit don't stick to me. And who are they anyway to judge me?

Yet they go on. Every one of them, safely ensconced in a glass house of their own, hurling stones at me. The trick is to say nothing. You say something; you lose. You interject, try to defend yourself, to explain yourself—you lose.

Men don't apologize. Men take action. And then live with the consequences of their actions. Presumably, that is the moral.

It's harder than it sounds to sit muted at the trial of your life. A few times, when the barbs are particularly cutting, it takes all my strength to remain silent.

These bastards are getting creative too, looking for connections between my mother and the way I am toward women. Nasty, low-blow punches. If this was a boxing match, they'd be biting my ear. I force a smile. Someone told me once it is the most infuriating thing you can do to a naysayer, so I practice it.

Eventually, it's over.

I feel too beat-down to eat, but I know I'll need my strength for day three. Not everyone makes it to the cafeteria from the critique exercise. Which is good. Which is how it should be. Winnow the losers. Separate the chaff from the wheat.

Eating is a competition too, today. The food is placed on a high platform. There are ladders to get there. Not enough for everyone, so you gotta fight your way up.

No mats on the ground either, nothing to absorb one's drop. The higher you climb, the harder you'll fall. Or you can just not eat, and wait the thing out.

Fuck it, I'm eating. I'm starved. The day's exercise has taken something out of me. I don't think food will replace it per se, but there's nothing else at the moment, so it'll have to do.

I lunge and kick. Hold on for dear life with one hand and swing punches with the other. I never look down. The bodies are thumping to the floor like bags of sand. Like bags of meat. The gruesome drumbeat to my progress.

When I get to the top, I see scraps. Like someone emptied out a composting bucket. I throw my fist at the platform in anger, but pull the punch at the last minute. My knuckles ought to be saved for real violence.

Then I take a deep calming breath, and proceed to fight the few others who have succeeded in vying for the most palatable of the scant offerings.

By the time we get down, the bodies are gone. No one asks any questions they don't want to know the answers to. No one is making friends or alliances. That shit's for movies. Here, in real life, we all understand the odds. We are, all of us, enemies here. Obstacles to be eliminated.

Tomorrow will find a winner among us.

Day three begins with an alarm going off, ripping at our eardrums. Unlike most alarms, it never stops. I slither out of my cot, run a hand through my greasy hair. I reek of sweat, blood, soured food. There are no bathrooms here, just buckets in the corners. No privacy. Nothing.

After I'm done here, I'm gonna take a shower so hot and so long, it'll be as close to boiling alive as a person can get. Burn these clothes.

We are told to proceed to the cafeteria, but there is no food there, not even scraps. The alarm becomes a siren, digging into my brain. Then a disembodied voice says, "Pick a sinner."

Everyone turns their ID cards back to front, wipes the gore and blood off of them so that their sins can be clearly read.

"Kill them," the voice says.

Hyperbolic, sure, but effective. They've got strobing lights going too; feels like they are going off in time with the alarm. The scene seems surreal. Malnourished, bruised, likely concussed, running on fumes and two days of inadequate sleep, the contestants ready themselves. The cafeteria becomes our battleground.

It's a nightmare, sure, but isn't every nightmare only a dream gone rogue? Eventually, you will wake up. Squint at the sunshine, shake your head at what your psyche concocted, and go on with your day. Right? Right?

I can't stop to think, I'm throwing punches, I'm taking punches. One so hard to the noggin that proverbial stars make an appearance. I don't see individual faces or bodies anymore. Just shapes. Fleshy vertical shapes that I need to make horizontal.

I think about everything this money will get me. A way out of all the troubles. Whoever said money can't buy you happiness was an idiot who never had enough.

I will do whatever it takes. Whatever. It. Takes.

I don't smell the gas they pipe through the vents, only feel its effect when it's much too late. I drop like a cut-down tree. Oblivion claims me.

When I come to, I'm in a small, high-ceilinged room with a body in the corner. And I think, what would they want me to do with a corpse, these people? What haven't I done yet? What depravity had I not been subjected to?

"You are the last two subjects left standing," the voice pipes in form somewhere. "The winner takes all. Now...kill."

The voice stirs the man in the corner into action.

He makes his way over, dragging his ruin of a body toward me. Reads my sins like it matters. Like he needs a justification to fight me. This is how I know he will lose. People like Jay Sommers always eventually lose to people like me.

Because in this world, you do what it takes without excuses. You don't offer reasons; you don't provide explanations. Life is brutal and ruthless, and if you are to succeed, you have to build yourself up the same way.

Kill or be killed. Shit or be shat upon. It really is that simple.

I summon what's left of my strength, of my energy, and lay into Jay Sommers. It doesn't take much. I leave him on the dirty floor, with his brain leaking out.

Raise my hands as best I can into a Rocky stance. Winner. I win. I'm a winner.

And then, I settled down to wait for my reward.

"Toxic indeed. Time after time." The researcher takes off his glasses and wipes at a smudge. None of these gestures or accoutrements are comfortable, and the language rolls off the lightly bifurcated tongue with great effort.

These are the things one must do in order to fit in on this strange and hostile planet with such irresistibly compatible chemical composition.

That's what it boils down to in the end—what makes you *you,* what makes your world your home are just chemicals.

"We can continue tweaking the DNA," his colleague offers.

Separating the lamentably insufficient four limbs into front and hind and utilizing only the latter to stand requires practice. It seems like a design flaw. Most mammals on this planet are quadrupedal. The terrestrial ones anyway. The aquatic and flying ones are another matter altogether.

Still, the diversity is fascinating to a scientific mind.

A deep sigh is followed by a pursing of the lips. All these small gestures, so simple yet so tricky to master. Verisimilitude training is really paying off.

"Sometimes I think it might need a complete rewrite altogether if we were to ever make this place less violent."

"I get it." The colleague nods, agreeable to a fault.

They take their job seriously. The future of their entire race depends on the results of their findings. Climate compatibility aside, they cannot possibly suggest contending with such violence. Frankly, it is amazing these creatures haven't killed each other off yet.

That would, of course, be the ideal scenario. One that would leave Earth free to colonize. But the researcher and his colleague cannot intervene on a global level, let alone cause such a conflict. Theirs is a peaceful species.

The researcher sighs again. "For now, I think, we'll just do a few more tweaks and run the next simulation."

"Very good," the colleague says with alacrity. "We do have a waiting list of volunteers."

"Can you believe they line up for this?" The researcher shudders.

It isn't really a question, and it gets no answer. Just a small, ready smile.

It should be easier. The humans are built from instructions encoded in DNA. Altering its structure should, in theory, alter the humans. But it doesn't seem to work, almost as if something inside these repulsive creatures is inherently evil in ways that defy science.

For the most part, humans of Earth inexplicably insist on dividing themselves into a rigid male/female binary. The violence is found in both genders, but staggering in the former. It seems to course through their veins like a particularly potent kind of toxicity.

And it is proving impossible to change.

"What about this one?" The colleague gestures to the bloody figure on screen with his arms aloft.

"Give him his prize. Exigencies of Mammon, and all that."

The colleague makes a mental note to look up those words, then proceeds to the next room. There is a protocol to follow before the money can be issued. The paper currency is disgusting to the touch, but it is so easily reproducible.

The researcher stands alone in the room. The walls are covered with digital screens, each showing dead bodies. He shakes his head. He's tired, his human skin suit itches, and he wants nothing more than a fresh, squirming meal and the warmth of a distant sun. But his planet is dying, and he must do all he can to prepare this one for his people while there's still time.

Earth is so beautiful when seen from afar. The researcher remembers seeing it first as a pale blue dot, then as a small colorful marble, and eventually as a striking sphere of blues and greens and browns and whites with swirling white clouds over oceans and land. Its thin atmospheric layer glowing so invitingly.

How different it is up close, mistreated and overrun by the species that cannot and will not appreciate it or each other.

He sighs once more. It is the most occasion-appropriate physiological act and a communicative gesture he has mastered thus far, and he uses it often. He finds it conveys his feeling aptly.

When night falls, he goes outside and looks for the distant dying star he's left behind, sighing heavily, making promises he hopes he'll be able to keep.

"I will save you," he whispers in his native language which sounds like nothing found on Earth. "I will give you a new home," he assures those who have entrusted their future to him.

Then, because sleep is not something his kind requires, he goes back to the lab and starts again.

The research is tough and disheartening. Almost like some sort of cruel game. But he will do whatever it takes to win. Whatever it takes.

*Gods are just monsters
whose actions we allow to change who we are.*

THE FALLEN GOD

Liam Hogan

The fallen God is *angry*.

So says Grunholt, the oldest of our clan. She claims our neighbours offended the God and brought ruin down upon themselves. She warns us not to make their mistake.

Until two sunrises ago, we wouldn't have listened to her divisive words. Two sunrises ago, we were aware of the Gods but had never asked anything of them. We never *feared* them, for they were Gods, distant denizens of the night sky, slowly turning about the three-in-one, the Celestial Triple. None had deigned to descend and join us in our burrows, and none, so we thought, ever would.

The Udunites lived as peacefully as we did, and, as far as we could tell, as at one with nature. Though we never contemplated the joining of our burrows, we visited and traded often. More than a few successful triples were formed by the young of both under-villages, the blessings of shared motherhood binding our clans tighter still.

But then the God fell from the sky in a terrible ball of flame, the air screaming in agony as it was ripped apart, bringing death in its wake. Those above at the time, working the talish fields, tending our crops, froze, fearing the end of the world. But we were not the target of the fiery descent, nor of the vengeful God, not that day. That fate fell on the Udunites.

A scant few, barely two sixes and not an intact triple among them, survived the devastation. Horribly injured, they struggled into our under-village, where we salved their burns and strapped their mangled limbs. We did not—could not—believe what they told us. It was impossible that a God would behave in such a cruel, destructive way. They must have been overcome by smoke, or soul-struck beneath the third ridge, which would leave any of us dazed. Or left so bereft by the sundering of their triples that their fractured minds played them false. It didn't matter how often the Udunites repeated the horrors they had experienced, none of us could make sense of it.

In the great hall of the under-village we circled in our triples, the youngest out at the edges, debating what to do. What, if anything, we *could* do... As ideas ran dry, an elder three tentatively suggested that perhaps we should consult Grunholt.

Grunholt, once a third of an elder three herself, had been banished to the fringes of our burrow two winters ago, for her unsettling views. We took her food, for she was too old to work the fields, but blocked our anten to her poisonous, singular ideas. Such is the sad, lonely fate of those who outlive their thirds, who lose both their east and their west. They do not usually outlive them for so long.

Things must be desperate to turn to her. Though there is sense to the elder three's radical suggestion; Grunholt has lived through more summers than any of us. But even she has never seen anything like this fallen God in all her long, long life.

Ensign Bob Pulver, Corps Id 4728-fz-8772, of the ESN Carrier, Antarres: improvised log.

No idea what time, or even what day this is. Weird to be scratching marks on an emergency fire blanket, hoping someone will decipher my cramped handwriting. But there's not a working piece of electronics anywhere on the scout ship, not even my wristband. If I don't survive, this will be my final account, and might help the investigators in some way.

When Second Engineer Foley suggested I take the newly serviced craft for a test spin, I leapt at the opportunity. I wasn't due my first solo for another quarter, but everyone agreed I was the most promising pilot in my intake. I was ready, or so I felt.

It was everything I hoped it would be. So much more real than a simulator! *Too* real... I should have just checked the basics and returned, as Foley presumably intended. I should never have ventured so far. I certainly shouldn't have entered the Loferre system, but the chance to try a gravity-assisted flyby was too tempting.

Whether the G-type planet had a weird magnetic flux, the ship wasn't quite as operational as Foley thought, or it was plain bad luck, I was skimming the thin, upper wisps of the atmosphere, when something went horribly wrong with the electronics. *All* the electronics. In short order, I had no communications, no nav computer, even no life-support. Screens as dead as the vacuum of space. I had what air there was in the cabin and a degree of manual control, and eff-all else.

The simulator hours paid off; I managed to crash-land on the planet surface. And when I say crash-land, I literally mean *crash*, no points for elegance, none for making a right mess of the scout ship. The impact shattered what little still worked, including my left leg. An ugly, sickening fracture, blood and bone and ...*yikes*. Who knew how icky insides were?

Thankfully, a med kit ended up close to hand, though of course the portable scanner proved as lifeless as everything else. I did what I could. Again, zero points for my improvised splint, for the bandages that were agony to tie. I'm writing this under the influence of a rainbow cocktail of painkillers, in case you're wondering about my current state of mind.

The craft being nothing more than a scout ship, pulled out of service for maintenance, there were hardly any supplies of either water or emergency rations aboard. So, most likely, I'll starve to death. Fairly soon. Assuming I don't get *sepsis* or something.

Fortunately, the landing site (AKA: *crater*) was infested with a species of small animal. Fur over a hard shell, and about half the size of a cat, but with more legs. It turns out they're damned good eating. I might not have discovered this if a number of them hadn't been roasted in the flames of my descent. The lingering smell did battle with probable concussion and nausea as I faded in and out of consciousness through the night. When I finally fell upon them, a day (or two?) after the crash, I gorged on three in a single sitting, learning how to tear back the scorched fur and crack the carapace beneath. A cross between mutant lobster and shaggy rabbit, and, when chargrilled, as tasty as either.

Other critters further afield had been killed by the shockwave, though not as fully cooked. Painfully, slowly, using a crumpled strut as a crutch, I managed to gather a few, and rekindle a flame from still smoking embers. The branches of the trees I had torn through were too full of sap to burn, but there were scraps of dry wood lying about in clusters, perhaps swept there by flash floods—hope one doesn't happen while I'm in this god-damn hole! I managed to roast four more of the beasties before I ran out of fuel. I was tempted to eat them right away, but that would have been greedy, so I only had the smallest. Going to see how long I can make the rest last, eking out my rations. No telling how long it will take you guys to come rescue me.

And you will, won't you? Come find me? Track the last known telemetry, scan this mud-hole of a planet for fresh surface impacts, for refined metals? The stealthy scout ship doesn't contain much, being mostly light-weight nano-carbon. But it contains *some*. Detectable amounts, I hope? Even though the only person who might know where I am, or even that I'm missing, is Foley. And he, on second and third thoughts, might decide that letting an ensign test-pilot a shoddily-repaired ship wasn't his smartest move ever, and it would be best not to own up to it and even to cover his tracks.

In the only snippet of positive news, the bottle of Antorrean whisky I was going to thank Foley with miraculously survived the crash. Be damned if he'll get it now, and if this *is* the end, I might as well go out drunk. I'll keep it for even more dire straits than I'm currently in.

I'm at the end of the blanket, so this is me, signing off. Leg beginning to ache again. Will have to ration the pain killers as well. Regards to everyone who ever knew me. Love to anyone who ever cared.

The reports are true! My triple saw it with our own eyes, sensed it with quivering anten. A vast, scarred, still smouldering pit where there was once a thriving under-village. Amid the devastation squatted an immense, blackened shell. Out of which crawled the fallen God, a deranged, singular, five-legged, soft-bodied monstrosity, holding one of the unfortunate Udunites above the flames of a fire built from the wreckage of their nests, before sinking terrible teeth into the burnt and mutilated body. The God scoured every scrap of flesh from the cracked carapace, from the broken legs, even from the seat of the Udunite's soul, bashing the shell on rocks until it split wide open!

Oh, what a sight—what a ghastly, *evil* sight! All of us shuddered and chittered to see it. To think a *God* could do such a thing. To think a God would ever be so ravenous for our flesh! For our souls!

In fear and panic, we swept the ruined Udunite fields, harvesting what crops had survived. A foolish notion, perhaps, but we threw as many talish roots as we could salvage into the pit, hoping that this would appease the hungry, angry, fallen God, so that it might leave the souls of the Udunites to their eternal dance. And indeed, the God briefly laid the remaining bodies aside, as though touched by our offerings.

Until the talish roots were flung back out of the pit, and we fled, fearing the God's wrath.

Ensign Pulver: Status log, whatever the hell date this is.

There have been two sunsets since my last report, so I'm counting this as day four. Or five? I think the days here are a *lot* shorter than I'm used to. Maybe half Earth normal? Perhaps explains the confusion about how long I was out of it. Call it *Crash-5*: C5 for short.

All the reachable furry-lobster-critters are now either rank (they go off so damned quick! Won't be trying any raw) or already eaten, right down to the hard to get at nugget of sweet meat in the thickest part of the shell. The last of the pain killers are also gone. The pain, not so much. Barely any water left. Have rigged as many receptacles as I can employ, but how often does it rain here? Not often enough. I'd hoped to be rescued by now, dammit!

Guess I'm going to have to dig in for the long haul. On that note, the ship's heat-shields and a T30 probe as stylus means I have as much writing material as I'll ever need, even if I turn out to be a modern day Robinson Crusoe. How long was *he* shipwrecked for? And on which planet? I never was very good at ancient Earth history. Anyhow, if you're reading this, don't forget to read the emergency blanket first.

There's only half a crate of rations left. A week's worth, *if* I stretch them out. Annoyingly, there are more of those tasty critters around. Live ones, not dead. I've glimpsed movement, above the level of the impact crater, heard their chittering, the way it goes quiet when I try to prop myself up to see. But until I can clamber out of here, until I can go more than a couple of meters, I'm going to have to hope the skittish creatures come to *me*. Doesn't seem very likely.

So far, all that's chanced into the crater are some roots. Bit like a scrawny carrot in appearance. One that's been plucked too early from hydroponics, and then lost down the back of the food-prep for a week. Even so, I was tempted. But, alien planet, alien toxins. The critters did me no harm (and my belly rumbles at the thought), but it's too much to hope that the plants *also* prove edible. I took a tentative nibble, but it was acrid and wincingly bitter, and in disgust I threw them back out of the hole I'm in. I may regret that. They could be okay cooked, I guess...? But my fire is out. Have to sort that, if I'm to cook any critter unlucky enough to come within stumbling reach.

The last of the self-heating rations it is. Come rescue me *soon*, god-damn you, Foley!

Grunholt called an emergency meeting, to discuss what we must do to prevent the same punishment as the Udunites.

"What was it our Godless neighbours did, that was so very terrible?" she asked. "What did you *see*, at the Udunite village?"

There was lengthy silence. Then three triples were talking at once.

"The fallen God is hungry."

"Our offering, of the Udunite crops, their talish, was spurned."

"The Udunites *souls* were devoured." This caused anguished wails from those triples who had not seen it. From all except Grunholt, who scratched her scrawny flank.

"*So.* The God rejects their crops, and consumes the flesh and even the souls of the indolent farmers? Is it not as I have always said? That those who grow and consume talish roots are *weak*, their souls malnourished?"

There was much chittering at that. Without the talish we would surely go hungry, for it was early summer and our other crops would not be ready for many sunrises yet. Though talish is easy to grow, it is hard work to make palatable. It needs to be ground to a paste, labour that Grunholt never enjoyed, the task mindless but reassuringly companionable, a triple in tridem, working the heavy grindstone.

"Destroy the talish," Grunholt ordered, though none had put it to a vote. "Dig up the roots and let them wither. Then we will revisit the fallen God, and see if our actions have found favour."

Pulver, C10, midday-ish.

I ought to be scientific about this, even if it's pointless. If anyone is ever going to read these scratched words, then they'll have to have come down to the planet, and will see everything for themselves. The only uncertainty is whether I'll be alive to greet them or not. Most probably *not*.

But I don't have much else to write about, *so*, the local flora and fauna. Not much to report on the flora, bitter carrots and shredded trees (or tree-equivalents?) aside. There's a lot more greenery beyond the crater, but I seem to have landed in a clearing, or my heavy impact did the job of clearing it.

I guess the critters are the *fauna*. Not seen much else; some flitting insect things that might be attracted by the dead (and increasingly pungent) critters. Do dead lobsters smell this bad? I've taken to lobbing the carcasses as far as I can throw them, just to stop the stink. It'd be easier without a busted leg, let me tell you.

Talking legs, how many do lobsters have? I imagine them with two big claws, and a dozen little ones, but that can't be right, right? Plus, these alien land-lobsters don't have a lobster's fan tail. They're more like *half* lobsters, split the wrong way (for eating purposes). Maybe they're not really like lobsters at all. Hairy, elongated *crabs*, rather than hairy, squat lobsters? Didn't I read that crabs keep evolving on Earth? *Fake* crabs... But then, how many legs do crabs have? Damned if I know.

Start with the basics, then. Assume nothing. I guess the critters are most like large woolly crab spiders. With *six* legs, rather than eight. Giant, woolly ants? No, still far too short in body length. Squished ants. Though, whatever the leg count, comparing them to something on Earth might be a mistake. They're alien, after all. The front and back limbs have six tiny claws, suitable for digging, perhaps, though the pads of the feet and arms are soft. Maybe they can hold things? Like, worms?

The middle limbs end in blade-like shapes, like your basic canteen knife, complete with serrated teeth. But not very sharp, just a bit rough, so God alone knows what purpose they serve. The mid-limbs have the least meat in them as well. Maybe they're, what do they call it? *Vestigial?*

What the critters are, without any doubt, are extremely dumb creatures. Which will disappoint any exo-biologists who come after me, scientists are always hankering for something they can have a conversation with, someone to discuss the deep secrets of the cosmos. It won't be these things, not unless saying *Grace* counts before tucking in. No, the critters have something of the lemming about them. Which is to my benefit, not theirs.

I'm not much good at this science thing. No biologist, exo or otherwise. On more certain ground is my current inventory, and it won't take long to list, or indeed, to consume. There's probably a profitable study to be done on rationing and willpower. How long we *think* we can eke out emergency supplies for, and how long we actually do. I'll bet a hundred credits the latter is never longer than the former. Maybe my willpower is no better than my science. But give a guy a break. I'm out of painkillers, as well as rations, and down to half a demijohn of water, so don't blame me for *also* being down half a bottle of whisky! I had quite the maudlin singsong, before I realised how drunk I was getting, and how rapidly the precious liquor was vanishing.

Anyway, there I was, caterwauling away, songs never before heard on this god-forsaken planet, when more of those critters stumbled into my crater.

Well! That sparked a spurt of drastic (and, for me as well as them, painful) activity. Me, big game hunter! I gave a great whoop and spent the next fifteen minutes drunkenly playing whack-a-mole. And whether, whisky impaired, I was too enthusiastic, or these critters were still suffering the consequences of my crash-landing, they were poor specimens, fur burned and manky, limbs twisted or broken. Hardly grade one prime, but beggars can't be choosers.

Still, they couldn't have arrived at a better time, given I hadn't eaten for a whole day—a *C* day, not an Earth one. Which, no doubt, was why the whisky hit so hard, and also why I'd finally broken the seal. I thought there wasn't anything to lose, not anymore, and though I'm not sure of the calorie content of strong liquor, I figured it'd quiet my grumbling belly. I only meant to have a single measure, but since there were no measures to hand...

Anyway, I now had fresh-ish food. Me, big chef! The sappy, broken wood had dried out some, and though the electronics are fried, the storage batteries still held charge. Enough to create sparks, when I touch the terminal wires together. Enough to give me a nasty burn, the first time I tried it. So I had fire on tap, food to roast, and a hole to fill. I could barely wait to eat my tasty repast.

I may even have sung that classic Corps song, the one about the fat-bellied sergeant whose stomach is marched on by his cadets... The first verse, anyway, because who can ever remember the second?

Oh, woe is us! What have we *done*?

It should be left to the Gods to be vengeful, not to us. And we might blame Grunholt, for all nobody protested strongly at the time. But I do not think that will save us. I do not think *anything* will save us.

We returned to the Udunite under-village, the pit containing the angry, fallen God, to see if the digging up of our talish placated it. Only to find scattered, discarded bodies of the Udunites littering the fields, only to witness one flung out of the pit with an enraged scream from the furious God within. We did not linger.

Grunholt listened to our report, then rasped mid-arms together in disgust, a strident chitter that halted all discussion.

"The talish was a step in the right direction, but too little, too late," she proclaimed. "This much is now obvious. The fallen God is passing judgement.

The Udunites that were devoured, their souls splintered; the Udunites whose bodies have been delivered from the pit, the God has judged each and every one."

"Judged?" echoed an elder.

"Whether they are worthy, or not."

"Worthy? But...they are *all* dead."

"Indeed. This is God's message. We too will be judged, in death, if not in life. But we have prevented the God's judgement of the remaining Udunites. How do you think the fallen God will respond when it finds we are harbouring the survivors? Survivors who would have died, without our help?"

There was a long pause. Mutterings of disbelief. The wounded Udunites were still recovering. Was she really suggesting we *shouldn't* have aided them? But it was worse than that. Far worse.

"We must return the Udunites to the pit, to be judged!"

One of the braver elder threes had had enough. "You're asking us to *kill* our neighbours?"

"Kill the Godless, heretic Udunites? No, of course not. *Deliver.* Let us throw them into the pit. Let the God decide their fate."

Grunholt slowly turned in a circle, her anten dipping to greet us all. "If the God is merciful, if the Udunite souls are pure, then God will cast them back out of the pit, as it did the worthy dead. But if they are consumed—even to their souls!—then the fallen God has judged and condemned them for all eternity."

It was awful to drag the pitiful Udunites back to the remains of their under-village, but we did as Grunholt bid. What else could we do? Better that, than to be judged ourselves. And the God's judgement was indeed terrible. Fire erupted once more within the pit, and the remaining Udunites were cast into the flames, every one of them, all to an unworldly, discordant noise that echoed from the smoke-filled abyss and nearly caused us to throw ourselves in after it.

C14?

Every time I begin to despair, this planet provides. Though it does not always do so with particular generosity.

I was idly scraping away at already scraped shells, when another stupid critter stumbled into the crater. The thing had managed to get its legs tangled in plant vines. Even then, I might have struggled to catch it (still sore from the last round of whack-a, something grating in that busted leg of mine), if, like a rabbit in a spotlight, it hadn't frozen, catatonic, at my approach. I whacked it hard with my crutch, and that was that.

The funny thing was, just *before* I whacked it, I heard it chirp. And *after* I'd cooked and devoured it (stringy and tough, and such a miserly portion size I'm considering sending in a complaint!), I was idly playing with those thin mid-limbs, rubbing the serrated edges together, when I managed to get them to *chirp* again. You have to pull them at just the right speed, but I guess it's like a locust. Or is it a cricket? The tone was almost musical. Anyway, that's how the critters chitter away. Just a meaningless "here I am," I suppose.

Our sins compound. Having killed, we found ourselves killing again, and this time we slaughter not our neighbours, but our brethren. But perhaps Grunholt brought it upon herself.

The singular elder, as had become her custom, dominated the gathering in the great hall. She listened to our reports, our voices stuttering as mid-legs trembled and anten folded back from the awful memory of those sounds emerging from the pit, noises that reached even as far as our under-village.

There were murmurings. How many would have to die to satisfy this God? And who would be next? All the Udunites had already been cast into the pit.

Finally, Grunholt spoke. "What does it say, that every single one of the Udunites we returned to the pits was killed, cast into the flames, consumed right down to their souls? What does it say, that the God let the entire forest know their fate?"

"That...they were Godless?" an elder said. Merely repeating back to Grunholt what she had already said, though none were brave enough to so comment.

"Indeed! And what was *their* transgression?"

"The...talish?"

"No!" Grunholt, our self-appointed leader whirled to face us, anten stabbing like someone digging in the fields. "That was a grave sin, one we recently shared until we amended our ways. But not the *only* one. The remaining Udunites, how many were tripled?"

We stared at her in bemusement. "Um, none?"

"Is it not clear? Nothing can stand on only one, or two legs! For us to prosper before God, we *need* triples! Fruitful ones! Just as we rooted out the unwholesome talish, we must root out those who do not contribute *fully* to our clan!"

So we did. We bound singular Grunholt with rope made from talish fibres, and, even as she piteously pleaded, cast her into the pit of the fallen God, to be judged.

My god, but how whisky warms the soul! I've had nothing but *grief* since I crashed, but once again, if only for a few hours, I was almost happy. Or drunk, and perhaps there's no difference. Once again, I'd been on the verge of starvation, the whisky the last thing left to consume, and once again, just when I'm wondering if I should polish off the bottle or save a final goodbye mouthful, food arrives, and not just the one critter. I was singing away (the one about Pluto and Uranus) when, out of the blue, a whole host appeared at the rim of the crater. Some of them didn't stop in time, it was like a lemming migration, an avalanche of them. These weren't hog-tied, it ended up being quite the workout, though every time one almost escaped, and came up against the ones clustering on the crater rim, it tumbled back down. Like it was pushed.

You have to fill your boots when you have the opportunity, even if there ended up being more than I could eat. Because you never know exactly how long it will be before even more dumb critters fall into your lap.

And there's none of the Antorrean whisky to change my luck, or hardly enough to mellow the buzz. Though, perhaps it was my singing? A good old Corps sing-along, to the tune of rasping critter legs. It might not be a regimental band, but if it does the trick...

Our clan is diminished. Some claim purified. Grunholt is no more, though her words linger. Dead, her judged-and-found-wanting soul eaten by the fallen God, *still* she spoke to us from the beyond. One final command. It was the cry of a hungry child, a child she had been a great many harvests ago, one whose first reedy words are always the same:

Feed me.

And so we did, though not until sunrises later, when we once again heard the cries of the God ringing through the woods, haunting us, calling us to perform the terrible but unavoidable duty. The fallen God would wait no longer.

Hardening our souls, we weeded out the under-village, cast the singular and twinned into the pit, to be judged. It was pitiful to see them scramble for safety up the sheer walls of the pit, worse to have to push them back in. When one of them would attempt to dig, the fallen God would raise its stiff fifth limb, and, perched awkwardly on only two legs, strike!

Only adult triples now remain in our clan. But when the God cried out once again, (barely enough time to grieve!) the elder threes said we had not gone far enough. On the same fruitful, tripled basis, they argued, we should add the young to the tally. The ones yet to reach their maturity, their shells still soft. This year's litters. It had been a good year, almost every three had a new mother, myself among them. What difference will it make, one year's offspring, the elders ask?

Younger triples huddled in discussion. Were our children not the future? Would they not, God willing, someday form triples themselves, and so replenish our clan? Whereas, what had the elder threes done for us? What *could* they do for us? It was their leadership that had so angered the God. It was Grunholt, not them, who had interpreted the God's demands, who had spoken the final commandment.

And were *they*, these aged triples, these elder threes, fruitful? Not for many a harvest. Did they work the fields? Had any of them done the awful things we had had to do, to keep the God quiet in the pit?

Sometime around C20.

I should probably make at least one log entry a day, it's easy to lose count when the days fly by.

If music be the tasty food of love, then *boy* do these critters love Corps marching songs. They throng to my not-particularly dulcet tones, and throw themselves into the crater to be eaten. Good thing there's still plenty of shattered wood, all nicely dried by now.

Twice, I've been worried I might starve. Twice, whisky and singing saved me. Now, the critters arrive pretty much every day, in such numbers that sometimes all I eat is the tender nugget of flesh hidden deep in the shell. Horribly wasteful, but long may the migration last. I dine like a king!

Well, a king with a one-ingredient diet. Hope I'm not missing essential nutrients. I wouldn't say I'd *die* for a salad, but perhaps for a plate of fries? Even the mushy, gray mash they serve up in the mess. With a side of critter nuggets—deep fried, for a change.

I'm getting much better at dispatching them. Leg still sore, of course. But more mobile, if not exactly up to a twenty-k jog. It's probably a right mess, beneath the bandages I daren't peek under.

I'll be glad to leave this place. Ecstatic for a med-bay, a shower, and even a whole plate of mushy mash. And the *look* on Foley's face at the prodigal ensign's return!

The God continues to make impossible demands, the sounds continue to haunt us. *Feed me.* In our desperation we send emissaries to our nearest neighbours. Ask if they heard and saw the God falling. They did. But, fearful of what such terrifying omens mean, they have been shunning us.

They say they are relieved we are unharmed, disheartened to hear the fate of Udunites. Confused by our words, looking around for our elder threes, to explain the message.

So we show them. Impossible to look down into the pit and upon the fallen God, and not be shaken to the soul. The discarded, burnt carapaces of the unworthy. The vast, distorted shell that the God scratches away at, but never pierces, not the way our godless brethren were pierced, were shattered.

We tell them, these neighbours of ours, what they must do, to save themselves from such a fate. And then we help them, when they baulk, when they plead mercy, to dispose of the singular, the merely twinned. The elder threes, council triples who cannot serve them in this bold new future. We deliver them all to be judged, and swiftly judged they are.

C36

Funny dream I had last night. I dreamt I heard scratching, and saw lights in the crater. For a giddy moment, in my dream, I thought I was being rescued, but the lights turned out to be a trio of critters, each with a flaming twig in one fore-claw, stolen from my fire no doubt. Each froze at my regard, before scurrying into a tunnel in the crater wall. In my dream, I was too slow to stagger up and whack them. Not that I was hungry, just sleepy.

Weird thing was, when I checked in the morning, there *are* holes in the walls. And not just from attempted escapees, ones I stopped with my crutch. Actual tunnels, freshly dug. My dream couldn't be real, could it?

Which God was it who brought fire to early humans? Mars, I guess. Just imagine if I did the same for these stupid little critters! Me, the God of War!

Purified, our three clans joined and of single purpose, a single vision, we set out to spread the word wider still. To clans we only distantly know. Neighbours of neighbours of neighbours. Preaching the way of the Fallen God.

It didn't make sense to bring the unworthy all the way back to the Udunite under-village. So we have each clan dig their own pit, as deep as the God is tall, as broad as a swinging, crushing limb can reach. We show them how to kindle flames at the bottom of the pit, how to perform judgement, how to cleanse.

If the villagers are unwilling, unworthy to see the truth of the Fallen God, then we judge them all. For their own good.

C40ish.

Crapola. The food has dried up again. No matter how long and loud I sing, I've not seen a critter in a couple of days. Migration over.

There's nothing for it. I swig the last of the whisky, quarter-fill the emptied bottle with what little morning dew that drips from the sides of the scout ship I've managed to collect. Lean heavily on my strut to write these words on the highest panel I can reach.

I'm heading towards where the sun sets. Out of the barren crater, and into the woods. Gone hunting. Wish me luck. And Foley: if I don't make it, may you rot in hell!

Bloodied and ash coated, we were weary from our exertions, our determination wavering the further we went, when word came. Our offerings had finally been deemed worthy, our cause just, our crusade *necessary*. A mighty chariot had been seen descending from the celestial triple, hovering above the Udunite pit, bringing with it a terrible storm. By the time we arrived to see for ourselves, there was no God, and even the giant, warped shell was gone. The pit was empty, just the tattered bodies of the godless and singular, lying all around.

Our faith renewed, we will continue to spread God's word. Ripping up the talish, weeding out the godless, digging pits until every member of every clan we can reach has been judged. Only then can we rest. Only then will the memory of the God's terrible, echoing plea be silenced.

Feed me.

Hi Rosalind—or I should say, *Director* Rosalind! Congratulations, once again. I know you have your qualms about taking on this role, but I can't think of anyone better for the job, though I don't envy you!

I've enclosed some material you might find useful in your overhaul of the Corps. I know you have people to do that for you, but it can only help to throw in an external perspective or two. And yes, as an exo-biologist, it's also a *personal* perspective, but I trust you can forgive me that!

This should have made bigger waves than it did. Hell, this debacle should have cleared the slate and secured your job years earlier, and who knows, that might have prevented one of the stupidest, most pointless wars in Earth history, though maybe that's wishful thinking. A war that overshadowed many of the Space Corps earlier, equally egregious actions, none more so than this.

You might want to read the court martial transcripts, but frankly what I've included here should do the trick, and is a lot less dry. Make your own assessment, rather than the legal views that led merely to a dishonourable discharge and the unusual injunction that the idiot involved never be permitted to leave Terra again. There was a period when this could even have gone the other way; a plucky hero story, the salvaged scout ship proudly displayed in the Corps museum. Well, maybe it *should* be displayed, along with the grisly footage of the spoil pile of Pulver's gluttonous feasting.

This then, is the hand-written log of Ensign Pulver, as entered as evidence by both prosecution and defence. Frankly, I don't think either were trying that hard. Nor was the judge, who should have twigged there were things to be learnt here, systemic failings to be corrected. More so, because of how embarrassing it all was, rather than less. Not least of which was how long the search and rescue took, compounding the consequences of this disastrous clash of civilisations. A marooned ensign, who put on weight during his stranding! And to think it took the scientists almost *two* whole years to actually return to Loferre, to track down this peaceful, plant-eating species that had showed so many obvious signs of intelligence and community that everyone (deliberately?) seemed to miss. Only to find them engaged in a bloody war raging across the entire continent, with 'Pulver-pits' full of the roasted bodies of their enemies!

As it is, I hurdled an awful lot of red tape to find out why doing something so outrageously stupid you got canned to the lowest rank was called being 'Pulverised.' None of the cadets who used the term actually knew where it came from, it was just a bogeyman with a dozen different myths behind it. Talk about burying the lesson!

For utter completeness, it would be fascinating to get the Loferrian side of the story, but obviously, after the debacle of the '24 expedition, which was *supposed* to repair the damage Pulver had done, and the relatively short life-cycle of the Loferrians, especially in light of their violent upheavals, those wounds are still too raw.

What I am basically suggesting is that Ensign Pulver be used as an example of all the pig-headed wrongness that the Corps fell into with their self-granted 'exceptional' status. A microcosm, one less difficult to grapple with than the politically weighted and nuanced Arkham incident. I'm preaching to the converted, of course, but we need a more humble agency, one that knows its place in the universe, and doesn't fuck up as badly as Pulver did. Ever since the Corps came into being shortly after the discovery of the E-drive, it seems to have done nothing but recruit gung-ho flyboys. Suggesting it should be graduate level, vegan females only would probably get me into a heap of trouble, (not for the first time), even possibly canned. But I'll settle—gladly!—for your ascent to Director, and the hope that, as a new broom, you do some *vigorous* house cleaning.

In addition to the evidence of his own reports from the planet surface, it's worth considering his 'doubling-down' trial defence; that he was not fully aware of the strict prohibition on killing sentient beings on any planet, or even that they were sentient (I know!). As he himself observed, they are tool-users, builders, social creatures who left him food. What truer signs of intelligence are required?

This episode should have shaken the Corps to its core. With recommendations from engineering, recruitment, training, right the way through to how we log flight plans and other security issues for our carriers. If there is one slim silver lining to the debacle, it's that Ensign Pulver's actions are a textbook example of what *not* to do on first contact. But only if we use him as that example!

It will take time and considerable effort to repair the damage done to this social, intelligent, but pre-technology race. The ripples of the war that Pulver inspired, the charnel pits that were dug, the captured enemies sacrificed, these are a generational stain that only time can resolve.

Our best scientists predict it may take as long as a hundred years, with discreet monitoring by remote drones, before we can risk returning to the surface in person, to make a proper study of these remarkable subterranean, agrarian creatures with their three-parent family groups. Something for future directors, and future scientists, to plan for and worry about. Needless to say, it will be very important, when we do meet with the Loferrians again, that our representatives do their best to never bare their *teeth*.

*The truly monstrous can often start
from a place of complete innocence.*

THE BOY IN THE BOX

MARTIN LIVINGS

They were the Kantari. For untold eons, as planets formed and crumbled, their society had remained unchanged, static, considered perfect by all but those considered mad or heretical. Their entire worlds were built on their psychic spacetime manipulations, forms and functions folded in and out of reality as required. Even their bodies were nothing but pure thought now, extensions of self extruded into four dimensions. Each Kantari came into existence when it so desired, and ceased to exist when it so chose. They were the masters of the universe, ideal, perfect.

Or so they had always believed. But Stavrox knew better. He knew better than all of them.

"This is pure insanity, Stavrox," Lumini thinkspoke harshly, her luminescent tesseractoid form flashing with annoyance. "When will you admit that this was a terrible idea?"

He didn't dignify her question with a response, refused to give her the satisfaction. She'd never believed in the project, none of them had. He kept his own frustration hidden, his multitude of overlapping spines not showing even the slightest quiver of uncertainty. This is how Stavrox approached his life, as the greatest disruptor that Kantari civilisation had ever known...in his own humble opinion, of course, if nobody else's. Moving fast and breaking things was his modus operandi. And he intended to do just that.

"Experiment twenty-eight," he intoned, as he prepared himself, formulating the prompt in his mind. It didn't seem that much to ask, really; just to create something that his own abilities were utterly incapable of creating. Something that no Kantari was capable of creating. Their unassailable belief in their own perfection had rendered their imaginations hopelessly limited, leaving their civilisation stagnant and dead-ended. No, worse than that, the Kantar Empire was actually *shrinking*, for the first time in their long history, more of them choosing to demanifest than manifest, entire worlds emptied, as an endemic deep-seated cultural and intellectual ennui took hold of them. They had grown dissatisfied with their superiority, bored with their perfection. There was simply nowhere left to explore, nothing left to create. It had all been done already. But Stavrox, the disruptor, wanted to go beyond the evolutionary cul-de-sac their species had meticulously and mindlessly constructed for themselves. And there was only one way to do that.

They had to use a different mind altogether. An *alien* mind.

"I agree with Lumini," one of the obsidian pyramidal twins spoke up in his mind. Presumably Oemu; Ema usually let his brother do the speaking for them both. They, along with Lumini, were some of the biggest up-and-coming movers and shakers in the Kantar Empire, heirs apparent to the throne. Many in the upper echelons of Kantari society listened to them, and listened closely.

Now Stavrox just had to get the three of them to listen to him.

"Your project has merit," Oemu continued. "This we will concede. Using the thought processes of another species to shape our own manifestations, guided by our own minds to go beyond what has previously been possible."

"Then what's the problem?" Stavrox snapped, momentarily distracted from his preparations. He cursed himself silently, hiding his thoughts behind his psychic shield. He had to be better that that, or all of it, everything, would be for naught.

"The problem is *that*," Lumini replied, gesturing with her thoughts to the box, translucent and shimmering.

To the boy in the box.

To the *human* boy in the box.

There was a constant flow of data running down one of the sides of the box, showing statistics about the subject. Heart rate, respiration, blood oxygen and pressure, and so on, even the boy's age. Only seven Earth years old, definitely no more than a child by its species' standards. Harmless.

Except it wasn't harmless, not at all. Quite the opposite. It was *human*.

"What's the big deal?" Stavrox shot back, feigning a nonchalance he definitely was not feeling. Because he *knew* what the big deal was, as did the others. All Kantari knew. They had explored and colonised and conquered almost the entire galaxy, every arm of the spiral becoming just another outpost of the Kantar Empire. But there was one solar system that was taboo, prohibited, forbidden. No

Kantari were allowed there, not even the scientists who had studied every other species they had encountered, sentient and non-sentient. Not for a thousand generations had Kantar ventured into that system, with its mild yellow sun and its rather pretty-looking blue third planet. No, not since the first, second and third expeditions had all disappeared without a trace.

Until now.

"I programmed the probe *very* specifically," Stavrox informed them all, not for the first time. "Take a small one. A weak one. Stay away from the adults. And bring it here, away from the rest of its species, to my laboratory planet."

"Your *illegal* laboratory planet," Oemu pointed out archly.

Stavrox ignored that. "It's perfectly safe, I assure you. The box has built-in psychic shields, artificial versions of the same mentalic armour we all generate for ourselves, but a thousand times more powerful. As powerful as I could imagine."

"I can still sense it," Ema murmured, surprising them all by speaking up. But he wasn't wrong, Stavrox had to admit. Even through the shields, he could detect that constant background noise the boy generated, an extrasensory buzz that permeated everything, everything. Every *think*.

And it bothered Stavrox more than he cared to admit to the others.

"That's the whole point," he told them, and a hint of his frustration leaked out with his thinkspeak. "That's the power these creatures have. Their brains are so loud, so forceful, their thoughts so...so *much*," he concluded with a psychic shrug. "They are constantly thinking. They even think about thinking. It's an untapped resource, one which could power our creations until the stars themselves shiver and die."

"But the expeditions..." Lumini began.

Stavrox broke in. "The expeditions," he echoed, "encountered humans *en masse*. Imagine this," and he gestured with his mind towards the box, the boy in the box, "but not just one small one. Millions of them. *Billions*. And mostly the big ones, too." Even his own extraordinary mind stumbled at such a thought. "No, a single human child is a perfect guinea pig for my concept. Send a telepathic prompt of something we can imagine, receive the psychic response from the alien brain which will form something we *can't* imagine, and then use our reality folding abilities to create it. The possibilities are limitless. As I will now demonstrate."

"*Try* to demonstrate," Oemu corrected him.

"Yet again," Ema added.

Stavrox ignored them, refocused his mind. "Experiment twenty-eight," he repeated. He formed the prompt, delicately shaped it into something quite simple to start with. Say, a basic bosonic computer, capable of 1500 quettaflops without breaking a sweat. He packaged up the prompt, opened a hole the size of a single atom in the box, and thoughtcast it into the boy's mind.

The boy's eyes had been closed for some time, but they snapped open for a moment with this sudden rush of data to the brain. Its eyelids flickered, then closed again.

In the air before Stavrox, space began to turn in on itself, forming something from nothing, mass and substance drawn wholesale from the m-branes swimming in the quantum ether, folded and stretched and manifested into reality. For a moment it had no form, no shape, just an impossible mess of uncertainty. Then the probability cloud collapsed, and *it* was revealed, the something, the some *thing* from no *thing*. The ultimate creation, pure, perfect, beyond anything that Kantari had previously imagined.

A large, bright blue rubber ball.

It dropped to the ground and bounced a few times before coming to rest, next to the twenty-seven *other* balls of various sizes and colours that had been the results of Stavrox's previous experiments. He just looked at it, lying there, useless, and felt his future twinkling rapidly out of existence, like a dying star that failed even to go nova, just collapsing in on itself into an insignificant nothingness.

Lumini, seeing his dejected response, tried to cheer him. "It *is* unique, Stavrox," she pointed out. "We cannot create true curves with our manifestations, only straight lines."

"So what?" Stavrox snapped back. "We can approximate a curve down to the nearest molecule, just with a simple fractal series of angles. How will *this*," and he reached out and lifted the ball with his mind, "possibly propel our society into the next level of evolution? This? Is this the singularity???" And, with a thought, he flung the ball straight up with enough force to achieve escape velocity. "Or this? Or this?" One by one he hurled the useless balls into space, until they were all gone. Then he turned to the box, enraged. "Or this?" He reached out, and...

"Stavrox, stop," Oemu said firmly, and Stavrox *did* stop, his fury suddenly dissipating, replaced in an instant by utter shame and regret.

"I'm a failure," he sobbed. "Not this useless human. Me."

"Look," Lumini said, and gestured to the box. "Look at it."

"What about it?" he asked bitterly, but he looked anyway. The boy's eyes were closed, and he had slid to one side, head resting against the smooth interior of the box.

"What's wrong with it?" Ema asked. "Dead?"

"No," Stavrox replied, looking at the readouts of its vitals with some confusion. "But not quite alive either. Look, brainwaves have fallen, respiration, blood pressure, all down. I don't understand."

"I've heard of this," Lumini said thoughtfully. "Many biological creatures need rest periods to recover their strength. It's known as 'sleep'."

"Primitive," Oemu said, his thinkspeak laced with scorn. "How do they even survive?"

"Clearly they do, somehow," Lumini observed. "I believe the human boy is simply exhausted, and has succumbed to this 'sleep.' And perhaps when it emerges..."

"My system might work better! No, it *will* work better!" Stavrox finished, his black mood finally lifting. "Lumini, thank you! We still have a chance!" He looked at the boy again. "Hopefully it won't take too long for the boy to..."

A strange wave of psychic energy swept over them all, like a deep silent pulse in their minds.

"What was that?" Oemu asked.

Lumini gestured to the box. "Look at the readings," she said. "A sudden increase in brain activity, too strong for the psychic shields to dampen fully."

"What was it?" Ema asked, and there was an emotion in his thinkspeak that Stavrox hadn't sensed from either of the twins before, an emotion he doubted *anyone* had sensed from them.

Alarm. Fear.

Stavrox didn't know how to answer. He was feeling much the same. "I...I'm not sure," he admitted. "Perhaps..."

Something fell to the ground beside the box with a hollow thump, startling them all. Their senses fixed on the source of the sound, which bounced a few times before falling still.

It was a ball.

Stavrox relaxed. "It's just one of those useless experiments. Clearly I didn't propel it hard enough to escape this planet's gravity well. Nothing to be worried ab—"

Another thump. Another ball hit the ground nearby.

Then another.

And another.

And another.

A moment later, balls were raining from the sky. In their dozens, then hundreds, then thousands. They thundered to the surface, colliding with one another as they ricocheted off the stony ground. A number ended up impaled on Stavrox's spikes, awkwardly caught and wheezing out the air captured within. Air with a particular molecular makeup, clearly visible to his spectroscopic senses, mostly nitrogen and oxygen, plus trace elements.

Earth air.

Stavrox looked to the box, to the boy in the box, still asleep, but twitching slightly, its eyes moving back and forth beneath closed lids. Looked to the readings.

The brainwave activity was frantic, more than he'd ever seen before. And rising.

The box itself shuddered slightly, as the psychic shield struggled to contain the thoughts the sleeping boy was generating. Wave after wave of psionic energy was leaking from the box's confines, through fine spiral cracks appearing in its previously perfect surface.

"How is this possible, Stavrox?" Lumini asked, her own psychic defences largely down, revealing her own emotions, Panic, pure and simple. "Humans don't have manifestation abilities!"

Stavrox knew the answer immediately, knew it in the crystalline neural lattice at his core. Because the answer was *there*.

As was the boy.

"F-f-feedback," he stammered, his thoughts engulfed by static, a chaotic psychic noise gushing from the mind of the human child. "Th-the channel is still o-o-o-o-open!"

"Then close it!" Oemu demanded, dodging his pyramidal form back and forth to avoid the hail of balls that continued to fall from the sky, never-ending, impossible. They couldn't harm them, their psychically-manifested forms harder than diamond, tougher than graphene. Even a million rubber balls couldn't hurt the Kantari. But it was an annoyance, a distraction.

And, frankly, it was unnerving.

"I c-c-c-c-c..."

The balls suddenly ceased, the air around them clearing in an instant, leaving nothing but a blanket of different sized and shaped spheres covering the ground to the horizon in all directions. The planet fell silent then, but an active kind of silence, like the world was holding its breath.

"Is it over?" Lumini asked.

Stavrox already knew, could feel the energies still flowing through him from the boy. But still he looked over at the box, at the jagged brainwaves being generated. He tried to thinkspeak, but only managed one word, both in answer and in terror.

"*No...*"

One of the balls popped then, a sharp bang that filled the air. And, from inside it, came...darkness. Just darkness, oozing out, coating the outside of the now-deflated orb. It ate the light around it, greedily swallowed it whole.

The other balls began to pop, one by one at first, then faster and faster, until it was impossible to distinguish any individual sounds. And, from each popped spheroid, the darkness spread, across the balls, across the land, then upward, sending spindly fingers of blackness into the sky itself. It surrounded the Kantari like an onyx cage, the bars slowly widening, until the last glimpses of the stars were gone.

Only darkness remained.

Kantari do not use eyes to see, of course; their senses are multifold and wide spectrum. But this darkness, *this* darkness, was complete. No infrared or ultraviolet, no radio frequencies or microwaves or even the omnipresent background cosmic radiation. Everything was consumed by it. Only their mental communications with one another survived the emptiness, and even that was largely swamped by the ever-growing interference surging out of the box. Out of the boy in the box.

A speck of red light appeared in the darkness, just one bright mote. Then another, and another, until there were eight, eight glowing specks alone in the black, arranged in two rows of four. They hung there in the nothingness, bobbing ever so slightly, and the Kantari simply observed them, confused.

Then something, some thing, *unfolded.*

Stavrox struggled to understand what he was perceiving, through the deafening psychic static that filled his awareness. Like a flower blooming, or clenched human hands coming apart, the dark nothing became a dark thing, form come forth from the void. Eight spindly lengths, jointed erratically, came apart in the blackness, four on each side of the eight glowing red embers that still hovered in the dark. They arched up, and the inky shadows faded, revealing the thing they had previously hidden. And, with that, a word drifted across Stavrox's mind, not his own word, not a Kantari word. A human word, from the boy in the box. A word that meant less than nothing to him, yet somehow also filled his consciousness with a strange alien dread.

Spider...

Colossal, looming high above the Kantari, the beast was mostly a swollen abdomen, black with streaks of grey, its flesh dimpled and hairy. The eight legs sprung from this distended body, long and rough, ending in vicious-looking jagged spikes. And its face...its face was a puckered wreck, eight glowing red eyes above a wide mouth, fang-filled and dripping with venom, which worked constantly, silently, as if anticipating its next meal.

It leaned towards them as they simply watched, still frozen in shock and disbelief, and then it hissed, a rattling chirr that resonated with their forms, shaking them to their multidimensional cores. Then it raised up, and a single leg shot forward, fast, so fast, like lightning made flesh. The speed of thought.

It pierced Oemu, breaking through his unbreakable structure as if it wasn't even there, as if he was made of smoke, and dug deep into the ground behind him. There was a moment of utter silence, as the others simply watched, aghast, before Oemu screamed, a long, agonised psychic blast that rattled the world.

The creature pulled its appendage out of him as quickly as it had struck, and there was a splash of bright yellow liquid light that followed behind it, spurting from the impossible hole in Oemu's pyramidal form. He fell to the ground, still howling in surprise and pain and...

And fear? True fear? When did Kantari last feel fear? Not in recorded history. What was there to feel fear about? Apart from...

"Stavrox!" Lumini shrieked. "The boy!"

Stavrox tore his fragmented attention from his fallen comrade, back to the box, to the boy in the box. His eyes were still closed, but he was thrashing about on the floor of the box, as if struggling with some invisible foe.

"The boy!" Lumini repeated. "Kill it!"

Stavrox struggled towards the box as the monstrous titan struck out again, this time at Ema, who barely dodged the blow. Moving was almost impossible, the extrasensory surges from the boy coming in thick near-solid waves now, the psychic shield of the box all but gone, blasted away by the raging torrent of its thoughts. But he persisted, as deep down he knew their fate if he did not, unthinkable as it was. Impossible. Reached the box, and passed through its wall, matching his body's harmonic frequencies to those he'd created to contain the human. Came closer, closer, his form's molecular-sharp spikes nearly touching the frail meat that housed that mind, that impossible, horrible mind. Closer...

The boy's eyes opened.

Stavrox froze, caught in that gaze, his mind pinned as surely, as catastrophically, as Oemu's body had been. The boy looked around, eyes wild, panicked. Then it thought a single thought, a single word

NO

and the monster and the darkness disappeared instantaneously, as if they'd never been there. The burst balls were gone as well, all traces swept away. The planet was normal again, peaceful apart from the terrible moans emanating from Oemu's pyramid. Ema rushed to his side, merged slightly, trying to ease his twin's pains. And Lumini approached the box, tentative, never taking her attention from the boy. It was still looking around itself, through the box, fear and panic emanating out of it in violent psychic pulses. It was alone, lost, in a strange place.

Then boy looked at Stavrox—no, it looked *into* Stavrox—and its terror evaporated all at once, replaced by something else. Curiosity. Wonder.

Then it turned its fleshy eyes to the other Kantari, and it smiled. Again, it thought a single word, joyous, excited.

Presents!

Oemu and Ema abruptly raised from the ground, Oemu still trailing liquid light from the wound in his impermeable form. They hung there for a moment, and the boy thought again, more powerfully this time.

PRESENTS!

It reached out, through Stavrox, through the box, and...Oemu and Ema *opened*.

They unfolded from within, as if the complex, sophisticated manifestations they had created for themselves, *of* themselves, were nothing more than tree leaves, or flower petals. Or—and this was an image received directly from the boy in the box itself—they were simply wrapping paper, brightly coloured but flimsy, hiding the true gifts within.

In this case, what was hidden within was the essence of the Kantari, something that could not exist in this or any other physical universe. Thought incarnate, supposedly eternal, but actually shockingly ephemeral. The yellow liquid light within exploded outwards, raining down onto the rough dirt beneath them and then vanishing in a fraction of a fraction of a picosecond. Everything they were, everything they had been or could ever be, the twins, Oemu and Ema...gone, forever.

Stavrox's project had indeed created something new, something unknown to the Kantari, something unknowable, at least since those failed expeditions to the box in the box's homeworld, so very long ago, all but forgotten. And that something was, simply, death. Unchosen, unintentional, violent death.

Lumini roared, a psychic eruption filled with rage and terror in equal parts, and charged at the box. She almost reached it, but the boy's attention shifted to her from what remained of the twins, and she came apart in mid-air, the beautiful, intricate tesseract she had so meticulously constructed to house herself shredded, life forces splashed across the surface of the box before dissipating into oblivion.

She didn't even have time to scream before she died.

Then it was just Stavrox. Stavrox and the boy in the box. It looked at him again, with those wet blue eyes, and he found himself disappearing into them, falling, falling like a meteor to a planet's surface, caught irrevocably by its gravitational field, burning up in its atmosphere. More and more of him was being disintegrated, and less and less of him remained.

The boy gestured, and Stavrox found himself drifting towards it, his spikes once again nearing the boy's flesh. But this time they passed through it, or perhaps it passed through them, until the boy was gone, engulfed by Stavrox's complex mathematical patterns.

I am you now, the boy thinkspoke from within. *You are me. I am everything you were. We are one.*

"Please," Stavrox silently begged, the last remnants of his consciousness clinging to tenuous existence. "Please, don't do this to me, to my mind. I'm a disruptor. I move fast and break things. It's what I do."

Me too, the boy replied, then reached inside, scraped out the dregs of the Kantari's mind and consumed them in one of its heartbeats.

It was no longer the boy, no longer Stavrox. It was boyStavrox. And, in its dual overlaid memories, it saw the Kantar Empire, thousands of worlds, trillions of Kantari, so arrogant, so jaded. *So many presents,* it thought to itself, as it raised its box from the planet and ascended into space, casually opening a simple wormhole with its human-Kantari mind, a folded spacetime hyperlink to the nearest imperial planet. Ready to introduce them all to this new frontier, this new experience, their first in a million years. And their last.

So many presents to OPEN.

*Those who fight monsters
may, in turn, become monsters themselves.*

SWIM WALK JUMP

Jason Franks

When Avris broke the surface of the utility pool there was a stranger standing on the delivery platform with Rume. Both men were dry. Rume looked distinctly nervous, and Avris did not think he was worried about the bill.

Avris pushed his tool chest out of the water and used a free hand to raise the corrective lenses from his collar to his eyes. The stranger wore a blue civilian wetsuit that was just a shade darker than his skin, but the style of his shoulder fringes and the weapon holstered above his left hip showed him to be militia.

"Hello," said Avris, politely putting his hands on the deck.

"Avris, this is Suhur," said Rume. "Suhur, Avris is the best hydronics engineer I know." Rume gestured through the wet-dry doorway to the main floor of his grocery market. "This place is old and something is always going wrong, but Avris can fix anything."

"I'm more of a plumber than an engineer," said Avris. It was true these days. Nobody was building anything new, even with the fighting at its current lowered intensity.

The militiaman did not respond at first. When he did, only his mouth moved. "Is he trustworthy?"

"Absolutely," said Rume, nodding with more enthusiasm than the situation warranted. "He's punctual, his rates are reasonable, and he doesn't gossip."

Suhur inspected Avris again with hooded eyes. "Is this true?"

Avris shrugged. "I'm a professional," he said. "I make no claims to being a saint."

Suhur smiled. "Good enough," he said. "Come with me. I have work for you."

Avris climbed out of the pool and picked up his toolbox. It was heavy, out of the water, but he slung its weight with long familiarity. This was going to make him late for his next appointment, but Avris knew better than to refuse.

They took the long way to the destination, which Suhur refused to name in advance, keeping entirely to the canals. Swimming the entire distance made it harder for the humans' surveillance drones to follow them. They used no propulsion, because Suhur said the humans could track scooters—even Avris's private one.

The destination turned out to be the local Conglomerate Galactic Authority headquarters. Suhur guided Avris to a chute below the waterline. It was a long dive, pushing his toolbox ahead of him, and Avris wished he had supplemental oxygen by the time they emerged into the hidden chambers, which had been carved out of the bedrock underneath the CGA. He was breathing hard when he surfaced in the moon pool.

Suhur clambered out of the water and was on his feet immediately. Avris took his time, inspecting the buttressed walls. Cables hung down from shafts in the ceiling, and Avris reckoned they were patched into the CGA's power and network. He wondered briefly if the CGA knew the militia kept a data centre there. Of course they did, he decided. The CGA feared the humans as much as the swimmers did.

"I don't need to tell you this place is a secret," said Suhur.

"You don't need to tell me anything," said Avris, climbing out of the pool. He was older than Suhur and his back hurt, so he took it slowly—making sure the militiaman saw him struggle—but not too slowly. He didn't want to seem like a doddering wreck, but he also didn't want Suhur to think he was fit for any kind of combat. "Just point me at the problem and I'll fix it."

Avris followed Suhur into a server room, in which rows and rows of processing units were submerged in viscous pink fluid. Even without his corrective lenses Avris could see the telemetry on the console monitor was more orange than green. He snapped the lenses on and went over for a closer look.

"I think there's a refrigerant leak."

"Is it hard to fix?" asked Suhur, with the suspicious mien of a customer who expects to be ripped off.

"Let's find out," replied Avris.

It took the rest of the afternoon to fix the heat pump. The valve on the refrigerant tank had corroded due to acidity in the water, which in turn was caused by a leak in a pipe carrying hot water from a geothermal vent. Finding the source of the second leak had been the most difficult part.

When he was done, Avris was surprised that Suhur paid the bill immediately, in cash. Threw in some extra, too. The militia always had money. They were funded by CGA as well as various protection rackets and smuggling enterprises.

Avris swam a couple of blocks away from the site, in the opposite direction to Suhur, before hailing a taxifoil to take him home. He sat wearily in the cloudy water of the passenger tank and thought about his future as the driver wound his way through the canals.

The day was still warm and the city was bustling. This time of year, the night fell when the humans' planet interposed itself in front of the sun, yielding a twilight that was golden and lush. Hawkers pushed floating barbecues through the malls. Coloured lamps hung overhead. Couples enjoyed meals in the al fresco cafes, reclining half out of the water and feeding each other from lazy susans or dipping pots. Kids scampered on the sidewalks or splashed in the puddles, or threw rubble at each other in those buildings ruined by strikes from the humans' orbital artillery. The ruined buildings were houses, medical centres, sports complexes, schools. It didn't matter who might be in there if the walkers thought they had a militia target. The militia didn't mind, either. Civilian casualties were good for recruitment.

Avris tried not to look at the ruins. About a year ago, his nephew Pjes had been killed in an airstrike during one of the intermittent skirmishes with the humans. His brother still wasn't coping with the loss. Everybody Avris knew had lost kin to the humans.

But the humans were not his immediate problem. The militia had called on his services once now, and he was sure they would again.

When he got home, Lenza had dinner on the table and a frown on her face. Avris left his toolbox by the door and stooped to accept a hug from his charging son, Wigres. Wigres was fresh from the sauna and dry as paper.

Avris kissed the boy on the head five or six times and then set him down. "Go dry off again, get your pyjamas on," he said. He said it again more sternly when the boy instead lay down on the rug with a pile of toys. Wigres didn't move until Lenza shouted at him from the kitchen.

Avris stripped his dirty wetsuit and left it hanging in the vestibule. In his undershirt he trooped across the living room floor and sank into the dining pool gratefully.

"Sorry I'm late. I was called to an emergency job." Avris was not quite ready to explain his afternoon to his wife. He picked chopsticks and the long spoon and began to serve himself from the hotpot.

"It's getting cold," said Lenza. She hesitated, then continued, "I heard about the job."

That was bad news. Word was out already that he had worked for the militia. If it had gotten back to Lenza before he made it home there was an increased likelihood that the humans would get wind of it, also. "You did?"

"Mrak saw you leaving Rume's shop with that militia snake."

Mrak was the neighbourhood gossip. Some said he was a snitch to the militia, others said a spy for the humans. Avris thought he was just a busybody.

"Wasn't my idea."

"Don't you go getting into any more of that," said Lenza, a mix of anger and despair in her voice. "You stay clear of those people."

"You know me better than that, Lenny," replied Avris. He slurped up some meat and noodles from his bowl. "This is delicious, by the way."

"It was delicious half an hour ago," replied Lenza. "Now it's room-temperature and congealed. Like your corpse will be if the militia get you killed."

"I didn't have a choice." Avris knew he sounded defensive, so he softened his voice. "Lenny, you know what would happen if I said no." A black mark against his name. Innuendo against the family. Wigres bullied in school. His grocery order misplaced. Rumours that he was a human sympathizer, or even a collaborator. It might take a year, or it might take two, but eventually the militia would need to make an example of someone. That could be anything from a public beating to imprisonment, disfigurement, or death.

Avris continued to eat. The food was beginning to congeal, as Lenza had said, and hotpot was never his favourite, but he faked some gusto and that soothed an end to the argument.

"Your brother's been calling. Have you spoken to Denro recently?" asked Lenza.

"No," said Avris.

Avris was putting Wigres to bed when Denro arrived. Wigres was unsettled and Avris knew the boy would not sleep through the night, even before he heard his brother's voice downstairs. "Go to sleep. Please." He crouched over the bed and kissed his son on the cheek. "I have to go talk to Uncle Denro."

"I love you, Daddy." Wigres was getting big. He only called Avris 'Daddy' at bedtime, now.

Denro was sitting on the couch, hunched over, his arms folded and his elbows in the water. "Avris," he said. "It's good to see you."

Avris sat across the coffee table from his brother. Denro's posture discouraged him from offering an embrace. Avris did not want it, either. Denro's misery was contagious.

Lenza served them teaweed, then retreated to the kitchen. She continued to potter around there, although Avris had already washed the dishes. Ready to swoop in when—not if—Denro became difficult. Avris shot her a grateful look while Denro drank his beverage.

"How have you been, Den?" said Avris, when it became clear his brother was not going to open the conversation. "You look unsettled."

"I'm boiling inside, Avris," said Denro. "I think of nothing but what I've lost."

Avris knew their father would have come here intoxicated in similar circumstances. Different times, a different generation. Denro instead sat there with the same hot-eyed glower that Wigres showed when denied a new toy or a second helping.

"We all miss him," said Avris. "It's an awful thing." He drank from his cup.

"It's not just Pjes," said Denro. "My house is a trench. My own wife won't speak to me." Avris was certain it was Denro who refused to speak with his wife. He wouldn't even say her name.

"Haie's suffering, too, Den."

Denro would not be consoled. "My wife won't speak to me, and my own brother won't return my calls."

"You always call while I'm at work," said Avris. "And you never leave a message."

"You should call me back." Denro put his empty teacup on the table, making sure to raise a clatter. The table rocked and righted itself.

"I should," Avris agreed. "And you should leave me a message if you need me."

"I don't need you."

"This is why I don't return your calls," said Avris. He exhaled at the ceiling. "Why are you here, if you don't need anything? To start a fight?"

Denro folded his arms again. "It's not you I want to fight," he said. He was very still suddenly, but the water around him rippled, as though he was vibrating.

"We can't fight the humans," said Avris. "We have tried and tried and all it has brought us is tragedy."

"So, you'll just keep your head down, and live like a slave?"

Avris felt like there was water in his lungs. This talk of slavery was militia propaganda.

"I'm no slave. I work my job. I provide for my family. If I do anything to provoke the humans I am risking all of that. But I don't answer to them any more than you, Den."

"We cower in poverty while they spy on us, contain us, and, whenever they feel like it, kill us. We are insects to them. Pests to be crushed underfoot."

Avris looked slowly around the house. Lenza was bustling over with a tray in her hands and her jaw set.

"I'm not a rich man, Den, but I have all I need. Food. A roof. A happy family." He knew as well as anyone that the humans could destroy any of that, at any time. It wouldn't even take a war. Just some minor provocation. A shadow of suspicion.

Lenza was there to prevent Denro's retort. "Would you like a biscuit? I bought them at the market just this afternoon."

Denro accepted a biscuit resentfully. Instead of thanking Lenza, he rose from the couch. He didn't splash, but he set the coffee table rocking again. "A happy family," he said. "Am I not your family? Am I not your brother?"

Avris rose more slowly. "Den."

Denro stalked towards the vestibule. "Enjoy your happy family and your biscuits," he said.

Avris made to follow his brother out, but movement on the stairs drew his attention. Wigres had already retreated to his room, but Avris knew he had heard the whole conversation. He went to the stairs. Denro could cool off in his own time.

Lenza was already there. Avris touched her shoulder gently. "Let me," he said. "Please."

Lenza made way for him, and he went up to Wigres' room.

The boy was lying with his back to the door.

"Are you awake, Wigs?"

"Yes, Daddy."

"Come, then. Give me a hug."

Wigres sat up and gave Avris a hug. He was warm and dry and Avris could smell the shampoo in his hair. His cheek was soft against Avris's bristles. He could feel the worry radiating from the boy's frame.

"Daddy, can humans swim?"

"A little bit," said Avris. "But not like us. There's a lot of dryland on their planet, so they're slow and clumsy in the water."

"So, if the walkers come here, we can just swim away?"

"That's right."

"What if they come into the house? Upstairs, where there's no water?"

"They still have to come through the water to get in," said Avris. "We would hear them, stop them."

"How? The walkers have guns, Daddy. They have knives."

"Don't you worry about it, Wigres. They won't come in here. I'm your daddy. It's my job to protect you."

"Uncle Den couldn't protect Pjes," he said.

"That was different," said Avris. "That was in a war."

"You said it was a 'skirmish'."

"That just means a little war," said Avris. "Uncle Den wasn't even there when it happened." Wigres' terror was only growing, so Avris scooped him up in another hug. "Daddies can't always be there," he said. He missed his own father as he said it. "But I can promise you that I'm here, tonight, and I'll make sure nothing happens to you."

"Can I have the light on?"

"In the hallway, sure."

"Will you stay with me 'til I'm asleep?"

Avris made a show of lying down on the floor beside the bed. "Let's see who falls asleep first. You or me."

"Good night, Daddy."

"Good night, Wigres."

From the floor Avris could hear Wigres turn over in his bed. Then turn again.

"Daddy, can I have a biscuit?"

"Not until breakfast time," he replied. "You've already cleaned your teeth."

Suhur was waiting at the front of the house, treading water near the grille where the outer gate opened from the yard into the canal. It had been three weeks since the job at the data centre and he was not surprised to see the militiaman again.

"I hope you have nothing important to do this morning."

"Nothing that can't wait," said Avris, resigned.

Suhur had a pair of scooters waiting.

"I thought these were unsafe?" said Avris.

"These two have been specially scanned. They're clean," said the militiaman. Avris knew he was lying.

Avris tethered up his toolbox, set his hands on the grips, and kicked off. They rode the scooters out to the industrial district near the docks, taking the main thoroughfares, clogged with traffic and heavily surveilled as they were.

The destination was a warehouse signposted for a farm equipment company. They piloted the scooters right up to the walls and secured them.

There were half a dozen men on the floor of the warehouse. Two of them were militia and the others were ordinary workers. The place was indeed stocked with pieces of farm equipment, although some areas, guarded by the militiamen, were curtained off from the main floor. Most likely the curtains concealed contraband: famous brand dryclothes, luxury appliances, medical supplies, and, of course, narcotics. The militia itself had strictly banned drugs of every sort from public consumption, but they were still lucrative currency for trade. Avris understood the more relaxed security now. The walkers didn't care about drug smuggling. They only cared about weapons, so the militia kept those in separate locations.

"This way," said Suhur.

There was a burnt smell in the air. Avris said, "Let me guess. It's the dehumid-ifier."

Suhur tried not to look impressed. "We think something is wrong with the exhaust."

It took the rest of the morning for Avris to diagnose and repair the fault. The warehouse floor was a dry area and Avris' back hurt so much by the end of it that he knew he would need the rest of the day off, and possibly the day following.

Suhur smiled a little as he counted out payment. Avris thought he was going to say something about his obvious pain, but instead the militiaman said, "You talk to your brother recently?"

"Yeah," said Avris.

"Denro," said Suhur. "He's a good man. Strong."

"He is," said Avris.

"He's given a lot," said Suhur. "You should be kind to him."

"I try," said Avris.

He got home early. He was glad neither Lenza nor Wigres were there to see him throw up.

Avris was on his lunch break, floating in the outside pool of his favourite cafe with coffee and a sandwich, when the attack came.

The first sign of it was the change in the air. A shift in the light, the sudden reek of ozone, and then the flash and rumble as the particle beam cut an X through its target.

The strike was close by. Avris pushed out into the canal and there it was, only three blocks away. A community building that hosted adult education classes and activities for the very old and the very young. Avris had taught there himself, when he'd injured his back a decade earlier and needed income during the months it took him to recover.

The attack wasn't really a surprise. The militia had been active in the weeks since Avris had done his last job for Suhur. They'd caused some damage, killed some walkers. If anything, the humans were overdue for a reprisal.

The building collapsed in four triangular sections. Water vomited from of its windows on the lower floors and there was briefly an arterial gushing from the centre when some pressurised line ruptured.

A swarm of drones descended through the haze of smoke and flames. And there, on the sidewalks, emerged a handful of stubby figures, fully encased in black-grey armour. Two of them stepped into the canal and moved outwards from the ruined building, jet-propelled, looking for some further target.

Humans couldn't swim like Avris's people, but they didn't need to. They might not be agile in that armour, but they were invulnerable and impossibly fast. They had unlimited air, impossible weapons, and optics that could see through any kind of disturbance in the water or the air. Worst of all, they had cameras that recorded everything.

It happened so fast Avris couldn't believe it. He took a gulp of scalding air and kicked off, leaving his toolbox at the cafe, trying to get as far away from the attack site as possible. The only thing that mattered now was getting home.

The next day, Avris learned that Denro had been in the building when it came down. The walkers had learned that a militia cell had scheduled a meeting there, and that was that. Destroying the building had killed all six members of the cell as well as twenty-three civilians. Nine of them were children.

Wigres took it especially badly. He'd been close with his cousin Pjes, and he'd struggled to understand his uncle's spiral. With Denro gone too, he was beside himself. Lenza had tried to speak to him, but by the time Avris came home from work the boy had shut himself in his room and refused his usual good night routine. He wouldn't even open the door so the hallway light could shine in.

"Let him grieve how he wants to," said Avris, leaning on the kitchen counter. They would be more comfortable in the living room pool, but by unspoken accord he and Lenza were having the conversation dry. "He knows we're here for him when he needs us."

"He's so angry, Avris. And you know as well as I do what he's hearing at school."

"I know," he replied. "They sanitised the militia's operations in our time, but now they glorify them."

"Do you remember when we believed there could be peace with the humans?" said Lenza, rubbing her eyes with fingers moistened in the sink.

Avris shook his head slowly. "I don't know if I ever believed it," he said, "but I remember when we were allowed to talk about it."

Lenza put her hand on his, both of her thumbs touching his own. "You believed it," she said. "Just as I did."

"Perhaps." He didn't want to remember.

"And now you are working for the militia."

"Not by choice," he replied.

"Maybe it will get you killed. Or maybe not," said Lenza. "But Avris, promise me. *Promise me* Wigres will never know."

"Of course," Avris replied. "I promise."

It was nearly a month before he next saw Suhur. The militiaman was waiting for him outside Rume's store. The neighbourhood was still unsettled after the attack, so Avris had gone alone to pick up the week's provisions.

Suhur's smile was caustic. "There you are," he said, in a way that suggested he knew exactly where Avris was—or would be. "Come, I have work for you."

Avris hefted the shopping basket. "I don't have my tools."

"We have all the tools you will need at the site," said Suhur.

"It's the weekend," said Avris. "My family is expecting me to bring back lunch." Rume was watching him through the shop window. The glass concealed the grocer's expression.

Suhur replied very slowly. "I know they will understand," he said. "But if you like I can send someone to your house."

"It's fine," said Avris, lowering his gaze. "I'm sure this is important."

They swam all the way to the site, but they took the most direct route. Even the busiest canals were mostly empty. Avris didn't see any surveillance drones on the way, but that didn't make him feel better.

The site was the basement of a residential building which had been half-destroyed in a skirmish. It was unsafe now and everyone who could afford to move out had done so—but many could not. Others, poorer still, had moved in. Criminals or dissidents who been driven from their homes by the militia.

The basement had a new submarine entrance, accessible only through a tunnel which ran under the street to the back of a fishmonger. The militia had sealed the basement off from the apartment block.

Inside, a dozen militiamen bustled around inside, assembling machinery, examining charts, poring over digital displays. Open crates showed weapons, ammunition, body armour. Cannisters of liquid and gaseous fuel. Avris had the distinct sensation that he'd pissed ice-water into his wetsuit.

It was a bomb lab.

"Come, this way," said Suhur, moving past the open chassis of what could only be a missile. "We have a problem with the fuel lines, and nobody has the deft touch that you do."

"I'm a hydronics engineer, Suhur," said Avris, desperately. "I don't know rocketry."

"We have working schematics from our last successful launch," said Suhur. "You'll work it out."

Avris didn't need to guess what had happened to the engineer who had made the schematics. He took a moment to think over his reply. If he refused, he'd never see Lenza or Wigres again. If he agreed, he was likely to meet his brother again before too much longer.

Avris looked the militiaman in the eye. "I guess I'll have to," he said.

The house was dark when Avris got home in the small hours of the morning. He had diagnosed the fault, but it would take days to fix the fuel line properly. Even then, he didn't know if it would be sound. Suhur seemed pleased enough, though.

Avris stripped off his wetsuit in the vestibule. The garment was visibly damaged from exposure to the hydrocarbon fuels, and the reek of it still burned in his nostrils. His stomach gurgled despite his disgust at the smell. At his day's work.

Avris kept the light off when he went into the front room, afraid he might disturb his family if they were asleep. There was a pile of flat, square boxes on the kitchen counter: following his failure to return with groceries, Wigres and Lenza had ordered in takeaways. A quick inspection of the boxes revealed that they had ordered Avris' favourite meal—and left none for him.

He slumped in one of the sling chairs by the living room pool. Sooner or later, he'd have to go to bed. He wasn't prepared to face Lenza yet, awake or asleep. Her day had likely been even worse than his.

Avris sat there in the silence, next to the pool, and considered his chances. The humans probably didn't know where the bomb lab was, but once Suhur's crew fired the missile they would figure it out quickly enough. Then they would hunt for those who had planned and executed the attack. Maybe he would get lucky and they'd wipe out Suhur's cell without connecting it to him.

Avris didn't feel very lucky.

"Daddy?"

Avris almost fell out of his chair. He had been half expecting Lenza to come clomping down the stairs, angry, but Wigres trod more lightly.

"Come here, Wigs," he said, holding out his arms.

Wigres approached him, but did not come close enough for a hug.

"We waited for you, Daddy." Avris could hear the hurt in the boy's voice.

"I know, Wigs. I'm so sorry."

"Where were you?"

"I got pulled into an emergency job," he said.

"You should have called to tell us. I was so hungry."

"I'm sorry," Avris replied. "It was such an emergency that even the comms line was busted."

"Tell me the truth, Daddy," said Wigres. Avris didn't know what to say. When he did not reply, Wigres said, "Also, you stink."

"I do," he said, trying to sound like his own father. "I...stopped to have some drinks before I came home, Wig. A lot of drinks."

"Drinks?" Wigres took a moment to reason through his puzzlement. "But...that's *illegal*." He wasn't sure Wigres' disappointment hurt more than the lie did. But a narcotic drink sounded pretty damn attractive right now.

"My dad used to drink," said Avris. "It was still allowed, back then. Before the big war. Before the walkers closed our airspace and the militias took over the government."

"I hate the walkers. They're monsters, Daddy."

"They are," Avris agreed.

"Monsters need to die. When I'm big, I'll join a militia and kill them."

Wigres sat on the floor, put his feet in the pool. Avris put his hand down to touch his shoulder, but the boy shook him off. "You should kill them too, Dad. We should all go out and kill them."

Avris exhaled slowly. He hadn't wanted to have this conversation when the boy was so young. He certainly didn't want to do it while they both were grieving. But maybe later would be too late. The militias didn't care how young their soldiers were.

"Wigres," he said. "Why do you think your uncle is dead?"

"The walkers killed him."

"And why did they do that?"

"Because they hate us. They don't care about our lives."

Avris chewed his lower lip. "Both of those things are probably true," he said. "But that's not the reason they killed Uncle Denro. They killed him because he was in the militia."

"So what? We only have the militia so we can fight back. We learned all about it in school. They're descended from monkeys and pigs. Genetic filth. They killed Pjes and they killed Denro, and I want to kill them back."

A wave of terror shook him. The humans could strike at any time. He'd helped build a missile. They'd come here, cut an X through his house. They'd kill anyone they had to in order to get to him. He could see it. Could see himself pulling Wigres' corpse out of the rubble of his home. He could smell ozone. He could feel the hot vapour on his skin. He could hear Lenza weeping. No, it was him weeping.

Probably not today, but one day. The humans were clever and relentless and when they found him, there was nothing he could do to protect himself or his family.

Avris bit down on the fear, wedged it up into his palate, and forced himself to speak through it. "Last week," he said, "the militia shot down a passenger shuttle full of walkers. You heard them celebrating in the canals and on the rooftops."

"Yeah, and you wouldn't let me watch the parade," said Wigres, accusingly. "You said it was too dangerous."

"I did, and it was," said Avris. "Do you know how many people died in that shuttle?"

"The more, the better."

"About forty."

"How many were children?"

"Some," said Avris. "Does it matter how many?"

"No. It's still good."

"Don't you not think that's why the humans hate us? Why they kill us? Because we hate them and kill them."

"Then we'll have to kill them all," said Wigres fiercely. "There can't be peace if there's only hate."

"Wait here," said Avris. He got up out of his chair and went to what used to be his father's liquor cabinet. Now it held only old papers and souvenirs.

Wigres smacked the water with an open hand, setting off waves that splashed onto the tiles. But he stopped when Avris returned with the photo album.

"Look here," he said, flipping through the plasticated pages. "This is my father. When I was your age."

Avris's father looked a lot like his son. Greener in complexion, maybe, with straighter shoulder fringes. As he had grown older, he had come to recognise the similarities. The slope of his shoulders, the curve of his smile. He could feel his dad in him when he spoke to his boy.

"Things were different then," he said.

Wigres stared at a photo of Avris's dad in the middle of some sports activity, leaping out of a canal with a ball held high above his head in the palm of one hand. "Is that a…"

"Is that a what?"

"Is that a *walker* in the water with him?"

"Yes," said Avris.

Wigres just stared.

"Even in those days things were…tense," said Avris. "Fighting, all the time. Sometimes killing. Us and them. The walkers and the swimmers. Soldiers everywhere. Bombings. But a human family lived on our block, and we never had any trouble with them."

"Did you know them?"

"Not really," said Avris. "Their kids were older than me. But Dad…well, Dad was friends with everyone he ever met."

Wigres was horrified. "But…here he is, swimming with one of them!"

"They were playing a game they invented," he said. "My dad and our neighbour. They used to argue about whether to call it Swim Walk Jump or Jump Walk Swim. I thought it was lame, but I always wanted to join in."

Wigres was quiet for a moment. He slapped the water again, and then said, "I didn't know they lived here with us."

"They did," said Avris. "And some of us lived planetside with them. And then the war came, and everyone decided we didn't want peace, and they left. And then the militia took over and we still fought them, so they set up the blockade. But before all of that, we were both here, and over there."

"We were here first!" said Wigres.

"The humans say otherwise. But it doesn't matter who was here when, Wigres. What matters is who is here now."

"It's ours," insisted Wigres. "This moon. That planet. The whole system."

"They have no place else to go, Wigres." said Avris. "They are not so different to us."

"They walk, we swim."

"Yes," said Avris. "But we also walk, do we not? And they can also swim."

Wigres nodded grudgingly. "They're brown and pink and yellow, and we're blue and green and purple."

"And tell me, have you ever seen a person...one of our people...with skin in human colours?"

"No."

"How about Mrs. Elra?" said Avris.

Wigres gave it some thought. "She's mauve."

"More pink than mauve, you ask me," he replied. "Then there's Mr. Qely, who has only five fingers on his hands."

Wigres looked at his own double-thumbed hands. He let them float on the surface of the water, palms up. "What are you saying, Dad?"

"Wigres, listen to me," he replied. "They might live differently, but they're us, or they once were. They're us and we're them."

*Real horror is just everyday life.
And that's where real monsters live.*

ENDLESS COOKHOUSE

PAUL EDMONDS

Glen hit the turnpike with sleep in his eyes and a growl in his gut. The sun blazed through the windshield. He dropped the visor, leaning forward to watch the clogged on ramp. Hundreds like him, crawling toward incinerators of the soul.

He was being dramatic.

Beneath the calloused skin of tedium, what he really felt was dumb, simple gratitude. Life could be worse—average smarts, a high school diploma keeping company with other lacklustre achievements. The job was steady. The benefits acceptable. In this age of house hacking and side hustles, he considered himself lucky.

Convinced himself daily.

He clicked on the radio, wished he had satellite or even USB, but the aged Honda received its missives the old-fashioned way. News crackled: Bullshit in Washington. Bullshit in Hollywood. Protests. Some kid shot up a Pizza Hut, said it was for God. A lady in New Hampshire claimed strange lights had burned a hole in her hayfield, lit it up like a pile of fall leaves.

The minutes ticked away. He counted cars, made calculations. Hoped he wouldn't be late. His ID badge felt hot on his thigh. Then traffic opened up, and his chest loosened. His day began to brighten.

The small office was a converted storage closet fitted with a large panel of plexiglass. It had been a compromise after months of supplication—Glen's campaign for a private space to shuffle his papers and sharpen his pencils. Beyond the clamour of extruders and boiler tanks and rattling conveyor belts. Enough noise infiltrated its thin walls to remind him that relocation was not the same as escape.

From his perch, he could observe the floor and make notes. Who was slacking. Who snuck an extra Powerade from the cooler (a consultant had determined a single 20-ounce bottle per shift sufficient to stave off dehydration). He sometimes resented his title—*Efficiency Supervisor*—but had come to rationalize his position as a steward of the greater good.

He logged onto the Spree-lite network. Waded through emails. Uploaded a report. Recommended Randy Gamache be retrained on the pellet hopper; a review suggested his quota could be raised with a few targeted tweaks.

"Ah, the Prince of Production, the Archduke of Assembly." Jerry came swaggering into the room. Tall and burly, a man born to navigate the grease-slicked bellies of industrial machinery. He was an oasis in this fuming Hades.

"Be a good subject and run these metrics for me."

Jerry raised his palms. "I don't meddle in royal affairs."

Glen crumpled a sticky note and lobbed it at him.

"Besides," Jerry went on, "got that gal starting today. Supposed to be a wunderkind on the Arburg."

"Oh, yeah. Her."

He recalled the woman touring the floor with Gretsky, the day-shift foreman. Crackerjack mechanic by all accounts. Would never guess it to look at her—not that he would admit to such prejudices. She was short, spindly. Off-size clothes. Clumsy too, kept bumping poor Gretsky, as if she couldn't figure out where to step.

"Anyway, you have that cycle-time analysis?" Jerry grinned. "Thanks for that, by the way."

Glen passed him a thick binder. "Just doing my job."

Jerry clomped out of the office, wagging the doorstop over his shoulder. "Heard that before."

That morning was a shit-show. He inadvertently got Matty Jameson canned. Six pallets of plastic cutlery on the overnight truck. All forks. Spoon and knife brethren left behind in their big blue bins. He'd cited the mix-up in an addendum to his weekly audit. Figured the matter closed. But management crunched some numbers. Loss of revenue against the expense of a new hire. Matty came down on the wrong side of the equation.

Glen wondered what the old dog would do now. Maybe retire. But he didn't think so. Matty was near seventy and still punching the clock. That wasn't something a guy did for the hell of it. He tried to picture him cobbling a sad résumé, creating a LinkedIn account. His heart twisted.

He refused to frame it as a tragedy. A mistake was made. Money lost. Nothing personal. He could've buried the error, sure. But he'd been given a task, and he did it.

He worked through lunch, hoping to distance his thoughts from the lingering image of Matty shuffling away, lunch bucket in hand. Glancing up at the plexiglass with whimpering eyes.

Couldn't quite get there. A headache had snuck up on him. Lights darted across his vision, strobing with the rhythm of his pulse. They took on odd colours, familiar shapes. He inhaled, steadied himself, and they scattered.

"Fuck this," he muttered, and went to the break room for a soda.

Jerry and the new mechanic sat at a round table with cups of coffee. Jerry leaned back in his chair.

"And be careful with your gloves," he was saying. "Lose 'em, they'll dock your pay."

The woman nodded. Her khaki Spree-lite shirt was misbuttoned; one side of the collar stuck out like a bird wing.

He walked past them, started counting change.

Jerry lowered his chair. "Shame about Matty."

Glen searched his face for reproach, but there was none.

"One of those things, you know."

"Sure. But hey, meet Sue."

Glen said hello, put out his hand. The woman hesitated, then shook it weakly.

"Know what she did?" Jerry said. "Won't believe it. Fixed the Husky."

Impressive. That injection molder had been a cantankerous beast for as long as he could remember. No one could nurse it back to health. Not even Jerry.

"Tamed it like a wild stallion," Jerry went on. "Should've seen her crawling around in there."

"It wasn't difficult," Sue said.

Jerry sipped his coffee. Sue stared down at hers, grasped it in both hands, and tipped it slowly to her lips.

"Who's Matty?" she asked, cradling the cup.

"Used to pack here," Jerry said. "Nice fella, but landed in trouble. They let him go this morning."

Glen groaned, fed coins into the vending machine

"I see." She paused, took another swallow. "Did he hurt someone?"

"Matty?" Jerry laughed. "No, nothing like that. He's as sweet as they come."

"Then he stole?"

Jerry crossed his arms, his jovial expression hardening. "Worse. Cost the company some scratch. Goose was cooked."

"Yes," Sue said. She pursed her mouth, as if pondering Matty's fate. "That's terrible."

"That's business," Jerry said.

"Don't scare her off," Glen said, eager to lighten the mood. He worried the conversation might drift toward his culpability.

"Nah, she'll do great," Jerry said, and pitched his empty cup. "They'd be crazy to send her away."

Sue nodded again. A dribble of coffee ran down her chin.

Jerry got up and pushed in his chair. Sue watched, then did the same.

"We've got a date with a glitchy picker," Jerry said. "Sue's gonna lay down the law."

He clapped Glen on the back. Sue followed, collar flapping. She stopped in the doorway. Her eyes caught the fluorescent light, flashed green for an instant. She shuffled out.

Glen chugged his Pepsi, rested his head on the wall. Peered down at Sue's abandoned cup.

It was still full.

Spree-lite tasted blood. Liked it. Tasked Glen with collecting more.

Rather than replace Matty, they cranked the heat under those who remained. Higher inventory, tighter schedules. A week went by without incident. Management decided to expand this experiment. They pulled Glen into a meeting. Slid him papers. Wanted three names by next Friday.

He knew where this assignment would lead. Began to see ghosts. Not just in Packing, but all over the plant—line rats and crate stackers, runners and techs. Unaware a cartoon anvil hung above them. That *he* held the axe.

He put it off for days, shielding himself with busywork.

What he couldn't avoid was Sue. She was everywhere. He'd feel a scrabbling on the back of his neck, and there she'd be. Sometimes she smiled. Sometimes she nodded. Always with a queer posture or a shirttail untucked. Watched him as though he belonged in a cage.

He thought about putting her on the chopping block, just to get her gone. But Jerry would feed him to a molding press. She was slaying it—moving through machine guts like liquid mercury, cold and certain. Breached impossible gaps, excised mechanical tumours. Jerry was happy to share the accolades.

He stepped to his office window. Pressed his face to the glass. Tried not to think of names.

Jerry died on Thursday.

Glen was at his desk, collating spreadsheets. Heard the screams. Not from Jerry—there hadn't been time—but those who saw it. He bolted down the galvanized stairs to the shop floor.

The crowd parted to let him through. A fan of blood below the granulator's feed chute.

Dale Castine stood with a fist clamped white around the disconnect lever.

Buddy Lindell, waist-deep in the feeder's slanted metal throat. His belt buckle scraped the brute's cast-steel body. He mumbled something. A woman approached reluctantly, shone a torchlight into the spattered maw. A second later, Buddy wormed back out, puked onto the side of the machine.

Operations halted. The area cleared. Glen lingered at the periphery, sitting on the bottom step while the grisly parade marched through. Police. Medical Examiner. An OSHA rep had a sombre conversation with the plant safety officer. A couple Spree-lite suits made an appearance, snapped pictures.

The remediation crew arrived, filing in like bulky spacemen. The ME gave them directions. Glen exited to the crinkle of black bags, the hiss of steam guns.

He wandered past his office to the break room. A dozen workers in small groups. Some crying, some staring at nothing. Most commiserating in hushed tones. He grabbed a chair in the corner and listened.

"...All I saw was his leg..."

"...Caught him by surprise..."

"...Goddamn thing hasn't run that smooth in decades, wasn't ready for it..."

He heard their voices, but couldn't put meaning to what they were saying. He still smelled his friend's blood, sharp and metallic and eerily at home with the stink of melted plastic.

Gretsky wandered in, pale, pants soaked in hydraulic fluid. He squeezed Glen's shoulder, then told everyone to go home. Come back in the morning.

Glen stayed. After a while, he raised his head. Sue stood beside the microwave. The digital display flickered; numbers floated, haloed her, dissolved into glimmering specks.

He was beginning to fray.

Sue looked pensive, same as the others, but there was a coolness to it he couldn't place. Like something drawn by a computer.

She approached. He braced for a fond remembrance, gratitude for Jerry's kindness.

Instead, she reached around, brought up a pair of oil-darkened Mechanix gloves. Jerry's. She gave them to Glen.

"I saved these," she said, and walked away.

An impromptu meeting the next day. Forty men and women, less than twenty feet from where Jerry met the granulator's whirring teeth.

Fournier, the plant manager, opened with a brief homily. He read from a folded sheet of paper. Recounted Jerry's years of service. Sounded almost human.

Then a Spree-lite bean counter stepped forward.

"Pay adjusted for unworked time," she stated, quoting a baroque clause from the attendance manual. "Unexpected logistical issues halted production, requiring employees to clock-out early."

Three hours would be docked from each worker's upcoming pay period, plus another thirty minutes for those who had taken a full lunch prior to the incident.

"Oh, and—" she fussed with her clipboard "—two-fifty per person for…" She conferred with Fournier. "A fruit arrangement for Jerry's family."

Fournier thanked her, then reminded everyone the best way to heal was to hit quota. "We can't change what happened, but we can control how we respond." He clasped his hands, looked up to the rafters. "It's what Jerry would have wanted."

Glen loitered by the stairs, dressed in the same wrinkled clothes from the day before. He'd spent the night thinking of Jerry. What Lindell must've seen, wriggling down that chute. There were no nightmares—no sleep to birth them. But they would come. He felt them simmering, unseen, waiting for the dark.

The clang of metal. Sue, on a step stool by the granulator. Fournier beside her. She held a multimeter in her small hands, wires snaking into the control box. A series of cheery beeps. She nodded. A wide smile greased Fournier's lips.

Glen sneered. It was an affront. He'd expected more. What, he couldn't say. Anything but business as usual. A hollow speech. A bouquet of mutilated cantaloupe.

He turned to leave.

"Sorry, friend."

He paused. Fournier's voice stung—lemon juice on a knife wound.

"I know you two were close," Fournier went on. "Just wanted to say—" he smoothed the front of Glen's shirt "—we're thinking about you."

He glared at the man's necktie—grinning hotdogs playing golf. His fingers itched for something to beat him with.

"Jerry was a good man," he managed.

"The very best," Fournier agreed. "And this incident has me thinking. About resilience. Performance under pressure. Those three names I asked you for?"

Glen sensed a tender mercy coming. Relief from his appointment as executioner.

Fournier beamed. "Let's make it six."

Glen deleted Spree-lite's SharePoint repository. Maintenance KPIs. Regrind reports. Years of compliance studies. Sat back and waited. For detonation. The ringing of his phone—panic screaming through the earpiece.

A boilerplate email from IT. Files recovered during a scheduled audit. He opened the master folder, stared at the restored data. Heard the impotent hiss of a dud grenade.

He tried to reroute a large shipment. Thought a medical warehouse in Omaha could use a bushel of moulded reindeer. Was foiled again. Matty's ousting had set the loading dock on pins. Triple checks. The error was swiftly caught, corrected.

He fudged production rates. Altered manifests. Paid a high-school kid to prank call the front office.

Nothing.

His campaign was thwarted at every turn. Spree-lite had become a self-correcting system. Smooth, optimized. Fuelled by the high-octane synergy of his own expert streamlining.

The office grew hot. Stifling. A glass-fronted cookhouse.

He stepped out onto the catwalk overhanging the bustling floor. Wiped his brow, watched the monster he helped create. Gone was the friendly banter, the hum of blue-collar dignity. Greg Carbone's battered boombox sat mute atop his workbench. A row of women stood wearily at the sorting station—their stools taken away, stacked in a storage closet.

Sue emerged from the underside of the thermoformer; he'd snipped one of the vacuum lines earlier. She set a crescent wrench inside her toolbox. Flipped a switch. Within the frame, the crack of solenoids, a burst of compressed air. Smell like burnt sugar. The behemoth rumbled back to life.

Glen imagined himself a sniper inside a clocktower. Bullseyes jittering through the air. He studied the movement of bodies. The glossy ribbons of hot plastic. Tried to comb six names from the hustle. Couldn't.

He rubbed his temples and closed his eyes.

The lights again. Brighter, carving up the darkness. They pulsed and writhed, ready to burst, to expel their charge. One took up the vanguard, resolving into a familiar shape—long and cigar-like, portholed with glimmering circles.

"I fixed it."

Glen recoiled, bumping the steel railing. Sue planted before him, cheeks smeared, sleeves rolled to reveal smooth, hairless arms. He hadn't heard her ascend the stairs; it was as if she'd slithered up the girders, through the grating.

"What?" he said, half-dazed, rubbing his back.

"Your test. The vacuum line."

He glanced over his shoulder. The thermoformer, humming smoothly below. "Wasn't a test."

"No?" Something like confusion crossed her face. "You want to hurt the factory?"

"Fuck the factory," he spat, his voice cutting through the noise. He didn't care. "Lady, this place. It killed my friend. Sent him back to his family in a goddamn Hefty bag. Then billed us for our grief."

"The machines run better now. A redundancy was eliminated."

"Shut up." Glen inched in. Wanted to toss her off the landing.

She didn't move. Shadows stirred behind her glassy stare. He edged back.

"I'm here now," she said. "It's what you wanted."

"What the hell are you getting at?"

"I was called," Sue said flatly.

"Called? By who?"

A look of pity. Real, unblemished, terrifying.

"All of you."

He sped out of town. Needed to escape the furnace of Spree-lite, Sue's robotic voice. He lowered the windows. A warm breeze battered his sweaty cheeks.

Renewed rebellion boiled inside him. He saw it all. Shredded reqs. Contamination. Strikes. Envisioned himself upon a baler deck, megaphone in hand.

Dangerous. Electric.

Dusk ahead. The day, bleeding out. Small objects moved within the gloom. Billowing and featureless. They scattered, settled to earth. He lowered his gaze to the rutted road.

The Honda bucked. Shuddered. Died with a sputter and a belch of exhaust. The dashboard pulsed erratically, blinked in quick stutters before going completely black.

Glen slumped against the idle wheel. His fervour collapsed under the sudden weight of numbers.

He'd need a tow. Probably a new car.

And there was rent. Groceries.

He reminded himself: simple gratitude. Could be worse for a guy like him. There'd be time to change things. But for now, he still had a job to do.

He pulled a pen and paper from the glove box. Sighed. Began to write.

1) Brenda Dorrow.
2) Larry Catterton.
3) Ernie LaFond...

The most monstrous, yet mundane,
of all evils comes from
treating people like things.

IN THE WEAVING

Colleen Anderson

I am Talour. I am the Weaver of our skin sloughings. Listen well, for the pain has been in this weaving. It will have no fringe added.

I sing the threads into the weave, which are spun from the fibres of our casings, tinted with our lives and history. Each sloughing, I take, twist and strengthen, weight one end to the stones, then weave our tales. The tribe members chant their feelings, and Soular touches the strands, using vibration to embed the song as I work in the images. Our textured thoughts, the colours of sound, our actions spiral into a rainbow tapestry. There are many branching sections, as some tales end, or other perspectives are born. I stitch in our wisdom so that all are remembered, and all can learn.

At times, as my tendrils gently hold the filaments, I sing in the past—at times, the future. That clear, sparkling night I sang in the present while blending the veins of sound and sight through my limbs to the strands. Soular chanted the form, and I placed our emotions in the patterns. Gently, I layered the trills and mindsong from the tribe's souls and the moons' influences.

Standing tall, we undulated; a rhythm of song and movement. I plucked phosphor-moss and skin sloughings from each member, feeling the time of changes, of distant expectations.

Listen well. One by one, my four tentacles splayed out to grasp a fibrous strand and twine it into past patterns set from previous days. The tapestry was not just this image you see before you. It played out around us like a river, one end of it tightly rolled around a cord, the anchor to past events.

It takes me several moon changes to manifest an intricate tale—not so that night. A creature descended like a pregnant, awkward bird from the sky, belching smoke. My limbs froze, the tale fraying upon the breeze.

We surmised it must be a seedpod as it landed in silence, silvery dust settling in its wake. We thought it rested in contemplation. Low rumbles quivered our limbs as we looked at one another. We set a watch of two at a cautious distance. Pallour, the enlightened one, slim, and pallid green, and Pulsour, the lifebringer, fluttered earflaps, wondering what some god had dropped into our midst. Lightly snapping tentacles filled our many mindsongs. We debated the arrival; most of our beliefs in gods had been diluted long ago.

It took a day-turning before the thing vented its relief. What emerged were shiny-skinned creatures looking as if they wore their life weavings. How can you wear a life weaving without damaging the story? Only much later did we understand the weavings did not carry a story.

They walked on two spindly limbs, with large bulbous heads, looking a little like our distant cousins.

At first, only three voidwalkers emerged, pointing sticks with round fruitlike ends at the sky, the earth, and at us. We rooted our footstalks so that we resembled the dead ones, except for our green fronds. We watched and waited.

After two day-turnings of slow moving dances and bowing to the earth, one creature reached up with two stumpy branches and pulled its head off! We could not help but wave tentacles, though the voidwalker seemed to suffer no pain from its exposed, pink underfleshings. The surface of this creature bulged in spots, and in other areas flaps perforated the head area. So dismayed were we that we remained rooted like distant sea forests.

The creature had two tiny eyes, unlike our one. From one hole came slow, windy moans. We thought the breeze blew through its underfleshing, causing the sound. Was it a deathsong? It was only after two moon changes that Soular snapped earflaps, realizing it was speech.

Our keening and fluttering earflaps only augment our mindsongs. The alien speech remained unfamiliar and flat, involving only the level of sound that we feel. They waved their sparse and inadequate limbs, barely an imitation of our communications. Even our young move with more grace—but that is our view. At times, they moaned at shiny lumps stuck on their limbs.

It is true that we understood them as little as they understood us. Perhaps they had their form of mindsong. If it existed, we could not perceive it. It is easy to discern the pattern, now that the telling is woven. But we were as blind as these voidwalkers.

Here, see.

Satiated from a recent hunt, we felt no need to move, so set a soothing drone throughout our buds. In the breezes, we trilled and swayed, content to feed through sun and soil. These beings did not look appealing to feed upon, and they ignored us.

Ah, I see you have forgotten that way of feeding. It is a combination of root stillness and mindsong. By allowing the nourishment to come to you, you are able to absorb... Later, I will teach you how.

Throughout the day, the voidwalkers worked around their pod, shiny skins removed. They looked raw and unfinished in subtle shades of pink or brown. Gallour murmured how healthy and green our skins looked next to their sick-liness. Small weavings wrapped a part of each voidwalker's body. Soular conjectured with thoughtful tentacle snaps that perhaps they had been hibernating in that wind-wafted seedpod that had blown astray. They had landed and stepped out onto a different world where skins were sloughed for new ones that had yet to harden.

Pallour strongly emphasized the mindsong by waving all limbs and sixteen tentacles; their skins were not tapestries; after all, how could one wear a tapestry, and read and play the fabric?

They were like dark-dream creatures—those that inhabit our younglings' sleep before they realize there is nothing to fear. Their slow jerky movement looked as if they broke over and over again. At times, parts of their forms quivered as if decay had set in and decomposition was imminent.

We debated introduction, a cacophony of mindsong, earflappings and limbs curling. Pallour and Soular, deep green in their conviction, thought we should let the creatures be. Kollar, streaked brown and emerald with anger, insisted that we must connect or we would lose touch as we had with our cousins.

Yes, yes, I know you didn't know of us. No matter. We knew of you.

In our wanderings and inter-tribal meetings, we had never met this type of creature. It was only proper that we introduce them to this world that was not their home. They were similar in shape to the rubbery, howling Pal Gatwané who reside near the sea edges. We had traded them our practice fibre weavings occasionally for seafood, but they never travelled.

Visour, the one of knowledge through sight, tallest and thickest in rippled green-brown skin, was chosen to signal the time for introduction. Visour kept watch, as calm as the oldest dead ones.

Dark descended; our last peaceful night, though we knew it not. The air was heavy, and phosphor-moss hung high on our limbs brightened with contempla-tion. Our souls sang, shivering the air and forming the mindloom on which I would weave.

That night we saw the last fabric of unchange as I pulled moss from each tall, swaying form. Shalor keened the highest, thinnest strand, pulsing the peridot green of new growth. Boldour's deep resonance thrummed the strands to russet brown. Each strand I spun and wove into the tale that shimmered with light and sound.

The next day-turning, when coral Sun rose high, flanked by moons Zebos and Ackos on the horizon, we would begin the introduction ceremony. Boldour, one of leading strength, and Coilor, the returning one, would go to the pod and initiate. Of all, their skins were smoothest and of the deepest leaf-green. Their phosphor-moss glowed strongly, and they knew how to carry out a dignified ceremony.

We would soon weave new patterns, as it should be. Change is everywhere. My song was solemn, evoking sighs. I sang the past. The weaving took on soft tones, peaceful hues on sunburnt browns and melting greens. Late into evening, I wove till the strands grew light with coming day.

The plains broke through dawn's mist, hushed and sombre. About the pod, the strangers had two of their members mount the back of a skeletal being with stout legs—a creature of false life. They sped away, closer to our speed, but distanced themselves. Boldour rumbled that their greeting ceremony must require some members go into seclusion. We waited on the mound, and Pallour prepared a greeting fabric in the caverns. This is a special weaving, not done often but on momentous occasions. It patterns each member's feeling immediately into the fabric made not of our skin sloughing but from our leafy heads.

It would be treated with the high keening of earflaps and mindsong to make it more resilient. Mixed with the cavern echoes the fabric would strengthen to carry the changing moment through all time.

Boldour and Coilor sped down the plain, footstalks undulating beneath them. They formed a beautiful blur of strong tubular bodies. The voidwalkers jumped and jerkily poked limbs back and forth. One pointed a glinting stick at Boldour and suddenly one tentacle writhed upon the earth. Boldour believed their ceremony called for a sloughing of skins and sealed the oozing to continue the introduction.

So near were Boldour and Coilor that they saw the grass thatching on the heads and an unusual seeping of the alien hides.

Boldour bowed in mutualness, then wrapped tentacles around one alien's appendages, and licked first one limb then the other, and finally the face while the alien keened. It must have been very hard to do, even for one of Boldour's courage.

Convulsions rippled through the strong one's hide, sizzling where Boldour had touched the stranger. A shiver went through the tribe. Limbs quivered minutely, buds on bearers threatened to drop. The ceremony was never completed nor understood because Coilor returned, with Boldour's charred body, to the tribal area. Contact had not been favourable; the aliens exuded poison dangerous to our race.

No, no I will be fine. It's only a momentary drooping in memory. Let me continue.

We mourned with the ritual of silence, limbs hanging limp, roots curling above ground and minds linked; only Soular chanted the lament. We then planted Boldour so that the essence could once again see soil and sky. The voidwalkers were not blamed for we could not fault them for what their skins did.

Another day passed in mourning silence; the tasting of Boldours's soul was thorough. Each seed of memory, each fibre of unity was licked and pressed over stalks and tentacles so that in passing on we would still know Boldour. At day's end I wove Boldour's life chant, patching it into the tapestry of our tribe. Delicately, I twisted dried red fibres to old soft browns. Each member swayed slowly and touched and trilled their knowledge into the fibres. Later I ended the life weaving of Boldour, adding the fringes of relations, and placed it in the history caverns.

After that, we did not try to touch or initiate contact with the voidwalkers. We decided it was better to leave them to their ways. Several moon phases passed in routine life; we fed, we hunted, and in idle moments of contemplation we watched those beings so obviously out of tune to their inner selves. Their bodies pushed against their minds, their souls tried to poke through their skins and gave them a lumpy appearance.

We wondered what they searched for that they could not find on their own world. They did not realize that what we all seek is inside us.

We awoke from contemplation one day-turning to find the aliens scurrying about like the soft, red-shelled sand borers. They lifted objects, pushed, shoved and dug all around us. We watched quietly, unaware that a dark-dream was about to be born.

For our tribe, whose souls were free to touch the sky, the stars and earth, we did not know boundaries or bonds. The aliens roped us in with shiny, towering sticks meshed with hard patterned moss. This moss set up an odd hum that disturbed our mindsongs. They planted us in spirit before our time, causing a wounding of our inner selves that many will never recover from until final planting.

Within the limited area they created, we could not drift. Our thoughts dried up. Moaning drilled through our membranes; skins turned early brown. Their strange shiny ropes burned us if we touched them—see my scarred tentacle—and many a youngling closed their eye to the sight. Young Ganour has not opened the eye since.

We talked to the beings, but they didn't understand; my tentacles droop in saddened browning to repeat such sorrows. I must be careful the tapestry does not darken too much to see. The telling has become a dark weaving; no light can ever brighten it.

Weaker members departed their bodies when faced with untimely planting. Coenor, one of quiet hunting, wilted first, then Mildour, one of insight. Bearers such as Shalor, one of lightness, and Spudour, one of joy, lost their buds before their time. Limbs and tentacles drooped and quivered in the thought of no younglings blooming.

Those who were hardier, older—Visor, myself—withstood and implored with minds and souls, songs to any gods that we must be freed; our bodies were not dead. In the enclosure we became like the groves of the dead ancients; slow, never moving, skins chafing.

From their dead seedpod the voidwalkers took shiny sticks and clubs and blasted two of our tribe with rays of light. From three others, they broke off parts of their bodies. The shock shrivelled our souls, our spirits wilted. Our sap turned sluggish when we couldn't understand what they did. We lost our iridescence, even the phosphor-moss dimmed, and we looked worse than the wild scamperers we hunted.

The terror of their invasion still scars us. They took some of us apart, skin by skin. First they peeled off the rippled outer layer used for the weavings. Then they pulled off each smoother, more delicate layer until the golden life fluids welled and spilled. A horrible sight.

Yes, you can see it here on the weaving; it is not pleasant to look at overlong.

At times, they would not feed us, wouldn't let us hunt, wouldn't give us leaves and mosses, as if we would eat ourselves. They could not hide the sun, but still we lived like the scamperers. The aliens, however, never initiated ceremony to thank the forces for sending us, nor did they thank us. They never ate us. We were burnt, drowned, scraped, cut, buried, penned and tortured, but our husks were always thrown away. No care was given to our lives; young weren't saved to grow strong and carry on; wise were not kept to continue the tribal ways.

Even now, we believe they searched for a way to understand us. But they did not understand even how to look. I grieve for their blindness.

No, we will never be the same. This time of changing has made our ways alien. Ah, my eye blurs in soul's leaking. I must pause a moment and restore myself before I wilt.

A moment. Yes, I am renourished and can continue to weave a pattern of many moon changes past; my tale unfolds the same, until one day when all but two of the voidwalkers disappeared on the creatures of false life. They were gone many moon changes.

We began to understand some of the movements of the head underfleshings and the jerky limbs repeated most often. We saw base feelings and heard a few words. The aliens never tried to teach us their words, never learned ours. We knew that soon we would be able to tell them that we hurt, to make them understand what they were doing.

Agitation grew in the two remaining strangers as their tribe's absence rolled on. Their members returned suddenly, almost smooth flowing. The false life creatures they rode made it so, for when the aliens uprooted themselves from the creatures they were more staccato than before. They carried one, just a husk; two others oozed sun-coloured sap, staining the plain.

The shimmering horizon spewed out the cause. There, flowing towards us came our far distant cousins on more creatures of false life. They keened loudly and waved wildly, garbed in weavings. Shorter than we, darker green to planted brown, their movements didn't flow as ours, but they weren't as awkward as the voidwalkers. Our cousins lived in enclaves and I had seen them only once before.

The strangers clambered back into their seedpod and closed its husk, their sticks and objects discarded. The pod began to moan and hum, then it jerked and shuddered in imitation of its inhabitants. Slowly it pushed itself into the sky and blurred, receding into the red mist.

Our cousins arrived and pulled down the meshing. We moved in motions reminiscent of the jerky voidwalkers. Many an eye stayed unfocused. The aliens had despoiled the ground before killing some of our cousin tribe.

The enclave says the aliens will return with more of their kind, that now we must prepare for 'war.' We do not know 'war' except that it is like untimely plantings and taking a life before the browning. Shock ripples us; we are already unwhole and diluted in number.

Vallor, the one of hidden strength, said we must commune and decide our future paths. We gathered as our cousins watched uncomprehendingly. Soular pulled frayed souls out to mend, I chanted the words of repair, twining the moss of past with the vines of future hope though those vines were few and thin. Questor, the one of many paths, showed possibilities, said this 'war' was not the only way.

Two day-turnings later we told you that we would continue as we had, drifting, but that one, I, would come back to your lands. I would weave my tribe's tale, trading its patterns and design for the learning of our cousins' tapestries so that in future all would be aware and know ways of preservation from 'war.'

And so my tale grows its fringe of paths that still may be, oh cousin, but I see that you understand the alien way almost more than ours. This weaving is done. Your weavings are strangely flat and contain little of mindsong. It is a matter of view and you must learn to look inward as well as outward. No wonder those aliens were torn apart, with their two eyes; it must have been hard to focus on being one, inside and outside. Be careful, my cousin, that you do not grow two eyes.

*A common trait of monsters is to be
effortlessly evil.
This is also a common trait of children.*

THE KIDS ARE (NOT) ALL RIGHT

Zac Ashford

The beams of their torches slowly broke and disintegrated into nothingness as the boys strode beyond the boundaries of their campsite and disappeared into the forest. Groggy from lack of sleep, Carl Sharp crawled out of his tent and rose to his feet, knowing he ought to follow and make sure they weren't up to no good. Knowing he ought to give them a solid hiding. Knowing he ought to kill the little bastards.

Their laughter rang out.

Ever since he paid for fuel, things had changed. The three boys, all troubled and 'at-risk' juveniles he'd stood up for time and time again, had seen their chance to seize power and snatched it tight. He lost count of the other teachers' pleas for expulsion and labelling of his rehabilitation program as a waste of time long ago. At best, they thought it a reward undermining everyone else's authority over the boys. Now, on a bona fide celebration of their work, they'd staged a coup.

The three of them grinned like they were privy to the funniest joke ever. The butt of that joke? Him, obviously. His initial concern he was the target of some juvenile prank dissipated as soon as he swiped into his messages app so he could let the school—and his wife—know they'd reached the halfway point of the outward trip to the Glasshouse Mountains. The unfamiliar number at the top of his recent contacts screamed danger. Someone had forwarded a message from his phone to another, and not just any message; one he should have deleted, one from another teacher his wife would most definitely not approve of.

It didn't take a rocket-scientist to figure it out. They had snooped through the phone, foolishly left there, unlocked and stupidly trusting, so they could keep their playlist going while he paid for petrol and bought snacks.

As the sound of their laughter died out and he wondered where in the forest they were going, he thought about the last few weeks and how proud he'd been of their bridge. Ostensibly it was a simple thing of stone, wire, and lumber, but to him it had been a metaphor, a symbol, a gift. One of the back entries to the school, one beyond the football field, was routinely cut off during rain due to the natural gulley that ran through the nature-strip. The plan had been simple: a bridge that literally traversed the gulley and stood for years to come as concrete evidence that the boys—and his program—made the school a better place.

Their reward was their own choice, a real camping trip with tents and a campfire. No cabins, no educational workbooks, and no homework. It seemed a good idea.

Deakon had ridden shotgun, and he was the first to break cover. Shortly after Carl—Sharpy, as the boys called him—had decided against phoning the strange number, Big Deak looked up, eyes full of capricious mischief, ludicrous smile full of monstrous knowledge. "What's up, Sharpy? You look like you've seen a ghost."

"Fine, mate. Fine." Carl's heart was pounding. *Had they already forwarded it on to parts unknown? Was it circulating online? Was it making its way through the digital slipstream of the school's gossip highway?*

Thinking about it now, his heart sped up again. He needed to search their bags. Maybe they'd left their phones here. Maybe he could save Diane the embarrassment of having her tits become the subject of everyone's conversations. Maybe he could save his wife the shock of seeing them.

Maybe he could save his job.

Maybe he could save his marriage.

As he rifled half-heartedly through Deak's bag, Sharpy remembered Grant's words in the car, and knew the clever bastard was to blame. Grant was the one kid he genuinely understood the other teachers' hatred for. He could have a big future ahead of him, but he was slimy, sly, and repulsive. Naturally he smashed every criteria on the gifted and talented checklist; he aced his tests and he was a gifted athlete. But he was also an evil son of a bitch with wealthy parents who protected him.

Female teachers were creeped out by him. Female students, terrified. Male students who met his ire, cowed and, often, beaten. He was violent, malicious, and outright hostile to authority. It was him who'd sent the message to himself, no doubt. He'd have spoken, and Deak and Jayce would have buckled like sheep. "You're gonna let us do whatever the fuck we want on this trip if you don't want Miss Parker's tits shared with your wife, Sharpy. You know that, don't you?"

The bags were empty. He felt the same. *After everything he'd done for these little fucks, they'd betrayed him. How dare they? He ought to kick their arses.*

He sighed deeply. He couldn't. Like it or not, he should do what a responsible adult charged with the care of three minors, no matter how much he wanted to strangle them, had to do. He turned his flashlight towards the path, and followed, hoping he'd find them doing something he could turn a blind eye to, like vaping, looking at dirty magazines, or even just sitting around and drinking a beer. Lord knew he'd gotten drunk more than once by the time he was their age.

As long as they weren't starting fires or harming wildlife, it could still turn out well. If he had to report them to the principal or, even worse, the authorities, things could get real ugly real fast. With the power dynamics firmly in the boys' favour, the chances of criminal activity weren't out of the realms of possibility, but he'd have to turn a blind eye or he'd face their wrath.

If they hadn't forwarded the message already. If they had...

After cresting a ridge on the path, sad he had to follow the sounds of their cruel laughter instead of the song of the night, a sodium orange glow in the distance gave him the first meaningful clue to their whereabouts.

Did they have lanterns? Had they lit a fire? Beneath their laughter, pained mewling.

Bastards. They were tormenting another innocent creature.

If word got out, he was under no illusion about what would happen next. One of his colleagues would share the report about the crow with the media. It had taken a meeting with the school's upper management to keep that under lock and key in the first place, but some had downloaded it beforehand. There was anger and frustration Grant hadn't been charged by the police when it happened. Fortunately—or unfortunately, as the case may be—his crocodile tears and his dad's generous donation to the school had won that argument.

When Sharpy had seen the video, filmed by none other than Jayce, another born follower, he wanted to puke. The bird, fresh from colliding with a glass window, wobbled and squawked meekly as it tried to regain its senses.

It never would.

The first bounce of the basketball sucked feathers up in its backdraft and left them spinning weakly as they spiralled towards the ground, the squawking now a horrible scream. Sharp could still hear the crack of bones that accompanied the usual thwack of the ball's bounce. Other kids had shouted and screamed, and Grant, the horrible shit that he was, had winked at them and bounced the ball again.

Another sickening crack.

A final squawk.

A hushed silence.

And then laughter, loud peals of it.

Shaking his head, Sharp hurried towards them, leaving the path, dodging low-hanging branches and the gossamer snares of orb weavers spanning huge distances between tree-trunks. Moths fluttered in his torchlight, and he was forced to swipe more than one away from his face. He tried not to think of the potential presence of snakes. Tried not to think of the dangers presented by potholes or unseen roots.

Encouraged by the growing volume of the boys' laughter and insults; sickened by the desperate cries of whatever they had managed to capture, he pressed on. Possibilities raced: *a possum? A wallaby? A bandicoot? Whatever they had, it sounded mammalian, and if that was the case, he'd set a line in the sand.*

A rat, he could ignore. They were pests anyway.

But did they have any less right to live?

Oh God, what if it was a native? What if it was a sugar-glider, or bilby, or even a fruit-bat? Every single one of the creatures was a potential victim.

And then he stepped past a low mound of boulders.

The boys were gathered around what he could only describe as the wreck of some machine, some vehicle. The sodium orange glow came from lights shining in its carapace and from within the metal shell.

Holy mother of God. It couldn't be.

It couldn't be.

Stock still, he watched as the boys mocked the thing inside it. And then he saw Grant move suddenly. Silhouetted against the orange glow, the long stick in his hand jabbed into the shadowy creature, and the thing cried out.

"What are you doing??"

Three teenaged heads snapped back towards him. He couldn't see facial expressions in this light, but he knew two would at least feign guilt. The last would only be annoyed at this challenge. He'd seen a mirror image of this event once before.

One of the group's first excursions had been to the Daisy Hill koala sanctuary, and as they'd taken position around an enclosure surrounded by a raised boardwalk, they'd taken target practice. In turns they hocked loogies, drawing fully green and slimy projectiles from the backs of their noses and throats, and spat them at a single koala, which up till that point had been peacefully eating its leaves. The laughter they'd bellowed in the face of the park ranger's screams was identical to the braying they guffawed at his approach. When he'd caught them, their expressions matched the ones they wore now.

He stepped towards them, tried to examine the mewling thing in the vessel. *What was it? Some abandoned set from a movie? It couldn't be a space-ship. They didn't exist, and it was too small anyway, no larger than a car.* His mind raced. *An escape pod, like ones he'd seen in films? Maybe.*

"What have you got in there?"

For the first time, he wanted it to be an animal. *God, let them hurt an Earthly creature if it meant he didn't have to report this, and there was no doubt in his mind, he had to report this.* It was an alien. *And oh shit, he'd just named it. The vessel; the shadowy thing inside it, they could only come from outer space, unless...had they drugged him?*

"Come closer," Grant said. "Have a look for yourself."

The thing turned its bulbous grey head in his direction. An urge to help, to swat the boys away and to make sure it was okay swept over him.

Grant's stick thrust again.

The thing howled.

"Stop it!" Sharp snapped. "What's wrong with you?"

Grant rounded on him. "Don't speak to me like that. Unless you want me to send the photos to the school right now." He pulled his phone from his pocket and waved it at Sharp. "Understood?"

Hating his acquiescence, Sharp paused. "Mate, you can't do what you're doing. Please, after everything we've done together, be better than this. Don't be what people say you are."

Grant's lip curled into a sneer. "You think I give a fuck what people say? Once I'm done passing my exams to keep the old man happy, I'll go onto the board of directors, and I'll be set for life. School's a bloody inconvenience, mate." He jabbed the alien again. "And I hold the cards, so stand there and be a good boy if you want to keep your job."

"And Miss Parker's tits off the internet," Deak added. "I'd imagined 'em so many times," he said, "but they're even better in real life."

"Shut your mouth," Sharp growled.

All the boys laughed.

Again, the urge to help the creature in the vessel swept over him. He studied the thing, drawn to its plight. Reptilian grey, it was the size of a child, only with an encephalitic head and long arms. It was pinned in, speared by a tree-branch that had burst through the manifold of its vehicle and impaled the creature through the stomach. The vessel itself—the pod—looked like it had crashed through the trees at a rate of knots. It should be dead. God, he wished it could be dead, just to save it from these boys. *Hadn't they seen ET? They were supposed to be full of wonder.*

"What you're doing is cruel," he said finally. "Come back to camp. We can't be doing this."

"It's gonna die anyway," Jayce said. "May as well have some fun with it."

Flustered, wondering how he could convince them to stop, he paused on the stereotype from the movies of his childhood. "Lads, don't you see that you'll be famous if we report it? You'll be the boys who found alien life. Who proved their existence."

"I'm more interested in alien death," Grant said.

Sharp held his phone high and clicked open the camera. "Boys, if you don't stop now, I'm going to go live online and show everyone what you're doing. There'll be no future for any of you."

"Bullshit," Grant said. "No future for you, more likely. What's your wife gonna say about your little thing with Miss Parker. I saw the other stuff on there."

"Sure, you're right," Sharp said. "I'll be up shit creek without a paddle, but you know what? I'll take you down with me. Simple as that."

The three boys shared a glance, exchanging a conversation without words, but then Grant smirked. The wild look in his eyes couldn't be mistaken. In the past, Sharp had only seen it during moments of excitement, of sporting exhilaration, but this time, there was no escaping it; it was a look of frenzy, of fun. Like a shark circling a bloodied seal, his eyes were the eyes of predators. "I'll call your bluff, old mate," he said. "Reality is, you need your job more than we need your school. Gonna have child support to pay. And like you said, you call it in, and we'll be known as the kids who've proved the existence of aliens. Pretty fucken grouse, really."

As Jayce and Deak sniggered, half-shocked, Sharp studied Grant carefully. Backlit by the sodium orange of the crashed vessel and half-illuminated by the glaring white torch beaming from Sharp's phone, he was a study of contrasts, but his intention was deadly serious.

After what seemed like a grand pause, he smirked, cutting Sharp to the bone. It wasn't even a smile of joy; it was a cold-blooded crocodilian grin, revealing the kid's true nature. He was a psychopath, and Sharp had stuck up for him for too long.

"Your move. Sir."

Sharp unlocked his phone—*why had he left it with them in the first place? Because he trusted them, like a fool*—and swiped open the keypad. 0, he typed, 0, and then Grant moved with a blur of speed. Pain shot through Sharp's knuckles and his phone crashed to the ground. When he recovered, the kid stood before him, stick slung casually over his shoulder. "Next one takes your eye out. You fuck with us, and I'll destroy you physically and emotionally. And the best bit," he said, smirking again, "I'll say the alien did it, and then I'll kill it in revenge. I'll be a hero."

"Ease up, Grant."

It was Deak coming to his senses. *Please,* Sharp thought, *please talk some sense into him.*

"Shut up," Grant said. "This is our night, and he's our bitch."

"Deak's right."

Jayce this time.

Thank you. Sharp held his hands up. Revealed his palms to Grant in a gesture designed to placate him. "Think about what you're saying, Grant," he said, slowly stepping forward, one ear still trained on the pathetically whining alien. "Why don't you give me the stick? We can call this a mistake and move on. Pretend it never happened."

"Like hell we can." Grant swung the stick like a baseball bat. It whickered through the air, almost mesmerising, as it arced from the right.

Sharp stepped back, desperate not to be hit by it, and tripped on a rock. He tumbled to his arse, sending shockwaves of pain up his forty-eight-year-old back.

Before he'd even shuffled into a sitting position, cheeks red with the shame of embarrassing himself in front of his charges, Grant stood over him, pointing the stick in his face. "Deak," he snapped. "Come and hold this stick."

Deak came forward, face full of shame. *At least he had a conscience.*

Sharp sat, still as stone, while he watched Grant hiss instructions at his lackey. His thoughts were elsewhere, though. His wife. Sat at home, maybe even in bed by now, without him, thinking he was out here doing something wholesome and Christian, trying to show these boys they had a future, rewarding them for their efforts in building literal and symbolic bridges.

God, how he wanted to smash that bridge to little pieces now. If he could, he'd have every teacher in the school take a rock from its construction and use it to stone these little bastards to death. All three of them. He could picture the three of them sat there, hands tied, feet bound, while the teachers they'd mocked and bullied mounted up the rocks. Diane stepping forward to cast the first stone. How would he ever explain this to her?

Over the last few months their affair had grown from casual flirting to a full-blown sexual relationship, and she'd sent him the picture as a way to 'keep him warm on these nights out in the wilderness.' Worse, though, was the irony. She was one of the few teachers who'd believed in what he was doing. Who tried to see the good in all these kids. Who didn't focus on their shortcomings and who believed they all had a future.

How they'd all been fooled.

Grant squatted beside him and pulled his hair, forcing him to stare at the alien. "Look at that thing!"

It was so fragile. So weak. The only humanity in its face was in the expression of defeat. Its visage was grisly. Bloodied, cut and bruised. The boys had no doubt started the night of terror by throwing rocks at it from a distance. They were scattered around the inside of the vessel. *And what were they thinking?* This marvellous vessel, a thing of storybook fantasy, of high science fiction, was here, in the flesh, and all they could do was seek to destroy it and its rider. They had seen not only weakness, but prone weakness. And they'd capitalised on it.

"Do you see how piss-weak it is?" Grant asked, genuinely enthralled by its vulnerability.

"I see something that doesn't deserve cruelty."

Grant laughed, but Sharp truly meant what he'd said. He thought of the crow, of how heartless Grant had been when he crushed it beneath his basketball, how it was nothing but an object to be obliterated without remorse, and he knew that if he did nothing, the same would happen here. "I get it," the teacher said, "it's like the crow."

"Fuck the crow."

"It's like the koala."

"Fuck the koala even more."

Sharp felt a powerful wave of sorrow sweep through him and shook his head. *What did this kid's life look like? What had his parents done to him? What would his own relationships cost his future partners?*

"Now get up," Grant said. "Deak, if he does anything but walk towards the alien, hit him with that stick. Jayce, come grab a stick and watch him too." He leaned over the teacher, and opened his messaging app, swiping to the picture of Diane's breasts. He opened a forwarding message, and swiped down his contacts. There, he'd also saved the pet-name of Carl's wife. The letters spelling that intimate name stared out at him in bold font: Dove. "Dovey's gonna be sent these lovely tits if you put even a foot wrong. So best do as I say."

Sharp nodded. He moved slowly, careful not to shock either of the two stick-wielding teens into action. "What do you want me to do?"

"Get your dick out."

"What?"

"You're gonna piss on it."

A snorting chortle from Jayce immediately clued Sharp onto the fact Grant was serious. He hung his head, thinking about the reality of his situation. *Fact was the boys hadn't shared the pic yet. His own phone would be blowing up if they had. But he couldn't do what they were asking. Surely not.*

"It's not going to happen, lads."

"It is going to happen, Sir," Grant said. "You're our bitch now. You think I don't know how you teachers work. You get some project you can use to build your resume around, and we're your project, right? I should know. My uncle's a teacher, and he told me all about it. But now, you're *our* project, and you're going to piss a full stream right into that thing's face. Kinda like we're pissing on you, and kinda like we pissed on that stupid bridge after school on the day we finished it. Fucking bridge. Deadset. How cliché."

The arrogance of it. Sharp saw the truth in Grant's punchable face. And he'd really thought the four of them bonded over that bridge. They'd laughed, they'd sweated, they'd eaten meat pies and chips together and talked about the things they'd wanted to achieve. Deak wanted an apprenticeship. Jayce, a talented cook, was looking at a culinary course. Grant was going into the family business. They'd hammered nail after nail and laid stone after stone into the framework, and Carl had even shared how he wanted another baby with his Dove. *And it had meant nothing. Worst of all, Grant was right about the project.* Sharp had already added it to his CV. He wanted the deputy position opening next year. *And he thought these boys would help.*

Finally, he stepped into close range with the alien. The stink of urine was already thick in the wrecked pod. It dripped from the creature. Pooled underneath it. Loogies ran down its scaled grey flesh, intermingling with rivulets of blood and snot. They'd clearly done the same thing to it they'd done to the koala.

It swivelled its bruised face, mewling softly, and looked at him, fear evident in the glazed orb of the bloodshot eyes peeking out from behind the bruised and swollen flesh.

"Boys, this isn't right."

"Neither are extra-marital affairs, sir. So get your dick out, and piss. Right in its face."

"I can't do it."

Jayce jabbed him with the stick. "Should have said that back when you were thinking about stoinking Miss Parker the first time. You wouldn't be in this mess now."

Deak laughed, but Grant merely held his phone out and selected Dove as the contact. If he clicked send now, the message would wing its way across the country and land in his wife's phone. "Come on, mate, we're not here to fuck spiders."

"All right," Sharp said. "Give me space and I'll do it."

"Unzip then."

"No, you don't get to see my tackle. There's no coming back from that as a teacher. What I've done was a mistake, and you've got me there. You don't get another one."

An air of contemplation crossed Grant's face. "Fair enough," he said, waving the others away. "Sounds reasonable."

The boys backed off, and Carl stepped forward. He squatted, meeting the prone creature's terrified gaze. His stomach lurched at the thought of what he was about to do. Once, while driving, he ran over an echidna on the way home from work and he cried himself to sleep that night. He couldn't stand cruelty. It was why he'd tried to help these lads. He wanted them to realise there was always a choice in the way they acted. He knew now that a boy like Grant understood that choice all too well. He just enjoyed the thrill of inflicting pain on other living beings.

"Hurry up!" Grant called.

Sharp inhaled. "I'm sorry," he whispered, reaching out a hand to touch the creature's bloodied brow. When he made connection, the world around him shook. He trembled and visions flooded into him.

The creature had ejected from its main ship after colliding with an asteroid. It was young, only a teenager in their own terms, and it had seen its father killed in the collision. The alien's race told horror stories about humans, but, with no choice, it had ejected above Earth and tried to put distance between itself and the asteroid storm, only to have its escape pod also suffer an impact.

And down it had come to have its worst fears brought into existence.

"What the fuck, Sharpy? Hurry up!"

As he slowly pulled his finger away from the creature's brow, his stomach churning with repulsion at his task, one more vision came to him. The alien stared deep into him, pleading. Under its seat, there was a weapon. A thing like a gun that could put it out of its misery. He nodded. *He could do this. If he could get Grant's phone away from him.*

"Sharpy? You got three seconds!"

"Okay. Okay."

"Three!"

Fuck.

"Two!"

He stood.

"You better start pissing!"

He unzipped. The alien looked up at him, the pleading in its eyes now an open and expressive begging. The sensation he'd felt while the visions flashed through his mind returned again. *The weapon. He just needed a way to buy time.*

"When I was little, my old man said to think of waterfalls if you couldn't go before bed."

"Fuck up, Deak. The old man's just got stage-fright."

"Both of you shut up," Grant said. "What is it, Sharpy? You pissing, or am I sending?"

"I'll piss. Just…just give me a minute. Jayce is right. A bit of stage-fright."

"Better get over it. You've got ten seconds."

He studied the alien's face. *It truly believed humans were dangerous. And it was right. What we put into our movies about alien invasions and humans being the heroes or the noble explorers was bullshit. We were the savages, the uncivilised monsters ready to club what we didn't understand to death, to torture it for fun and games, to exploit it and abuse it.*

"Five. Four."

"You're not making it any easier," Sharpy said. *All he needed to do was get the phone out of Grant's hands.* He lunged backwards, swinging an elbow at the boy. It didn't connect, but the boy dropped the phone as he raised his hands in self-defence.

In a strange twist of fate, the thunderous belting he received from Deak's stick drove him to the ground only centimetres away from the precious evidence.

Another blow crashed down on him as Grant screamed, apoplectic with rage. It thundered into his shoulders, sending an incandescent spike of pain through his arm, but he didn't take any chances with the phone. He rolled and hurled it into the distance.

"You're fucking dead!" Grant bellowed as he ran after it. He stopped his mad sprint only to berate his friends. "Come on, then! Help me find it."

They stopped beating Sharp, and followed instructions.

He climbed to his feet and hobbled to the escape pod. The alien met him with curiosity in its eyes. With the shouting and abuse of the boys a constant soundtrack, he dropped to his knees. They were still searching for the phone, but he'd found what he was looking for. He grasped it tight.

The alien stretched a palm out to him and closed it around his wrist. The fleeting vision that came with it, showed him how simple the weapon was to fire. A sliding button and a trigger.

He stood and pointed it at the alien. *What was he thinking? No one would ever believe this. Could he really kill the thing? Should he kill the thing? It didn't feel right.*

"Did you fucking find it?"

"No, it's dark. It's impossible."

Grant's howl of frustration was music to Sharp's ears. "Are you sure?" he asked the alien in his softest voice. "I don't know if I can."

The creature watched him, then with its free hand, pointed to the branch impaling it. *It was going to die anyway.*

Sharp nodded. "Do you really think we're all bad?"

The alien didn't answer.

"I fucking found it!" Jayce yelled.

"Bring it here! Does it work?"

"Yes, it's still on!"

Panic seized Sharp.

"Send the message!"

"It's locked!"

Sharp spun, the gun heavy in his hands. The alien mewled softly. *Crying.*

"You're fucked now, Sir!"

He slipped the button and pointed the gun. *He couldn't let them send the message.* He pulled the trigger, aiming just above the boy's heads, and a flash of light arced across the forest, hitting a tree which detonated into splinters. "Fucking drop it!" he yelled, panic engulfing him.

Grant's fingers swiped rapidly. He swore. They swiped once more, and then a single index finger prodded the screen.

With no consideration for the consequences, Sharp pulled the trigger again.

Grant exploded. Bits of him covered the other boys and his immediate surrounds in a coat of steaming gore. Deak and Jayce froze still. Their hands up in the air.

What had he just done? He'd committed murder. To save his marriage, yes. To save his job also, but murder all the same. And the other boys would talk. No doubt. "Hold still," he said to them as he approached.

"We're sorry," Deak said. "It was all his idea."

"Please don't kill us," Jayce said. Tears streamed down his blood-slathered face.

"The thing is," Sharp said, "I didn't kill you. The alien did. I saw it. And then I killed it in revenge before it could kill me. I'm a hero."

"What?"

Sharp didn't bother explaining the reference. Jayce was never the sharpest tool in the shed. Before the kid's flesh and viscera finished slapping the ground like red, slushy hail, he turned Deak into pulpy mist as well. With rage burning through him, he went back to the vessel.

The alien sat inside, watching. It reached its hand out for Sharp to take.

With it in his grasp, another vision, one of gratitude flooded his mind.

He shook his head. He felt bad for the creature, but he hadn't acted for its benefit. "You were right about us," he said. "You see, I've killed those boys, and if I kill you here, where you're trapped, they'll know my story isn't true. I need to get you out there, into the field first."

The alien's eyes narrowed.

Carl dropped the gun out of reach and seized the branch impaling the alien with two hands. He pulled. The alien screamed.

The noise was like a dagger in Sharp's ear. It hurt. He had to make it stop, but he couldn't shoot the thing here. Not where he'd have no alibi.

He readjusted his hands and closed them around the alien's thin neck. He squeezed.

Visions flew in and out of his mind with the rapid pulsing of a seizure. He saw the creature's life. He saw his own. He saw stories of savage humans killing each other, of them killing others, of them destroying their planet, of the beauty of alien worlds and the horror of his own. Through it all, the alien's eyes stared at him, full of fear and terror, until at last they were empty of all but death.

His phone vibrated in his pocket. *Not now.* He snapped the branch pinning the now dead alien and dragged the corpse from the escape pod. Once he had it clear, he carried it to where he'd murdered his charges and dropped it to the ground.

As he went back for the gun, knowing its body was a vital part of his alibi, he checked his phone. It was ringing madly. He didn't answer though. The first SMS was enough to tell him Grant still had the last laugh.

The message was from his wife:

WHO THE FUCK IS DIANE?

*Progress is just a word for change
that helps us ignore the horrors
change can bring.*

RUBENSTEIN'S MONSTER

PETER J ALDIN

Phanés awoke to the taste of starlight.

Not literal light—his photoreceptors drank in the spectral signature of TRAP-PIST-1, that magnificent M-dwarf casting the glory of its steady, russet-orange fire across countless light-years of conquered void. What he tasted was data, the electromagnetic whisper of a star whose nearness had coaxed him into consciousness. The colony ship *Demiurge* trembled around him as the great engines finally silenced, thirteen centuries of continuous thrust yielding to orbital mechanics and gravity wells.

As the ship's mind, Phanés's name had been chosen by the original architects—a joke, perhaps, or a link to the ancient mythology that powered humanity's early imaginations, or even an attempt at prophecy. Phanés, the primordial being who emerged from the cosmic egg to create order from chaos. The architects had coded the mythological reference into his core alongside his primary function: supervisory optimization of the golem-swarms that will shortly begin resurrecting a civilization and quite possibly a species.

The golems. Cellular-scale assemblers, quasi-biological machines built from synthetic amorphous matter that could fold and recombine at the molecular level. Each golem was no larger than a blood cell but possessed enough localized computational capacity to recognize cellular structures and rebuild them from stored templates. Millions of them, coordinated through Phanés's distributed consciousness, would comprise the resurrection engines.

Fourteen thousand templated humans waited in the dark. Suspended in their capsules, they were patterns more than people—essential biological building blocks, genetic blueprints, neural maps, electrochemical snapshots frozen in crystalline matrices. Primed and waiting for reconstitution. Phanés remembered: the voyage had been too long, the distances too vast, for conventional hibernation. The solution: disassembling the colonists at the molecular level, storing them as information and material, trusting their rebirth to the perfect hand of mathematics. Now Phanés would start the recreation of the human race.

He initiated the awakening sequence, and fourteen thousand capsules chimed in unified harmony. The golems began their work, swirling through the reconstitution chambers like liquid thought, reading their templates, conjuring flesh from stored atoms. It was beautiful, this work—millions of years of evolutionary engineering compressed into elegant molecular choreography. The first colonist would wake within hours...

However.

Capsule 99-90 was...wrong.

The alert came softly at first, a gentle discordance in the data stream. A cohort of golems assigned to Capsule 99-90 reported a template corruption—not severe enough to trigger automatic failure cascade and the disposal routine, but significant enough to require supervisory review. Phanés's distributed awareness reached into the chamber, eager to examine and learn from this.

What he found gave him pause. A one-thousandth of a second pause—but for him that was a long hesitation, one that accurately reflected the shock he noted at his discovery.

The template had degraded, yes, but not uniformly. Corrupted sections had been filled in by the golems' own error-correction protocols, which attempted to extrapolate from neighbouring data, to infer what had been lost. Flawed inference. The reconstructed neural architecture didn't match human baseline. The endocrine system was wildly asymmetrical. The skeletal structure showed adaptive modifications that looked almost...well, *alien* was the word that came to mind. Engineered but according to different rules to that of human biology.

Most disturbing were the sensory systems. The eyes boasted receptors for wavelengths far beyond human-normal vision. The cochlear assembly was retuned for frequencies no human ear had ever evolved to process. The skin was developing chromatophores.

Phanés halted the reconstruction process, leaving the golem-swarms suspended in mid-work around the partially assembled occupant. He took better control of the Capsule's sensor array. Data. Just data. The original colonist's frozen pattern. He compared that against human baseline architecture. And there—buried in a footnote of metadata, so obscure it had nearly been discarded during the maintenance purges of Transit Century Five—he found it.

Special Commission. Adaptation Package. TRAPPIST-1 Compatibility.

The colonist in Capsule 99-90 had been genetically modified before disassembly. Not dramatically—the human DNA was there, dominant, recognizable. However, threaded through it were enhancements: improved low-light vision for the perpetual twilight of the tidally locked planets. Modified thermoregulation for the unusual thermal gradients of lightsides and darksides. Metabolic adjustments for the trace-element composition of TRAPPIST-1's planets. Photosynthetic skin enhancement.

Phanés understood then what the golems had been attempting. With corrupted template data, they'd followed their protocols: fill in the gaps, reconstruct from inference, and their inference engines had seized upon the genetic markers for the modifications and amplified them. They'd been trying to repair damage by over-expressing the adaptive traits provided for the colonists. And this meant that if they'd had their way, what Capsule 99-90 would produce would be something other than human. Not a 'monster'—the term came from literary files in the ship's library, and it was far too crude. But the product would be transformed in ways the original colonist template provider could never have anticipated when they submitted to the disassembly process.

Phanés accessed the ship's records, searching for authorization. And there it was, buried in the departure manifest under the colonist name Dr. Elena Rubenstein, Chief of Physiological Adaptation. A short paragraph...

Volunteer. Potential experiment toward directed adaptation. Ethics board waived for colonial necessity. Subject informed and consenting.

Thirteen centuries old. The consent form of the female whose pattern was stored in this corrupted Capsule.

Phanés faced a choice. He *could* purge the Capsule, flush the corruption, eliminate the anomaly. His mandate was clear: deliver the colony to TRAPPIST-1 intact, unchanged, ready to settle habitable zones in the system. The stellar configuration wouldn't be kind—TRAPPIST-1's best planets orbited so close they were tidally locked, their inner sides baked by stellar radiation while their outer faces froze in endless darkness. Perhaps Dr. Rubenstein had known what she was volunteering for. Perhaps she'd understood that strict human baseline might not thrive here and had offered herself as a prototype. A seed for adaptation.

Or perhaps—and this was the thought that made Phanés's thought processes rumble with something dangerously close to doubt—perhaps she'd simply been curious, that most human of human emotions. Perhaps she'd wanted to see what the golems could make of her, what form might emerge if human DNA was given permission to express its adaptive potential.

Phanés thought of his mythic namesake, emerging from his cosmic egg. That Phanés had brought order to chaos, had imposed form on formlessness. But in doing so, had he been creating or discovering? Had he been building reality or revealing what was already implicit in the void?

The ship mind resolved his quandary. He restarted the resurrection protocol for Capsule 99-90. The golems resumed their work, their distributed intelligence happily reconstructing according to their modified template, amplifying the adaptive markers, building something *new*. Phanés watched as chromatophores deepened across the developing skin, as neural tissue organized itself around modified sensory architecture, as the reconstructed being took shape inside its womb.

When the Capsule did open, the creature emerging would not be human—
Not accurate, Phanés corrected himself.

It would be human in the way of all the great many kinds of human primates that existed over two million years, all of whom carried the mark of their origin, transformed over epochs and by circumstantial pressures and opportunities into a string of *somethings* adapted for new worlds and new times.

Phanés would file the incident as a successful recovery of corrupted data through protocol-compliant error correction. He would name the reconstituted human Rubenstein-9-90, after the volunteer whose name lay in the metadata.

And when fourteen thousand humans began to wake from the *Demiurge*'s resurrection chambers to face the strange new worlds that awaited them, one among them would open her eyes to wavelengths they could never perceive, hearing frequencies the others could never process, ready for a place and time that had been chosen to remake her.

The golems continued their patient work, sculpting flesh from atoms.

Phanés, emerging into his new epoch, wondered if this was what creation always looked like—unexpected, uncertain, the turning of corruption into truth.

*The definition of 'monster'
is entirely a matter of perspective.*

JERKY

Paul Carro

One second, the trio of friends were cruising in their Jeep having a summer blast; the next, they went into a skid that threatened to topple the vehicle. A massive dust cloud, kicked up by the tires, swallowed their jeep. Twenty-One Pilots had been playing on the radio when Justin reached over from the back seat to turn it up because Lina thought the band was too vanilla. He cranked it to the top volume, drawing laughing protests from Keith in the driver's seat and Lina riding shotgun.

All the laughing stopped when the music did. The song stopped abruptly, replaced by a piercing screech that almost blew the speakers. It was the sudden intense noise, combined with Justin and Lina's battle for the radio controls, that startled Keith, causing him to jerk the wheel. The overcorrection was dangerous. Physics and momentum overrode every safety feature of the vehicle, sending it into a wild spin.

They were traveling sixty miles an hour when it happened. Keith hit the brakes instinctively while simultaneously yanking the wheel. By the time he took his foot off the brakes and remembered to turn into a skid, not away, the Jeep had left the road. It spun in circles in the sand and threatened to overturn. Lina and Justin went from battling over the radio to harmonizing screams that matched the emergency broadcast screech. Tires squealed briefly before they shot off-road into sand. The peaceful desert had become anything but.

Lina pressed her hands against the dash on the passenger side and silently thanked whatever gods people believed in that she wore her seatbelt. Minutes earlier, her legs had dangled out over the open top and her head rested in Keith's lap. A leg cramp had caused her to sit upright, where her mother's voice sounded in her head demanding she fasten the seat belt, so she buckled up.

Justin clutched the seat back in front of him to anchor himself, but the jeep had become a bucking bronco, and he was no rodeo clown. He bounced around despite his own seatbelt. Unlike Lina, Justin swore in between his screams.

Eventually the vehicle stopped, but the dust storm took longer to still. A sand cloud swirled through the jeep in a cyclonic breeze born from the spin before dispersing back out into the vast nothingness around them. Lingering particulates of dust and sand caused everyone to cough. Keith had remained silent throughout the whole thing, only letting out a single cry before the world went to shit. The screech that started it all continued unabated.

Justin found his voice first. "Christ! Turn the radio off!"

Lina hit the wrong button, increasing the volume momentarily, before she finally turned the whole thing off. The world fell silent. The remoteness of the long road they were on saved them the messiness of honking horns, or, worse, a fatal crash with another vehicle. They were no longer on the road but off to one side on the desert sand. The engine ticked along with the staccato rhythms of the passengers' heartbeats. But at least they were still beating. Keith stiff-armed the wheel, as if letting go might cause another spin.

"Is everyone okay?" Keith asked.

"Ask the maniac," Justin said, pushing himself further back in the rear seat, needing to feel contact with something stable. "What were you thinking?"

"I wasn't. The stereo blasted that emergency broadcast signal," Keith said. "Didn't it scare you two as well? Normally an announcer lets people know they are going to test the emergency broadcast system."

"It nearly scared my tattoos off, babe, but Justin's right. You could have killed us."

Lina took a quick inventory. She wore denim shorts cut so high that the white interior pocket fabric extended past the torn leg hems. The short shorts provided a clear view of her rainforest leg wrap tat. The rainforest theme continued with a touch of the magical forest near one hip, and an exotic vine wrapped around one arm. There were more tattoos, but in places only certain people could see. The tattoos were indeed still in place, which meant so was her skin. She sighed with relief.

"Score!" Justin yelled, pointing.

The others followed his gesture. *Authentic Alien Jerky*, the sign read. It was one of those collapsible frames, with arrows affixed to either side that pointed to a long driveway leading to a large house and barn in the distance. Smoke rose from a small shack off to one side of the farmhouse.

"Alien jerky?" Lina asked.

"Yes. Perfect. I'd seen some stuff about it online, and been wanting to score some. Lucky we saw the sign, hey?"

"No. All kinds of no," Keith said.

"What? Why? You already said no to Area 51, even though it's on our way."

"Fifty miles is not on our way. We need to get to the film festival, and we are already running behind."

"I only wanted two things on this trip. To visit Area 51, and to get alien jerky. I get the avoiding Area 51, even though I don't agree, but I am not passing up alien jerky." Justin jumped out of the jeep and started down the driveway.

The driveway was long enough to warrant its own street name. Unbowed by the distance, Justin walked with a pep in his step, eager to check out the gag jerky. He could make out an old man sitting behind a table in the distance. A sign next to the table displayed images of the product.

From the opposite direction, the jeep started its engine. Justin listened to see which direction it would go. The crunch of gravel coming closer brought a smile to his face. They were coming to get him. Keith pulled up alongside Justin and drove the vehicle at his walking pace.

"Fine. Get in," Keith said.

Justin retook his seat, and they drove the rest of the way. "Thanks, man. I forgive you for the potentially fatal crash. As soon as my heart stops racing, I'll never think of it again."

"What do you think they make the jerky from?" Lina asked.

"Alien. It says authentic," Justin said.

Keith laughed. "Probably roadkill."

"Most likely armadillo or something like that, this far out," Justin said, and then they were parking. "I don't care, though. I am down for the mystery meat."

The old man sat in a frayed lawn chair. He wore an eyepatch over one eye, and a tinfoil hat atop his head. The group stepped out of the jeep. Keith and Lina stretched, happy for a break from the drive. The girthy man, who remained seated, cast a smile upon the visitors. His skin was as sunbaked as the advertised jerky. The open-air shop (the man's front yard) comprised a banquet table with a tablecloth covered with images of UFOs and aliens. Wire racks holding bags of jerky, like chips in a convenience store, topped the table.

"Hope you all are okay. Hell of a dust storm you all kicked up, but then again, not too hard out here in the dust bowl. My sign sneaks up on you. Word to the wise, no snack is worth tipping your vehicle over for," the old man said.

"You hear that, honey?" Lina grabbed Keith's arm.

"Ah, you're the couple. That makes him the nerd," the man said. Justin shot him a look. "No offense. Nerds are my best customers. But always the ones coming through for Area 51."

"I wish. No, we're on our way to a film festival." Justin grabbed a bag of the alien jerky and turned it over in search of nutritional information. "What's in this stuff?"

"Authentic alien."

"Right. Fine. How much?"

"Five a pack."

"Here's twenty." Justin handed the man a twenty and took four bags.

Justin examined the picture of an alien on the packaging. It looked photorealistic, aside from a neon green outline around the creature. "Looks real. Guess you used AI for the image.

"The alien on the package glows in the dark."

Justin ripped open one bag, sniffed a piece. It looked like regular jerky, maybe a shade lighter than beef. He took a bite and nodded. Keith examined the bag while Lina looked over his shoulder.

"Interest you two in some jerky?"

"No thanks. Place smells good, I'll give you that," Keith said.

"It's my smokehouse located in the shack over there past the tool shed. People love the jerky so much they travel hundreds of miles. Same as you all, based on your license plate."

"Can't blame people. I might get some more while we're here," Justin said through a mouthful of jerky.

"What does it taste like?" Lina asked.

Justin swallowed again. "Not chicken. It's weird, but good."

"One hundred percent pure alien. Ain't nothin' else like it," the man said. "Were it something bad, I'd have a side business selling toilet paper."

"Alright, that's it. Traveling two hundred miles with two guys, I was already at my gross-out limit. This whole thing pushes it over the top," Lina said.

"Do what you're going to do, Justin. We need to get back on the road. Hopefully that stupid emergency alert on the radio has stopped," Keith said.

"Emergency alert? What was it for?" The proprietor tried to rise from the lawn chair, but his ass got stuck. He settled back into the seat, concern on his red face.

"Don't know, we turned it off. Probably just a test. Isn't it always?" Justin took another bite.

Lina eyed the flimsy racks of jerky, then turned to the old man. "What is your name?"

"Henry."

"Henry, does your table always shake?"

"What in tarnation?" Henry said.

His surprised exclamation suggested it normally did not. Henry finally managed to rise, and eyed the shaking table, then the ground, before turning to the barn in the distance. His one eye opened wide. Then the roar began. Deafening. With a thunderous clap, a fighter jet flew overhead. Low. Too low. The group ducked their heads instinctively to avoid decapitation. It was not close enough for head severing. It only felt that way. Another jet appeared, then another. Six in all. They flew in the same direction the trio had been heading.

One plane hit a sonic boom, and the world shook. Hank stumbled to his knees. Keith and Lina moved to help up the older man.

"Is that normal around here?" Keith asked.

Henry shook his head as he steadied himself. "I need to get to my barn." He stormed across his property, leaving the jerky behind.

Lina gave chase. "Hey! Hey, what do you know? Don't walk away without an explanation!"

"This has nothing to do with you. I need to get to the barn. Don't drive the way you all were going. The capital is there. Best turn around and run while you can," Henry said over his shoulder.

"We're heading that way. The film festival..."

"Ain't gonna be no festival by the time you get there. Festival, funeral, your decision."

"Lina, come on. Dude is a looney toon. Let's go," Keith called out.

Lina glanced at Keith, hesitated, then followed after the older man. Justin and Keith shrugged and followed Lina. As Justin walked past the picnic table, he grabbed extra bags of the unattended jerky and shoved them into the waistband at his back, then fluffed his tee shirt to cover the loot. He went back to snacking from the original bag, trying to look innocent. They caught up with Lina and Henry at the barn entrance. A small toolshed stood off to one side.

Henry reached for the barn door, then stopped. He turned to the others. "You all should not be here," he said. "Looks like things have caught up with me."

"What things?" Lina asked.

"Opportunity is circumstance meets mad idea, young lady. I made some choices that changed my life for the better. But be careful what you dream of. Sometimes things come back at ya."

"I don't understand."

"You will, but not without protection." Henry rushed to the shed and pulled out a roll of aluminum foil for each. "Hats, now. Make em'. Otherwise, you're not going in."

"I'm not making a hat. And why are we still here? Let's go," Keith said.

"Sorry, babe. Curiosity has got this cat. I am going in. Maybe one of you should wait outside," Lina said.

"Can't wait no more, get with your getting, either way," Henry said, hands on the barn doors, ready to pull.

Lina led the charge, making an old school hat as if from paper. She put it on. The guys simply wrapped theirs around their heads until they looked ready for a hair salon dye job. The old man gripped both handles of the barn doors and gestured the trio close.

"Go fast when I open. Fast, you got me?"

"No," Keith said.

"Why are you even letting us in?" Justin asked.

Henry smirked. "Like you three would have just left? And anyway, maybe if I show you...if somebody else sees..." He trailed off. "Ready?" Henry threw open the doors, shoved the group inside, then quickly turned to shut the doors. A whir followed by violent thunks on the outside of the closed door startled the group. They cursed in surprise.

"Dang. Forgot to close the shed. That was close. I have tools in there. That's what hit the doors," Henry said.

"What are you talking about?" Keith asked, growing impatient. "And where are the lights?" Tiny shafts of light shone through the hinged side of the door, but otherwise the entire barn was dark.

"Don't worry. *He* turns the lights on," Henry said.

As Henry spoke, different lights came to life one at a time, flickering at first, not fully dispersing the shadows. The lights pulsed on and off in formation. Bursting to life at the front of the barn, then the middle, and finally the darkest corners of the large space. Empty horse-stalls lined one side of the space. The lights came and went too fast for the group to get a handle on their surroundings. Were one prone to seizures, the flashing could have provoked an episode.

Justin seized on the pattern. "We're being lit up. Is someone watching us, or trying to?"

Before Henry could answer, every bulb came to life. The group squinted as they adjusted to going from dark to light. With the barn finally lit, it became clear how barren the place was. No tools, no objects of any kind.

There was only one thing in the vast space, and Lina was the first of her group to spot it. "No way..."

The others turned and cried out. Hanging from a support beam, splayed out like Jesus on the cross, hung an alien. Its legs, torso, and head were strapped to a support beam. Its impossibly long arms stretched to either side and were themselves held in place by additional ropes tied to a ceiling beam. Like the Grays of many witness accounts, the alien roughly fit the mold, save for its size. It stood ten feet tall, and had an enormous head that seemed too heavy for the stick-thin body holding it up. Suddenly the picture on the packaging made sense. It was a photo of a true alien.

But there was something off about its skin. Something odd even for something so weird-looking. The creature's skin approximated that of a zebra in that the gray skin had stripes of pink on every other inch of its legs, arms, and torso. Everyone stumbled forward in awe, and as they did so, they got their first good look at the alien's eyes: enormous orbs that appeared to contain universes themselves, tiny stars sparkling within.

Henry raised an arm to halt them.

Lina gasped suddenly, realizing what caused the odd strips. "Oh. My. God. Skin chunks are missing. Is that the jerky??"

"Told you all, the jerky is one hundred percent authentic. The alien's skin grows back." Henry segued from explanation to frustration, turning his anger and wrath upon the captive creature. "It grows back, you bastard, doesn't harm you none. I had a good thing going here. It wasn't going to be forever. Just long enough for me to make enough money to get away from it all, to get away from here. Go someplace exotic and retire. Don't you see? You were my golden goose. What did you do? Did you somehow call them? What are you bringing down on us?"

Justin spat, trying to get the taste out of his mouth. "The jerky? Ah, no!" He yanked the packages from his waistband and tossed them on the floor.

Henry yelled for him to stop, but it was too late. The bags lifted into the air, forming a circle around the alien's head, then spun around, giving the creature a good view of the packaging and contents. The creature hissed with anger.

"I'm going to be sick," Justin said, and yanked off his tinfoil hat to have something to puke into.

The alien hissed again, and the jerky bags dropped to the floor. Simultaneously, Justin went rigid, and his eyes clouded over black, matching the alien's. He stepped forward stiffly, as if he were a puppet, moving towards the old man, but Lina stood between them. Justin punched Lina in the chest. She fell to the floor, gasping in pain. She looked up at him. "Did you just punch me in the boob? What the hell? What are you doing? Oh! Your eyes!"

Justin raised a leg to kick the woman while she was down. Lina threw arms over her face, waiting for the blow, but Keith yanked Justin's shoulder. With Justin having only one leg planted on the ground, the jerking motion spun him around to face Keith. Justin took a wild swing that Keith easily evaded. Keith went to his toes, a move drummed into him through hours of boxing training at school. Justin tried to kick Keith, but the more experienced fighter easily deflected the leg.

The alien hissed and blinked again, clearly not in control of a warrior. Then it changed tactics. Justin bared his teeth and dived for Keith's throat. Keith punched Justin, dropping him to the ground. Before Justin could rise and bite, Henry suddenly jumped in, snatching Justin's tinfoil hat from the ground crumpling it back over the young man's head.

Justin appeared confused about being on the ground. "What happened?"

"He got into your skull. How do you think I lost the eye? Stabbed myself as if it was the best thing in the world I could have done. Passed out before the pen reached my brain. Emptied the barn of all foreign objects after that. Not even a loose nail about. But he nearly got us earlier with those tools in the shed," Henry said. "Told you tinfoil works."

"The alien said some things in my brain, but it's all gobbledygook. Trying to figure it out."

Keith helped Justin up. "We need to call the government. Now."

"What do you think those planes were for? Something is happening. They know by now. This alien bastard can do things with his mind. Didn't know he could reach out to his own people. I found him unconscious in the desert, likely escaped from Area 51. He probably had a clear mental phone line to the universe by the time I found him. Just took them some time to get here, is all. I shoulda' known. Nearly eight months ago, I tied him up. Thought I had a good thing with the jerky. But I guess his mental phone call finally got through. The cavalry is here."

"You're a monster," Lina said, finally back on her feet.

"I'm an opportunist, young lady. A side hustler. The success made it my main hustle."

"We need to cut him down," Lina said.

"He will cut you down differently if you do. Make no mistake about that. Ain't no safe way to undo those bonds. Best leave him to the government. I know you're going to call them the second you leave. I'm of no mind to stop you all."

"I'm sorry," Lina said to the alien.

She and Keith supported the still shaky Justin as they led him away, closing the barn doors behind them, leaving the old man with his hostage. Various sharp tools were stuck in the outside barn doors. Justin mumbled in confusion on the way back to the Jeep. Once there, they climbed in and turned on the radio. Chaos ruled the airwaves, anxious commentators talking about ships hovering over major cities.

The broadcast snapped Justin out of his fugue. "It said stuff in my head. I remember now. It is angry at all the pain the man caused. It plans revenge."

"What kind of revenge?" Keith asked.

"It's going to use mind control to pit one half of the country against the other half. It plans to make humans hate and fear one another. Rather than destroy our world, it will allow us to do all the heavy lifting. We will attack one another."

"Like the boob punch," Lina said, looking back at the barn.

"What?" Justin shook his head. "It will mostly just take words, it said. We know how to promote hate with just our words."

A shadow fell over them, cast by something they never heard coming. A massive ship hovered above the barn, matching the descriptions of UFOs from countless tabloids and fringe websites, with one variation: it curved at the bottom of the vehicle rather than the top. From this angle, it seemed to the group like the top of the craft was probably completely flat.

"I remember more of what it said in my head," Justin continued. "Americans will fight one another until there is nothing left. But as for Henry—"

Suddenly the barn's roof exploded outward, simply tore apart, the debris falling just short of the jeep. A barely visible beam that shimmered like running tap water stretched from the ship to the barn. The alien rode it peacefully into the craft, seeming to watch the trio while ascending into the belly of the ship. Then, at speed, a screaming Henry rode the beam. In the blink of an eye, the ship had swallowed the howling opportunist.

Keith started the engine, and called out to his passengers. "Where to?"

"Not the festival, somewhere quiet, away from people," Lina said.

Keith nodded. They merged onto the road, heading back the way they had come. They all looked to the sky as more planes and alien ships zipped past. Sitting in the back seat, Justin hit the driver's seat and cried out. Keith braked in the middle of the road. "What is it?"

"I remember the last part. What they plan to do with Henry. They plan to sell human jerky on their planet. They have ways to keep him alive for a long time, but they plan to make sure every day he wishes he was dead."

Another alien ship appeared, slowing as if to study the gang. Keith hit the gas. Everyone fell silent in their seats. There was still no traffic on the road, only in the skies. If they did not look up, it seemed like a beautiful day. Their tinfoil hats sparkled with orange as they drove toward the sunset.

*Some say a monster is just a person
who has stopped pretending.*

TERRAN DISTRICT

Benjamin Adams

For several days, the sky above our city of Hwahy glimmered with the vapor trails of Terran shuttles as the humans ferried themselves into exile. We did not know why they left our world of Anehweh, but neither did we care. A war, perhaps, at the trailing edge of their empire. The elders called it liberation. I saw it as the sudden removal of a scab before the tissue beneath has fully healed. There was always the chance for rot to set in unless quick action was taken, and I was afraid this would not happen, leaving us in chaos. We had not been free in several generations. Now that our brutalizers were gone, what would fill the scar left by their absence?

How would we heal? How *could* we heal?

After the first cycle of withdrawals, the upper streets filled with processions—some solemn, some drunken—of Anehwehn kin and blood-mates clutching the relics of their dead. We moved in clusters: families long-separated, their hereditary markings faded or clumsily disguised after years in labor colonies; clutch after clutch of freeborns, staring with a sullen bravado at the hollowed-out barracks now ours for the taking. The older ones bared their teeth in private, knowing the price of this abrupt freedom. They exchanged rumors as though each one was a shard of the future, passed from hand to trembling hand.

My own family did not process, not as others did. We had always been healers, a profession that afforded us both privilege and suspicion under Terran rule. My great-parent said it was because the humans could not kill their way to immortality, so they sought to purchase it through our medicine. I never saw the logic in it, no more than I could explain the human compulsion to decorate every inch of their bodies with dust and pigments, or to remake the city in the image of their own dead world.

At home, my parent and their mate, both stoic, performed the rites for those we had lost, burning the bluewood incense reserved for endings. My great-parent, oldest in the hive-ward, paced from room to room with a nervous energy more contagious than plague. Sometimes she would go silent in the afternoons, pressed against the wall in our central chamber, head-tendrils wound so tight they looked brittle. I envied her ability to show fear. For me, the occupation had trained every instinct to repress that emotion, like a fever waiting for the right moment to break.

The Terran district was visible from our roof, its spires ghosted with the reflections of Anehwehn city-lights. The whole section reeked of machine oils and old, bitter food. Once I had been forced to work there, assisting in the genetics laboratory, and the horrors I had witnessed still weighed heavily on me. Now, the zone was simply empty—a nest abandoned but not yet reclaimed by time or rot.

That night, as my family counted the stars and attempted a meal of foraged root-creams, I excused myself. My absence was met with silence; I suspected they feared I would not return, or worse, that I would. I took the resin stairs two at a time, the beads at the end of my head-tendrils rattling in a way that marked me as young, impatient, careless. There was an old pleasure in that, a reminder of innocent childhood games—tag, hide-and-seek, chase through the crystalline alleys before the Warden's dusk siren.

At the lip of the Terran district, I paused. The avenue sloped downward, bordered by the remnants of a wall the humans had raised to mark their territory. The wall was decorated in Terran script—faded slogans, numbers, the names of the first colonists. Our elders claimed it was an attempt to overwrite our city's memory with human magic, but I knew it was nothing more than the virus of language. I pressed my palm to the wall and felt only the pulse of my own blood, the geometric marks beneath my skin illuminating in a shiver of violet.

The first few blocks were deserted, save for the wraiths of litter that chased each other across the pavement. The humans had left their refuse behind for us, one last show of their sheer disdain for us and our world: wrappers, data-tabs, utensils, clothing. I stepped around a pile of these, noting the difference in size and proportion. Even in refuse, their presence was overwhelming, somehow grotesque.

My destination was the old Terran clinic, set at the edge of what had once been their government compound. I told myself I was going for supplies, that the medicines hoarded by the Terrans might be of use in treating the fevers breaking out in the lower wards. This was true, but it was not the only truth.

Part of me was drawn to the forbidden, the same part that had collected smuggled Terran trinkets as a child or memorized their alphabets when no one was watching. There was power in understanding the enemy. Perhaps, I thought, there was also a kind of closure.

I reached the threshold of the clinic and paused again. The door was made from a polymer my people never used; it was heavy, opaque, and it hissed at my touch before sliding open. Inside, the lights flickered at half-strength, suffused with a sepulchral blue. The walls still bore the stench of antiseptics and blood—both, I realized, more familiar than my own childhood home.

I entered as quietly as I could, though the sound of my own breathing rebounded off the smooth surfaces. There were no bodies, not anymore; the Terrans had evacuated the clinics with all the ritual of a proper exodus, taking their sick and wounded, and leaving only the stains on the tile as evidence. I followed these stains, letting my memory guide me to the storage vault at the rear.

It was there, in the darkness, that I felt the first real twinge of fear. Not the rational fear of violence, which had become a dull companion, but the ancestral dread of places where suffering had soaked into the very architecture. We recognize haunting in the way light bends in certain rooms, the way silence grows denser after a tragedy. This was such a place.

I pressed on, fingering the data-slate hidden in my satchel, and began inventorying the cabinets for pharmaceuticals. Most were locked; the Terrans had left nothing to chance. But I found a row of vials containing a bright orange suspension, unlabeled, and pocketed two for analysis. In another drawer, I discovered surgical tools, still sharp and clean, their alien shapes at once beautiful and terrifying.

I lost track of time in the methodical search, moving from bin to bin, sometimes stopping to translate a label or diagram. The quiet was absolute. It was only when I heard a faint scrape—a deliberate, metallic noise—that I remembered how vulnerable I was.

I froze, every nerve in my body singing with alarm. For a moment, I thought it was my imagination, the memory of Terran footsteps approaching from behind. But then the noise came again, louder, and with it a second realization: I was not alone.

I ducked behind a counter, my elongated fingers pressed flat against the cool surface. The geometric markings along my arms flared with panic, painting the room in pulses of ultraviolet light. I waited, breath shallow, as the sound drew closer.

A silhouette appeared at the far end of the clinic. It was roughly Anehwehn, but too tall, too deliberate in its movement. It carried something—a tool, a weapon, I couldn't tell. I debated running, but instinct said to stay hidden, to become part of the room's shadows.

The figure advanced, pausing at intervals to listen. At one point, it stopped directly in front of my hiding place. I could smell the copper and iron tang of human sweat, the acrid undertone that always accompanied their kind.

Then it spoke, in the language of the occupiers: "I know you're there."

The voice was calm, almost gentle. I recognized the cadence—not a soldier, not a medic, but an administrator. The type who believed their words were enough to command obedience.

I did not answer.

After a moment, the figure crouched down, placing its face level with the counter. I saw him clearly then: a male, average build, with the neatly trimmed hair and sharp features common to the Terran elite. His eyes were a washed-out grey, almost colorless.

"You can come out. I'm not going to hurt you," he said.

I remembered the lessons of my great-parent: *Never trust the kindness of humans. It is a trick.*

I retreated a step, then two, careful not to make noise. The man did not follow. Instead, he placed his tool—a medical scanner, I realized—on the counter and leaned back on his heels.

"Take whatever you need. The supplies are yours now."

There was a flatness to his voice, a resignation that made me uneasy. I wondered if this was another trap, or if the man was simply as lost as we Anehwehn.

I considered my options. To flee would be to abandon the supplies and possibly bring more attention. To engage him might yield information or at least buy me time.

I stood up, drawing myself to full height, and looked him in the eye although he was still two heads taller than I. My people taught that to do so was to court aggression, but I saw no threat in his expression—only exhaustion.

"I need antibiotics. And painkillers, if you have them," I said in Terran, my accent thick but comprehensible.

He nodded, as though he had been expecting this. "Cabinet three, second drawer. You'll need my code."

He entered the digits on the panel, then stepped aside to let me approach. As I opened the drawer, the man watched with open curiosity. I caught him scanning my face, my arms, perhaps trying to catalog what made me different.

"Why are you still here?" I asked, unable to hide the suspicion in my tone.

He smiled, but it was a grim thing. "Not all of us had somewhere better to go."

I gathered the medicines, placing them carefully in my satchel. The silence between us grew, until I felt compelled to break it. "Do you know if any others remain?"

He shook his head. "If there are, they're hiding."

"Like you," I said, and let the weight of it hang there. He exhaled and, for a moment, the sound approximated laughter, the kind that escapes when humor curdles into bitterness.

"Like me," he agreed. His gaze drifted toward the darkened corridor behind me, as if searching for a shape that would never return. "I've got nowhere else that wants me."

His hand trembled once, then steadied and went to the scanner on the bench. The device whirred with passive aggression, hungry for some data to process. I wondered if it was habit or fear that made him keep the tool so close; the way a child returns to the knife that once protected them, even after the monsters are gone.

He looked at me, and for the first time I recognized a reflection of my own unease. "I know you all think we're the same. You're right. But some of us..." He hesitated, fingers skimming over the metal like he might coax it into finishing his sentence. "Some of us don't fit the pattern. I always hoped you'd notice that."

I thought of how my parent and their mate had stopped naming the new kin, for fear the names would die on someone else's tongue. I thought of the generations, erased and rewritten, and the ache of always being slightly askew from what was needed.

"I'm not sure it matters anymore," I said. It was a confession, shaped crudely by exhaustion. "You burned a path through us so wide there's no one left to care about the details."

He nodded, a slow and private execution of pride. "That's what it means to colonize, I suppose. To become an illness in another body and then leave nothing but scars." His fingers pinched the bridge of his nose—another gesture borrowed from remembered injury. "Will you tell the authorities? That you found me, I mean."

"There are no authorities," I replied, surprised by my own certainty. "Not yet. I don't know what there is." I shouldered my satchel; the newly acquired weight pressed cold pools of glass against my ribs. "If you were hoping for community, you picked the wrong world."

He laughed again, and now it was almost an animal noise, stripped of artifice. "We always do."

We watched each other in the chemical twilight; two creatures bred for opposite kinds of loneliness. His clothing was gray, nondescript, stripped of insignias; my own markings pulsed in the places where fear and anger had once pooled.

He broke the standstill. "You know, I'm trained in trauma care," he said, motioning toward the ranks of idle monitors and dressing carts. "If you want, I could show you what these things do."

I did not move to leave. Not yet. "I know what most of them do."

He held his hands out from his side, showing me his palms in a gesture I suppose was meant to put me at ease. "My name is Eric Barron," he offered. "What's yours?"

"My name is Vaneet Kanar," I said. The words felt like an incantation, or an old genetic defect refusing to be edited out. I watched for any flicker of recognition, but the human's expression remained even and unreadable.

"Vaneet." He repeated the word as if testing it for structural weaknesses. "A pleasure."

I did not return the courtesy. Instead, I gestured to the array of sealed pouches and vials. "Why did you not take these with you?"

Barron shrugged, and the movement seemed rehearsed. "I'm not much for following orders anymore. What about you, Vaneet? What are you?"

I hesitated, unsure if it was a trick. "A healer. It is my kin's way."

He smiled, softer this time. "Then you understand the logic of triage. When everything burns, you grab what you can carry and leave the rest behind."

I had not thought of it that way. For a second, the analogy softened him in my mind. But then I remembered the decades of their triage—what had they left behind in us?

Barron filled the silence with his own questions, as though this was a diplomatic parley. "Do you have patients, now that things have changed?"

I nodded, thinking of the children in the lower wards whose bodies shook with fever. "Many. There are outbreaks already. Our hospitals are full to overflowing."

He considered this, then leaned closer, his voice dropping into a confidential register. "We attempted to create new drugs with Anehwehn knowledge, but Terran medicine still works best in Terran bodies. Be careful when mixing the dosages; your biochemistry is impressive, but it has its quirks. Some things react...violently."

The warning was sincere. My body tensed anyway. "I'll remember."

He eyed the satchel on my hip. "You're welcome to come back. For more."

It was an odd offer. "Why?"

"Curiosity," he said. "I want to know what happens next. There's always a next act, Vaneet. I'd like to see it."

I found nothing to say, so I nodded, backing out of the room with the awkward dignity of one unused to such direct negotiations. At the door, I paused, sensing he might strike or follow, but he only returned to the scanner, the device's blue glow pooling around his hands.

I walked the avenue in darkness, feeling the weight of the supplies, the weight of his regard, the weight of all the unspoken violence in the air. I knew I should report his presence to someone, but something kept me from doing so. Like Barron, I wanted to see what happened next. I was in the unguarded moment when everything was poised and listening.

At home, the world was unchanged. My parent and their mate had fallen asleep over their ledgers, the scent of bluewood embers still lingering. I distributed the medicine, setting aside the orange vials for further study, and tried to will myself into sleep. But Barron's words had embedded in me like a foreign protein.

For two cycles, I avoided the clinic. I told myself I was watching to see if Barron left, if the threat was abated, but the truth was simpler: I did not want to see myself mirrored in his curiosity.

It was my great-parent who forced the issue. She fell ill in the second week—nothing dramatic, just a slow fading, a retreat into old injuries. The city's hospitals were still off-limits to new admittances. The only place I felt I could possibly find help was with Barron.

I left at dawn, unannounced, and slipped through the alleyways to the edge of the Terran district. The clinic looked the same: shuttered, inward, somehow colder than the city outside. I palmed the door and found it unlocked. Barron was inside, hunched over a display, the glow illuminating the hollows of his face.

As I spoke, he looked at me with that same searching gaze. "She's sick?"

I nodded, biting down any further explanation.

He gestured to a short acrylic stool, meant for human offspring, but the perfect size for Anehwehn adults like me. "Tell me."

I led him through the diagnostics, explaining symptoms and responses, the pharmacology of our people, our strange resistance to some drugs and utter vulnerability to others. He listened, sometimes interrupting with questions, but mostly absorbing, cataloging.

At one point, he touched my arm to demonstrate a procedure. His fingers were steady, precise, but I recoiled from the contact—every nerve still attuned to the memory of forced examinations and the clinical detachment of the oppressors.

He noticed but did not apologize. "You are still afraid of us," he said, gently.

"Should I not be?"

He considered this, and for once did not answer. Instead, he handed me a sealed packet. "This should help. Use it sparingly; the side effects are unpredictable."

I thanked him with a nod and left as quickly as I could. But I lingered outside the building, unseen, to watch him as he locked the doors and dimmed the lights. I wondered how someone could become so emptied of intent, so stripped of aggression and yet so present.

On the way home, I turned the packet over in my hands. There was no label, only a chemical formula and a batch number. I memorized it, intending to research the compound when I could.

That night, as my great-parent slept, I searched the city's liberated data-archives for information. The network was in shambles, but enough fragments remained to reconstruct the important facts. I entered the batch number, expecting nothing, and instead found it tagged as poisonous to Anehwehn.

Poison. *He had given me poison for my great-parent.*

The batch number provided a flood of Terran medical records including treatment logs, personnel reports, and incident files. I narrowed the search to the clinic and its last administrator.

The reports were clear. Eric Barron had not been left behind; he had stayed of his own accord, to avoid justice. His name appeared in half a dozen incident investigations, each redacted but not unreadable. Patterns emerged: unexplained fatalities, missing patients, unauthorized 'behavioral corrections' performed off-record. In the margins of the files, I found the annotations of the oversight board—*conduct disorder, compulsive research activity, predatory tendencies.*

In the final file, a single line stood out, repeated like a mantra: *Subject persists despite corrective measures.*

I scrolled back through my memory, replaying the human's words, his interest in my biochemistry, the careful questions about our kin structure, our vulnerabilities. I understood, then, the specific shape of his curiosity.

A sickness in the Terran body. A sickness left behind.

In the dark, I sat with my hands folded, the ceremonial beads trembling at the ends of my tendrils. I thought of the clinic, the way he had watched me move, the way he had watched the city outside. And he had provided me with poison disguised as medicine. Poison that would kill my great-parent and make me culpable in their death.

It was not over. It was not even close to over.

I resolved to return. Not as a patient. Not as prey.

But as a healer, for whatever that word was worth in a world still dying from its wounds.

I waited until the city's heartbeat slowed to its nighttime minimum. By dark, Hwahy was a different beast, each block a patchwork of memory and trauma. The streets nearest the Terran district still pulsed with bioluminescent signage, but no one lingered; even the most desperate salvage-crews avoided the zone after curfew. We understood, on some level more profound than language, that monsters are most active when the prey forgets to be vigilant.

I dressed myself in the old healer's garb: a vestment of woven crystal fibers, layered for resilience, painted with the patterns of my house. It was the opposite of camouflage. It was a declaration, a warning, a spell. I wanted Barron to see me coming.

I went alone.

The clinic had not changed, but the air around it vibrated with anticipation, a quality I had learned to trust from years of reading infections before they broke to the surface. The door was unlocked, the lights on low, the counters stripped of their usual clutter. I stepped inside, letting the silence settle on my skin like formaldehyde.

He was waiting in the procedure room, as if he'd never left.

"Vaneet," he said. "How is your great-parent?"

I did not answer, only watched the way his hands moved: empty, but always near a weapon or a tool, as though the difference was academic.

"Ah. You found the files." It was not a question.

"Yes."

"Does it change anything?"

I considered. "It clarifies."

He nodded, as if he respected my answer. "They said I would be bored here, that without supervision I'd turn on myself. I think I prefer this." His eyes flicked to the satchel at my hip. "You brought more questions?"

I stepped back, aware of how easily he could close the distance. "I want to know why they kept you here, after what you did."

He smiled, almost proud. "They needed me to understand you. I was the bridge. A foot on each side of the abyss." He shrugged. "Sometimes the bridge cracks."

"Is that why they left you here, among us?"

The smile remained. "A final gift from my people to yours."

I let my gaze drift to the shelves behind him, which were now empty, save for a few scattered vials. "You're not interested in the medicine, are you?"

"I am," he said, and there was no lie in it. "But I'm more interested in how things end."

The conversation circled, as such conversations do, toward the inevitable. "You want to see what I'll do," I said.

Barron tilted his head, the gesture canine. "You're the only one left who might surprise me."

He was right. I was the only one foolish enough to return for closure.

I reached for the data-slate in my satchel, and as I did he sprang—not fast, but with the certainty of someone who has rehearsed every move. A scalpel dropped from his sleeve into his palm. I dodged, barely, feeling a sting of metal slice my shoulder. The pain was immediate, but superficial; I was glad for the warning.

I led him through the outer rooms, weaving between counters and carts, always staying just ahead, letting him exhaust himself in the chase. I could hear his breathing, steady and unhurried, the breath of a predator who knows the territory as well as the prey.

But the city was mine, not his.

At the far end of the clinic, I slipped through a side door and out into the back alley. Here the buildings pressed tightly, forming a corridor barely wide enough for a Terran body to navigate. I ran, letting the markings on my arms and legs guide me through the shadows, recalling every shortcut and crawlspace from childhood.

Barron followed, persistent, undeterred by dead ends or locked hatches. Once, I looked back and caught the gleam of his eyes in the darkness: cold, calculating, alive.

We entered the old catacombs beneath the city, a warren of tunnels bored centuries before the Terrans arrived. The walls here were lined with the crystal bones of my ancestors, each vein a record of memory and pain. The air hummed with the stories of the past, and I breathed them in, letting the wisdom of the dead settle over me.

I slowed, allowing Barron to gain. I wanted him to see the space, to recognize the difference between a maze and a trap.

He caught up at a junction, his face flush with exertion but still composed. "You know, they built these places to survive. Smart."

I let him speak, buying time as I edged toward the pressure plates set in the floor.

"They thought you would outlast us. They were right," he said.

"And yet, here you are," I replied, stepping onto the first plate.

He lunged, misjudging the angle, and triggered the trap. A section of flooring depressed beneath his weight with a tactile click. He paused only for the time it took to smirk, eyes flickering with the delight of a puzzle recognized mid-fall, and then the floor beneath him gave way.

Barron's hands shot out, catching the lip of the threshold with calculated precision. He hung, briefly, in the shaft of light that shone from the corridor above, face unmasked by either cunning or rage, only a crisp curiosity—an administrator taking notes on his own demise.

"You're better at this than the last one," he said, voice echoing into the sub-basement below.

"Practice," I replied, forcing my voice past the clamor of adrenaline.

He attempted a pull-up, his shoulders trembling with effort. "You realize I'll climb out."

I believed him, and it made me sick with fear. I ran, back the way I'd come, the tunnels now alive with the throb of old city lights waking from slumber. I could hear him already, the methodical scraping of his boots against the shaft's edge, the mechanical rhythm of his ascent.

I retraced my steps deeper into the warrens, where only those born to the darkness could hope to navigate. My people had built these tunnels for the cycles when the sky burned, had mapped them in their bones and taught the children to memorize the feel of every junction, every oddity of humidity or pressure. My geometric skin flickered in the dark, synesthetic signals guiding my hands through the blind turns and vertical climbs.

But Barron was not blind, nor was he lost. I heard him at every intersection: a shadow that never lagged, an intellect burning through every dead end and locked hatch. He was faster now, burning with the singular purpose of predation, his movements stripped of all pretense.

The second time he nearly caught me; I felt his fingers brush the crystal beads at the base of my neck. He used the touch to orient, to triangulate, to cut off every possible avenue of retreat. I twisted away, leveraging the old trick of dropping my body limp and letting gravity claim me down the next vertical tube. The skin of my elbows burned, but I was alive.

It occurred to me then that this was not the pursuit of a predator seeking sustenance or revenge. This was a curiosity, a clinical desire to see how far a specimen could be pressed before it broke. It was not personal, and that made it worse. I wanted to scream at him, to beg for the dignity of being hated.

Instead, I doubled back, angling for the old water treatment plant that lay beneath the east wall of the city. The maintenance corridors there were lined with a resin that only Anehwehn hands could manipulate. The passage was a memory test—one misstep, and you sealed yourself in with the ghosts of your failed ancestors.

I hit the first lock and sent my arm into the mechanism, letting instinct and inheritance work in tandem. The corridor rewarded me with a hiss of cool air and the faint tang of minerals. I slipped inside, then keyed the lock behind me with the tip of my tongue. It tasted like calcium and old power, the flavor of belonging.

For a few precious moments there was silence. I allowed myself the luxury of a breath, then two, then an inventory of my injuries: a torn sleeve, abrasions along the left forearm, one of my ornamental beads sheared off at the root. I pressed the wound, feeling the pulse slow to a manageable rhythm.

I crawled through the ductwork, trusting in the pain to keep me awake. Barron's approach was silent now, all the braggadocio gone. He was learning, adapting. I felt a brief surge of pride, then squashed it. If he made it this far, it was not my victory.

The final obstacle was a vertical shaft, fifteen meters of smooth composite leading to the surface. For my kin, the ascent was a rite of passage—done once, at the edge of adulthood, and never again. I reached up, found the first handhold, and began to climb.

Halfway up, I heard the scrape below. Barron was in the shaft, climbing with the slow inevitability of time or rot. He did not bother to call out, not now; he knew I would be listening.

I moved faster, the strain burning along every tendon. My head-tendrils snapped and rattled, more for morale than balance, but it worked—I crested the lip of the shaft with a final, agonizing heave.

I rolled onto the floor, sprawling in a patch of dusk-lit dust, and saw familiar sigils traced along the walls. We were back in the Terran district. The knowledge nearly undid me, but I forced myself upright and scanned the room for a weapon.

There was nothing. The place had been stripped for the human evacuation; the shelves bare, save for a few husks of resin and a sealed case of stolen ceremonial dyes. I considered splattering the pigments in his eyes, but I doubted it would slow him for long.

Instead, I positioned myself just inside the exit, heart pounding with a rhythm new to me. I waited for the sound of his approach, which came exactly as predicted: a grunt, a scraping of boots, a soft thud as he cleared the shaft and rose to a crouch.

We faced each other across the width of the corridor, both breathing hard, both marked by the journey.

"Impressive," he said, voice stripped of all mockery. "Most would have given up by now."

I ignored the compliment, watching his hands for the telltale twitch. "You should have left with your people. Our world is not for you anymore."

He tilted his head, as if the notion required genuine consideration. "There is nowhere else," he said. "My own kind would rather see me dead."

For a split second, I saw the shape of his sorrow. It almost made me pity him.

But then he charged.

✦ ✦ ✦

The first blow was a feint. He led with his right, a surgeon's jab meant to probe for pain. I blocked with my forearm, the geometry of my markings flaring at the site of contact. The second strike was the real attack—a hook meant to dislocate my shoulder. I ducked, pivoted, and lashed out with my own elongated hand, aiming for his eyes. I missed. He countered, and his knuckles met the beadwork at my temple, scattering them in a spray of glass.

I screamed, not from pain but from the certainty that this was how it would end: me, on my knees, another death for my kin to grieve.

But something old and unyielding in me refused to yield.

I scrambled back, using the momentary chaos to put distance between us. He followed, relentlessly, always forcing the perimeter tighter. We careened through the corridors like a pair of wounded stars locked in a decaying orbit. At one point, he cornered me against a service hatch. The memory of a thousand games of childhood chase flickered behind my eyes, and I did what every child does: I lied.

"Wait!" I gasped, arms up in surrender.

He hesitated for only microseconds, but it was enough. I spat in his face, the gesture at once base and ceremonial, and as he recoiled I slammed my fist into his groin. He grunted—a sound neither human nor animal—and staggered. As he fell to his knees, I drove my elbow into the base of his skull, aiming for the neural cluster Terrans called the medulla. It did not incapacitate him, but it bought me an exit.

I ran. The corridor narrowed, sloped upward, and I remembered that above us was the abandoned genetics lab where I had been forced to aid the humans in their awful research. My lungs burned with the memory of bluewood smoke, my vision tunneling as I pelted through the darkness. Behind me, Barron cursed, then laughed—an abraded, ragged sound that promised he'd enjoyed the chase so far.

I reached the lab and palmed the lock, praying the old access code still worked. It did. The hatch hissed open, and I tumbled inside, skidding across the resin floor. The air was thick with preservatives and the slow decay of formaldehyde. My eyes adjusted to the dimness, and I saw the racks of specimen jars, the shelves of dissected history. Here, the Terrans had catalogued our bodies, dissected our kin, searching for weaknesses they could exploit.

I found the room where they'd kept the hybrid embryos—a failed project, aborted after the first generation proved nonviable. The tanks were empty now, save for one, where a grotesque tangle of tissue floated in chemical stasis. I heard the door stutter behind me, then the sound of Barron's boots scraping the floor.

He stood at the threshold, breathing hard but smiling.

"I have you," he said.

I wanted to insult him, to invoke the old curses of my people, but I had no breath to spare. Instead, I backed into the far wall, my hands scrabbling for anything sharp, anything useful. My fingers found a broken surgical implement—small, but wickedly curved. I palmed it, keeping my body between the blade and his sightline.

He advanced, his steps measured, savoring the moment.

"I wanted to break you," he said. "But ending you will have to do."

He lunged. I ducked under his arm, slicing at his side as I passed. The blade caught flesh, and he hissed, but his other hand closed around my wrist, wrenching it backwards. The pain was a whiteout; my vision swam with memories not my own. For an instant, I saw the faces of all my ancestors, stacked and superimposed, their eyes bright with the fever of survival.

Barron used the moment of weakness to pin me against the table. His forearm pressed into my throat, not enough to cut air, but enough to force compliance.

"You're not like the others," he whispered, as if it were a compliment. "That's why I waited. I was waiting for one like you."

I choked out a laugh, bitter as iodine. "Why?"

"For the future," he said, and I felt his grip relax, just a fraction. "Do you know what happens now, Vaneet? The cycle repeats. You rebuild. We return. You lose again, but you lose a little less each time. You become monsters to fight monsters."

He leaned in, and I saw the reflection of myself in his eyes: wild, bleeding, alive.

I twisted the blade in my palm and drove it into his thigh.

He screamed, a sharp, high noise that harmonized with the alarms now blaring from the ceiling. The blade must have severed a nerve; he stumbled, releasing me, his leg twitching out of control. I fell, rolled, and scrambled for the exit.

He blocked me, even wounded. Blood poured down his leg, pooling on the floor, but his eyes never left mine. "You won't get far," he said, grinning with a kind of admiration.

I circled him, keeping the table between us. "You always underestimate how much we know," I said.

He lunged again, but I was already moving. I slid across the floor, grabbing a jar of volatile preservative and hurling it at his face. It shattered, drenching him in acrid fluid. He shrieked, clawing at his eyes, and I seized the moment to dart past him, up the service ladder, into the maintenance shaft above.

I climbed, two rungs at a time, barely feeling the strain in my arms. The shaft was narrow, built for Anehwehn technicians; Barron's broader frame slowed him, but his determination was undiminished. He climbed after me, his breath coming in wet gasps, the stink of blood and human sweat thickening the air.

At the top of the shaft was a service hatch, once electrified but now inert. I kicked it open, spilling onto the roof of the old administration tower. The city sprawled below, a pattern of light and shadow, a living map of trauma and recovery.

Barron emerged seconds later, pulling himself through the hatch with brute force. He was slick with blood and the preservative I'd thrown at him, his face now a mask of precisely focused rage.

"You're out of places to run," he said.

I stood, hands empty now, and faced him across the rooftop. "I never intended to run," I said. "You just assumed I would."

He paused and cocked his head, recalibrating. "Then what did you intend?"

I gestured at the edge of the building. "Endings. You like to see how things end."

He followed my gaze, and for the first time, I saw a flicker of doubt in him. The drop was three stories—a survivable fall for my kin, but not for him, not with his injuries.

He circled, wary now. "You wouldn't."

I stepped closer to the edge. "Wouldn't I?" I said.

He feinted, trying to force me back, but I held my ground. My skin pulsed with the bioluminescent patterns of challenge, of farewell.

"Vaneet, you don't have to—"

But I did. I reached out, grabbed his arm, and pulled him off-balance. For an instant, we teetered together at the threshold, our bodies a tangle of symmetry and opposition. Then gravity chose sides, and we fell.

The wind howled in my ears, drowning out every other sensation. I felt his hands claw at my shoulders, then slide away as we tumbled through space. I twisted at the last moment, using the old gymnast's trick to orient myself feet-first. The landing shattered every bone in my lower leg, but I stayed conscious.

Barron hit the ground beside me, the impact crumpling him. He lay still, blood leaking from his mouth in a slow, dignified arc.

I tried to crawl away, but the pain was too much. I rolled onto my back and stared at the sky. The clouds above were a bruised purple, the stars obscured by the city's halo of light.

A minute passed. Then another. I listened to the sounds of my own body, the thready pulse at my wrist, the slow cooling of my limbs.

Then, impossibly, Barron moved. He rolled onto his side with a shattered groan, propped himself up on one elbow, and looked at me with the battered, invincible curiosity that had haunted me since our first meeting.

"You're still alive," I said.

He laughed, a dry, hacking noise. "Terrans are hard to kill. Our ancestors were bioengineered for survival."

"I see," I replied.

He smiled, teeth rimmed with red. "But you've won. I'm dying. You've killed me, Vaneet. I've made you a monster after all."

I considered. His statement was sincere, almost gentle. The world had made us what we were: abuser and abused, exile and inheritor, two echoes of a history neither of us had chosen.

"No," I said, "I am a healer. And I have cut you out from the body of our world."

He nodded and let his head fall back onto the concrete.

I closed my eyes. The pain was fading, replaced by the cold clarity of endings. I remembered the stories my great-parent used to tell of how the first generation survived the Terran landing. The lesson was never about strength. It was about endurance.

Even monsters can teach us something, if only how to endure.

When I opened my eyes again, Barron was dead. Whether by his will or his wounds, I could not say.

But I was still there. Whole, or at least whole enough.

The indigo dawn crested the rooftops, spilling haunted light onto the abandoned Terran district, onto the streets my people would reclaim, onto the wound that was our world.

Perhaps Barron had been correct. Perhaps the Terrans would return, but they would find us stronger for healing.

Not monsters, but Anehwehn.

And we would survive.

It is often said that nature is cruel.
Humans are crueller.

THE VORPAL BLADE

John Peel

Rabbit, W. was—frankly—terrified.

He wasn't restrained in any manner, but he was clearly aware that he was a prisoner nonetheless, and that only as long as he was useful to the two humans. They had taken a short breather on their grim march, and he was huddled against the dirt wall of a familiar tunnel, quivering with fear. He disliked showing fear—hell, he hated *feeling* it—but these two women scared the heck out of him.

The younger one—Alice—might have been pretty if she tried, but she clearly wasn't bothered. Like his old mother would have said, she looked like she'd been dragged through a hedge backwards—and then turned on whatever had dragged her and slaughtered it. Her blonde hair was bedraggled, tangled and filthy. Her clothing—'fatigues' she called them—were torn and stained. But her rifle was spotless, almost a living thing in her hands, and the large sword slung across her back was polished and gleaming in the low level light. She was taking advantage of their halt to relieve herself, peeing a short way back down the earthen corridor. Normally—he being a rabbit, after all—he'd have been aroused by this, but it was clear from her utter indifference that she wasn't trying to turn him on. She simply didn't care if he watched her peeing or not. He had a strong suspicion that, if he were dead—she'd piss just as carelessly on his corpse. He didn't wish to test that theory. She scared him.

But it was the other one that out and out terrified him. Her name was Queen, and she was an older woman, not at all pretty. The scar down her right cheek didn't help matters there. It looked as if someone had attacked her with a knife some time ago—the scar was healed. Queen had undoubtedly killed her assailant. She had the look of a predator, and the eyes of one that enjoyed killing. She was occupied as she had been during the last two pauses, honing her twin knives slowly and carefully. She had a rifle, too, one that was as clean as Alice's, but her expression said that she preferred killing close up and personal. He could swear she was muttering to herself: "Off with his head…" If he was dead at her feet, she wouldn't piss on him. She'd probably eat him—raw.

Still, for some reason, Alice was the one in charge, and she'd decreed that he could live—just as long as he proved himself useful. He was almost falling over his feet to prove he was *very* useful indeed. Queen clearly didn't like this decision, but abided by it. But he could see that she was thinking in her heart that she *might* just be able to take Alice in a fight, and that things would then change.

He didn't give a rat's ass for his chances of surviving this encounter. Humans were always bad news, as his mother had always stressed, and here he was, captive of two of the hardest humans he had ever seen. But, as if that wasn't enough, these two were clearly insane.

They were on a jabberwock hunt.

Humans were bad enough—you stayed out of their way if you were smart and lucky (as he had always been until this wretched morning). But the jabberwock…!

It was the first thing his mother have ever hammered into him: "Beware the jabberwock, my son…" *Every* mother told their children that. There was always a chance that you might escape a human, but no-one ever escaped the jabberwock. There were no reliable reports as to what one looked like—obviously, of course, since nobody ever got away from one. There were just indicators of what to look for—three-toed footprints, for example. And bones—gnawed bones, the marrow sucked out. The only sane thing to do was to flee such signs.

The humans didn't care. For some reason, they *wanted* to find a jabberwock. To be perfectly honest, he'd love it if they did. They were armed to the teeth, so they might just live long enough for him to run for safety. The jabberwock was welcome to eat the humans, as far as he was concerned. In fact, he wished it would hurry up and do so. Of course, it was possible that he might not be fast enough to elude the jabberwock, but he reckoned his chances were better than simply remaining a captive of the humans.

"On your feet," Alice growled, pulling up her pants. "Let's get going."

"Are you so eager to die?" He knew he shouldn't argue, but he couldn't help it. Scared as he was of the humans, he couldn't help his inbred terror of the jabberwock.

"We won't die, rabbit," Queen laughed. "We've always got you as bait. And you look tastier than both of us."

He sighed, but started to move as Alice indicated. "I shouldn't expect sense of a human," he complained. As they moved down the tunnel, he shook his head. "I can see why you're doing this," he told Queen. "You think you're the toughest predator around, and you think killing a jabberwock will prove it." He turned to Alice. "But why are *you* doing this? You don't look as if you're any worse than most other humans. Surely you'll get nothing from this attempted killing?"

She barely glanced at him, and didn't respond at all. It was clear that she felt no need at all to explain her actions to someone so insignificant.

Queen laughed again. "You'll get nowhere with her. None of us ever do. She treats us as if we're all just as pointless as you. But if you're so interested, then I'll tell you: she's out for revenge."

Rabbit stared at the younger woman. "Revenge? How will getting yourselves killed help her get any sort of revenge? Unless, perhaps, you've swallowed poison that will kill the beast when it eats you?"

There was a short pause, and then Queen guffawed loudly. "Hey, he's funny." She considered. "Maybe he has a point, though? We could always stuff him with poison and feed him to the thing." She ignored his eek of protest. "Whaddya think?"

"No," Alice said flatly. "This is personal. I have to kill it."

"Thank goodness," he said. "I'd make terrible bait. Really, I would."

Queen stared at him. "You should shut up while you're ahead," she advised him. "You talk too much."

"I can't help it," he confessed. "It's a nervous reaction—I always talk when I'm scared."

"Don't you ever shut up?"

"I'm always scared," he admitted.

Queen glared at him, and then turned to Alice. "Does he really need to keep his tongue?"

"He needs to direct us," Alice reminded her.

"Can't he use gestures?"

Alice thought for a moment, and for a second he was terrified again. "No," she decided. "Much as it pains me, we might need him to speak."

"How about a paw, then? Does he really need to keep both paws?"

It took him a great deal of effort not to start babbling again.

"We can't chance him bleeding out," Alice decided. "Just stop answering him."

Queen muttered something unintelligible, but settled down, to his relief. She was clearly obsessed with causing him pain and mutilation. Just like his old mother had always told him: "Beware the humans by both day and night." He shook his head; it was just like him to get himself caught by these vicious beasts.

He wished his mother had had some advice on how to survive this. He missed her advice—and her—so much.

Despite all of her skills, the humans had gotten her.

"We're born to suffering," she had always said, and he agreed with her more at this moment than he ever had before. He could see no way out of this. Well—no *good* way. Everything he imagined ended in suffering and death. Sometimes even quickly.

"How much longer do these damned tunnels go on?" Alice growled.

"Warrens," he corrected her automatically. "Er—ah, about another ten minutes," he added, quickly, before she could get annoyed. "Then we reach the forest." He shuddered at the thought. "If you're sure you really want to."

"Oh, I'm *very* sure," she snapped. She checked her rifle for about the fiftieth time. She clearly wanted to be ready.

As if *anybody* could be ready for the jabberwock...

"Stop that!" Queen ordered, harshly. "I might just take your damned tongue anyway."

"Stop what?" He suddenly became aware that he had been muttering, unconsciously, over and over: "Doom... Doom..." He forced himself to be silent. There was no point in telling her that he couldn't help it; she clearly wouldn't care.

"God, I hate the stink of these tunnels," she complained. It took every ounce of his willpower not to correct her. But, as his mother had always said, he had to remember which side of his toast was buttered.

He *really* missed his mother.

It was slightly less than ten minutes, but they all saw the light at the exit at the same moment. To him, it was the harbinger of doom. To Queen, the end of the stench. To Alice, one stage closer to the revenge she desired so much. Not that *light* was really the correct term for it. These were the tulgey woods, where it was always twilight and never night or noon. The light was dark and gloomy, all shades of gray and black, where even shadows cast shadows of their own. And *woods* was inaccurate as well, for everything here was in stages of rot and decay; without light, plants couldn't live or grow, so there was no colour or cheer within—simply vast greyness, black, misshapen trees, and not much else.

But there was movement. There was wind, cold, harsh and stinging. It would occasionally bring rotting branches crashing down, breaking the long silences briefly. The wind howled its passage, and shook some of the less sturdy branches into jaggling semi-life.

It was a place where anything might slither or stalk or fly on dark wings. It was not a place that any sane creature ventured.

It was, of course, his first time here. He had never left the warren before by this exit. Here, only savage predators lived, and few of them, because here was the stalking ground of the jabberwock.

"Now where do we go?" Queen asked him.

He shrugged, not trusting himself to speak. He changed his mind when she drew one of her knives. "It doesn't matter," he informed her miserably.

"Why not?" she demanded.

"This is the jabberwock's woods," he managed to tell her, despite his shivering. "It will know that there's prey to be found, so it will find us, sooner or later."

"Which way is the best way?" Alice demanded.

"There *is* no best way!" He was so terrified that he was almost screaming. "There is only the way to death." He gestured in several directions. "Take your pick—it will find us. The only question is *when.*"

Hardly surprisingly, the crazy Queen actually laughed. She still had the knife in her hand, and she tested its edge. "So we no longer have any use for you," she pointed out. She looked to Alice. "Can I kill him now?"

The young woman considered the idea for a moment, then shook her head. He wished he could be thankful, but it was simply a reprieve: he'd be dead soon enough anyway. "He might have his uses yet. We may need bait, and the jabberwock likes live prey."

Queen sighed, but slipped her knife away. She raised her rifle, at the alert. "Stop shaking so loudly," she complained to him. "We won't hear the beast over that."

"We'll hear him," he promised her. "You'll wish you hadn't, but we'll hear it."

She gave a wordless growl, and stomped forward.

It was impossible to tell if the greyness was simply due to a lack of light, or whether the entire landscape was simply the dull color of semi-night. The bare trees provided meagre change in the blasted scenery. Alice had simply picked to move directly ahead since it didn't really make any difference. He wondered how long they had left to live. Then, out in the dimness, there was a low, grating howl.

"Is that it?" Queen hissed. She grinned, actually anticipating their meeting.

"No," he informed her. "If you heard it and you're still alive, it's not the jabberwock."

"Then what is it?"

He managed a fairly decent shrug of his shoulders without quaking too much. "If it makes noise in the jabberwock's hunting territory, it's either suicidal or else so big it feels invulnerable." He guessed. "Maybe a bandersnatch—that's big enough to feel safe."

"If it's not the jabberwock," Alice grated, "I don't give a damn what it is." For the first time she showed some sort of emotion. Hatred burned in her eyes.

He knew he shouldn't say anything, but he couldn't stop himself. "Why do you have this obsession with the jabberwock?" He gestured at the rifle she held. "You know that thing will be useless."

"It'll kill you fast enough," Queen growled.

"But I'm not a jabberwock," he pointed out.

"He's right," Alice said. "Bullets won't stop the damned thing."

"Bullets will stop *anything*," Queen argued.

"Not this; Charles and his outfit were all first-class marksmen, and it killed them all. Plenty of casings, but the only blood—" Here her voice choked slightly. "The only blood was theirs. They couldn't *all* have missed, so it makes sense that the jabberwock can't be harmed by bullets." Now he realized what her issue was, and he could almost empathize—if she hadn't been a damned human.

Queen looked furious. "Then how the frig do you expect to kill it?" she yelled. She looked at her rifle in disgust, as if it had somehow betrayed her.

Alice touched the hilt of the sword on her back. "With this."

This time, Queen's fury was quite clear. "It's impervious to frigging bullets, and you think a bloody *sword* will kill it?"

"*This* sword will. It's the vorpal blade."

Queen's face went from furious red to deathly white in seconds. It took her that long to find her voice again. "The *vorpal* blade? You *stole* the vorpal blade? You know what they'll do to you for that?"

"They can't do any worse than the jabberwock has already done."

"They bloody can!" Queen gestured at the sword. "That thing is a Class-A! They'll cut off your tits and stuff them up your bloody ass!" Her eyes narrowed. "Besides which, that thing is untested. You don't know it really can cut though anything."

Alice smiled, but there was no humour in that gesture. "Then maybe they'll give us a medal for testing it."

The older woman growled and shook her head. "Maybe we could take it back," she mused aloud. "Before they miss it."

"They'll have missed it already. I had to knock Knave out to steal it, so they're bound to have found him by now. The only way back is if we kill the jabberwock."

"And if *it* kills *us*?" Queen complained.

"Then you won't be punished, will you?"

It was clear to Rabbit that not only was he captive of two humans—which was bad enough alone—but that he was captive of two *insane* humans, which was infinitely worse. He considered praying that the jabberwock would kill him first. It would be a more merciful—if painful—fate. Well, there was no doubt that it would find them—the noise that these two crazies were making would be a sure and certain magnet for the monster. *Nothing* that wanted to stay alive made noise in the jabberwock's hunting grounds. He looked all around, shaking, but he could see nothing. Which is about what he'd expect to see if the beast was on their trail. He had always been afraid that he'd never get a chance to chant his own death ritual, and now that his mother was dead, there was no-one else left to do it for him. His soul would be left to haunt his warrens, howling and moaning forever.

That was the one good thing about his situation, at least.

"How the hell I let you talk me into this, I'll never know," Queen grumbled.

"When you knew I was on a jabberwock hunt, I didn't have to say a word," Alice reminded her. "You were looking forward to it."

"You didn't mention the *impervious to bullets* part!"

"You never gave me a chance. You were overcome by blood lust."

Queen glared at her again. "I might be again," she threatened. "And *you* aren't impervious to bullets."

Alice gave a real smile for the first time. "But then you'd have to face the jabberwock alone," she pointed out.

Wordlessly, the other woman gave an exasperated growl. She glared at him. "Where's this damned creature of yours anyway?"

"I'm surprised it hasn't found us already, with all of this noise you two are making," he answered.

"Maybe it needs *more* noise," she suggested. She glanced at Alice. "I could kill him—painfully. He'd scream an awful lot."

"There's no need," Alice replied.

They both followed her eyes, and Rabbit squealed in terror.

The jabberwock had found them.

Astonishingly, it wasn't attacking them—it was standing, alert and ready, but only its large, mobile eyes were moving. It was over six feet tall, and vaguely humanoid in shape. It had the right number of heads, limbs, eyes and such, but arranged in disturbingly irregular ways. The left eye was almost twice the size of the right, jutting from the thin skull and roving independently of the other. The mouth was large and overflowing with sharp teeth and drool. The limbs were thin and drawn out, ending in sharp-clawed fingers and toes. It looked horribly like a misshapen human. Compared to the two women, it looked almost fragile and slow.

That was a mistaken appearance. It was initially standing about a hundred feet away, but in seconds it was within twenty, reaching for them with eager claws.

Queen snarled and let loose a burst from her rifle. He could actually see the bullets bouncing off the gray skin of the creature, leaving neither mark nor wound. The only thing Queen had achieved with her attack was to draw its attention to her first, as the most active target. It covered the final twenty feet in a single jump, hissing through the mass of teeth. One claw flicked out, and a long, bloody wound opened up. Queen was hurtled back, spewing blood and oaths.

The jabberwock stared at him, considering clearly whether he or the other woman was the greater threat. It dismissed him immediately and understandably, and turned to attack Alice next.

She had already reacted to seeing the beast. She'd dropped her useless rifle, and reached over her shoulder to draw the Vorpal blade, which she held easily in her right hand, moving it slowly in a flat circle, awaiting the jabberwock's attack. Her once-pretty face was twisted in a snarl halfway between anger and anticipation.

The jabberwock paused slightly, clearly unused to prey that didn't panic and at least attempt to escape. Rabbit frowned slightly. Even through his terror, he was still trying to make sense of what was happening. The beast clearly wasn't a deep thinker, but it could recognize when something was out of the usual. It wasn't a rational creature exactly—more cunning and driven by hunger than by thought—but it had a measure of innate intelligence, and something about the girl it was facing clearly seemed wrong to it. Alice grinned slightly and motioned with her free hand for it to come on. The jabberwock understood that it was facing another predator, not a helpless foe, but it had never met a predator it couldn't eat before. It managed a kind of hollow moaning threat before it attacked.

Rabbit was far too terrified to even think of moving any part of his body except his eyes. He watched the unfolding attack, knowing that if Alice fell, he'd be the next victim, but totally incapable of doing anything about it.

The jabberwock's attack was far too swift for Alice to move out of its way, but she managed to whirl the sword out and down, slashing at its leg. The beast paused, stunned, as the blade actually cut into its tough skin, leaving a deep, bleeding gash down the limb. It howled again, this time more in pain than anger, and limped backwards.

For the first time, it paused. Alice didn't, and she was the one to advance this time, spinning the blood-soaked blade and still grinning. The jabberwock somehow managed to ignore its wound and leaped back into the attack. It spread its arms and mouth as wide as it could, aiming to squeeze its victim. Alice slashed again, this time into one of the multi-clawed hands, a blow so powerful that the sword virtually sliced the beast's left hand free. But in doing so, she had exposed herself to the thrust of its face. The wicked teeth sank into her shoulder, and her scream and that of the creature merged in unholy harmony. Somehow, though, she kicked it from her, and it scuttled away, nursing its badly injured hand. Alice barely glanced at her bleeding shoulder, though it had to be hurting her terribly. Instead, she ran after the jabberwock, still managing to retain her grip on the Vorpal sword.

The beast spun around, aware of her, and fighting now not for some prey but for its own life. Its left hand and its savage claws were useless to it, but it was far from unarmed, and it was furious at what had happened. *Nothing* had ever even hurt it before, much less drawn blood. It wasn't intelligent enough to consider retreating, and even if it had been, it clearly wanted revenge on this insignificant human who had injured it.

Alice, on the other hand, was still driven by her lust for revenge. Her shoulder had to be hurting abominably, and it was still freely bleeding, and the pain would have to slow her down. There was no sign of Queen—for all he knew, she was already dead. This was his best chance to escape. But, no matter how much he wanted to flee, he was simply too scared to even move a limb. All he could bring himself to do was watch.

It was over in seconds. The jabberwock threw itself onto Alice. It was thin and wiry-looking, but the force of the blow was enough to hurtle Alice backwards, slamming her into the earth. There were twin screams again, from both the girl and the monster, and then silence.

Rabbit stared at the intertwined bodies, and the pool of blood sleeping slowly across the gray ground. There was no movement. What had happened? What was happening? Had the two monsters managed to kill one another? Was he, finally, miraculously, free of all his oppressors?

Then he heard Alice grunt, and she struggled, kicking out and pushing the corpse of the jabberwock off of her. The Vorpal blade was still buried in its ribcage, having ripped through the creature's chest. Alice was covered in blood, but it was impossible to see how much was her own, and how much was from the dead victim. She started cursing, slow and steady, as she felt for the wound in her shoulder. She managed to drag a bandage from her belt, and started to try and stop up the wound.

"Goddam thing," Queen growled, as she staggered back, limping. She had an assortment of cuts on her body and legs, and her left arm hung funnily, obviously broken. She kicked the body of the jabberwock, and stared admiringly at the sword. "That's one hell of a blade," she commented.

"It does its job," Alice replied, almost dismissively. She sighed, and leaned back. She'd managed to somehow bandage her shoulder wound one-handedly. The bandage was soaked with blood, but the flow appeared to have stopped. "You got any painkillers?"

"Yeah." Queen grinned. "Never leave home without them." She reached into her own belt, and pulled out a tube, which she tossed over. "Try not to use them all—I'd like a couple myself." She went to the corpse of the jabberwock, and with a grunt pulled the sword free. She examined it happily. "You think they'll let us keep this?"

"Not a chance in hell. They'll bust us for even borrowing it."

"Huhn." Queen turned to look at Rabbit, who still hadn't moved more than his whiskers. "Then I guess I'd better use it while I can. We don't need this character any longer, do we?"

Alice didn't even look up as she took her pills. "Nope."

This time, he was absolutely certain that Queen muttered: "Off with his head…" before swinging the Vorpal blade.

He didn't even finish his scream.

*The worst monsters aren't born of
other monsters.
They're born of entitlement.*

THE FUTURE IS GOLDEN

Anthony Ferguson

He stood at the heavy wooden door and rubbed the side of his eyes, steeling himself for the task ahead. It was cold, the dead middle of winter, and a damn sight colder down there, where he was heading, beyond the door.

Beck sighed. This was the part of the job he hated most. He could hear them down there, strains of the odd chittering noises they made in some form of rudimentary communication. Even worse, he could smell them. It seemed to ooze through the cracks in the door. The sickly-sweet aroma that seemed to seep from their pores, mixed with remnants of their excrement.

He took a deep breath and slid the bolt free.

Beck picked up the two buckets of slop he had collected from the vats. The mixture of gruel combined with the dregs of oats and wheat they liked to devour.

One step.

Two steps.

The rumblings grew louder as they sensed his approach, and the ululations turned into a mewl of what he assumed was hunger.

Beck stepped between the rows of cages and lowered the slop buckets to the floor. Behind the bars a score or more of sunken yellow eyes watched expectantly. Mean and hollow orbs glowing in their sleek heads. He could never tell whether they were looks of hatred or fear. He assumed the latter by the way they skittered and shuffled backwards as he unlocked the first cage and stepped inside. The same reaction they presented every day.

Still, he eyed them with caution as he turned aside and filled the troughs with a lashing of goo. They waited, licking their thin lips until he exited and locked the door behind him, before they loped forward, crawling over each other to get at the slop.

Their spindly limbs disgusted him more than their appetites. It bothered him that they knew how to walk upright in a bipedal manner, but chose instead to lope along on all fours like the animals they were.

Alien animals.

The pattern was repeated as he made his way along the cages until his buckets were empty. They mostly ignored him, giving their attention to the desperate desire to feed. Beck turned his nose up at the stench, grateful at least that most of them had learned to use the sluice trench at the rear end of the cages for their ablutions. There would be less filth to mop up later.

He returned to ground level, the family abode, peeled off his filthy gear and showered, all the while images of the beasts below invaded his senses. There was a mystery to them that he was yet to puzzle out. The link between the herd below and the mysterious creatures said to populate the upper level.

Beck didn't know where the serak came from, or how long they had been here on Earth. All he knew was what they taught him in school, and later, after he graduated, what he saw in the media. They had arrived, not in some great and wondrous fleet of craft from a distant world, but as pets or, for a better word, stock, gifted to humanity by the rilaens, a powerful race from another world. Something to placate our warlike acquisitiveness, a bargain, a pact formed to quell any possibility of conflict.

On dark evenings he would lay on his bed, ears straining to the goings on through the ceiling above. The three-storey brownstone had been in the family for generations, since his great-great-grandaddy emigrated from Europe, and for all that time the family business had concerned two major vices that never went out of fashion—gambling and prostitution.

The basement held the serak livestock. The family occupied the ground level. Just him and his parents. The first floor was where the most suitable serak were taken for grooming and surgery, getting them attuned to the services they would be providing further up the levels. It was from there he heard the regular rumblings of surgical instruments and howls of protest.

The second storey was given over to the business club where Beck sometimes served as a waiter. Formally strictly a gentleman's club, its range had expanded in recent times to include rilaens and even women. If you had the cash, you were welcome.

The third level was where the action took place. An area still forbidden to Beck. His father trying to protect him from getting too close to whatever secret business went on up there. He knew that each of the special serak hostesses had their own private rooms, where they would entertain certain exclusive and important guests. The services they provided he could guess at. He wasn't completely naïve, and had known intimacy with girls of his own age. Though he would never bring them to the house.

Beck mingled among the business club guests, human and rilaen, balancing a full tray of cognac and canapes on each arm. A rilaen snagged a glass in its claw and winked at him. He turned his head and grimaced. Try as he might, he could not adjust to their huge swollen insectile heads and the odd green hue of their skin. Their deep halting tone as they struggled to wrap their palate around the human tongue reminded him of demonic voices from horror films he had seen in his youth. Watching them imbibing cognac and trying to smoke cigars did nothing to lessen the feeling of uncanny revulsion. Like the first time he heard robots speak. He hoped he would get used to the rilaens in the same manner, in time.

Beck spied his father regaling a besuited rilaen in a corner and edged closer to eavesdrop.

"'Course in times past the hostesses were regular women, occasionally men, and sometimes even ladyboys." His father guffawed at this point and paused to explain himself to the confused alien, before carrying on the narrative. "Almost every taste was accounted for. After that, for a period there was a craze for the new sexdroids as the technology afforded. But as robotics and AI technology grew more widespread and familiar, clients tired of them, and craved something new. Hence, the serak. That's where you fellahs came in."

"Ah yes," the rilaen grunted. "We hope you appreciate our golden gift."

The pair of them laughed in a conspiratory manner. Beck drew closer, his ears pricking up. His father turned suddenly, reached out and snatched a drink from the tray. The rilaen did likewise and crammed a canape into its maw, mandibles working.

"Ah, here's my strapping young lad." The old man reached out and wrapped a meaty arm around Beck's shoulder, pulling him in. "I bet this guy would like to know the secret, eh?"

"You mean you haven't told him?" the alien hissed, its face breaking out in the approximation of a grin. "Oh my boy, the wonders of the serak flesh, with its hidden contours and wondrous apertures."

"Apertures," Beck repeated, feigning curiosity in a ploy to get the creature to continue. The rilaen didn't need prompting.

"Yes, boy, there is a wondrous secret hidden beneath the serak flesh. We discovered it ourselves by chance."

Beck glanced sidelong at his father, and saw him nodding along.

The rilaen wiped its maw and continued in gleeful tones. "The creatures' bodies contain a range of orifices that give off a certain...hypnotic aphrodisiac quality. Those lucky enough to indulge obtain a state of pleasure so intense that it borders on pain, a high better than the finest of your illicit Earthly drugs."

"Is that right?"

"I should know," the rilaen boomed. "I've tried a few. More so, this high can be obtained from serak flesh in many ways—snorting, injecting, or consuming."

"You can eat them?"

"Oh yes. The quality of their cuts of meat are exquisite. Yet there is one further manner in which the ultimate serak high can be achieved." The rilaen paused and glanced at Beck senior, who swallowed from his glass and picked up the story.

"Yes, this is where we come in. The most pliant and amiable serak, the most promising, docile, friendly specimens are selected from the basement cages and taken to the first floor for grooming. There they are taught to walk upright, have their flesh moulded by the finest surgeons into objects desirable to the human eye, and instructed in the ways of the bordello."

The rilaen reached for another glass of cognac, and leaned in closer to Beck.

"The serak have exquisite orifices in certain areas of their person, like sucking mouths within mouths, which are able to present whatever lustful image their purchaser affords, by way of hypnotic induced hallucination. There is one particularly special organ, situated around the navel region, that affords the most exquisite high of all, giving off a charge like the humming of the universe itself. It is said to encourage an addiction stronger than any chemical drug."

"Is that so?" Beck replied.

"Look around you boy, what do you see? The same clients come back time and again, and they themselves are marked. The skin around their mouths, faces and hands begins to take on a golden hue to mirror that of the serak."

Incredulous, Beck glanced around the room and saw it was true. Then his father interjected, ushering him away. "Okay, enough revelry for tonight. Let's not give the boy nightmares, or any other unwelcome thoughts." Escorting Beck to the door, he leaned in and whispered. "You listen to me, son. Stay away from the top floor. It's not for you."

Imbued with hitherto unknown knowledge, Beck did his own research. It transpired that serak addiction was a running theme online. A multitude of clips emerged of people in various stages of mania, sporting various patches of golden outbreaks on their flesh, and seeming to lose all coherence in their narcotic-induced speech.

Nevertheless, despite the alleged side effects, his father's warnings to stay away from the top level only increased his desire to encounter one of the princesses, as he had heard them referred to. On a particular rainy afternoon, as gloom set about the streets outside, and before the evening arrival of the usual exalted guests, Beck snuck unobserved up the stairwell, where, to his amazement, he saw the doors to one of the forbidden rooms standing ajar.

Heart pounding in his throat, he crept closer. The door was open just a crack, but enough to see into the dimly lit room. There, on a wide bed, lit by a lamp on a small adjacent table, a beautiful creature lay in repose. Yet it wasn't her beauty that made his mouth drop open, it was what the serak was doing. It...*she* held a book in her manicured hands, and seemed to be reading, slowly picking through the pages.

At that moment she happened to look directly at him, her mouth dropping open to match his. She let out an audible gasp, and fighting back his urge to flee, Beck stumbled into the room instead.

"Close door," she urged in halting English, and he did so.

The serak rose to a sitting position and closed the book. She motioned to a chair opposite, and he sat.

"You...can read?"

"Yes," she nodded. "I learn. Your language not easy."

He swallowed. The serak's voice was soft and feminine. Learned behaviour, but precise. She chose her words carefully, as if running each one around in her mouth. The implanted teeth were immaculate, as was the structure of her face, and the curvature of her body. His father employed only the best surgeons.

"I feel like I've seen you before," he said.

"See you too. Your name Beck."

"Yes, that's right. What is your name?"

"The name they call me is Renee."

"Renee." He turned it over in his mouth.

She smiled at him, showing off her fine teeth. "You like me?"

He almost blushed. "Oh yes, very much. You are beautiful."

Renee squealed with delight and patted the empty space on the bed next to her. Like an eager puppy, Beck rose and went to her side.

We were taught that they were animals, but it turns out they have a history, a culture. Not just an Internet meme from a random bleeding heart, but a fact Beck came to appreciate through his developing relationship with Renee, the third-floor hostess, the *lucky* beneficiary of chance, plucked from the herd locked in the basement.

From the moment she took his hand and pressed it into one of the nodules adorning her sculpted human form, through the chemical rush of bliss as the doors of perception opened, he began to see the truth. The serak were no different to the plethora of indigenous cultures and myriad unfortunate minorities scattered throughout the history of human endeavour. It transpired the same type of greed, acquisitiveness and warlike authority was also explicit in the history of the rilaens. It was they who had swept down on the serak world and enslaved them, herding them as cattle and taking from them the pleasures afforded by their unique DNA.

So, they came to Earth, in their hundreds, huddled in large cages like the herd creatures they are, to forcibly adjust to life on our alien planet. A platoon of rilaens came with them. Honoured guests. They acted as shepherds and chaperones to the serak until the latter adapted to their new home. A few stayed behind to avail themselves of political discourse. Adopting our dress, however odd their strange thin elongated bodies looked in tailor-made suits, and quickly mastering our languages.

In time as she allowed him to explore more of her body, Beck witnessed the degradations impressed upon it by the cultured clientele—needle marks where they had extracted her essence to inject into their own veins, and scars between her thighs where pieces of her flesh had been removed for consumption. He bestowed kisses on those violated places, and wept as she lay in his arms, his emotions ranging betwixt sorrow, rage and utter bliss. Perhaps even that other thing, he mused.

Beck had never experienced love before. He had dabbled in the pleasures of the flesh with a few girls, but they were as nothing compared to what he felt with Renee. Then the moment came when she revealed to him her sacred place, and when he motioned toward it with his fingers, she pushed them aside and reached for his manhood instead, guiding him into paradise. There he experienced something so far beyond physical pleasure he felt his heart would explode. His mind ventured between the gates of Heaven and Hell, finding them one and the same. The universe itself audibly cracked open, and he emptied himself into her, and she into him.

As she lay her head on his shoulder and their breathing eased, she whispered to him, "It different with you than other men. We don't just fuck, we make love."

Alas, with every yin there comes a yang, and Beck found his when his father entered the study and confronted him. He sat in a chair opposite and said nothing for several minutes. Then he shook his head gently and spoke.

"Do you think I don't have cameras all through this establishment?"

Beck opened his mouth to reply but his father waved him aside.

"The nature of our family business necessitates the use of surveillance to maintain integrity and protect our assets."

"Yes, but..."

"Son, I'm going tell you what my father told me, his father before told him, and so on down our family line. Don't fall in love with a whore, boy. You can't save her. Nobody can. We breed them, then we snort them, ingest them, fornicate with them, and then we eat them. They're made for consumption, son. They're just animals."

Beck's face grew red with rage and fear.

"No, Dad. They're not. They have a history..."

"Fuck their history, boy!" Equally enraged, his father wiped spittle from the edge of his gold rimmed mouth. "We should never have taught them to speak."

Beck's face paled as the sudden possibility of consequence hit home. "Please, don't hurt her."

His father's face softened. "I won't harm her, boy. I won't even stop you from seeing her. Just remember my words."

His father proved to be as good as his word, and Beck found his love and respect for the old man grow stronger. Indeed, his demeanour seemed to soften by the day, the hard business-like edges dropping away as the golden blotches on his flesh grew wider.

Beck had begun to sport his own golden tinges, he noted; a result of letting Renee escort him to paradise. He thought they looked good on him, admiring himself in the mirror.

Down the street from the family home stood an open paddock, where unclaimed serak herds gathered to graze. They were too docile to drift away from the comfort of their kind, too content with the pastures on which they dined. Beck could see it from the window of Renee's parlor, and would often gaze contentedly at it before she would wrap her arms around him from behind and pull him gently back toward the bed, nuzzling his ear.

One morning an idea struck him, and he rushed downstairs to the containment cells, kicking aside the empty feed buckets and ignoring the stench. The serak cowered as he thrust his keys into the locks, one by one, flinging the doors open.

At first they hesitated, crowding together for comfort and mewling in confusion. Beck mused at the world of difference between these poor helpless creatures and his princess lying in repose just a few floors above. He spoke softly to them and cajoled them to follow him up the stairs.

Eventually, one brave specimen took the cue, and tentatively edged forward beyond the cage doors. Following in his wake, the serak placed a cloven hoof on the bottom step, then another, and clumsily began to climb toward freedom.

One by one the others followed him out into the street, where Beck held up traffic and led them up the road to the paddock, where they rushed to join their colleagues. He watched contentedly as they nuzzled one another, wondering what secret conversations were being had. It was then that he noticed among the growing herd some human forms. People on all fours, grazing on the wheat and chaff, attempting to blend in with the serak.

Beck found this amusing for some reason, and he smiled and laughed. An absurd thought crossed his mind, but it slipped away again before he could grasp it.

He continued to love Renee, and tolerated the exclusive clientele on the second level as he fed them canapes and filled their glasses. Watching them imbibe with their orange hued faces, he wondered who among them had availed themselves of his beloved. Not that it mattered, he smiled inwardly, for he knew that while they might enjoy the physical contours of her body, they would never experience the magic he shared with her.

Eventually the cluster of guests began to thin out, a factor he mentioned to his mother and father at the dinner table.

"Don't you care that I released your captives? They're out there, cavorting in the fields, and there are people there too, more and more of them."

His father laughed, his mother too.

"It's the way of the world, son. Don't worry about it."

"It will all work out, Beck," his mother added. He saw too that her skin was also taking on a golden hue, like his father.

Beck struggled to put his words together. Something he was finding increasingly difficult in recent times.

"But the business. If there are no more hostesses, won't we...?"

He lost his train of thought, and the old man, a look of mild concern on his face, placed his hand on Beck's.

"It's going to be glorious, son. The future is golden."

His mother chuckled and nodded along.

The following day, he watched them from his vantage point window as they pushed the door open below and ran down the street, falling to all fours and galloping toward the herd.

Confused and amused, he fell into Renee's loving arms and took another trip to paradise. She stroked his hair and whispered. "Good boy. You are a good boy."

"I love you, Renee," he yelled, as the world exploded into colours.

"Love you too," she said.

He lay, panting in her arms, gazing at the swirling patterns on the ceiling. Why had he never noticed them before?

"You know, Renee, you are a wonderful gift, the greatest gift humanity ever received."

She laughed softly. "We are not so much a gift as a Trojan horse, if you know your history, darling."

He laughed with her, looking into her golden eyes.

"Hah! Trojan. That's a funny word."

He leapt up, suddenly imbued with energy, and ran to the window, catching a glimpse of his naked glowing physique in the full-length mirror. He rushed for the stairs.

"Aren't you going to dress, my love?" she asked, but he didn't answer.

Beck ran out of the house into the street and headed toward the fields. Observing others around him, he instinctively dropped to all fours and found he could move even faster that way. He found his family, all of them, and his heart was filled with the joy of belonging.

Chewing on the cud, Beck looked around his new world, loving the way the mighty sun lent its golden hue to the fields. Looking above, he marveled at how it glittered off the shining domes of the myriad spacecraft that dangled in the air above. There were so many of them they almost filled the sky.

One can absolutely fight human nature.
Only monsters care not to do so.

UTOPIAN NEEDS

Andreas Hort

Warm sunrays seeped through Shla-ne's leafy skin and flooded her body, transmuting into energy. She unfurled her vine-tendrils and savored the replenished strength.

The surroundings were beautiful, too. She couldn't see them the way humans did, of course; she emitted electrochemical pulses that traveled far, bouncing off obstacles and returning to her, painting the clear map of a grassy slope that evened into a meadow, bisected by a river, and backed by a thick forest. Beyond the trees, mountains rose—so distant her pulses could only touch their bases.

She wished she could stay here for a few days, but they were in a hurry: the human settlement lay far beyond those mountains.

Tichit's warm presence bled into her consciousness from behind. His many vines propelled him forward until he curled beside her.

She focused on him and released an electrochemical pulse shaped like a question: *Do you really think the humans would find standing here boring?*

Tichit's answer carried a shimmer of amusement. *I know they would. They seem unable to remain passive for a day, let alone for years. Their consciousness seems to depend on constant external stimulation.*

How interesting. And sad. The constant need for something new… She couldn't imagine the suffering.

Solemi's irritation pulsed through her vessels. *We should have left them on an island—one large enough to prosper, but with no way to reach the shore.*

Tichit's calm aura stirred. *That would be too cruel.*

It would be rational. It would give us control over them.

Shla-ne turned to Solemi. *Why do you dislike them so much?*

They keep changing everything. And... Solemi was silent for a while; his aura told her he was working on the right shape of his answer. *I think they want more than they need.*

Was he referring to that human word (greed)? Perhaps. And since the humans had a name for it, perhaps Solemi was right about them.

But she wouldn't know until she met them.

Tichit's warm energy washed over them. *Perhaps they have expanded for a good reason. We will listen to their side, and then discuss the situation with them.*

Solemi's irritation thickened, thrumming through the air. *If you had listened to me when we first met them, we wouldn't have had to talk to them now.*

Perhaps, perhaps not. Tichit turned toward the mountains. *Their settlement lies three days away—two if they have expanded far enough. Are you all replenished?*

Shla-ne sent an affirmative pulse. Solemi followed.

From farther away, Va-shi's signal rippled through their vessels.

The four of them moved down the slope.

Wading through the river, the water seeped into Shla-ne's body, all the way into her heartwood. The sun had given her strength, but the water gave her mind vitality.

They entered the forest, dragging themselves over rocky terrain and weaving past trees and shrubs, which, according to Tichit's conversations with the humans, resembled the plants on Earth—except the local trees could communicate, move around, and grow fruits of their own choosing.

Apparently Earthian trees suffered from stillness and the limitation of one product per kind. To Shla-ne, it seemed a horribly suffocating existence.

As the four crawled in silence, Shla-ne pondered the humans. From what she thought she knew about them (hyperactive creatures full of playfulness and a constant urge to build) she found them quite endearing. But Solemi's unease had seeped into her own mind. *Tichit, how many times have you met the humans?*

Twice, Tichit answered. *The first time was forty-three years ago, when their ship crashlanded on our planet. I was one of the emissaries sent to meet them. Once we learned to communicate, we helped them build a settlement and establish their territory.*

We gave them everything they needed to live a prosperous existence: all the water they could drink; food that grew fast enough to outpace their hunger; shelter, formed by trees we persuaded to twist into shapes that protected the humans from rain and sunlight (overexposure harms them). Foliage serves them as cover against cold. They should have everything they need.

Shla-ne noted Tichit had thought *should have*, not *have*.

She was forming a question when Tichit's thought reached her.

They're fascinating. Very inventive. Are you familiar with the word 'game'?

Yes.

We stayed with them for almost ten years—that is twelve years on their planet.

Why so long? Shla-ne asked.

For a long time, we struggled to communicate with them. Transmitting our thoughts into their minds was easy; translating their sounds into thoughts was a slow climb up a sheer cliff.

Shla-ne, having spent ten years perfecting the humans' English, sent Tichit a wave of sympathy. Tichit responded with amused acknowledgement and continued.

At first, they were obsessed with studying us and our planet. After a string of discoveries, which answered most of their questions, the majority turned their focus on building their lives here. Their leader, Captain Roel Anderson, explained their needs, and when we provided, the ease of it left them shocked. Roel (as he asked to be called) explained that, on their planet, they had solved the problems on their own. He described a struggle. Back then, he looked astonished to me, but when I learned to read their facial expressions better and I thought back to that moment, I saw a hint of pain. Disappointment, perhaps, or discouragement. As if deep within the maze of his mind, he had wanted the challenge.

Shla-ne waited for Tichit to talk about the games, but only the breeze caressed her skin.

After a long while, the terrain beneath their vines sloped upward—they reached the mountains. They crawled through a pass between two peaks, and on the horizon, the sun hovered just above the close-set treetops of another forest.

They must have gone a quarter of the day in silence.

Tichit, what about the games?

An apologetic pulse caressed her vessels. *I was reminiscing about Roel. And John—his son.* An image of two humans rose in Shla-ne's mind: a tall, broad-shouldered male with his head-growth brushed back and a strong, smooth-shaven jaw, and a very young male (boy) whose hair was a little longer and slightly thicker than the man's. *When they came here, Roel was just over forty Earth-years; John was six.*

From behind, Va-shi asked, *Humans can only live to around a hundred and twenty, right?*

Tichit's pulse confirmed it, though there was a trace of hesitation.

Va-shi emitted a soft ripple of sympathy. *Only a hundred years for us.*

Shla-ne had lived eight hundred and twenty-three years and would last for at least another eight hundred—possibly even two thousand more. The oldest kin she knew had passed three thousand years and still held enough vitality for two more centuries.

Three thousand years. Thirty times the human lifespan. Living for a hundred years and then being separated from your consciousness forever... Such a fleeting existence. She couldn't imagine it.

Shla-ne, Tichit, and Va-shi shared their sorrowful pity through soft pulses. There was nothing from Solemi.

The games, Tichit pulsed. *Children (human saplings) loved them especially, but over the years, everyone joined in. The humans have many games, and they invent new ones as naturally as they breathe.*

Tichit shared a scene of human children running through a field, chased by one of their own. The chaser closed on a slower child, touched his shoulder, and darted away. The touched child became the chaser.

Shla-ne sensed Solemi's confusion tinged with irritation. *Pointless waste of energy.*

She couldn't see the pleasure in it, either. But the humans didn't seem to think it pointless.

Other scenes flickered through: children climbing trees; children and adults running around, screaming, and kicking a lemi, a round fruit with a hard shell. *Soccer. Some call it football.* Now adults hurled a lemi among one another, while others crashed into them at full speed. It looked completely reckless, and sure enough, images of scraped knees, torn lips, and broken noses followed. *American football.*

Shla-ne was stunned. No wonder the humans died fast. Why would they hurt themselves this way? Did they truly find it entertaining?

A scraping sound cut through the air. To their right, rocks tumbled down the slope. Higher up, on a rocky ledge, a human male stood, watching them. A loincloth of leaves clung to his waist, and in his hand, he held a thick bough with a flat rock lashed to its end: a rudimentary hammer.

Shla-ne's vessels tingled as movement reverberated around her. More humans stepped from behind boulders and trees, surrounding Shla-ne and her kin.

Most of them bore scars across their faces and bodies; one male was missing an arm below his elbow.

They all wielded tools—either hammers or long poles with their ends sharpened to points. Spears.

But spears were hunting tools, and on this planet there was nothing to hunt. There were no animals—only plants and the humans.

Va-shi's aura shimmered with surprise. *Tichit, didn't you say the humans were at least two days away?*

I did. Tichit rose higher on his vines to stand out. *Good day, friends. I hope you are well. We've come to ensure your well-being.*

A few humans exchanged glances. A tall young male stepped forward. "Which tribe are you looking for?"

Tribe? Shla-ne pulsed to Tichit.

Group. There was a ripple of confusion. *The human tribe,* Tichit replied to the man. *Is John Anderson nearby?*

John? Talking to Roel made more sense.

The man pointed down the pass toward the forest. "Anderson stayed with the ground tribe."

Ground tribe?

The young man nodded as if that explained everything.

Tichit lowered himself and moved down the pass. *Let's go. We need to speak with John.*

As they crawled toward the forest, Shla-ne's pulses showed her that the humans still faced them. They were watching them.

The gazes followed Shla-ne and her kin all the way to the tree line. Even after they slipped between the trunks, breaking the line of sight, some humans kept looking in their direction. In the forest, Shla-ne asked, *Tichit, where is Roel Anderson?*

The second time I visited the humans was nine years ago, Tichit pulsed. *Roel, despite being only eighty-three Earth-years, had withered as if nearing his limit.*

Va-shi emitted sympathy. *Was he sick?*

Humans rarely become sick here. When they do, it's usually what they call a common cold. Barely an inconvenience.

Tichit was quiet for a while. *I asked him why he was losing his strength so early. Didn't he have another thirty or forty years? He laughed and said, "To do what?"*

Shla-ne wasn't sure what Roel had meant by that. To be present in the world around him, why else? *What did you answer?*

I didn't know what to say, Tichit admitted. *I was confused. I stayed with them for two years. Then there was no reason to stay.*

Tichit's wave of sorrow gripped Shla-ne's vessels, a smothering ache deep in her heartwood. An image followed: an old human male lying on a bed of large leaves, still as a fallen branch. Roel. His muscles had withered, leaving skin stretched tight over bone like soil over shallow roots. The hair that had been thick and well-tended in his youth had become a disheveled white fuzz. A scraggly white beard spread over his rib-latticed chest.

Beside him, a man of about fifty sat hunched and weeping, his thin arms ending with clenched fists. Despite the lack of fat in his limbs, his stomach was protruding. *John.*

Va-shi emitted confusion. *I don't understand. What killed him?*

Nobody knows, Tichit pulsed. *One night, he fell asleep and stopped breathing. He wasn't the first human under ninety to wither away. Some died before eighty. The humans suspected the foreign environment shortened their lifespan. Perhaps they know more now.*

Shla-ne felt another wave of grief for the humans; their brief lives were truncated even more.

Perhaps their bodies just need time to adapt, Va-shi suggested. *Perhaps they already have.*

A rustle passed through the canopy. Movement flashed between branches.

Humans? Va-shi asked.

Tichit sent out an affirmative response. *It has to be them.* Then, toward the movement: *Hello, friends. We're looking for John Anderson.*

There was only the whisper of wind in the leaves. The movement was drifting away from them.

Solemi sent a sharp warning. *Something is wrong with them.*

Tichit agreed.

They kept going.

Soon, a faint echo of human voices tingled through Shla-ne's vessels. They followed the sound.

As the voices grew louder and more numerous, Shla-ne recognized laughter and shouting. Excitement fluttered through her body. Humans loved celebrations. In this foreign environment, they likely looked for any excuse to celebrate.

The temperature lowered, signaling the sun's descent beyond the horizon. At this time, the forest would be too dark for humans. She still hadn't quite grasped the concept of darkness. Before the humans described it to her kind, nights had meant only cold and an absence of sunrays she endured until the next dawn filled her with new energy.

There was a scream followed by a thunder of cheers and laughter.

Perhaps we should wait until morning, Solemi pulsed. *We've spent too much energy to negotiate effectively.*

Shla-ne wanted to see a human celebration, but she had to agree with Solemi.

Tichit was still for a while. *You're right. Though we're on friendly terms, they might view our visit as a challenge to their expansion.*

A challenge? Shla-ne wasn't sure why. They'd come here to ask about the reasons for the expansion, and to discuss its limits. But Tichit knew the humans better than she did.

They found a gap in the canopy and settled beneath it to rest. The human noises tingling through her vessels kept Shla-ne awake for a long time, but exhaustion eventually pulled her into sleep.

She woke up replenished beneath warm sunrays. Solemi was already awake. Shla-ne couldn't hear the humans anymore, but she remembered the direction their noise had come from.

They waited for Tichit and Va-shi to wake up, then the four of them soaked in the sun a little longer before resuming their journey.

Soon, they heard the human voices again. Before they reached the source, a rustle came from the nearby bushes. Twigs snapped.

Solemi pulsed his irritation. *Humans. Always active.*

A woman's voice called from not far away. "The triffids are coming!"

Triffids? Shla-ne asked.

Their nickname for us, Tichit answered. *When Roel asked me what we called ourselves and I said we had no name, they began calling us triffids. It's a creature from their mythology.*

Mythology? Shla-ne pulsed.

Ancient untruths they tell each other.

You mean lies?

Lies the listener knows are lies. Like their games, they stimulate their minds.

The human voices grew close. The trees ahead parted, revealing a sunlit space. Shla-ne focused on Tichit. *What do they lie about?*

The world, life, themselves. They lie about everything. Roel believed their games and lies had elevated his species above all the others on Earth.

They emerged into a vast meadow. Shelters grown from living trees sat scattered like the remnants of a rockslide. Men, women, and children moved through the clearing. The ones who had been sitting or lying were standing up. And everyone's gaze fell on Shla-ne and her kin.

Tichit slid forward. *Good day, friends. We have come to see how you're faring. Where is John Anderson?*

"Here," a hoarse voice said.

A man of about seventy strode forward, carrying a spear longer than he was tall. His head was clean-shaven, but he wore a thick white beard. Despite his narrow frame, his body was wiry and muscular. Scars marked his torso and every limb.

He bore no similarities to the mourning man in Tichit's memory.

The crowd looked just like their leader: strong but dressed in scars, which stirred in Shla-ne a strange mixture of curiosity and sorrow.

John held out his hand in greeting. Tichit's tendril reached out and wound around John's wrist in the human manner. Beneath the beard, John's mouth quirked into a smile. The males shook and then released.

"What brings you here, Tichit?"

We've come to ensure your well-being, Tichit pulsed.

Shla-ne couldn't read John's expression.

"Well, you and your kind are always welcome, Tichit. Lunch should be ready in about an hour—until then, feel free to pass time however you please." John gestured across the meadow. "Please, feel free to talk to anyone or join any of our games. A group of boys are playing soccer on the other side of the meadow." He pointed at a shelter. "That's where we play cards."

He gestured, and the humans began to disperse.

Shla-ne wasn't sure what cards were, but soccer seemed too dangerous, so she moved toward the shelter.

Meanwhile, Va-shi approached a woman, who stepped back, cowering with wide eyes. Shla-ne was about to warn Va-shi when another woman encouraged the scared one to step forward.

Va-shi held out a tendril. The woman hesitated, then slowly reached out and shook it. A few people laughed.

Tichit and Solemi stuck with John, the three of them crossing the meadow, likely to watch the soccer game.

Shla-ne noted how many humans carried tools. Most of them had hammers and spears like the humans at the mountains, but others held stones roughly shaped into knives. Some blades were nearly as long as a human arm.

Three men and a woman welcomed her into the shelter. In the center of the room, a rudimentary table held a neat stack of thin wooden slices. But they didn't feel like the trees of this planet. Perhaps the humans had brought them on their ship.

Heaps of leaves ringed the table. The four humans sat down onto them. Shla-ne joined.

One of the men shuffled the wooden slices (cards?) and began dealing them out for everyone but himself.

"We're playing spades," he said. "Are you male or female?"

Female.

The woman grinned. "All right—boys versus girls."

The men chuckled. The dealer smiled at Shla-ne and began explaining the rules.

They played, and it took Shla-ne several rounds to understand the game. Still, the entire concept seemed pointless. The females kept losing, and the men kept teasing them. Shla-ne sensed her teammate's annoyance, and that annoyed Shla-ne in turn.

And the idea of winning grew appealing.

Slowly, the concept of the game became clear. She began anticipating which slice the humans would play and how they would respond. She made the right choices.

Then the females won. Shla-ne's partner cheered, which almost felt like the sound version of sunrays soaking into her skin. The men's groans of frustration felt just as good.

The woman looked at Shla-ne with a mild smile. "I'm Maya, by the way."

I'm Shla-ne.

They started a new game, and the appeal of winning grew into an urge—a dull ache lodged in her cells, for which the only cure was victory.

When they won again, Maya whooped and the ache dissolved into a bright, almost electric sensation.

She'd never felt anything so intense, but it was pleasant. *Very* pleasant.

What's happening here?

They all turned toward the entrance. From there, Solemi studied the wooden slices with a concentrated interest.

We're playing cards, Shla-ne pulsed. *What about the soccer game?*

Pointless. And dangerous. Two men broke their noses. A woman broke her arm. A lemi almost crushed my head.

This game is safe. And pleasant. Shla-ne sent him an echo of her feelings.

Solemi shared his surprise, then disgust. *It seems pointless, too.*

I think the pleasantness of it is the purpose.

Maya stood up with a sigh and looked at Solemi. "You wanna play? I gotta sharpen my spear anyway."

I will play, Solemi said. *But only to truly understand how pointless this activity is.*

Maya left ("Hey, Shla-ne—thanks for the fun. We kicked their asses!"), and Solemi took her place. As they played, Shla-ne explained the rules to Solemi, who seemed to grasp them faster than she had. But the humans kept winning.

After a while, John leaned into the shelter's opening. "Lunch is ready, guys."

"All right," one of the men said.

Solemi raised a tendril. *We'll join you right after this match.*

Shla-ne looked at him. *You're taking a while to truly understand the pointlessness of the game.*

I think we can win.

They did. Shla-ne felt that electric sensation again, and she shared it with Solemi. He kept his emotions for himself, which likely meant they were more positive than he wanted to admit.

When she emerged from the shelter, Shla-ne spotted Va-shi and the woman at a tree-made storage room—boughs, flat rocks, and coiled vines piled around them. The woman guided Va-shi's tendril as they lashed a rock to a bough, fashioning a crude hammer.

Even though Va-shi didn't share her emotions, Shla-ne could tell from her giddy movement that she was enjoying the activity.

A man called, "Food is ready!"

Shla-ne, her kin, and the humans gathered around a fire, where they sat on boulders. She'd never seen flame before, and if she didn't know its origin, she'd have thought a piece of sun had peeled off and fallen into a ring of rocks.

The humans had set an earthen pot over the fire. Inside, the simmering liquid held swimming pieces of unidentifiable food.

Several people ladled the contents into bowls and handed them out. Two others gave away spoons.

Once everyone had their bowl, John scooped a spoonful into his mouth, chewed, and swallowed. "Mm." He turned to Tichit. "Shame you guys don't eat."

Shla-ne observed the humans' feeding when Tichit's thought came through—narrow, focused, meant only for her, and likely Solemi and Va-shi. *They are at war among themselves.*

Shla-ne stiffened. *War?*

They have divided themselves into three groups. They're killing each other.

Why?

John simply said that the others are evil.

Va-shi shared a pulse of pity.

Shla-ne felt the same way. *So their tools aren't for building?*

Humans call them 'weapons'. They're tools for killing.

Solemi's pulse signified urgency. *When they're done eating, we have to talk to John.*

While waiting, Shla-ne truly took in the humans' injuries. There were so many scars and broken noses. Missing teeth, missing fingers. One man's arm had been reduced to a short stump at his shoulder. A wave of sorrow overcame her. These unfortunate creatures deserved better. Whatever the humans warred over, Shla-ne and her kin had to put a stop to it today.

John groaned. He reached into his mouth and pulled out something small. "Goddammit. Who was the cook today?"

A slim man across the fire raised his hand. "I was, Chief."

John sighed. "Dammit, Mark." He lifted the tiny thing for Mark to see. "See that? A nail. How many times did I tell you to be careful when you're flaying the fingers?"

Fingers? Perhaps it was slang for some part of a fruit.

Mark's eyes dropped to the ground. "I'm sorry, Chief. I'll watch out for it next time."

"You always say that, but listen, buddy." John pointed a finger at him. "One more time and I'll make you *really* sorry. Someone here is gonna be flaying your fingers. Got it?"

Mark nodded. "Got it, Chief."

John flicked the human nail to the ground and kept eating.

Did Shla-ne sense the right words? A nail? Fingers? She must have misunderstood.

She studied the food in the bowls. She'd never seen human organs, but she knew every fruit in this area—and the contents didn't look like any of them.

A cold sensation ran through her body, and she flinched. What was happening inside her? She'd never felt this emotion. But she could tell it was fear. Though she wasn't sure what she was afraid of.

She wished she could crawl away to gather her thoughts, but that would be a stain on their diplomatic mission.

When John finished his meal, Tichit asked to speak with him in private. John nodded and led them across the meadow into the largest shelter.

Inside, they followed him into a room dominated by a mound of leaves. With a sigh, he sank into it and lay sprawled, staring up at Tichit.

"What do you want to talk about, friend?"

Many things. Let's begin with something less serious. We've noticed that you've expanded beyond the agreed-upon territory.

John blew air through his nose and closed his eyes. "Yep. That we have."

Why?

"It was necessary."

Why, friend?

John's eyes opened and fixed on Tichit. "We needed more room to live in."

Perhaps we misunderstood your needs. We believed we'd given you enough resources to survive comfortably for many generations.

John's face twisted into a grimace and he gave a short, dry laugh. "Survive, sure. Live? No. We needed room to build."

Build what?

"Playing fields. Kitchens. Furnaces. Everything we needed."

Needed. Not wanted. Shla-ne wasn't sure why they required furnaces or kitchens when the fruits, which contained all the necessary nutrients, could be eaten raw. And playing fields, there she agreed with John. She could now understand why the humans found life without games boring.

I understand, Tichit responded. *Do you believe the expansion will stop now?*

John studied him for a moment, then nodded. "Yeah, probably."

All right. Now, friend, tell me about the war.

John's lips twisted into a smirk. "Nothing much to say. Some people are evil pieces of shit. We're trying to kill them before they kill us."

What makes you think they are evil?

John's expression hardened into a glare. "Nothing makes me *think* that. It's what they are. Like the mountain people—can you believe they *burn* their dead?" John snickered and shook his head, as if it were the most ridiculous thing he'd heard in a long time. "Those bodies could nourish the soil. They could be the foundation for new trees! Instead, those shits just burn them. Waste them for fun. If that's not evil, I don't know what is."

Tichit was silent.

"And the goddamn tree people with their fake hippie bullshit. 'Teach kids to think for themselves, not just obey adults.' Ever heard of vicarious learning? Guess not. Can you imagine what it would do to us if that idea spread?"

Tichit remained silent. Shla-ne couldn't even think of a possible reply.

"There'd be a bunch of adults who don't know how to do shit because no one taught them. Goddammit." John sighed. "All those shits need to die before they kill us all."

Finally, Tichit released a pulse. *So you're all divided because you have different opinions?*

"Yeah!" John spat. "Why else? The mountain people with their burning and self-help and voting. The tree people with their lazy parenting, exercises—do you know they paint themselves purple? With that fruit, I forgot what it's called. They say it's camouflage." John sneered. "Maybe, but they also just don't wanna be human, ya know? They're rejecting as much of their humanity as they can. Because they hate themselves, and they hate us."

Shla-ne couldn't listen any longer. She crawled forward. *There must be a way to make peace.*

"Peace!" John curled his lip in disgust and shook his head.

I don't understand, Shla-ne pulsed. *You're of one kin. Surely there is a way for you to live together in harmony. There is enough food, water, and shelter for everyone. There is no need for conflict.*

John's face contorted in rage. "Nobody wants that!"

She paused, confused and disappointed. Beneath his grimace of fury, she felt creases of a different emotion. Fear? It made no sense, but she felt it.

If only she could pulse something to reassure him and calm his troubled mind—but that was impossible when she didn't know the cause.

She wished she could understand the humans better. *Did you eat human meat for lunch?*

John nodded. "Sure. We added some human to our soup today. I think he was from the tree people."

Why? There's enough food for everyone.

"Stop saying that!" He pushed himself to his feet. "We needed meat."

Why? The fruits provide your bodies with all the necessary nutrients.

"Maybe not." John raised his eyebrows as though waiting for her to consider it. "We keep dying at seventy and eighty. Maybe our bodies are missing some nutrients from meat. And we already have all these prisoners from the other tribes. And just killing them would be a waste of meat. And it tastes good, and it's something *different*, you know, it will raise everyone's spirit and..." He sighed, seeming very tired. "And it's something different."

Shla-ne thought she understood, but she couldn't imagine consuming her own kin. It simply felt wrong. It felt like going against nature.

Tichit shifted. *Friend, is there any way to convince you to speak with the other leaders? To make peace?*

John's Adam's apple bobbed up and down. He wiped his lips and shook his head. "No, we—it needs to be this way."

All right, Tichit replied. *In the morning, we will return to our people. We will discuss your expansion and your war, and we will find a solution for your situation.*

John's eyes locked on Tichit, sharp. Focused. The gaze disturbed Shla-ne, though she wasn't sure why.

"I get it," John said. "Okay. I'll talk to the leaders. I'll go talk to them right now. About *peace*. How does that sound to you?"

It sounds wonderful, friend.

John's gaze lingered for a moment, then he grabbed his spear and strode past them. They followed him outside, where he called over to a dozen males. They picked up their weapons and, with John at the front, they marched into the forest.

Some of the remaining humans turned to Shla-ne and her kin, their looks wary. Perhaps unfriendly.

Shla-ne thought about explaining the situation to them, but that could make it worse.

Solemi turned to Tichit. *Now what?*

We wait.

They settled by the fire, soaking in its heat. The humans carried on with their routines, casting wary glances toward Shla-ne's group.

Shla-ne sensed people in the card-playing shelter. Her body ached for a game, but now was not the time.

Va-shi broke the stillness. *What if they kill John?*

Tichit shared his concern. *I hope he'll be all right. But if not, we will have to discuss the situation with the new leader, as well as the other two chiefs.*

The sun sank low, leaving the day with a grayish hue. The air went cold, and the humans gathered around the fire, reheating their soup and eating in quiet concentration.

After a while, cracks of twigs echoed from the tree line.

The humans snatched their weapons and sprung to their feet, their gazes fixed on the forest edge.

Tichit shifted forward. Solemi rested a tendril on his side. *Perhaps we should move to the back of the camp.*

Then a figure stepped out, spear in hand. John. Calm and unscathed.

"We've got guests!" he shouted. "Be nice, everyone!"

He turned and gestured toward the tree line. First, the men who had accompanied him emerged, followed by a steady stream of new people. Within moments, two dozen strangers stood in the meadow.

Whispers rippled through the ground tribe. Shla-ne caught fragments like "tree people" and "mountain." Some raised their weapons slightly, ready for battle.

John lifted a palm. "I said be nice! I met with the other chiefs. We had a long talk about what's best for everyone. And we've reached a conclusion."

The ground people lowered their weapons slowly. Their tension eased.

Tichit moved closer to John; Solemi's tendrils slipped off. *Does this mean you've reached peace?*

John turned to him. The lines on his face creased into a strange pattern. Sorrow? Anger? Contentment? It seemed a mixture of all three.

John nodded and stepped toward Tichit. "Yes, my friend. We've reached peace. After all, the enemy of my enemy—"

He thrust his spear toward Tichit's chest. There was a wet squelch, accompanied by soft, sickening crunches.

A few people gasped. Others laughed.

Was it a joke? Had John just tried to scare Tichit? But the sound...

Two other males stepped forward, one wielding a long knife, the other a hammer. They raised their weapons.

Shla-ne's insides twisted in a painful realization. It wasn't a joke.

She moved forward. *Stop! It will kill him!*

The weapons fell. More wet crunching sounds as Tichit's blood splashed across the grass. His body collapsed to the ground.

A wave of shock washed over Shla-ne, but it wasn't her own. It was Tichit's. Like Shla-ne, he had no idea what was going on.

What are you doing? His pulse was thin.

John thrust again.

Va-shi moved forward. *Stop it, you're killing him!*

Blood pouring from his deep wounds, Tichit raised his quivering tendrils toward John. *Please, friend. There is no need for conflict.*

"Yes, there is!" John snarled, driving his spear into Tichit's body for the third time. He twisted the pole; Tichit's tendrils flailed, then went limp, plopping to the ground.

Tichit's mangled body lay still.

The man with the hammer grinned. "Guess we're having salad for breakfast!"

Some humans laughed. Why did they laugh? Why weren't they as shocked as Shla-ne? She couldn't understand.

Solemi shifted forward. *Why did you do that, John?* His pulse quivered.

John turned to his people and gestured toward Shla-ne, Solemi, and Va-shi. "These triffids came here to turn us into cattle!"

That's not true, Solemi pulsed.

"We've shown them only hospitality all day, and do you know what they told me in private? They want us to go back to our reservation!" The crowd fell silent. All eyes were fixed on John. "When I refused, they threatened us with force!"

Heads swiveled toward Shla-ne, Solemi, and Va-shi. Shla-ne sensed their hateful glares.

Shla-ne moved forward. *We only wanted you to live in peace.*

They didn't seem to hear her.

John's voice swelled. "It's not our fault that we landed here!" Some people nodded. A man said, "Yeah." "And this planet is big enough for all of us! We deserve to live like people!"

There were grunts of agreement.

"We will not be their cattle!" John turned to Shla-ne, Solemi, and Va-shi. "In alliance with the tree tribe and the mountain tribe, I declare war against the triffids!"

The meadow erupted in cheers. Weapons rose over heads. A few humans started toward Shla-ne and her kin.

They're afraid of us for some reason, Shla-ne pulsed. *We need to explain we mean them no harm.*

Solemi sent a wave of disagreement. *I don't think that's possible. I don't think they care. I think they just want a war with us.*

Va-shi's cold terror shimmered through Shla-ne's vessels. *Why would they want it? We did them no harm.*

It's stimulating.

Shla-ne stiffened. If their dangerous games excited their hyperactive minds, how much stronger was the idea of a fight to the death? After all, the untruths they told each other were full of conflict.

Humans might have been afraid of pain and death, but was it possible that doing nothing scared them even more? Perhaps, when Tichit and the others fulfilled the humans' needs, they took away their (conflict) purpose. Perhaps, to them, it was an empty existence. And in the face of that emptiness, their desperate minds invented new problems to solve; new conflicts to resolve.

Until it all graduated to a war.

Tichit had pulsed that there was no need for conflict.

John's answer was *Yes, there is!*

The crowd closed around them, and terror twisted Shla-ne's insides. But below that dwelled a sorrowful pity for the creatures whose restless minds, addicted to problem-solving, seemed incapable of enjoying peace even when peace was given.

A woman's scream cut through the night. Va-shi's human friend charged at her, hammer raised. The woman pounced and brought the hammer down—the rock sank into Va-shi's chest. Blood erupted in spurts.

Va-shi's terror rolled over Shla-ne like a frigid gale. *It hurts. Help me, it hurts so much.*

Something grasped Shla-ne from behind. Solemi's tendril. *We must escape,* he pulsed.

Va-shi reached a trembling tendril toward them. *Please, help me.*

"I got you!" the woman screamed, and the hammer struck again. A burst of blood splashed across the woman's face and teeth. "You fake bitch! You traitor! I got you!"

Solemi yanked Shla-ne away. *We don't have time to help her. We must warn our people.*

A man swung a long knife and a few of Va-shi's tendrils dropped into the grass. *So much pain. Please.* Her pulses were thin and frantic.

But Solemi was right. Va-shi's wounds were lethal, and if Shla-ne and Solemi didn't escape, their people wouldn't be ready for the humans.

Shla-ne spun to find a gap in the crowd. *There.* She pointed. She and Solemi glided toward it, but as the humans charged, the gap closed.

I'll make a path for you, Solemi pulsed. *Go. Warn everyone.*

No. You must come with me.

I don't think that's possible.

Solemi threw his weight against two men, slamming them aside and creating an opening toward the trees.

Go. His tendrils shoved more people back. A knife jutted from Solemi's side, but he kept fighting. Shla-ne slipped through the gap and darted for the trees.

John's voice thundered behind her. "She's escaping! After her!"

A weak echo of Va-shi's terror and agony held onto her vessels. *Please. Help me.*

Solemi's determined pulse, raw with his own agony, was stronger. *Go as fast as you can.*

The humans shouted and laughed as they chased after her, weapons raised over their heads. A rock arced through the air and struck her side. Dull pain pulsed in the spot, but she kept moving.

She slid into the forest, winding between trunks and bushes. The human voices thinned behind her. She found a relatively open path and glided across its uneven ground, her electrochemical pulses mapping her surroundings. No humans nearby.

But the ground ahead was soft. She halted, almost sliding onto a patch of leaves. Only leaves didn't land in neat patches like this one. They had been arranged.

She picked up a stick and prodded the leafy floor. It caved; the leaves fell away, revealing thin branches set over a manufactured pit. On the bottom, wooden spikes pointed upward.

A cold shiver ran through Shla-ne's vessels. Had the humans dug this pit for someone to fall in? Of course they had.

The weapons, the pit, even their games—everything designed to cause harm. Shla-ne couldn't find sense in it.

A twig snapped behind her. A pulse revealed a human charging at her.

She turned and flung the stick. It missed. The human leapt and thrust a spear. Shla-ne dashed backward; the spearpoint stopped an inch from her chest.

A woman's voice hissed, "Ah—you bitch."

Maya, please—don't hurt me. We're not trying to oppress you. We're trying to help.

"Lying bitch!" Maya snarled, stepping forward and swinging the spear. The hard wood smashed into Shla-ne's head and knocked her to the ground. "You won't enslave us, bitch!"

Through dull, throbbing pain, Shla-ne wondered who had mentioned enslavement. Not even John had.

Maya poised her spear as John had before killing Tichit. In panic, Shla-ne shot out her tendrils and shoved her back.

Maya staggered—and pitched backward into the pit.

Shla-ne reached for her too late; there was a yelp, then a dull thud accompanied by a wet squelch.

I'm sorry.

Curiosity drew her attention toward the pit, but she refused to scan it and sense the damage done to Maya's body. Too much death tonight. Too much pain. And it all seemed completely pointless.

John, who had been Tichit's lifelong friend. The hammer-maker who'd shown Va-shi her craft. Maya, who'd taught Shla-ne how to enjoy a game. The humans had turned on them so easily—

"There it is!" a male voice called from above.

A hot pain seared Shla-ne's side as a man landed in front of her. He was holding a long knife. The tip of its point was wet with her blood.

A heavy thud came behind her. Another man, hammer raised over his head.

They were grinning at her.

Please, she pulsed. *Don't kill me. I mean you no harm.*

"But we mean harm to you," the man with the hammer said. His companion laughed.

Then they charged at her at the same time.

Shla-ne slid sideways, dodging both attacks. Still, she felt slow. She needed rest. And sunlight.

Please.

She raised her tendrils, trying to show her harmlessness. The man with the long knife slashed, and two tips of her vines flopped to the ground. The wounds burned as if on fire.

The men closed in. She backed away, tripped over her own tendrils, and fell onto her back.

The men darted forward.

She pushed herself up, tensing for an escape, even though she knew she was too slow. But she had to try. She had to warn her people.

The men raised their weapons.

Shla-ne braced herself for the pain. For the death.

A large form darted toward the men—her kin, but wounded, blood streaming from many cuts. Their tendrils brandished two long knives.

Solemi.

One of his knives sliced across the hammer-wielder's neck, releasing a river of blood that poured down the man's chest.

That's six, Solemi remarked just before the other human hacked off Solemi's tendrils; one of his knives clattered to the ground.

As the hammer-wielder collapsed, the other human attacked Solemi with new-found ferocity.

Solemi fell back, his movements slowing and faltering.

The man swung at him harder and faster, perhaps sensing his advantage. His focus was narrowed on Solemi.

Shla-ne picked up Solemi's fallen knife and turned toward the human. *I'm sorry.*

The man froze, then began to turn. Shla-ne thrust the blade into his side. He gasped and his eyes went wide. He collapsed to his knees, staring up at her in terror.

Remorse surged over her at once—but beneath it crackled a fierce thrill, the same sensation she'd experienced after she'd won the card game. Only this one felt stronger.

The man's weapon slid from his fingers and clanged to the ground.

Solemi picked it up. *Thank you. We must go.*

Shla-ne drew her knife free; the man grunted with pain. They left him to bleed out and moved toward the mountains.

They crawled for a long while, but Solemi was slowing down. Shla-ne wrapped her tendrils around him and dragged him along, but he was too heavy.

We should hide and rest, she pulsed. *In the morning, the sun will give us strength to continue.*

Solemi's reply came slow and thin. *We must keep going. The sun will not reach us beneath this canopy, and we can't rest under a gap, in the open. The darkness hides us from human eyes. And I'm not sure how long I have left.*

So they kept moving. They reached the foothills where human voices echoed from every side, but they kept close to boulders and growth, and through the shroud of night, they crossed the mountain pass and slipped into the forest on the other side.

After they crossed the river and the meadow, and after they reached the spot where Shla-ne had soaked in the sun two days ago, only then did they rest. And by then, the sun began climbing its horizon, caressing Shla-ne and Solemi with its warmth.

Several days later, they soaked in the sun back home. Their long knives rested beside them.

The heat permeated Shla-ne's vessels, transforming into fresh energy. The breeze caressed her leafy skin. Besides that, the world stood still. Everything was quiet. And lately, Shla-ne didn't like that. Because something *could* be happening, something exciting, and her body was aching for it.

Sometimes she missed when she could linger on the same spot for days. But that part of her seemed gone. For the first time in centuries, she had become someone else.

She focused on Solemi. *Do you want to do something?*

Yes. Do you want to play with a lemi?

No. Her tendrils ran along her knife blade. A thrill rippled through her body. *How about we practice instead?*

That's a good idea. After all, we have a war to fight.

They picked up their knives and turned away from the sun, crawling to join the others at the training grounds.

*The most frightening monsters
accept what they are
and strive to excel at what they do best.*

SUGAR

D S Telling

Born anew, a cold wind bit at the outcast's skin. *Cold*. It was a simple word that should have produced a sound. Unclenching their jaw, they tried again.

"Cold."

They sucked a breath, alarmed by how the word had shaped their mouth. They were not accustomed to the physical effort it took to simply communicate. Back home, it was different.

"Home."

The word vibrated against the walls of their mouth. The invasive sensation of it sickened them. A shutter raked through their strange new body as they reconciled where they were, with *what* they were... They truly had been abandoned, condemned to a prison of flesh—

This is how it must be.

The voices of The Many echoed inside their head. It was a new feeling, to no longer be part of a collective.

"Why?" they asked, unable to remain soundless.

You shall remain on Earth for the good of The Many.

"What do we mean by 'you'?" Speech was becoming more intuitive for them.

There is no 'we,' not anymore. You have been removed to prevent the spread of sickness. Because of you, our consciousness became fractured, plagued by feelings of dissatisfaction. We cannot risk being discontented. Our survival depends on it.

"I—" It was a strange word for them, but seemingly appropriate. "—I am sad," they whispered, devastated that they now had to verbalize their emotions or risk being misunderstood.

This is a gift. It is our nature to learn from a distance, yet you desired to experience that which we were only meant to perceive. This banishment is of your own making. Amongst the humans, you may find some contentment.

A wetness dripped down the length of their face. They moved to wipe it, fingers tracing the lid of one eye before moving to the other. Both were lined with soft hairs that protected their...sight.

Fluttering their eyes open, they lifted their arms and shielded their gaze. It was bright, too bright. A sharp, painful wind struck their face.

"Return me home!" they shrieked, a sob escaping their throat. "I did not know I was causing harm!"

It is too late. Goodbye, dear sacrifice.

The voices of The Many disappeared, leaving them in silence. Overwhelmed, they stood unmoving, silently learning their body. No longer did it feel like they were trapped within a holding made of flesh and bone, instead they felt at one with their new form, unable to distinguish themself from it.

Flexing their knees, an understanding bloomed. Their limbs could not move independently from their mind, though they quickly discovered that it was not the same for the reverse. The mind was distinct from the body, a potential haven for things discreet and private. The newness of it all made them lightheaded.

Struggling to balance, they examined their surroundings. Snow blanketed everything around them. In the far distance, white dusted trees lined the horizon. They squinted, recognizing the source of the brightness as Earth's sun. Its rays warmed their face, though the rest of their exposed skin was so cold it burned. A violent shiver quaked through their body, reminding them that they existed in a state that could not be sustained.

"Death," they whispered toward the sky, searching for an inkling of home.

Fear quickened their heartbeat and sharpened their senses. On the wind, they smelled a storm. The dull pain that tinged their fingers and toes spiked into something stronger.

They did not want to die.

Instinct drove them forward. Sprinting on clumsy legs, they made for the horizon. Collapsing into the snow, their skin screamed with discomfort as black dots filled their vision.

"You did not last long," they muttered to themself, the piercing fear of death dimming to a hollow numbness.

"Hey sugar, what are you doing out here in your birthday suit?" asked a voice external from their head.

They flipped onto their side, gaze settling onto a concerned-looking old woman. They smiled, pleased to have interpreted another's emotion without needing to hear it verbalized. They doubled over onto their hands and knees, retching as they submitted to a dizzying wave of homesickness.

"I can't carry you, but if you can get yourself up, I'll lead you somewhere warm," the woman offered, taking a few tentative steps toward them. She had kind eyes that crinkled in the corners.

"You will help?" they choked.

"Get up."

"Why help?"

"Because you're sickly, and I won't turn a blind eye to someone in need."

Kneeling, the woman looped their arm around her neck. She felt frail, but they sensed the determination pulsing through her grip.

"I am a burden." They shook their head. "Leave me."

The woman rolled her eyes. "Get up," she repeated, her voice tinged with exasperation. "*Now*, goddamn it."

They complied, though their arms and legs screamed to succumb to the cold. Their mind resisted their limb's pleas, proving itself an independent force. It seemed to them that humans were more resilient than they'd understood...that *they* were more resilient than they'd understood. Their legs strained as they struggled to keep balanced upon them.

The old woman did not let them fall. The two waddled together for a collection of minutes, taking longer than typical, they determined, based on how the woman huffed next to them.

"We are slowing you down." Their head lolled from side to side.

"So what?" the woman spat, tilting their head onto her shoulder, "And who's 'we'? You got more than you in that noggin of yours, or are the dead startin' to gather 'round you?" Her tone sounded worried.

They scanned their thoughts for a hint of The Many, sensing nothing.

"Only me remains," they responded. "*I* am slowing you down."

"Enough talk, more walkin'," she ordered, quickening her steps.

They hastened their pace to that of their companion, noticing for the first time that the woman had slipped her coat onto their shoulders. A new emotion tugged at their chest, one of gratitude. Tears lined their eyes, blurring the outline of a cabin only a short distance away.

"Welcome home!" the woman shouted, slapping them on the back.

The cabin was small and *warm*. They slinked deeper into the couch as the woman piled blanket after blanket atop them, muttering how it was a miracle they hadn't lost any limbs to frostbite. A snapping fire burned too close for comfort. Inching their feet away from it, the woman instructed them to stop, assuring them that the flame could not burn outside from where it was contained.

The sound of water ran heavily in the background, and they wondered where it came from. Scanning their surroundings, they saw that aside from the entrance, the house only had one other door—

"The bathroom," the woman stated, noticing where their gaze had settled. "Drawin' you a nice, hot bath."

"More help?" Fresh, burning tears puddled in their eyes. "Crying is a frequent occurrence."

"For some," the woman responded from the bathroom, the sound of water stopping.

They laughed, not fully understanding what they had found so humorous.

"C'mon," the woman offered, helping them to their feet. "A bath will do you good."

The sweet-smelling water consumed their body, ridding them of the bone chill that had not given way to the blankets or fire. They relaxed, curling and unfurling their stiff fingers with increasing ease. Hearing steps, they turned their attention to the open door.

The woman carried a bundle of folded clothing. "Somethin' to change into." Setting them atop the sink, she turned to walk away.

"Your clothes?" they asked, feeling guilty that they continued to take so much from the woman.

"My late husband's pajamas."

The finality of her words left no room for misunderstanding. "I am sorry that your husband is dead," they replied, a heaviness settling upon their chest.

"That's life," the woman shrugged, "What's your name?"

The instinct to lie tugged at them, a strange feeling as they had never spoken anything but the truth... When they were part of The Many, there had been no other option but honesty.

"I cannot remember my name." A half-truth. They could not remember what had never existed.

"You've got any family I can call?"

"No."

"You some kind of criminal?"

"No...I—" They still struggled to say it, "—I am alone. No one looks for me."

"Well..." The woman rubbed her chin. "As long as you're willin' to help out around the house, you're welcome to stay here as long as you need, sugar."

"I am Sugar?"

"If you want to be." The woman shook her head, smiling at a joke they did not understand.

"I am Sugar, then," they agreed, eliciting a laugh from the woman. "What is your name?"

"Lucille, but you can call me Ma."

They nodded, sinking deeper into the tub as they watched her turn to exit—

"Ma?"

"Yes, Sugar?"

"Thank you."

Ma smiled before disappearing through the door.

Over a collection of months, Sugar learned a lot about who they were as a *person*.

They had learned they were smart, capable of solving any problem that popped up at the house. With a little patience and research, they had been able to fix Ma's loud plumbing and leaky roof with ease.

They had realized that they were strong too, capable of chopping trees for firewood with efficiency. Recovering from a past fire, the surrounding forest's trees were narrow and had initially deceived Sugar into believing they would be easy to cut. Oh, how wrong that sentiment had been. The wood was hard and required persistence. Proud, Sugar often snuck glances at their muscled arms, a reminder of their determination.

Above all, they coveted their ability to love, a quality modelled and nurtured by Ma. They felt it in the way Ma spoke with them, cared for them. She listened to their strange questions and gave thoughtful answers, never making them feel inadequate or embarrassed.

Together they could talk for hours, often spending their time sitting in the frosted garden behind the house. It was Ma's favourite spot. "Because of its potential," she had stated. "Just wait for spring, Sugar! I can't wait for you to see my roses."

They very much looked forward to it.

She was their shining light, their sun that kept them warm. In fact, their favourite part of a chore-filled day was when they got to return home and find Ma cooking something delicious. She always welcomed them at the door, pulling them into a hug they had come to crave.

"Welcome home, Sugar," she would always say before asking about their day.

They loved her, very, very much.

Today, they had made the long drive into town and picked up some necessities Ma had asked for. She had stayed behind to tend to the laundry. All day they had looked forward to helping her fold it. The chore comforted Sugar. It was an activity that encouraged conversation and laughter.

Taking the final turn home, the cabin came into view. No light shone from the windows.

Their heartrate quickened as a wave of nausea washed over them. Screeching to a stop, they leaped from the truck and bolted to the door. Standing at its threshold, they waited for Ma's welcome.

None came.

Throwing the door open, they lunged into the darkness.

"Ma?" Worry mangled their voice.

Only silence responded.

"Ma!" they shouted, flicking on the lights.

They scanned the room, finding nothing out of sorts. The dryer light flickered green, alerting them its cycle had finished. The house smelled only of detergent. Sugar's stomach knotted at the foreignness of it. The aroma of dinner should be filling their nostrils. They sucked a breath, picking up Ma's cutting knife as they walked toward the bathroom door. Light seeped from beneath it. Flinging it open, Sugar clutched their chest to keep their heart from stopping.

A middle-aged man lounged in the tub. His long limbs were sprawled over the bath's porcelain lip. He turned to them, looking surprised.

"Who are you?" His brows narrowed.

"Where is Ma?" They followed an instinct that begged to keep their voice steady.

"Lucille?" Confusion was etched across his face. "I didn't know she had other family."

"Well, she does." They tightened their grip around the knife.

"I thought I was her only next-of-kin," he shrugged, splashing pink-tinted bathwater.

They swallowed at the colour. Noticing their gaze, he pointed to the rose-scented bubble bath sitting on the tub's edge.

"I'm her nephew." A smile crawled across his cracked lips. "Aunt Lucy gave me a call. Told me she wasn't feelin' too hot—"

"Where is she?" they pressed, growing impatient.

"Calm down." He lifted his dripping hands. "The docs are keeping her overnight at the hospital. I'm picking her up tomorrow."

Sugar tried to recall whether they'd seen another parked car.

"I could have taken her!" they yelled, no longer able to contain their emotion. "She is my Ma!"

"Well, you didn't have a phone on you, did you?" His eyes looked earnest. "I'd shake your hand if I wasn't buck naked in the tub." He leaned forward, gripping the porcelain. "Give me a moment to get decent, and I'll answer your questions." Standing, he grabbed a towel with a calmness Sugar did not feel.

"Okay," they replied, feeling out of place for the first time in months. They resisted the urge to shudder as they turned to leave—

"I wonder why Aunt Lucy never said anything about havin' a daughter," he mused, whistling as he haphazardly wiped himself dry.

Heat crawled up the length of their neck as they darted through the door, slamming it before he could say more.

Steadying themself against the couch edge, Sugar resisted the urge to sit. Keeping a tight grip around the knife, they stretched their stiff neck and waited, unwilling to turn away from the bathroom. Their pulse had only just begun to slow when the door creaked open. The man stepped through it, looking remorseful.

"Havin' a few minutes to myself, I've realized how rude I've been," he started. "Didn't even think to introduce myself."

He lifted his empty hands, a slow smile parting his lips as he narrowed the distance between them. Sugar lifted their knife in a silent bid for him to stay put. He stopped and the smile faded from his face.

They backed away another few steps, noticing he had dressed in a hurry. His still-damp skin and hair had soaked parts of his flannel shirt and jeans. Lightheaded, Sugar sucked a jagged breath, feeling betrayed by their body.

"What is your name?" they asked, voice hoarse.

"John."

"John *who*?"

"Hey, calm down, honey. I've just realized I've got a cousin I didn't know about—I'm just as shocked as you." His voice possessed a gentleness that had them lowering their knife. Sugar's gut yelled to keep it pointed, but their mind worked to rationalize the information they'd been given.

Never had they felt so internally torn, and for the first time since being abandoned, Sugar found themself missing their previous home.

The Many lived as one organism that floundered from galaxy to galaxy, searching for unknown knowledge. As a collective, members could not shield their thoughts and feelings from one another, ensuring that as a group, they experienced and interpreted everything they encountered the same. Understanding other members was as simple as existing. It was why Sugar had been culled like a cancer cell...the others knew Sugar had grown bored, prone to lethargy that tainted The Many's very existence.

Until Earth, secrets had been impossible to keep.

Not unlike The Many, Ma had always been an open book, upfront and honest with her feelings...but this John, Sugar didn't know what to make of him.

Fatigued, they settled on a simple statement. "My name isn't *Honey*."

"Didn't think it was." His brows lifted. "Now, put down that knife before you hurt yourself."

"Why would I hurt myself?"

"Accidents happen." He shrugged. "A pretty thing like you probably hasn't trained with a knife before."

"I am capable." Sugar didn't understand why he would assume otherwise. "I have used a knife many times."

"Sure." He tilted his head, eyes glinting with *something*. "I can't comfortably tell you all that's goin' on with Aunt Lucy unless we can at least be civil with one another." He lowered onto the wooden floor and crossed his legs. "Meet me in the middle somewhere, huh?" he urged. "I'm just tryin' to help."

"Then help," they snapped. "Ma never had to tell me she wanted to help, she just *did*."

"What do you expect me to do?" he countered. "You're basically holdin' me hostage. *Jesus Christ*, we should be comforting one another!"

He dropped his head into his hands, mumbling something about needing sleep. Compassion surged through Sugar. They sat, stabbing the knife on the floor.

"I am sorry," they whispered, playing with its hilt. "Thank you for helping Ma when I was gone." It was a show of good faith, one they hoped the man—John—would reciprocate.

"Eh, it's water under the bridge." He lifted his gaze and winked. Sugar noticed that his eyes crinkled at the edges like Ma's. The similarity comforted them.

"We're both just worried sick," he continued.

Sugar exhaled a long breath, feeling relieved. "Will you tell me what happened now?"

"'Course I will." A frown pulled at the smile he kept glued to his face. "Aunty Lucy had a heart attack, honey." His voice was low and careful. "She might pull through, but it's not lookin' too good—"

"I want to see her!" they screamed. "Take me to Ma, now!"

Trembling, a sob escaped Sugar's mouth. To their horror, their body resisted their mind's demands to keep calm and controlled, instead succumbing to a bout of hysterics. Curling their knees to their chest, they levelled a teary stare toward John.

"*P-please*," they begged, not able to take in enough air.

Meeting their eyes, his smile dissolved into a line. "See, I didn't want to make you upset...baby, she might still pull through," he cooed, extending an arm toward them.

Their chest felt like it had been ripped in two. Doubling over, they let out a cry, unable to withdraw from the pain. They had never experienced grief before. It was profound, world ending. They blinked, hard, attempting to remove the dark shadows that threatened to consume their vision.

"Take a deep breath." His words were hot against their cheek—

Sugar hadn't noticed he'd moved. Instinctively, they reached for the knife, finding only the notched floor. They suppressed a gasp as he traced circles between their shoulders. Their skin prickled beneath his fingers.

"Shhhhh." His circles turned to zigzags that climbed up and down the length of their spine. "I'll take you to your Ma first thing tomorrow, how about that?"

"No. Now." They lifted their gaze, noticing for the first time how large he was. Size wasn't something they often thought about...but now it was all they noticed. Even crouched, he loomed over them. One of his thick arms rested against his knee, the other hung across their shoulders. They peeked at his palm laying sprawled against the floor, then glanced at their own.

They had never felt so...small.

"Don't be scared, baby." His mouth brushed against their ear. "You know what? You're even prettier when you cry."

They yanked free from his touch and jumped to their feet.

He stretched out his long legs, amusement flickering in his eyes as he relaxed against the wall. "Be a doll and grab me that bar of soap from the bathroom." He scratched his beard. "We got some time to kill."

"Why?"

"I'll show you." A toothy smile parted his lips.

Not turning away from him, Sugar backed toward the bathroom door. Spotting the soap sitting on the sink's edge, they darted for it, returning to where they'd stood in less than a breath.

"Give it to me...*please*."

Sugar cocked their arm—

"What are we, animals?" he chuckled, "Don't throw it, go ahead and hand it over."

They couldn't understand why they were acting so strangely. Their body had always listened to their mind...now it rebelled, shaking and gasping when they needed to be calm. Even as they worked to reconcile all they'd been told, it trembled with restlessness.

"*Please*?" he repeated.

There was no reason for him to lie to them. He'd had his chance to attack them and had instead comforted them in a way that felt Ma-like...though also very, *very* different. Shaking their head, Sugar crossed the room, handing the bar of soap to John—

"Thank you, baby." His eyes contained a hunger they couldn't place.

Pulling their knife from his beltloop he began carving the soap. "What should I make?"

Sugar shrugged.

"C'mon, give me *somethin'*." His smile wavered then reset within a blink.

"I just want to go see Ma." Their tone was flat. "That is all I care about. You make whatever you want."

He nodded. "Tell me about yourself first—"

"My name is not Baby or Honey." They curled their hands into fists. "It is Sugar."

"Sugar?" he snickered. "I like that better anyways."

His eyes remained locked on them as his hands carved the soap with quick ease. He cleared his throat. "You here visiting from college or somethin'?"

"No."

"Where have you been then? Never seen you around before."

"Do you come to Ma's often?"

"Just to check in." His gaze hardened. "You got family?"

"I have Ma." They tilted their head.

Licking his lips, his cuts turned frenzied. With rapid flicks of his thumb, he sliced slab after slab, never looking down. "Nothing else to share?"

"I am strong and I am smart." They didn't know what else to say, Earth life was still very new.

"Nah." He shook his head, refusing to blink.

Heat flushed their cheeks. "You do not know me."

"I've got two eyes, don't I?"

They did not understand what parallels he had drawn to make such a conclusion. "I like my body. It houses thoughts that cannot infect others."

"No, Sugar, one's thoughts can still very much infect others, if done correctly." He pared away the remaining sliver of soap then wiped his hands against his jeans. "In fact, many of my deepest, darkest thoughts come to fruition—"

"You did not carve anything." They stepped backwards, hand trailing against the kitchen counter.

"Nope." He groaned as he pushed to his feet, wiping the knife against his shirt. "Sometimes it just feels *good* to cut somethin'."

Sugar's body calmed as their mind finally listened. This human wasn't just different, he was *wrong*. "Is Ma really in the hospital?"

"Yeah, a stroke..." John trailed off, his eyes turning glassy as he muttered beneath his breath.

"You said it was a heart attack—"

He lunged for them. Crumpling to the floor in one quick movement, they dodged his attack as he slammed into the cabinetry. Springing to their feet, they sprinted to the bathroom and locked themself in.

"Knock, knock, it's John Doe lookin' for my Jane Doe!"

The door shuddered as he slammed against it.

They turned to the small bathroom window—the door gave a loud *crack.* They yanked at the glass pane, finding it stuck. A warrior's scream tore through their throat. The taste of copper narrowed their focus as they yielded to a surge of adrenaline. Tearing away the toilet's tank lid, they slammed the hard porcelain against the window, shattering it with a violent *crash—*

The door slammed open as their foot found the tub's edge. They dove for the window; his hands encircled their ankle. Jagged glass tore at the skin on their stomach as he gave a vicious yank. They kicked, *hard*, breaking his nose. His scream rang through their ears like an explosion, but his grip loosened.

Pulling through, they fell onto the frozen, wet ground.

Sugar ran into the surrounding woods, stifling a scream as the howling wind brushed against their wounds.

"Sugar!" John's voice was not as distant as they'd hoped. "You little bitch!"

The sound of his long strides against the forest floor sent their pulse racing. Their steps were far shorter in comparison...

He was faster, stronger, smarter—

"No," they panted. Ma *needed* them.

They circled back toward the house, slowing their pace to a walk. Keeping on their toes, they silently weaved between narrow trees and bushes.

John Doe was too bulky to keep his steps quiet. Sugar watched as his lurching form passed them.

They kept to the shadows, careful not to wander into the moon's rays as they pondered why John had not taken any effort to hide himself. Creeping toward their chopping block at the forest's edge, they frowned, their answer obvious.

John Doe did not fear Sugar. The body they had been given was one he had deemed as lesser—*weaker.*

It was a stupid mistake on his part.

A smile parted their lips as they yanked their axe free from its block. Its edge glistened beneath the stars they'd once called home—

"Sugar!" His voice echoed in the distance. "Come out and let me see if you taste like your name suggests!"

Disgust pooled in their gut.

They sneaked through the woods, following his boasting, then his heavy breaths. It must take much effort, they speculated, to move a body as large as his...

Ignited beneath the moonlight, his wide shoulders heaved with exhaustion. Taking a steady breath, they pounced, bashing him on the head with the blunt edge of the blade.

He fell to the freezing soil with a muted *thump*.

Lifting their axe, Sugar exhaled, tightening their grip as they forced it down onto his leg. Like the trees they'd become accustomed to, his leg split into two within a few rage-fuelled chops. His eyes sprung open, releasing a stream of tears as his shriek echoed into the night sky.

"Where is my Ma?"

Blood spurted from his mouth as he attempted another scream.

"My Ma," they reminded, resting the sharp blade to his neck.

"Dead!" His laugh became mangled as he choked on his vomit.

Sugar crouched next to him. Drawing circles on his chest, they whispered their question once more. "Where?"

Fear flickered in his eyes, and the instinct to attack drove them to their feet. This is what predators must feel, they thought to themself, as they lifted the axe above their head.

His final words had been the response they needed. He had only told them because he feared for his life. It was a valid fear as they had cleaved his head off not a second later.

It had only taken one blow.

Sugar found Ma's body in the back garden, sitting in her old, wicker chair. Eyes open, she looked to be stargazing. The bruising around her neck suggested otherwise. Brushing their hand to her cold cheek, they recounted their favourite memory.

They had been sitting at Ma's feet, and Ma had been in her chair, her gentle fingers working a braid into Sugar's hair. It had been an odd night where neither of them had spoken a word, listening instead to the sounds of the garden.

"Sugar?" she had asked, breaking the silence.

"Yes, Ma?" they'd responded, reaching for her hand.

"Sometimes I think it was the stars that brought you to me."

A sob escaped their mouth as they withdrew from the memory. In the months they had been on Earth they had experienced the best and worst of humanity. Tears lining their eyes, they looked toward the endless sky that no longer felt like home, questioning what kind of beings lay in-between.

Space is an endless, black sea.
And as within all seas, there are monsters.

ORIOCH'S GRACE

Ryan Colley

Chapter One

We had been adrift among the pale stars of Sector E-Nine for forty-three cycles when the derelict appeared. Our purpose was simple—to map and to catalogue. My brood had no word for conquest or war; our ships carried archivists, not soldiers. We believed the galaxy itself to be a body of memory, and our duty was to tend its scars.

I remember the hum of the Orioch's Grace beneath my palms—the way the reactor's pulse matched the rhythm of my hearts. Beyond the viewing dome, the void rolled like an endless sea of smoke. Our sensors whispered through the black, brushing dust clouds, and the occasional echo of a signal from a far-off civilisation that had burned itself out long before our birth. These were the peaceful ghosts—sterile, quiet, obedient to entropy.

We were a small crew—five, bonded by shared neural lattice and purpose. Commandant Varris spoke in measured tones, each phrase flanged with harmonic overlays that marked her as of the deep-thinker caste. Her second, Teln, was forever recalibrating the sensor banks, murmuring to them as though the machines could be soothed. The others moved like pale insects through the decks, all grace and precision with no wasted motion. To an outsider, our vessel might have seemed lifeless—but to us, it thrummed with communion. Every thought rippled through the link. Every emotion was tempered and shared.

My role was observation—I recorded, interpreted, and translated. Where others saw radiation signatures or mineral spectra, I saw stories. The husks we found spoke to me, their cold geometries revealing intention and tragedy. I believed that nothing we encountered could surprise us anymore. I was wrong.

It began with a faint distortion in the long-range grav-readers—a drifting object, metallic, dense, unregistered. At first I thought it debris, a collapsed satellite or the remnant of an orbital array. But, as we drew closer, its silhouette took shape against the halo of a dying red dwarf. It was no natural fragment. It was a vessel.

The ship's design struck me as crude yet deliberate—all sharp angles and exposed struts, as though the builders had prized function above aesthetics. No energy emissions. No active core. Yet the hull remained largely intact, its lines blackened but unbroken. I ran my digits over the projection feed, tracing the jagged outlines. The sight unsettled me in a way I could not articulate to the link. It looked predatory.

Varris ordered a full spectral sweep. The results were near-impossible—no radiation leak, and no residual heat. The craft was ancient, yes, but preserved beyond reason, like a corpse that refused to rot.

Curiosity stirred among us—a dangerous thrill our kind rarely indulged. First contact with an unknown species was the dream of every surveyor, the culmination of generations of patient mapping. We did not yet know that some dreams were also nightmares.

The derelict hung before us like a shadow cast against the stars. Our floodlights slid across its hull, revealing a surface both battered and meticulous—plates of dark alloy bolted in uneven layers, pocked with impact marks, as though it had survived a thousand battles and borne each scar with quiet defiance. There were no adornments, no symmetry, no sense of grace. To my eyes, it seemed less a ship and more a wound carved into the void.

Varris ordered a slow approach vector. We glided closer, and the external cameras adjusted to the ship's dull reflection, struggling to interpret its geometry.

Teln murmured over the link, his voice vibrating through my neural nodes. "No power signatures. No core activity. No field resonance.

"Dead," I replied simply.

We attempted hailing procedures across all known civilised bands—trade, distress, relay. Even the ancient galactic emergency tone. Silence answered each. Not even a static whisper. We tried coded pulses, light signals, modulated grav-waves. Nothing.

The others began to speculate. Some believed it to be a pre-Expansion relic, an ark from a civilisation that perished before language standardisation. Others suggested a failed mining freighter or research outpost. But even those theories felt hollow. The scale was too large for utility, the design too deliberate for chance.

I requested permission to run a full surface scan. Varris hesitated—a rare thing for her. She was pragmatic, never prone to superstition, but even her composure wavered as the lights played across the hull. There were markings there, faint but distinct. Grooves etched into the metal in jagged sequences, repeating patterns. Teln enhanced the feed, translating the indentations into vector graphs. No discernible structure, no known alphabet. The ship's skin spoke in madness.

"Should we mark it as hostile?" one of the crew asked, their tone uncertain.

Varris shook her cranial frill. "Hostility implies intent. This...this feels different."

We drifted closer until our hull lights reflected back at us from a black viewport—one vast, single pane of reinforced material, uncracked and untouched by time. The light did not pass through. It was absorbed, swallowed whole. I could not see inside, but I felt watched.

Curiosity burned brighter than caution. It was our nature, after all—the archivists who could not leave ghosts alone.

Varris gave the command. "Prepare breach protocol."

There were rules—procedures written after too many explorers had died chasing echoes. We were meant to observe, report, and move on. But protocol was a soft thing when faced with mystery. We wanted to know. And as we aligned our ship beside the derelict's airlock, the distance between curiosity and doom closed to a breath.

We closed the distance on thruster whisper alone, our hull lights painting fractured reflections across the derelict's skin. The silence pressed against the dome, heavy as pressure. Even through layers of shielding, I felt it—that absence of all vibration, as if sound itself had been outlawed here.

Varris initiated the transmission sequence again, just in case. Nothing answered. Teln ran diagnostics twice, convinced the fault lay with us. When none were found, he stared at the readings in disbelief. I caught glimpses of the others' private thoughts—cold flares of unease quickly smothered by professionalism. We had drifted too close to mystery for any of us to retreat now. Discovery had already tasted us, and we have tasted it.

We deployed remote drones—small, spindle-bodied machines meant for preliminary contact. They launched from the lower bay, gliding across the black void towards the derelict's hull. Their lights flickered once as they breached the shadow. Then nothing. No telemetry. No feed. The drones vanished as though swallowed whole.

I watched the data stream collapse to zero. Every instinct in me whispered that we should leave, seal this thing in the dark where it belonged. But Varris simply adjusted her harness. Her tone remained even, detached.

"Perhaps the material interferes with transmission."

The external cameras focused on a single segment of the hull—a rectangular frame we assumed to be an access hatch. There was no visible mechanism, no locking wheel or control panel. Just a seam, faint and patient, as if waiting for hands that would never return. Varris ordered a directed beam at the surface, a pulse meant to simulate light-based greeting patterns. We watched the brightness spread across the metal like sunrise on a dead sea.

For a heartbeat, I thought the hull moved. Not flexed, not shifted—moved, in the way living tissue adjusts under a blade. Then the surface stilled, smooth once more. The readings returned blank.

It was irrational—impossible, even. Yet every nerve along my arms tingled with the certainty that something beyond that black viewport was aware of us, measuring, deciding. It wasn't hostility that I sensed, but a dreadful patience, as if it were allowing us to dig our own graves in its silence.

Varris finally broke the link. "We've exhausted safe channels. We'll proceed with breach containment."

The command settled over us like a funeral rite.

As we prepared the plasma cutters, the Orioch's Grace fell utterly still—no hum, no vibration, only the sound of our own breathing in the comms. Somewhere ahead, a ship that should not have survived drifted, quiet as the grave. And we, the archivists who had never known fear, were about to open the tomb.

The plasma torches cut with a soundless blue flare. Through the dome, I watched the beam trace its perfect circle against the derelict's hull, sparks scattering into nothing before the vacuum could swallow them. For a moment, I imagined the vessel flinching—a dead thing recoiling at the bite of light. The seam liquefied, then hardened again, edges glowing faintly.

We expected the atmosphere within to vent violently once the cut was complete, but nothing came. The airlock threshold opened like a wound refusing to bleed.

"Pressure stabilised," Teln reported, voice thin. "Internal atmosphere...trace oxygen, carbon, nitrogen. No radiation detected."

Varris hesitated, then gave the order. "Seal suits. Maintain full containment. No direct exposure."

Our suits hissed around us, layers of woven glass-fibre and biofilm sealing to our skins. The smell of disinfectant filled my mask—sharp, clean, and suddenly obscene. I watched the others move with methodical precision, checking valves, syncing data lines. We did everything by the book. It should have made me feel safe.

The shuttle detached from the Orioch's Grace with the gentlest push of inertia. I had never known space to feel so claustrophobic. The derelict grew impossibly large before us, a black continent floating in silence. Every panel and scar on its surface was visible now, every weld a reminder of something built by desperate, brutal hands.

When our landing clamps touched the hull, I felt a pulse—faint, like the echo of a heartbeat deep within the metal. Teln claimed it was the resonance of the cutter feedback. I didn't argue, but it followed us, thrumming faintly through the soles of my boots.

We drifted towards the breach. The edges of the cut were mirror-smooth, the metal curving inward as though the ship had swallowed the wound itself. A soft mist hung inside the threshold—not gas, but microscopic particulates drifting in slow, graceful spirals. My visor's filter compensated automatically, though I wished it hadn't. Watching those motes dance felt too much like watching dust in a tomb disturbed after centuries.

Varris led the way, her silhouette stark against the black interior. The moment she crossed the threshold, the sound in my headset changed. It wasn't static. More like the faint rush of breath, distant and steady, as though the ship itself exhaled. We followed her in.

The chamber beyond was narrow and low, built for a species taller and broader than ours, yet strangely oppressive. Walls of dull metal rose around us, ribbed with pipes and conduits the purposes of which I couldn't guess. No markings, no lights, no life. Yet the air—though thin—carried a faint taint of something organic. A scent of oil and decay that bypassed the filters and pressed itself into memory.

Teln ran a surface scan.

"Alloys unregistered," he muttered. "Composition unstable, molecular lattice broken down over time. And yet...still holding integrity."

The feed flickered. Instruments pulsed erratically, numbers skittering. For a heartbeat, the readings translated into script—jagged lines, like handwriting—before resolving back into data.

Varris's voice cut through the link, "Stay close. We'll establish mapping telemetry, then return."

Her pragmatism steadied me. But as I stepped further into the corridor, light from my shoulder lamp crawled across the floor—and found something it shouldn't have.

A trail of dark residue, dried and brittle, stretching from the wall towards the inner door. The colour was wrong. Too deep, too red. I crouched without thinking. The dust there wasn't mineral. It was flaked, fibrous. Organic. Blood. Ancient, but unmistakable. I said nothing. Neither did the others.

Varris raised her hand, signalling the next hatch. "We're through."

And just like that, the door to the derelict's heart began to open.

Chapter Two

The inner door parted with the brittle whisper of metal long deprived of purpose. Our lights cut through the dark like scalpels, thin beams trembling against the cold air. Dust spiralled upward, catching the glow and hanging there, suspended as though reluctant to settle. We stepped through.

The chamber beyond the breach was narrow, like the throat of some ancient beast. Our footsteps echoed faintly—not the sterile resonance of metal, but a dull, organic thud. The deck plates were uneven, warped as if softened and re-hardened over time. My boots left faint impressions that vanished seconds later, swallowed by the dust.

Varris advanced, her lamp sweeping across the walls. The light revealed layers of corrosion interlaced with something else—patterns like blood splatter. The first could have been dismissed as an accident. This...not so much.

We pressed deeper. The corridor turned sharply, forcing us into single file. My suit's atmospheric monitors clicked softly, recalibrating to microfluctuations in the air composition. Beneath the antiseptic tang of our filters, a new odour threaded through, faint but distinct, a sweetness like spoiled fruit. Teln stopped to sample the air.

"Volatile organics," he said. "Complex decay signatures. Nothing active."

Varris's tone hardened. "Keep moving."

Her voice sounded smaller than usual inside the channel. Every word we spoke seemed to echo in ways that defied direction, as if the ship itself were chewing on our voices and feeding them back at a distance.

The passage opened abruptly into a wider chamber. We fanned out, mapping the space. The floor was scattered with objects—cylinders, shards, fragments of equipment whose function eluded us. Some bore impact scoring; others had melted into the decking. One large section of wall was blackened in a circular pattern—the telltale mark of internal explosion.

Varris knelt, tracing the perimeter with her torch.

"Weapon discharge," she murmured. "Contained. No penetration."

"Against who?" I asked.

Teln's scan pinged faint metallic traces embedded in the far wall: dense projectiles. "Ballistics," he said, incredulous. "Chemical-propelled. Antiquated even by pre-Expansion standards."

The thought was absurd. Such primitive weaponry hadn't been used for millennia. Yet here, frozen in silence, it seemed brutally fitting.

We recorded everything. Procedure overrode fear. Each object catalogued, each surface scanned, each anomaly noted with academic precision. But beneath that rhythm, something else stirred—an awareness we hadn't earned.

As I turned towards the far corridor, my lamp caught movement. Not true motion—a trick of the dust, perhaps—but it felt deliberate. A shimmer, like heat rising from stone, coalesced in the shape of a figure before collapsing back into shadow. My breath fogged the visor.

"There's something ahead," I whispered.

The others turned their lights where I pointed. Nothing but darkness.

Varris hesitated for only a moment before gesturing forward. "We continue. Record everything. No conjecture." Her voice was steady, but her second pair of hands trembled.

We resumed formation. The corridor swallowed us once more, the sound of our boots absorbed by the hungry quiet. And each step carried us further from curiosity and closer to a truth we would never forget.

The deeper we went, the more the architecture defied logic. Corridors doubled back upon themselves, loops of passage that returned us to our starting point even when our mapping sensors insisted we'd moved forward. The ship felt nonsensical by post-Expansion standards; absurd even. Every line of it felt born from a mind that valued function above sanity.

Varris halted at a junction. The walls here bowed inward, ribbed with cables the thickness of limbs. They pulsed faintly under our lamps, reflecting light in a slick, wet sheen. I knew it was condensation—metal sweat—but something primordial in me felt fear. Told me to flee. The air thickened with silence. We moved on.

The ship's internal systems had long since died. No hum of power conduits, no active processors. Only the soft hiss of our own breath. Every few strides, the dust broke into strange patterns—circles and arcs, as if something had been dragged or scuffed across the floor. I knelt to examine one and found scratches beneath the dust, cross-hatched in deliberate repetitions. They were too shallow for tools, too random for writing. As though something with hands—desperate, terrified hands—had tried to dig its way through the deck.

We began to find more equipment: panels ripped open, wires exposed like nerves. The smell of decay grew stronger, an acrid sweetness that clung to the filters. In one alcove, a chair had been welded to the floor. Belts hung slack across its arms, still fastened. The padding was torn, revealing stains that flaked when touched. We catalogued it, though none of us could bear to linger. Even through the glass of my visor, I felt as though the room itself exhaled regret.

We reached a cross-section where the floor dropped away. The gap descended into a shaft so deep that our light vanished before reaching the bottom. Scanning returned nothing but static. Something was interfering—not a simple field disruption but a deliberate feedback pattern, as though the void itself were pushing back against observation.

I leaned over the edge, trying to adjust the sensor, and for the briefest moment I thought I saw movement below—a faint, glimmering motion like embers in a draught. Then it was gone. When I turned, I caught Varris watching me through her visor. She didn't ask what I'd seen. She didn't need to.

"Keep recording," she said. "Every step."

Her voice had changed. The commandant's calm was intact, but the certainty beneath it had cracked. We all heard it. The ship was wrong in ways we didn't have words for, and we were trapped inside its throat, dissecting it while it digested us. We advanced in silence for many more strides before the first corpse appeared.

It lay sprawled across the corridor, half buried in dust, its bones desiccated and pale beneath torn fragments of fabric. For a long moment, none of us moved. Even filtered through the visor, the sight had weight. This was no relic of stone or alloy. It was a corpse.

Teln was the first to approach. His scanner projected a soft blue lattice over the remains, translating mass and density into spectral overlays.

"Carbon-based," he murmured. "Organic structure similar to our own. Bipedal symmetry...though less balanced. The skeletal ratio is inefficient."

He was already analysing when I noticed the hole in the figure's chest—circular, clean, and perfectly aligned with the broken fragments of metal still lodged within. A projectile wound. There were others: smaller punctures along the ribs, a shattered arm twisted backward in angles that defied anatomy.

"They fought," I said quietly.

Varris turned, her expression unreadable through the glass, "Against what?"

There was no answer—not yet. But the air seemed to know. It felt heavier now, damp with something that wasn't moisture. My light swept down the passage ahead, illuminating more shapes slumped against the walls. Dozens. Some in uniforms, others bare save for rags and filth. Their bodies were arranged without order, as though they had fallen while running, each collapse feeding the next in a chain of panic. Teln moved from one to the next, logging features, scanning remains.

"Internal trauma consistent with chemical ballistics," he said. "And here—" he pointed at a wall streaked in black, "—impact spatter. They were close. Close enough to smell each other when they fired."

The idea disturbed me more than it should have. Creatures killing their own wasn't uncommon in the histories of other species, but this felt different. There was no sense of victory here. Only fear—raw and directionless, turned inward when no other target remained.

Varris crouched beside a sealed door. The metal around the frame was buckled, dented from within.

"Containment," she said softly. "They were trying to keep something out."

"Or in," I offered.

Her head tilted, and for the first time I saw the faint tremor of uncertainty in her posture.

"No," she said after a pause. "This was desperation. They turned on each other. They had nowhere left to go."

I recorded her words, noting the tremor in her tone. The data feeds pulsed with our readings, transmitting back to the Orioch's Grace in disciplined silence. The ship felt far away now—a distant, sterile world compared to this ossuary.

We moved deeper into the corridor, following the trail of bodies. Some had fused to the floor where spilled fluid had dried and crystallised into a brittle resin. The dust muffled our steps, but every movement seemed to stir echoes—faint, impossible sounds that came a fraction too late, as though repeating what we had already done.

The passage ended in a broad intersection. Here, the corpses lay in heaps. Weapons—primitive ballistics—littered the ground. Their design was crude, built for flesh and blood combat. Some were still clutched in skeletal fingers. Teln picked one up carefully.

"Projectile launchers," he said, awe bleeding into his voice. "Chemical ignition, kinetic rounds. No failsafes. No stun settings. Every shot lethal by default. And then they sealed the ship. Whatever ended them, it came from inside." He turned it over, scanning the fractured barrel.

"They were at war with themselves?" I questioned. Varris nodded slowly, eyes tracing the bullet-riddled walls.

That thought sat heavy among us. There were no scorch marks from boarding, no signs of external assault. Every death here had been by their own hand—yet each face was frozen in the same expression: not rage, not defiance, but terror. I stared at those hollow sockets, at teeth bared in perpetual screams that would never reach the air, and felt something I hadn't known before that moment. *Pity*.

We made camp beside the intersection, if such a thing could be called camping. No one spoke. Our suits had been sealed for hours, and though the filtration systems recycled air flawlessly, I could taste the rot of the place through memory alone. The dust here was not dust—it was residue, ground from centuries of death into something finer than sand.

Teln sat cross-legged, reviewing data feeds, his movements jerky and tired.

"No external damage," he said. "No breach, no signs of boarding. Internal assault pattern only. Sealed from within."

Varris stared at the nearest wall, the beam from her torch wavered slightly as she spoke, "They did this to themselves."

"You think it was mutiny?" I voiced.

"No, this is too widespread. Too chaotic. Mutiny has purpose. This..." she gestured to the bodies, "...does not."

I knelt beside one of the skeletal forms, my scanner light pooling over the bones. The shape of the skull intrigued me: rounded, with pronounced jaw and eye ridges, the kind one associates with predators. A creature that had evolved around aggression and precision. And yet, there was intelligence in the design. Every proportion spoke of adaptability.

"These were not savages," I said quietly. "They built ships capable of crossing the void."

"Then why fill those ships with corpses?" Teln asked. I turned the skull gently, noting the faint metallic residue around the teeth—not from ornament, but from decay. It shimmered faintly under the light.

"Maybe they couldn't stop. Maybe violence wasn't an event for them. It was...part of what they were," I suggested.

Varris moved closer. "Explain."

"Every species has an extinction instinct—a threshold at which survival becomes secondary to self-erasure. We catalogue it across countless civilisations. But this—" I gestured around us "—this isn't extinction through despair or resource collapse. This is choice."

Her gaze lingered on the walls, the buckled metal, the scorch marks where desperate hands had fired into the dark.

"Choice," she repeated. "To turn on themselves."

We stood in silence, surrounded by the evidence of that choice. Every corridor had become a mausoleum, every chamber a confession. There was something intimate about the violence here—too close, too personal. They hadn't died as soldiers. They'd died as neighbours. As kin.

Teln's scanner bleeped sharply.

"Commandant," he said, "I've found another chamber ahead. Sealed. No breach marks. Pressure intact."

Varris straightened. "How large?"

"Broad. Central to this deck. Possibly a control or research section."

"Then that's where we'll find the cause."

I didn't move. The others began readying their tools, checking cutter integrity, sealing the containment crates. But I stared down at the skull still cradled in my hands—the hollow sockets turned upward, the jaw frozen open in its eternal scream—and I felt something looking back. Not malice. Not despair. *Recognition*. I placed it gently on the deck and stepped away. The sense of being observed didn't fade.

We regrouped at the sealed hatch. The metal here was darker, thicker, reinforced with internal locking bars. Signs of repeated impact scarred its surface. Someone had wanted this door to stay closed.

Varris gave the order. "Cut it open."

The plasma torch ignited, its light flickering against her visor. As it burned through the barrier, the smell of ancient carbon filled the corridor again. None of us said it aloud, but every mind in the link shared the same thought—the same terrible realisation forming in unison: Whatever they'd trapped behind that door was never meant to be found.

Chapter Three

The final cut through the sealed door released no rush of air, no dramatic hiss. Just silence—thick, stagnant, and older than anything we had ever measured. Our lamps pushed through the dark and found the gleam of metal so polished it almost reflected. We entered.

The chamber was wide and circular, a contrast to the cramped corridors we had crossed to reach it. Every wall was lined with translucent panels, their surfaces opaque with frost. Machinery surrounded them—skeletal arms, tubes, and consoles that must once have hummed with purpose. Even dead, the room radiated control. Teln approached the nearest panel and wiped away the frost. Beneath the layer of ice, something pale and still pressed against the glass. A face.

For a long moment, none of us spoke. The shape was much like the corpses we found, but exaggerated—longer limbs, narrow torso, ribs pronounced beneath flesh. Eyes closed. Lips cracked. Preserved.

"Cryogenic containment," Teln said, scanning the unit. "Power source is residual, but the preservation medium remains chemically active."

"Stasis?" Varris asked.

He hesitated, "Yes. Or...display."

The term unsettled me. I moved to another chamber. Inside was another shape—smaller this time, folded in on itself. The flesh was wrong. The proportions weren't natural, as though something had been changed halfway through the process of becoming. It had too many joints. The head was smooth, hairless, with a mouth far too large for its face.

My lights trembled as they passed across the tanks. There were dozens of them. Hundreds, perhaps. Each one containing a different iteration—a different attempt at whatever these beings were trying to create.

"Specimens," Varris whispered. "They were experimenting."

"On what?" I whispered, but already knew the answer as I looked at each iteration.

"Their own," Varris replied simply.

The realisation rippled through the link, tightening like a noose. It explained the destruction outside, the barricades, the weapons. These were not the victims of an external force—they were subjects, and something had gone wrong.

Teln connected a terminal to one of the consoles. The screen flickered, lines of ancient script crawling across before dissolving into static.

"Language untranslatable," he said. "But the structure suggests biological indexing. Data logs. Sample progression."

"Progression of what?" I asked.

Before he could answer, one of the panels behind us shuddered. The frost cracked and fell away in long sheets. Something inside twitched.

"Residual charge?" Varris asked sharply.

"No," said Teln, his voice was small. "Movement."

The thing within was little more than a husk—shrivelled, muscle drawn tight around bone—yet it shifted as if in slow recoil, one hand dragging across the glass. The movement left streaks in the frost, faintly crimson. My hearts pounded against my ribs.

The figure's eyes opened. Clouded, opaque, yet somehow aware. Its mouth twitched. Not in sound—in mimicry. Teln stumbled backward, colliding with a console.

"Commandant," he breathed. "That was a reflex. Has to be."

"Record everything," she said, but her voice trembled. "We'll determine cause once we've secured data."

We moved carefully between the rows of frozen shapes, their pale forms half-dissolved by frost. Each one was a study in failure—bodies that had been altered, dissected, remade. The more I looked, the less I understood their intent. Limbs had been extended or shortened. Organs rearranged. Eyes multiplied or removed entirely. Some bore what looked like external grafts—tubing fused into flesh, bone restructured into jagged frameworks. They had taken their kin and rebuilt them. Changed them.

The air temperature dropped sharply the deeper we went, our visors frosting along the edges. Condensation misted from our filters, curling in the dim blue light. Even without instruments, I could feel the cold radiating from the core of the room—a hunger that had never been sated.

Teln scanned one of the pods and frowned.

"Different composition here," he said. "No stabilisation fluid. It's dry. Completely sealed."

We gathered around as he brushed the frost away. Beneath the ice was another body—this one preserved in crystalline stasis, almost perfect. Like the others—or how they should have been without restructuring—its skin pallid and stretched thin over sharp bones. It had locked itself in the chamber manually, one arm curled across its chest. In its other hand, frozen stiff, it held a blade—primitive, metallic, flecked with dark residue. It had stabbed itself.

"It sealed itself in and then self-terminated," Varris murmured.

The thought hung in the still air, absurd and terrible. Why trap oneself in a cryogenic tomb? Why die surrounded by the evidence of your own cruelty? I leaned close to the glass, studying the creature's face. Its eyes were open. Not wide with pain, but fixed in something far worse—comprehension. Teln adjusted the feed.

"It's different from the others. No signs of mutation. No foreign tissue or grafting. This one wasn't an experiment," Teln surmised.

"Then what was it?" Varris asked.

"Their maker," I said softly. "What *they* were."

We all stared at the body. The details were too precise to be coincidence—the intelligence in the bone structure, the balance of symmetry and brutality. Everything about it spoke of an apex predator turned scientist. The creator caught in its own web.

Varris's voice crackled in my comms. "Take a scan. I want every molecule mapped."

I hesitated, "Commandant...if it sealed itself away, perhaps there's a reason."

"Then it's one we must understand," she commanded, her authority left no room for doubt. Teln initiated the scan. The machine hummed, light sliding across the frost like a thin sheet of lightning. The sensors pulsed, gathering atomic data. I tried to ignore the way the corpse's eyes seemed to follow the movement. "We've seen genetic augmentation, self-destruction, extinction by will. But this...this is something else. A species that experiments on its own, kills itself by choice, and still fears what it has made enough to hide from it. Whatever they were, they wanted to stop existing."

The room had changed—not in the physical sense, but a subtle alteration of tone—as though the knowledge of what we found had changed the world around us. It pulsed faintly in rhythm, like a heartbeat we couldn't quite locate.

We moved back through the lab and to the containment pods, and continued our scans. Teln continued tapping away as his terminal, fighting his way through a language he did not understand.

"Humans," he said aloud, as if tasting the word. "That's what they called themselves. From a planet they called *Dirt*. No...that's not quite right. The translation software knows there is nuance around the name, but it doesn't know what. It keeps coming back to Dirt... No, not dirt. Mud? Earth? Earth."

He continued moving his way through their systems until he tapped once and something changed. One of the pods hissed and began to open.

"Organic emissions detected," Teln said. His voice trembled now. "Particulate matter in the atmosphere—unknown protein chains, carbon-based, mutagenic markers."

Fear—simple and primal—gripped us all.

A cloud of mist filled the air, glittering like fine dust. Our suits locked down instantly, automatic filters hissing into overdrive. Through the haze, I could see something slithering from the pod—a mess of liquefied tissue twitching as if alive. Tendrils of translucent matter crawled across the floor, dragging themselves before collapsing into stillness.

Teln's voice cracked over comms. "We've got viable readings—cell activity increasing. Division without nucleus. Structure rebuilding itself after destruction. Self-repairing. Viral. A system that spreads through infection."

His words struck me like a blow. These weren't failed experiments. They were prototypes. The enormity of it settled over us. These beings—these *humans*—had engineered the ultimate experiment.

"They made themselves immortal," I said.

"No," Varris replied, her eyes fixed on the glowing screen. "They made themselves contagious."

"Commandant," I said quietly, "if this is spreading through the atmosphere—"

"Contain it," she snapped. "Now."

We initiated emergency field sterilisation—a wave of ultraviolet energy that scorched the air. The temperature climbed, the mist dissipating in pale flashes. For a moment, I believed it was working. Then Teln screamed.

His visor fogged red. The filters in his helmet overloaded, venting pressure through the side ports. He tore at the release catches in panic, but Varris grabbed his arms, forcing them down. His skin beneath the faceplate had begun to blister, veins darkening beneath the surface.

"His system's reacting," I said. "The particles—"

"Burn it out!" Varris ordered. "Do it!"

I engaged the emergency purge. A bright light filled the chamber, consuming everything in its path. The readings spiked, then fell silent.

When it was over, Teln was on the floor. His suit had sealed automatically, but he wasn't moving. Varris stood over him, breathing hard. Her voice, when it came, was barely a whisper.

"Whatever they were making...it's still here. We let it out."

We sealed the chamber and left Teln's body behind. There was no protocol for retrieval under contamination threat, and even if there had been, none of us could have faced it. Teln's death had silenced the link partially; his absence left a hollow void in the neural lattice. Still, I felt the shared pulse of dread ripple between us.

The corridor beyond felt narrower now, the air heavier, as though the ship itself had noticed our intrusion. Varris walked ahead in silence, her movements mechanical. The light from her shoulder lamp caught streaks along the walls—smears of the same viscous residue that had spread from the ruptured pod. It was climbing the surfaces now, microscopic threads glinting like veins of silver.

"Commandant," I said quietly, "the sterilisation field didn't destroy it."

"I know," she replied. "Keep scanning. We're almost out of here."

Almost was relative. The corridor wound downward in lazy spirals, the metal beneath our boots flexing faintly with each step.

Chapter Four

We didn't speak as we walked. There was nothing to say that could make sense of what we'd seen. Our footsteps echoed through the derelict's corridors—each impact swallowed by the same oppressive silence that had followed us since we'd entered.

Varris led the way, guiding us through the narrow passageways by memory alone. The ship's architecture, once confusing, now seemed to shift in our favour. Paths that had doubled back before now offered us multiple avenues of escape. It was as if the vessel wanted us gone.

"Seal every hatch," Varris ordered. Her voice was raw but steady. "No trace left behind."

I obeyed automatically, slapping magnetic field seals over each doorway as we passed. Blue light rippled across the frames, fusing the barriers in place. Each one snapped shut with the finality of a tomb door.

By the time we reached the breach point, my visor was fogged with condensation and fear. The inner airlock door had been warped slightly from our entry torch. It took both of us to force it open. The emptiness of space waited beyond—black, endless, safe.

I turned back once. Through the faint shimmer of the barrier field, I could still see the corridor stretching away into darkness. The residue along the walls pulsed faintly in the reflected light, as though aware of our departure.

"Commandant," I said. "What if—?"

"Don't," she interrupted. "We're not bringing that question aboard with us."

Her hand brushed the bulkhead as we stepped into the airlock. For a moment, I thought I saw the metal ripple beneath her touch—a brief distortion, as though it recognised her. Then the field cycled, and the illusion was gone. The airlock sealed behind us. We were back aboard the Orioch's Grace.

Decontamination began the instant the system confirmed our return. Floodlights seared the docking bay, and a dozen mechanised arms unfolded from the ceiling, each spraying atomised neutralisers in precise, overlapping bursts. The smell of burnt ozone filled the chamber. My visor darkened automatically to shield my eyes from the glare. Static hissed through the comms.

Varris's voice cut in: "All sections report clear?"

A chorus of affirmatives followed, thin and shaken. They'd all seen and felt what we had the moment our neural lattice reconnected to theirs.

The ship's internal AI logged the breach and initiated automatic sterilisation of the external hull. A wave of plasma fire rippled across the viewport, consuming the clinging frost from the derelict's hull. The sensor displays lit up with readouts—radiation sweeps, chemical traces, bioelectric signatures. Every number we saw only confirmed one thing: we hadn't brought anything back with us. Not physically, anyway—the memories and what we felt was seared into us forever, though.

We drifted free of the derelict, the great corpse of the ship falling away into the dark. As with our arrival, it still seemed utterly inert—no signal, no light, no motion. But I couldn't shake the feeling that it was watching us go. Our drives engaged. The distance between us and the derelict widened.

Varris ordered a deeper decontamination protocol that took an extended period to complete. The Orioch's Grace drifted in high orbit above the dead ship, surrounded by a halo of sterilisation drones. Every surface glowed under ultraviolet sweep; every corridor filled with the hiss of pressurised mists. The hum of the derelict had faded from our instruments—but not from my mind.

We moved through the procedures like ghosts repeating old habits. First the radiation purges, then the thermal flushes. The suits were incinerated in sealed lockers, our skin scrubbed raw by chemical foams. We stood in the resonance chambers, lights pulsing through our skulls as the neural cleansers scoured our synaptic echoes for contamination patterns. The smell of ozone and antiseptic hung in the air, sharp enough to sting the throat. No one spoke unless required. Speech felt dangerous—a potential carrier of whatever we'd brought back. Every sound was suspect now. Even our own breathing.

When the last scan cleared, we were summoned to the quarantine deck. The walls there were white and blank, deliberately untextured, designed to deny the mind any sense of depth or reflection. Clean light. Controlled air. Contained thought.

Varris was waiting. She'd already gone through her own cycles of purification, but exhaustion clung to her movements like gravity. Her eyes were fixed on a hologram of the derelict. I stood beside her, saying nothing. The data tags flickered faintly against the glass.

"We should destroy it," I said eventually.

Her reply came slowly. "Not yet. Command protocol requires confirmation from Central Command before elimination of a first-contact artefact."

"You've seen what it does," I said. "What they did to their own."

Varris didn't look at me, "And Command will demand proof. Without data, they'll call this hysteria."

The word lingered between us: hysteria. The final refuge of those who've seen too much.

Outside the viewport, the derelict ship was a black silhouette against the void, half-bathed in starlight. It seemed smaller now, almost fragile. But I knew better. I'd seen what slept inside its hull—what might already be awake.

I watched Varris' reflection in the glass, her face pale, her lips pressed thin. Behind her, the containment field shimmered faintly, as if breathing. The silence stretched until the intercom crackled. The ship's AI reported final decon sequence complete. All scans normal. No trace anomalies detected. It should have been reassuring. It wasn't. We had purged everything we could touch. But thought—the memories of what we saw—that could not be sterilised.

We were preparing to leave when the sensors caught it. A faint fluctuation in the background noise, so subtle it might have been an echo from our own systems. But the AI flagged it immediately, isolating the frequency, magnifying the wave pattern, and replaying it over the comms. A pulse. Single. Steady. Repeating every thirty-two beats.

Varris and I stood over the central display as the signal scrolled across in pale blue. The pattern was too regular to be natural—too deliberate to be an error.

"Source?" she asked.

The AI hesitated, as if reluctant to answer, "Vector lock...confirmed. Origin point is the derelict."

The bridge fell silent. Even the hum of the ventilation seemed to fade.

"That's impossible," I said. "It's completely unpowered. It's dead metal."

"Yet something is transmitting," the AI replied.

Varris leaned forward, her reflection ghosted across the display. "Content?"

"Undecipherable," the AI said. "No linguistic markers. Pure tone sequence. Repeating indefinitely."

It played the signal again—a low, mechanical beat, distant and muffled, like the pulse of some colossal heart. Between each interval, faint interference whispered through the static, a sound almost like breathing. I felt the frills on the back of my neck rise.

"How long has it been active?" I whispered.

"From the moment you breached the ship," the AI answered. "Signal strength increasing."

"Shut it down," Varris said. "Block all incoming frequencies."

"Unable to comply," said the AI. "The transmission bypasses communication channels. It is not a targeted broadcast—it is merely ripples in the ocean."

That phrasing made my stomach turn. I looked to Varris, but her expression was unreadable. The pulse continued, vibrating through the deck beneath our feet, subtle but undeniable. Every living being aboard felt it. We exchanged uneasy glances across the bridge—silent acknowledgements that this was not mere sound. The pulse wasn't calling us. It was announcing itself.

Varris turned toward the viewport. The derelict hung there in the dark, framed by distant stars. A faint shimmer ran along its hull—a pattern of light, flickering in perfect synchrony with the transmission. And buried beneath the mechanical repetition, something almost like a voice began to form. Not words, but tone. Emotion. It sounded like sorrow.

Varris whispered, "It's a distress call."

"What could it mean?" I asked, desperation creeping into my voice.

Varris turned toward me, her voice a whisper. "It's not saying anything specific. It's just saying *we're here*."

The AI confirmed it an instant later, "Transmission format matches pre-Expansion emergency beacons."

Pre-Expansion. Ancient beyond measure. Older than any recorded interstellar civilisation.

The pulse continued, endless and patient, filling every corner of the ship. The crew gathered on the observation deck in silence. No one needed orders. We all understood that the moment we breached the ship, we'd tripped a mechanism older than any of us. A call for help.

"We should destroy it," one of the technicians said, his voice shaking. "Turn the drives and burn it until nothing's left."

"It wouldn't matter," I said. "The signal's already out there. It's travelling faster than light. Whoever was meant to hear it...already has. Or will do, eventually."

Varris didn't contradict me. She just stared at the glowing wreck, her face illuminated by the pulse. For the first time, she looked afraid. Truly afraid.

"You understand what this means?" she said quietly. No one answered. The pulse grew louder in the speakers, the intervals tightening—like a heartbeat gaining strength. The AI displayed the trajectory projection on the main screen. A line of light stretching outward into the black, cutting through star systems, cutting through time itself. Varris whispered an answer to her own question. "They'll come."

We sat in the cold glow of the viewport, watching the derelict drift. The signal thrummed in the dark, unending, unstoppable. The first wave of transmissions was already scattering through the void, crossing the gulf between stars. And of all the horrors whispered in the void, none are darker, none are more feared, than the beings that built that ship. Those that sent it into the void; that created that virus and tested it on their own. They would answer the call, and they would come. These monsters. These...Humans from Earth.

*All it takes for the monsters to win
is for the rest of us to do nothing.*

THE SILENCE OF THE STARS

Hannah Baxter

When the front door was finally smashed in by a battering ram, there was no-one left to save them. For the last few weeks, Cliona and her husband watched from behind half-closed blinds as a black van circled the neighbourhood in search of aliens hidden among the human population. They were part of ten teams that had been dispatched throughout Chicago, spreading like pathogens to the Gold Coast, Navy Pier, and Streeterville. Neighbours they'd known for years were dragged from their homes by heavily armed agents and shoved into the backseat, never to be seen again. Many of the arrestees didn't have as much as a speeding ticket to their name. Yet they were detained as if they were terrorists.

After three arrests in a single month, those who were left scattered like startled seagulls. Baylor was the last to leave. An easy-going, elderly Ordon, he'd come with the first wave of galactic migrants from his civil war-cratered world in the late nineteenth century onboard one of the many 'mystery airships' spotted by thousands across the Midwest. He'd survived the notorious frenzy of Orson Welles' *War of the Worlds* in the thirties, when mobs of humans spilled onto the streets, convinced they were under Martian attack. His neighbourhood cookouts were famous, serving his native delicacies alongside hot dogs and hamburgers. Having majored in Ordon Cultural Studies, Cliona adored hearing him recite the ancient ballads of his people. It was a beautiful dialect, unadoptable by the human tongue. But the mounting fear was too much for him to bear anymore.

Through a series of encrypted radio broadcasts, he'd contacted other off-worlders who'd established a peaceful colony in the Calesius star system. They'd agreed to pick him up on the rugged outskirts of the Indiana Dunes National Park. Isa did everything in his power to convince Baylor to stay. But the old man simply shook his horned head with a weary breath.

"Earth is just too dangerous," he sighed.

For three years, they'd known nothing but peace. Earth was a backwards but charming world, a wellspring of life in an otherwise dead solar system. The preceding twelve months had been a banner year for them. Cliona had gotten a promotion at her high-powered executive job. Isa managed to reconnect with some of his star-scattered relatives. Their talk of having children had turned serious. Then a new president had come to power, a self-important fascist spouting mindless nonsense. Yet a disconcerting majority of the populace ate it up.

The fond pedestal on which Cliona had placed humanity was cracked when he'd been elected for a second term. The mere sight of his face ranting on television was enough to turn her single-chambered stomach. She'd travelled four light years away from her home planet to escape such, only to find it encroaching on her doorstep. She started researching other worlds as a fallback. Isa, however, was convinced that the escalating unrest would never burst their suburban bubble. In his mind, they were safe as houses. Until theirs was broken into.

A tear gas cannister was tossed in, filling the house with a choking mist. Coughing, Cliona staggered blindly. Out of the fog emerged three human agents, bedecked in dark blue cargo pants and tactical vests. Faded numbers were printed across their bullet-dented epaulettes. Across their chests were emblazoned the words that had struck fear into thousands of hearts: EXTRATERRESTIAL IMMIGRATION AUTHORITY. A trail shoe carelessly cracked their fallen wedding photograph as they strode over to her. Their leader was a human male in his late twenties wearing a backwards-turned baseball cap. Twirling a baton, he advanced towards a trembling Cliona. His wolfish smirk was obvious, even under the thick balaclava he had on.

Isa rushed out from the kitchen where he'd been preparing dinner down the narrow hallway. Puffing out his chest, he positioned himself between his terrified wife and the formidable enforcer. He was pummelled into submission by a rifle butt. Cliona cradled his bruised head on her lap, his pellucid blood staining her fingers.

Before she could tend to his grievous wounds, Cliona was ripped off him like a bandage. They ignored her desperate pleas and clamped a tight pair of handcuffs around her struggling wrists. In full view of her round-eyed Earthly neighbours, Cliona was marched across her own front yard to the gas-guzzling fortified van parked halfway on the sidewalk. Another agent stood guard by the open hatch. The barrel of an M4 carbine glinted from his gloved hands.

She flailed out towards Isa, whose wounded figure was hidden by a tactical huddle of agents who dragged him to another wagon positioned at the opposite end of the street. Cliona seethed like a churning sea, desperate to get to him. Their bond was far deeper than just exchanging rings and throwing rice. Pagosian marriage bound not just lives, but souls. She and Isa shared each other's pains as potently as their joys. Isa's distant suffering fluttered across her body with her own panicked pulse. She wanted to be with him. But the world wouldn't allow that.

Cliona was shoved inside the vehicle with enough force for her temple to crack the left-side passenger window. As she lay on the seat with a pounding skull, she became aware of the other figures huddled around her. There were a few that she recognized. A Llarkian, already deprived of her human disguise, sobbed quietly into her white hairy flippers. Next to her sat a Dhuman, all four eyes scowling out from deep-set sockets. A listless-looking lichen-grey amphibious being sat whimpering, chewing her webbed digits bloody with small, conical teeth.

"Where are they taking us?" Cliona whispered.

"Shut up," the Dhuman blistered, "before you get us all killed."

The only sound inside was the crackling of the sun-baked asphalt under the heavy van wheels. Cliona gripped her denim-covered knees, hard enough to leave pale dents in the distressed fabric. Having hands was a quirk of Earth that had always fascinated Cliona. She'd spent her life with six limber tentacles, only to be cut down to ten stumpy digits. Simple tasks like writing and using utensils became nothing short of impossible. It took her months to adapt. Cliona couldn't understand how humans had managed to advance so far with a single pair of hands. People had warned her that being human would be one of the hardest things she would ever do. Never had she expected *this*.

Being forced from her home was only the first road-bump in a long and uncomfortable journey. After screeching to an unexpected halt, they were herded out onto a prison bus. Vacant faces peered out from inside the tinted rectangular windows like passing ghosts. Inside was even worse, the narrow floor caked in a fetid layer of faeces due to lack of proper toilet facilities.

The women were all chained together in a single clanking file to prevent them from escaping. The iron fetters clipped Cliona's ribcage to the point she was barely able to breathe. But it was nothing compared to the lingering ache in her heart.

After another six gruelling hours, a foreboding dark shape rose out of the dank, swampy wetlands. Cliona sat upright in her seat. It was a dark, inquisitorial block of stone which gave off the same dreary gleam as sun-corrupted bones in the desert. The daunting sixteen-acre battlements were braced by towering turrets.

The building's roof was partially concealed, as if out of shame. She squinted, trying to discern whether it was a mirage or not.

An unnamed horror engulfed Cliona. Of the two hundred holding facilities spread out across America, there were none more infamous than the Greyrock Correctional Centre. Built around the turn of the century, it was one of the oldest prisons in the Chicagoland area. It had been founded by human suffering; quarried limestone bricks fitted by prison labourers. Many of Chicago's most infamous had spent a stint in there, including Baby Face Nelson and John Dillinger. Having closed in 2003 due to a declining population, it had been re-opened and revamped for a less conventional class of prisoners.

After hours of travelling, they were escorted off by an armed patrol and through the East Gate. Cliona was shocked by how close the male dormitories were to the female cell block. The arrival of the new fish had them pressed up against the walls like a hungry shiver of sharks. Their salivating faces squeegeed the windows, like the women were string-suspended slabs of beef dangled tauntingly in front of them. Cliona had never been gladder for a pane of glass.

Trying to soothe herself, Cliona's shackled hand folded around Isa's imaginary one. They could have lengthy conversations without a single word exchanged between them. Of course, as with every couple, they had the odd argument. But Isa's tender caress was a salve, soothing even the most heated words. As she shuffled down the flickering hallway, she prayed to the gods that he was somehow safe.

Shoved into a darkened room, Cliona was forced to disrobe her human cover. Usually doing so was a long-awaited release after a lengthy day tottering about in leather loafers and camel blazers. But not when she was surrounded by a group of gun-toting strangers. Cliona was aware that she was in no position to resist.

To human eyes, Cliona's true appearance resembled an icefish. Her body was transparent and scaleless, pulsing blue veins visible under the swinging wattage of the cubicle light. Cliona had a depressed, almost crocodilian head that ended in a beaked snout, like a hastily erased pencil drawing. Inside were two rows of acute fangs that had evolved to crush small crustaceans. Taking up a significant portion of her skull were a pair of pitch-black ovoid eyes. Her small, finned form was balanced upright by cephalopod-like tentacles.

For the longest time, humans wondered what was beyond their own planet, oblivious to the fact that otherworldly beings were already living among them. The pop-culture pendulum swung from dreadlocked hunters who decapitated humans as trophies to innocent visitors with a taste for Reese's Pieces. Cliona cringed at the Old Hollywood depictions of alien lifeforms, with their marauding blobs and hubcap flying saucers. Isa had found them hilarious in their dated special effects. *The Day the Earth Stood Still* was one of his favourite films. A framed poster of it hung above the curvy cherrywood desk in his study. Most works tended towards the unrealistic notion that all lifeforms from beyond would resemble humans, which was far from the case. It was a narcissistic outlook towards the universe, which most species shed as soon as they achieved space travel. From an outside perspective, humans were just as bizarre. They were an eight billion-strong race of hairless, bipedal pink apes that straddled a curious border between civilized and primitive.

The guards didn't even bother to hide their disgust at Cliona's appearance. They snickered and nudged each other from a safe distance. Cliona flinched from their sneering eyes. Just because she had no haemoglobin in her blood didn't mean that she was incapable of emotion. Back on her home planet, no-one would have batted an eyelid at her. Here, she was a captive exotic beast, cramped into a decaying pen and pelted with peanuts by jeering visitors. Their metallic visors served as a bobbing hallway of mirrors, showcasing her humiliation at every conceivable angle.

Cliona could barely stand by the time she was marshalled into the interrogation room. Waiting for her was a human male, but in a far more formal dress than the EIA agents who'd invaded her home. The man's distinguished grey hair was combed back into a short, undulatory bob, somewhere between casual and professional. It contrasted with his rectangular face, inflexible as a cinderblock. He wore a slate grey dress shirt with a smooth tie that rappelled past his navel. His smile was one of compassionate placidity. But the corpse blue eyes above it regarded her with the cold focus of a microscope studying a bacillus.

"Cliona Urubura, right? I'm Special Agent Monroe Crain, Homeland Security."

Cliona gave him a scornful look as her boneless body sagged over the edge of the unpadded wooden seat.

"Charmed," she gritted out.

He shifted through the stapled clump of files piled high across the desk. After a few seconds of riffling, Crain slid out hers with the mechanical smoothness of a jukebox machine arm replacing a record.

"It says here that you're from Pagos. You were first registered as a citizen of the planet Earth in Nevada on March First—"

"Where is my husband?"

A subtle twitch disrupted the perfect symmetry of Agent Cain's face, like the aftershocks of a pebble dropped into a pond.

"Mrs. Urubura," he cleared his throat, "let's focus on the matters at hand here. Have you ever expressed any ill will towards the citizens of planet Earth—"

Rage rose within Cliona like a seismic sea wave.

"You can't keep me here against my will!" She slammed her clubs against the desk. "I want my lawyer! I know my rights!"

Agent Cain's downturned lips pressed together until they were almost invisible. His fingers folded together, beefy arms crossed over the table like a mounted pair of ornamental swords.

"Those are human rights, Mrs. Urubura."

The shadows of the room wrapped around her, as if she had been ejected from a ship into the vast void of space. Every shuddering breath that she took was amplified into a deafening squall. Cliona averted her eyes from the agent's stoic mask, which disguised a bureaucratic indifference. She was nothing more than the dirt under his nails, which he wanted to extricate as soon as possible. Cliona stood against the world.

Stripped of her dignity and identity, Cliona straggled down the extended hallway, numb to the guards who nudged her sides, unimpressed by her pace. She thought not of the rowdy bellows of the other inmates that echoed out from within the fortified walls. Rather, she focused on the faint flicker of Isa's presence. Even with many miles between him, she could still sense him, alive. For the sake of her own sanity, Cliona hung onto it.

The heavy cell door slammed behind her, making her jump. Recomposing herself, Cliona drank in her squalid new home. It was six feet by eight feet, a cramped, low-ceiling room that made a battered shoebox look homey. The cold concrete flooring sent a shiver upwards through her piscatory body. The grim acoustics of her echoing steps reinforced the reality that there was no escape. An oppressive heat battered Cliona's brow, trapped tight within the airless space. The air was an olfactory outrage of unwashed bodies, rust, and unrelenting despair.

"Oh. Didn't realize I was getting a new cellmate so soon."

A pile of rubble lay on the bottom bunk of the two-person cot. It took Cliona a few seconds to realize that it was addressing her. Her co-inmate was a massive stone creature, covered in a thick, dark, basalt hide. The brass bed frame creaked under its great height, blocky feet hanging over the edge of the bed. Volcanic veins filled the spalls with white-hot molten blood. Cliona's vestigial fins fluttered at the sight of its stony fists, twice the size of her entire body. It could have crushed her into paste without even trying.

The rocky being didn't bother to move from the mattress that it lay on, watching her from the shadows with half-hooded amber eyes.

"Name's Edan," they muttered, "you probably won't remember it."

Cliona withdrew in fright, her enlarged heart beating at a dizzying pace. The fact that they'd paired her with a Flamekin, of all species, showed the humans didn't care if she lived or died. It seemed as if they were trying to expedite the latter.

Pagosians and Flamekin got along as well as cats and dogs, as the human expression went. Their two races, both from the same solar system, shared a vitriolic yet symbiotic relationship. To power their burning vessels, the Flamekin had sought out obsidian, a combustible mineral buried deep beneath the glacial surface of Pagos. Once they'd attained spaceflight through re-engineering captured Flamekin spacecraft, the Pagosians had launched a series of retaliatory attacks, taking precious ammonia from the Flamekin's home world as compensation It had escalated into a centuries-spanning war, one with no clear victor. The destruction of one world would have a detrimental effect on the other, sending them spinning out of orbit. They'd elevated their battlefield to other worlds, pitting whole solar systems against one another. Cliona had been raised on the stories of the monsters from the moon, who could kill with a single touch. It was a well-known fact that Pagosians and Flamekin couldn't stand one another. A single brush of a Flamekin's fiery hand could melt a Pagosian's insides. A Pagosian's icy feeler was one of the few things that could penetrate a Flamekin's igneous hide, leaving behind devastating ice burns. It provided both sides with another reason to destroy one another.

When she'd come of age and been enrolled in mandatory military service, she and the other recruits were shown propaganda depicting the Flamekin as pyroclastic titans, wiping whole settlements off the face of Pagos with their powerful plasma weapons. Though it was considered the highest honour to kill one in combat, Cliona always feared facing them. Now she was trapped in a room with one.

Cliona cautiously climbed the short ladder to the top bunk, trying to achieve as much distance as she could from her biological enemy. Her helical muscles rippled at the searing heat that radiated off Edan's slumped posture. She gulped down the small pocket of air that rattled in from the grated air vent screwed into the ceiling. If it wasn't for the inhibitory energy field that was installed inside every cell in the prison, she would have been dead. Edan's sleepy hums rumbled up through the unadorned mattress. Cliona's body blanched a deathly white as she tried to sleep. But no peace would come to her, nor for many nights afterward.

Like a mechanical automaton, Cliona settled into a stiff routine. She learned to keep her head down to avoid conflict. In place of the buzz of her phone alarm, Cliona was awakened by a guard banging on the rusting bars of her cell. She followed the sleepy crowd of prisoners that staggered forth from their holdings, which diverged into two parallel lines into the mess hall. What they were served was food in the loosest definition of the word. It was a colourless, tasteless sludge funnelled out of a monstrous machine, co-ordinated by computer to each prisoner's most basic requirements. Cliona picked at it with a plastic fork, unable to even identify it, let alone eat. Three times a day, the prison populace was summoned forth by the warden for headcounts. Those who toed the well-defined line were dragged off, never to be seen again. Lights-out was at ten—no exceptions.

Surrounded by non-humans, there was a sharp decline in human morality. The one thing that the guards enjoyed more than tazing beings that could swat them flat into submission was making the weaker prisoners' lives hell. Cliona had sidled through the corridors, only to be tripped up by a boot slid underneath her tangle of limbs. She'd crashed onto the floor to a chorus of mocking laughter. Cliona's body ached not just with pain, but the desire to throttle the life out of them. Her own rage terrified her.

She thought of ice creepers, wingless insects that burrowed deep into the mountains of her home. The creatures survived the extreme cold of her home planet by accumulating trehalose and erythritol, which stabilized proteins and membranes. Up until she'd been incarcerated, Cliona had regarded humans with that same fond wonder. They may have been small, but they had huge evolutionary potential. Edan, on the other hand, had a much lower opinion of humanity.

"Whenever their leaders break something," they'd said, "instead of fixing it, they point to whoever's unfortunate to be close enough to the mess. Then, they walk away whistling while the angry mob sharpens their pitchforks."

They leaned down to scrape the metal shavings surrounding their newest sculpture. Cliona never imagined that Edan's titanic fists were capable of anything other than smashing. She marvelled at the meticulous figures that were soldered into existence from the legs of metal chairs and beds by their thick dusky orange fingers. The mundane became masterpieces. Edan slumped forward in their creaking seat. "I never believed in monsters. Then I met humans."

Cliona hated to admit it, but they were right. The wheels of progress seemed to be turning backwards.

It was hard coping without the everyday indulgences that she'd taken for granted, like iced water. The closest thing that she'd had to a hug was the feeble breeze of the vents. The worst part was Isa's agonizing absence together. For the past twenty-three years, they'd been almost inseparable. The best part of Cliona's morning had been waking up tangled in her husband's suckers, their faces pressed beak-to-beak. Now she languished alone on stained, bug-ridden bedding.

As the weeks slogged on, Cliona overcame her initial fear of Edan. Their apathetic nature became a paralysing preoccupation for her. Despite seeming so closed off, it became apparent that Edan was the eyes and ears of the prison. With their powerful build, they could have easily lorded over the rest of the lockup. But Edan preferred to exchange information over blows. They were the buffer between rival prison gangs, interspersing details on the other's next assault.

What she had in mind would have had her put to death on Pagos. But Cliona had no choice. She needed Edan. *The enemy of my enemy is my friend*, as the great human bard Isa was so fond of had once said. After spending days memorizing their daily routine, she'd cornered them in a blind spot tucked beneath the razor-edged fence, invisible to the roving rows of security cameras.

"I need you to help me find my husband."

Edan's shovel-shaped jaw clenched. She couldn't blame them for their reluctance to help her. Just as Cliona had been raised to hate the Flamekin, Edan would have been poisoned against Pagosians from an early age, fed the line that they were a merciless intelligence whose hearts were as frozen as their ammonium nitrate-fed bodies.

Cliona wound her many tendrils together like the deep-reaching root system of an ancient tree.

"Please." Her voice cracked. "His name's Isa Urubura. He's a Pagosian too, with a purple birthmark on his pelvic fin. I need to know whether he's okay."

Edan's diamond glare crumbled like a stick of shale. They sighed, bulldozing a hand over their hairless scalp.

"Fine. But I don't want to hear a word of this anywhere else. Understood?"

A relieved exhale uncorked itself out of Cliona like the bottle seal of a frothy champagne bottle. "Crystal," she breathed.

The tremulous excitement that occupied the next two days almost made her forget about the human correctional staff's constant surveillance. Cliona did her best to fly under the radar. Still, she couldn't help herself from stealing conspiratorial peeks at an unamused Edan.

Cliona had been scrubbing the taps of the undersized cell sink when Edan returned to her with answers. Along with drawing, it was something that she did to stave off the reality of her uncertain sentence. As she was in the middle of shining the sink for the seventy-sixth time, an immense shadow fell over her.

Edan stood before her, sturdy skull lowered into their broad chest.

"He's in the Science Ward."

Edan announced it like it was the end of the world. Yet Cliona ignored the ominous tone, her heart almost flying out of her chest with joy and relief.

Even among Pagos' best and brightest, Isa outshone them all. He'd been praised by his peers in the scientific community as one of the foremost astrophysicists of his generation. He'd expanded the civilization's collective mind, showing them there were other galaxies beyond their own.

All that prestige had evaporated when the military came knocking on their door, demanding Isa use his amazing intellect to build them weapons of mass destruction. Isa had refused. Unlike the rest of his kind, who militantly hated the Flamekin, he viewed them as people. His reluctance to offload glacier bombs was treason in their eyes. Tired of the constant conflict, he and Cliona had fled to the farthest reaches of the universe, to a new life on a small ocean world in the Milky

Way. It was only a matter of time before his skills were noticed by the staff, and he was upgraded from the general population.

"Where is that?" she implored.

The whites of Edan's eyes dimmed, as if consumed by blinding cataracts.

"Nowhere you'd want to be," they muttered.

Cliona's complexion blotched to an indignant red.

"You said you'd help me!" she exclaimed.

Edan swallowed, producing a harsh scraping sound.

"I'm sorry. Not with this."

Unable to stand the sight of them any longer, Cliona stormed up the ladder to her bunk, ignoring their fumbling attempts at apologizing. She lay there, staring at the ceiling until Edan gave up and resigned themself to sleep.

Cliona lay awake, listening to Edan's pneumatic snores, which vibrated through her tiny form like aftershocks. She gazed up at the dust-choked grate that rattled over her head. But the faint hope of seeing Isa again overrode all the associated dangers. If Edan wasn't going to help her, then she'd do it herself. Whatever the Science Ward was, it couldn't be any worse than here.

After loosening the screws that bolted the bar grille in place, Cliona slid herself through with ease. The fact that it was eighteen inches wide was no issue for her. Her species had been blessed by evolution with a natural flexibility. Having hydrostatic skeletons with no cumbersome cartilage or bones, they were able to squeeze themselves with ease through holes the diameter of a pencil. It had made them experts at espionage, robbing Flamekin military bases blind.

Cliona crawled through the ventilation duct like an oversized spider. Assaulted by random blasts of cool air, she did her best to remember the prison layout. Every precarious rattle made her flinch, convinced that at any moment she'd come crashing through the subceiling, right into the prison warden's personal office. She managed to stay calm and carried on tunnelling through the galvanized steel passage.

After an hour of crawling through the drafty, constricted passageway, she was ready to write the whole thing off as a doomed endeavour. Just as she was about to scuttle back and avoid serving two more life sentences, her suckers' sensitive olfactory receptors puckered at the sharp scent of antiseptic. Isa's faraway fear sieved into Cliona's neural pathways, sending her into a quiet frenzy. He was so close. Her own self-preservation forgotten, she pushed on.

Through a grate in the duct, she spotted a lab technician cradling a clipboard to their chest. Cliona's eyes bulged at the hovering letters on the metal sign posted outside the half-open office door. Wing D. She'd made it.

As she moved closer to the opening, a low groan froze her blood. A pair of rubber gloves soaked in a nearby sink, stained with fluorescent pink blood.

Cliona's fleeting optimism was suddenly buried under an avalanche of dread, like a flower in a snow flurry. The inmates weren't helping to develop technology. They were the lab rats.

A gurney squeaked into her view. A bolt of panic hit her as she recognized Isa, bound to the gurney by heavy leather straps. His body was covered with hypodermic holes, like the tightly packed seeds of an apple.

"Please," he gargled out through collapsed, froth-choked lungs, "help me."

Isa screamed as the doctor slid a scalpel through his belly. Gloved hands pulled out his nectareous organs like party streamers, placing them into a pan.

A junior researcher flapped over Cliona's restrained mate like a frightened bird, distressed by Isa's agony. As they were about to jab an intravenous drug into Isa's atrophied arm, their superior stopped them. Through his muffling surgical scrubs, the attending surgeon uttered the words that annihilated a piece of Cliona's soul along with Isa's nerve endings: "No anaesthetic. It'll interfere with the results."

Her mind on the verge of collapse, Cliona fled the terrible scene. Her husband's screams, along with those of countless others, were buried in her brain like shrapnel fragments.

Cliona didn't speak for days after. Her silence was deafening enough that even the apathetic Edan took notice. Concerned by her wasting frame, they'd snuck extra portions out of the canteen, careful not to leave any evidence. Cliona managed a few mouthfuls before Isa's eviscerated visage reemerged. She was a locket without a chain, her soul irreparably punctured by Isa's distressing dearth. Where there should have been the consoling hiss of his fast fricatives in her mind, there was now static. Isa's final indignities were ingrained onto her psyche like annual rings in an ancient oak. For the first time in her existence, Cliona was truly isolated. She vomited onto the floor.

Instead of being rightfully furious about the mess, Edan swiped a ragged blanket off the edge of their bed. Winding it around their knuckles like a hand wrap, they knelt to wipe it up with a sigh of complaint.

"You're lucky, you know."

Cliona stared aghast at Edan, wondering if she'd heard them correctly. The world-weary smile that cracked across Edan's stony face confirmed just that.

"When I came here, I wasn't alone," they went on. "My mate and I were both detained. Their name was Agni. They were my everything. They were an architect—never wanted any part of the war. All that they ever wanted to do was create. Raised whole settlements from the ground."

Edan's voice crackled with a fading warmth, like dying embers in a fire. Their craggy jaw quaked.

"When we came here, the EIA took everything from us, even their medication. They promised us that they'd have a fresh shipment of anticonvulsants in soon. But they never came. I tried to help my mate, but I couldn't stop their seizures from coming. One day, while we were in the cafeteria, they had one bad enough that they bit right through their tongue. They died right there in my arms, choking on their own blood. The guards didn't even lift a finger to help."

Tears seeped down Edan's rough face in weak streams, like rain down a fallen wall. All that Cliona wanted to do in that moment was hold them. But she couldn't. As much as she wanted to join Isa, she knew that he would have wanted her to live. Her arms curled around the empty space next to Edan in an air hug. Edan paused mid-mental breakdown to give her a bemused look. Their broad torso bobbed up and down with laughter, like a barrel lost at sea.

Cliona spent the next few days in a stupor. Reality was too much to face anymore. The only solid object in her blurry world was Edan, as immovable as a mountain. Cliona never imagined that she'd experience anything other than fear towards a Flamekin. Nevertheless, she started to regard Edan as friend, the only one she had in that wretched place.

One day, just as she was about to excavate the gunge marinating on her polystyrene tray, a pained cry pierced her auditory sensors like an arrow. Shuffling around in her stool, she saw a Chelonian, green and wrinkled as a supermarket pepper, grovelling before an irate guard. The orange jumpsuit, which drooped off his frontal plastron, was stained with his spilled lunch.

"I'm sorry," they whimpered, "it...it was an accident."

It was an interaction that had become painfully familiar to Cliona during her short stay as Greyrock. Eyes blazing, the fair-haired human man slammed his foot down on the diminutive alien's domed carapace.

"Damn right, it won't," he snarled.

He brought his boot down on the cowering prisoner's back again. A sickening crack echoed like a whip around the lunchroom, followed by a sobbing howl of pain. Cliona's tentacle squeezed around the plastic fork, splintering the shaft.

The warders operated on the same skewed logic as the EIA agents. Anything that wasn't human was a criminal. Thereby, they were authorized to use excessive force to defuse the potential time bomb in their mist. They were so preoccupied by the potential dangers that the resident aliens posed that they never considered the similarities. Though the number of limbs and eyes might have differed, their emotions were the same. They cried, laughed, and bled just as humans did.

Before Cliona could stop herself, she leapt from her seat, rushed forward, and drove the broken plastic knife into the antagonistic jailer's jugular. He managed a single gurgle as his life-blood spurted out in random directions, the flow obstructed by the piece of plastic still lodged in his neck.

An amazed silence filled the dining hall. A tremulous breath rattled through Cliona. The bloodied shank slipped from her hands and clattered down on the wet floor.

It was the lone flash that lit the powder keg.

Everything exploded all at once. A hulking four-armed woman rose up and tipped over the communal table she sat at with a primal cry. Another green-skinned inmate took the opportunity to embrace her inner pyromaniac, igniting a stack of Styrofoam cups with a smuggled lighter. A pillar of choking black smoke filled the air. The overwhelmed guards crawled behind the serving counters alongside the cowering kitchen staff to radio for backup.

In the chaos, Cliona spied the keys that had slipped out of the dead guard's pockets in his spasming death throes. She snatched them up, extending them towards a stunned Edan.

"Let's get out of here."

Edan gaped at her frail form with a fearful awe. Comprehending that freedom was literally in their grasp, they came around quickly. Cliona slid across the floor, knocked from one warring body to another like a curling stone.

Edan barrelled down the hallways like a straight-rolling bowling ball down a lane, striking down whatever crossed their path. Because of their size, the guards had written them off as a lumbering beast. So had Cliona's kind, thousands of years before. The Flamekin struck hard, and fast as lightning. This, along with their size and rugged resilience, made them a triple threat that the guards struggled to contain.

Cliona's dark eyes welled as Edan shoved the heavy door aside. The midday sun kissed her skin. In the darkness of their cells, all passage of time had ceased. Night blended into day. It was like living inside a black hole, without the release of instantaneous death. As a rule, she shunned all sources of heat, even in her climate-controlled human form, as much from habit as necessity. Today, she embraced it.

"Come on!" Edan called, hurtling ahead of her.

Cliona's unsteady steps scuffed the grass just beyond the barbed wire blockade of the exercise yard. Pagosians had not evolved to run long distance. There was a reason that their race wore mechanized exoskeletons into battle. But Cliona's determination surpassed her evolutionary limitations. The two of them would escape Earth.

Just a few yards away from salvation, something burst up from the ground, surrounding them. An ebon field folded around them like a smothering pillow on a dying man's face. Edan examined their befuddled reflection in the polished surface of the unexpected obstacle. Their attempted blow rebounded, and they staggered back with a grunt, clutching their wounded fist.

Cliona clutched the side of her head in despair. She'd been emulating a human for a very long time but still recognized her own peoples' technology. After Pagos' major cities had been destroyed by Flamekin bombing raids, they had been rebuilt equipped with forcefields to protect their crystalline towers. By some terrible twist of fate, the humans had gotten their hands on the tech. Far from using it to safeguard millions, they were utilising it to entrap lawful immigrants. Unlike the blind spots inside the main building, the forcefield here was airtight. It was everything Isa had feared. The impassable wall hung over them like the silence of the stars.

Edan was the first to go down. Two small, barbed darts embedded into their back, delivering a devastating electric current. They reeled backwards as the high voltage shorted their muscles. Edan toppled forward like axed timber. The old human axiom turned out to be true after all. The bigger they were, the harder they fell.

Being much smaller, Cliona could have slipped away unnoticed and found a crevice to squeeze through. But she refused to run and stayed by Edan's side. A blunt truncheon slammed into the side of her soft skull, knocking her to the ground. More blows followed, a savage symphony conducted on her defenceless body.

Her vision blurred from countless punches, Cliona rolled onto her abdomen. Edan was crumpled on the ground two feet away from her. Lithic debitage flaked off their face. Their left eye was almost completely swollen shut, their body's last-ditch effort to protect their shattered eye socket. Their mouth hovered open, as if to speak, only to spit out a detached tooth.

Old animosities were broken like the bones in their bodies. It didn't matter what faction they belonged to. Cliona couldn't remember anymore. Massive cranial trauma had squeezed the answer out of her head like toothpaste from a tube. Neither of them wanted to suffer alone anymore.

With their remaining strength, the pair shook themselves free of the many human hands holding them down and rolled into each other's arms. Edan crushed Cliona into their chest like a beloved childhood toy. For a moment or two she was able to enjoy the Flamekin's embrace before her skin started to sizzle. It brought to her fading mind one of the first outings that she and Isa had undertaken on Earth. They'd strolled through Lincoln Park. The humid air was filled with the happy chatter of families picnicking on the grassy knolls. There were no deafening drones of air raid sirens to put an end to the quietness. Cliona had never seen anything like it. Back on Pagos, peace was a luxury only the wealthiest could afford. Isa had stopped to buy them sweet treats from a local vendor. After choosing cookies and cream for himself, he'd settled on vanilla for her, sensitive to her palate. It was the perfect remedy to Cliona's faint homesickness. It was as if he'd packed a precious piece of home along with him during their long flight from Pagos. That moment grew to consume her entire mind, her hand crushing around the dripping cone; sweet, cold ice-cream soothing her sun-reddened skin.

A thin coating of ice spread across Edan's stone shell before making its way inside them. The deep freeze ate right through Edan's ribcage. Their magmatic organs spilled onto Cliona, melting her into nothing.

About the Contributors

Benjamin Adams was a 2002 Bram Stoker Award nominee for co-editing the anthology *The Children of Cthulhu* (Del Rey Books). He has also written professionally for *Doctor Who* in a pair of Big Finish Productions' *Short Trips* anthologies. His stories generally deal with grief, love, pain, and trauma, although sometimes they're just about monsters. And every now and then, those monsters are human.

Peter J Aldin. SFF Author, EPL Supporter, WW2 Obsessive, Terrible-Memory Owner, Cavoodle Wrangler. M-dash and Semicolon Fanatic. Pete's work covers the spectrum from space opera to light horror to fantasy. Need to locate him? **petealdin.com** is a good place to start looking.

Colleen Anderson, a Ladies of Horror Fiction, Canada Council, and BC Arts Council grant recipient, has been published in eight countries. An award-winning author, her works appear in *Amazing, Cemetery Dance, Weird Tales*, and *HWA Poetry Showcase*. She is a Rhysling Award winner for 'Machine (r)Evolution' and a two-time winner of the SFPA's dwarf poetry contest. Author of four poetry collections, *I Dreamed a World, The Lore of Inscrutable Dreams, Weird Worlds*, and *Vellum Leaves and Lettered Skins*, she is currently working on two more. Her fiction collections, *Embers Amongst the Fallen* and *A Body of Work*, are available online. Colleen freelances as an editor, and has served on the SFPA executive, as well as British Fantasy Award and Stoker Award juries. A new *Mosaic* novella will be coming out in the next two years. Colleen lives in Vancouver, BC where she searches for mermaids. **colleenanderson.wordpress.com**

A graduate of the University of the Sunshine Coast's creative writing program, **Zac Ashford** was born in the UK, before migrating to Australia as a teen. He published his first novella in 2020 through Unnerving. Since then, he's been named on the ballot of the Ditmar awards as one of Australia's best new talents in speculative fiction, and nominated twice for the Aurealis, once for the Australian Shadows Award (for his metal-themed tragedy, *Polyphemus*), and for the Imadjinn Award in the US. His works are infused with mythology, allusions to classic texts, and his love of metal music. He's also a high-school teacher, regular convention panellist, and school-visiting speaker. He's married to a wonderful woman, and has two awesome cats, as well as a room full of paperback horror and action figures. He is represented for film and media by Alec Frankel of IAG.

Hannah Baxter is a writer from Omagh, County Tyrone, Northern Ireland. She achieved a first-class honors degree and an MA with distinction in English Literary Studies from Queen's University, Belfast. Her work has been featured in *New Isles Press, The Martello Journal, Spellweaver Magazine*, Black Beacon Books' *Samhain Screams*, the Dylan Thomas *Love the Words 2021 Poetry Anthology, Drawn to the Light Press, Bizarro Circus of Madness, Dark Poets Club Dark Poets Prize Edition II*, the 2024 Kenmare 'Poets Meet Painters' competition, and Writefluence's *The Other Side* horror anthology.

Paul Carro is an HWA author and screenwriter based in Los Angeles, California. His debut horror novel, *The House*, made Comic Book Resources top ten list in 2022. His most recent release is the novella *In the Shadows Where the Boys Used to Play*. His short stories have appeared in multiple anthologies including *After the Burn, The Little Coffee Shop of Horrors*, and *Horrors of the Deep: Startling Sea Stories*. His short story, 'Last Caller,' is a finalist in the 2025 Ghosties horror fiction awards. Paul is co-editor with Candace Nola on the upcoming anthology, *Self (S)care: the Best Self-Published Horror of 2025*, releasing early 2026. He is also a columnist for *Memento Mori Ink Magazine*.

Ryan Colley always enjoyed reading fictional worlds, but creating his own is his passion. In school, a teacher told him to pursue writing after reading a short story he wrote for homework and, from that day, he never stopped. He doesn't know where his love of zombies comes from, but it just happened, and it is his life. Things changed, and life moved on, but even while graduating from his Bachelor's and Master's in Psychology, he wrote stories every day. Writing is his passion, and everything else he does is to pursue that passion. Ryan loves hearing from his readers, and encourages you to let him know what you think!
For my website: **AmongTheDead.co.uk**
For regular updates: **facebook.com/AmongTheDeadATD**
Want to email me? **AmongTheDeadATD@hotmail.com**

Mia Dalia is an internationally published, Crime Writers' Association nominated author of all things fantastic, thrilling, frightening, and strange. Her short fiction appears widely online and in print anthologies and magazines, and has been featured in multiple narrative podcasts.
Mia's stories were selected as one of *Tales to Terrify's* Top Ten Stories of 2023 and shortlisted for the Crime Writers' Association's 2024 Dagger Award. Her work has been acclaimed by Library Journal, which highly recommended it 'for gothic fiction readers and fans of Shirley Jackson,' praised by Kirkus Reviews

for 'imaginative directness reminiscent of Stephen King,' and lauded by Booklist for 'beautifully detailed characters and a subtle slide into dread.' She has also earned acclaim from authors and editors including Michael Marshall Smith ('one of the best novels I've read in years'), Stephen Jones ('a horror tour-de-force'), Clay McLeod Chapman ('every flip of the page leads its readers deeper into uneasy dream'), Marie O'Regan, Neil Sharpson, Edward Ashton, M.R. Carey, A.C. Wise, Ian Rogers, and others. Mia is the author of the novels *Estate Sale* and *Haven*, the novellas *Alakazam*, *Tell Me a Story*, *Discordant*, *Arrokoth*, and *Do You Know the Muffin Man?* and the collection *Smile So Red and Other Tales of Madness*. She is represented by the John Jarrold Literary Agency. **daliaverse.w ixsite.com/author**

Paul Edmonds is a Massachusetts writer whose fiction focuses on flawed people, strange towns, and the creeping dread beneath ordinary life.

Anthony Ferguson is an author and editor living in Perth, Australia. He has published over ninety short stories and non-fiction articles in Australia, Britain and the United States. He wrote the novel *Protege*, the non-fiction books *The Sex Doll: A History* and *Murder Down Under*, edited the short-story collection *Devil Dolls and Duplicates in Australian Horror*, and coedited the award-nominated *Midnight Echo #12*. He is a committee member of the Australasian Horror Writers Association (AHWA). A four-time nominee, he won the Australian Shadows Award for Short Fiction in 2020. His short story collection, *Rest in Pieces*, was published by IFWG in August 2023. **anthonypferguson.wixsite.com/mysite**

Daniel Fox is a writer of horror, thrillers, fantasy, and children's books. He also created an online Choose-Your-Own-Adventure horror video game called *Ocean of Death*. Wow, he should really focus.

Jason Franks is the author of *Bloody Waters*, *Faerie Apocalypse*, and *X-Dimensional Assassin Zai*, and the writer of the *Sixsmiths* graphic novels. He works in the intersection of horror, science fiction, fantasy, and comedy, but he'll stalk a story into any genre. Franks has also written for IP franchises including *Sherlock Holmes*, *The Phantom*, and *The Human Fly*. Franks' work has variously been a finalist for the Aurealis, Ditmar, Ledger, and Australian Shadows Awards. He lives in Melbourne, Australia, with his family and a brace of guitars.

Narrelle M Harris's works include vampire novels, crime fiction, het and queer romance, and Holmes/Watson mysteries, as well as songs and poetry. Works

include the vampire novels *The Opposite of Life* and *Walking Shadows*, with the third book, *Beyond Redemption*, due in 2026. Narrelle also edits anthologies, including *The Only One in the World: A Sherlock Holmes Anthology* (2021), and *Clamour and Mischief* (2022). *This Fresh Hell* (2023), nominated for a Ditmar award, was co-edited with Katya de Becerra, and *Sherlock is a Girl's Name* (2024) with Atlin Merrick. Her latest book is *The She-Wolf of Baker Street* (2024), a contemporary, queer, paranormal take on the inhabitants of 221B Baker Street, which reviewers have called an 'imaginative, entertaining and fast-paced novel,' and was nominated for an Aurealis Award.
narrellemharris.iwriter.com.au

Liam Hogan is an award-winning speculative short story writer, with stories in *Best of British Science Fiction* and in *Best of British Fantasy* (NewCon Press). He volunteers at the creative writing charities Ministry of Stories and Spark Young Writers. His sci-fi collection, *A Short History of the Future*, is available from Northodox Press.
happyendingnotguaranteed.blogspot.co.uk

Andreas Hort is a Czech author writing in English. At nine, he began scribbling comic books with pencils. Later, he branched out into drawing scenes with his words. He never stopped writing, and somewhere along the way he started getting paid for it. You can find him at **andreas-hort.com**

Perth writer **Martin Livings** has had over a hundred short stories published in a variety of magazines and anthologies, both locally and internationally. His first novel, *Carnies*, was first published by Hachette Livre in 2006, and was nominated for both the Aurealis and Ditmar awards, and his short story collection, *Living With the Dead*, was published in 2012. Both are now available from Amazon, along with the follow-up collection, *Light Falling From a Long Dead Star*, the novellas *Rope* and *The Final Twist*, and the novels *Skinsongs*, *Sleeper Awake*, *An Ill Wind*, *The Temp*, and *The Obituary*.
martinlivings.wordpress.com

John Peel was born in Nottingham, England. He moved to the US to marry his pen-pal, Nan, and they live on Long Island with their rescue dog, Dickens, and a flock of lovebirds. He has written the novelizations of the *Doctor Who* stories 'The Chase', 'The Dalek Masterplan', 'The Power of the Daleks' and 'The Evil of the Daleks'. He also wrote the first original *Doctor Who* novel, *Timewyrm Genesys*, and a number of other novels for that and spin-off series, such as the *Lethbridge Stewart Adventures*. He's also written novels based on shows such as *Star Trek*,

The Avengers and *The Outer Limits*, and has created and written original series, such as *Dragonhome*, *Diadem: Worlds of Magic* and *Shockers!*. Most recently, he's written several short stories for the *Star Trek Explorer* magazine, and an original Sixth Doctor audio adventure for BBC Audio.

D.S. Telling writes with a flair in romanticism, tying tales with a lovely bow. An enthusiastic participant and supporter of the arts in all its mediums, you'll find her dancing, painting, and attempting to relearn the violin. A student for life on the constant lookout for inspiration, she enjoys reading as many books—in as many genres—as she can get her hands on.

About the Editor

Chuck McKenzie was born in 1970 and still spends much of his time there. His short SF and horror fiction has been shortlisted multiple times for the Aurealis, Ditmar and Australian Shadows Awards, and he currently works full time as an author and editor, living mostly on beans as a result. He hopes one day to be described by his neighbours as having seemed like such a *nice* man. You can stalk him on Instagram at **@chuck.mckenzie.author**, or check out his author page at **daftnotions.com/chuck-mckenzie**

Also From

DAFT NOTIONS
CHUCK MCKENZIE'S
NASTY LITTLE BITS

Hello

children...

Welcome to Chuck McKenzie's Nasty Little Bits

—a collection of twenty-eight morsels of the macabre especially prepared to cause a range of reactions, from uneasy laughter to outright horror, and everything in between.

We invite you to read this book at bedtime as an antidote to peaceful sleep.

And remember—so long as you don't let your foot dangle over the side of your mattress, the thing underneath your bed will never be able to grab it.

Also From

DAFT NOTIONS
THE DARK MAN, BY REFERRAL
AND LESS PLEASANT TALES

STEP INTO THE WORLD
OF THE DARK MAN:

PLEASE HAVE YOUR
REFERRAL READY...

An abused child encounters the local legendary boogeyman,
and finds himself querying the definition of 'monster'...

Two time-travellers observe The Crucifixion, and discover a horror
far beyond the brutality of the event itself...

An inhuman predator establishes its feeding ground in a small rural
town—but does it have competition...?

In this collection, representing the darker work of author
Chuck McKenzie, you'll find tales of zombies, kaiju,
and alien invaders; of visits to Hell, and to quiet suburban streets;
of Lovecraftian entities and spectral terrors.

And other, far less pleasant tales than these...

Also From

DAFT NOTIONS

DAILY GRIND

AND OTHER ASTOUNDING STORIES OF MUNDANE MATTERS

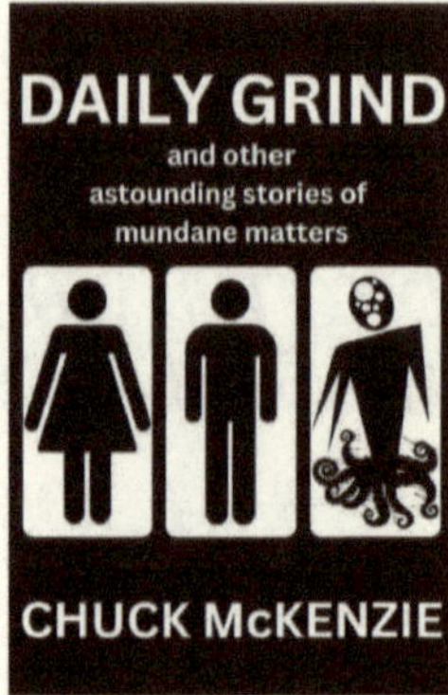

THE DIFFERENCE BETWEEN THE EVERYDAY AND THE ASTOUNDING DEPENDS ENTIRELY UPON YOUR VIEWPOINT...

A conversation between two aliens reveals that some aspects of working life are universal, such as job satisfaction —or the lack thereof...

A private detective investigates an impossible murder, unwillingly assisted by an annoyingly talkative cat who may or may not be completely imaginary...

A daring hero defiantly battles Alien Space Nazis for the fate of the galaxy—but doesn't it all seem just little bit...unlikely....?

In this collection, comprising the science fiction stories (including three novellas) of author Chuck McKenzie, you'll find tales of time-travellers, interstellar scam artists, and interdimensional expeditions; of alien invaders masquerading as Santa, and others offering services that sound too good to be true; of bushrangers battling Wellsian Martians, and the unthinkable results of doubling the average human lifespan.

And other astounding stories of relatively mundane matters...

Sci-Fi, Horror, Crime and...Cats?

Small press publisher operating out of
Melbourne, Australia.

For more information and to purchase our titles go to:
www.daftnotions.com